Red Dawn

D0165414

Also by Level Best Books

Available at
www.levelbestbooks.com

Cover Photograph by Katharine Langenberg
taken at Plum Island, MA
www.katharinelangenberg.com

Best New England Crime Stories

Red Dawn

Edited by
Mark Ammons
Katherine Fast
Barbara Ross
Leslie Wheeler

Level Best Books
Somerville, Massachusetts 02144

Level Best Books
411A Highland Avenue #413
Somerville, Massachusetts 02144
www.levelbestbooks.com

text composition/design by Katherine Fast
cover photo © 2015 by Katharine Langenberg
Printed in the USA

ISBN 978-0-9838780-6-3
Library of Congress Catalog Card Data available.
First Edition 10 9 8 7 6 5 4 3 2 1

Red Dawn

Contents

Contents

Contents

Introduction

It is with profoundly mixed emotions that we write our final introduction to a Level Best anthology. It's been a great ride!

We're intensely proud of the editions of *Best New England Crime Stories* we've produced. One reason is the public recognition our authors have received, including an Edgar® nomination for Judith Green, an Anthony nomination for Sheila Connolly, and Agatha nominations for Kathy Lynn Emerson, Barbara Ross and Sheila Connolly (twice). Stories from our collections have won two Derringer Awards, for Ray Daniel and Kathy Chencharik, and have appeared on Derringer shortlists eight times, recognizing authors including James T. Shannon, John Bubar, Adam Purple, Peggy McFarland, Mo Walsh, Adam Renn Olenn and Mary E. Stibal (twice). Stories by Ray Daniel, B.B. Oak and Woody Hanstein have been named Distinguished American Mystery Stories by Otto Penzler in the *Best American Mystery Stories* series. The collection as a whole was a finalist for a Silver Falchion Award by Killer Nashville. And, we've published five winners of the Al Blanchard Award: Bev Vincent, Lee Robertson, VR Barkowski, Michael Nethercott, and John Bubar.

This year marks the first that an author has won the Blanchard a second time. We're thrilled to include John Bubar's provocative and timely tale of hackers caught in a deadly game, "Tell the Others," in this volume.

Every year we've published stories by well-known New England authors and this volume continues that tradition with classic whodunits, "Singed" from Dorothy Cannell and "Last Mango in Paradise" by Lucy Burdette (aka Roberta Isleib). "Brotherhood" by Gerald Elias offers a symphony of backstage murder, while Gary Braver (aka Goshgarian) turns the art of the "Acceptance Speech" on its head. Chris Knopf takes us for a sexy but harrowing boat ride in "Kill Switch."

And, maybe most important, in every volume we've had the pleasure of introducing several new voices to our readers, offering first fiction publication to many who have gone on to have successful mystery series, including Ray Daniel, J.A. Hennrikus (Julianne Holmes) and B.B. Oak. Who will be the breakout stars this year? No way to know, but we offer you "Foolproof" by Bruce Robert Coffin giving macabre new meaning to "bottom of the barrel," Annelisa Johnson Wagner's creepily hypnotic "No Aura," a jolt of backwoods skullduggery in "Devious Doings in Dallas" by Sanford Emerson, and Deborah Dolby's bloody sleight of hand with "The Intruder."

Some authors have built whole worlds with Level Best, with memorable characters reappearing year after year. Judith Green, the only author to have a story in all thirteen volumes, continues her tales about Margery Easton with a modern version of an epistolary story, "Dear Manuel." Alan D. McWhirter gives us another installment about ex-New Haven cop and current PI Joe Chandler in "Old Doc Sloan," and Margaret Press brings us an update on her psychopathic working mother, Rhode, in "Paradise Lost."

This year's historical stories include Cheryl Marceau's haunting seventeenth-century mystery, "Druid Hill," and Angela Gerst's taut "Fibonacci Sequence," set in the Cold War world of spies.

We're fond of the off-beat, captured in this volume by Peggy McFarland's deliciously bizarre, "Breakfast," the twisty ending, conjured by Vy Kava in "Hero," and the lingering question, posed by both Dale T. Phillips in "Hope It Fits," and by Alan Vogel in "Lawyers, Drugs and Money."

Christine Eskilson shows us what happens when love goes disastrously wrong in "The First Wife," while A.J. Pompano reveals the flip side when it goes breathtakingly right in "The Bucket List." An outsider threatens love in Stef Donati's "Call Off the Search," but familial love and friendship triumph in Rae Padilla Francoeur's, "Hello?"

An author finds a cure for writer's block that's both grisly and surprising in Gin Mackey's "The Demise of My Wives," while another writer makes the mistake of marrying an adoring acolyte in Shelly Dickson Carr's "Words Can Kill." A Sherlock Holmes wannabe finds inspiration at a murder scene in Louise Clerici's "Baker Street, Boston."

Three former Level Best editors make a contribution to our final year. Ruth M. McCarty spins a tall tale with "The Wrinkle Curse." Susan Oleksiw returns to the hypnotic rhythms of South India in "High Crimes and Slick Demeanors," and Kate Flora shows us why they always finish last in "Nice Guy."

The soon-to-be former editors contribute as well. A rookie cop has a wild night in Katherine Fast's "The Wedding Gift." A wife makes a startling discovery in Leslie Wheeler's "Gone, But Not Forgotten," and a young woman struggles between warring desires in Barbara Ross' "The Perfect Woman." As the final icing on the cake, Mark Ammons outdoes himself with his nano-pico-zepto-yocto flash "Relax, It's Not Loaded," beating even last year's record for fewest words (but you're welcome to provide a few of your own).

Thanks to everyone who has helped us produce six years' worth of high-quality short crime fiction: the former editors, Skye Alexander, Kate Flora, Ruth M. McCarty and Susan Oleksiw, Sisters in Crime New England, Mystery Writers of America New England and especially the New England Crime Bake, the official launch pad for the anthologies. But most of all, thanks to the hundreds of writers who have entrusted us with their stories, and you, dear readers. Your appreciation, loyalty and support have meant more than we can say.

Mark Ammons
Katherine Fast
Barbara Ross
Leslie Wheeler

Tell The Others

John Bubar

They came for me just before sunrise. Classic timing. Between midnight and dawn, significant biological changes occur within the body: temperature drops, heartbeat slows, blood pressure falls. People with normal schedules would be at their least alert. Me, I'd been up for twenty-four hours, hacking the encrypted email system of a Fortune 100 company, chugging energy drinks, searching for inside information on possible mergers.

Classic timing, a wasted first thought. Not being normal—I'm a hacker-for-hire—was going to get me killed. My second thoughts were more analytical and survival oriented. How had they gotten by my neighbor's dogs? Who was behind this? How did they find me up here in Vermont's Northeast Kingdom? I'd created elaborate false trails in Boston, leaving no trace northbound. Please, could we talk?

There were three of them: Black SWAT-team outfits, black balaclavas, black pistols in black Kevlar holsters, and black knives in black Kevlar sheathes. This matte-black cloud engulfed me. As I struggled, the two big ones pinned my arms to my side and the slender one, whom I took to be in charge—had the body of a woman, body language of the leader—said with a quiet, throaty firmness, "Stop that, Harold. It won't hurt so much."

I took her advice, hoping my compliance might lead to a negotiation, those words having served as an introduction of sorts, an icebreaker if you will. Then I felt the needle in my neck.

I woke with sand in my mouth, naked, back burning up, and a

warm liquid tugging insistently at my lower body. All those years of disbelieving. I burrowed deeper into the sand, instinctively trying to hide in Hell.

What persuaded me to open my eyes were the unmistakable sounds of a party and the familiar whiff of my old friend Mary Jane. First thought: I was on a tropical island: sand beach, lagoon, bright sun, blue water, palm trees, jungle forest, and, in the distance, cliffs with breakers, crashing against the rocks below. Second thought: OK—so maybe not Hell—but the injection site on my neck was throbbing, so maybe not Heaven either.

Arriving at a party naked is not my usual come-on. After a few steps, I realized the sand had invaded more than my mouth, so I stepped back into the lagoon to wash out the gear. The cool water felt good on my back, but also guaranteed gear shrinkage. I worried my first impression would be SOA—Short On Arrival.

But no one seemed to notice. There were five of them in various shapes and sizes, all dressed in orange jumpsuits, Australian bush hats, wraparound sunglasses, and black flip-flops. All geeks—takes one to know one—and all stoned or drunk or some combination thereof. Beer cans, nickel bags, munchies of all sorts lay scattered around. Clearly they wanted not.

The muscular little fireplug, who'd been holding court as I approached, turned, rummaged around in a large wooden box, found an orange jumpsuit, tossed it to me, then threw the uniform accessories after it. First thought: Glad to be dressed. Second thought: Who are these guys?

Fireplug tossed me a can of warm beer and said, "You must be Ibis."

My attempted poker face dissolved. Ibis is my name in hacker-world, my persona on the Darknet.

"Looks like an ibis." The blond with the pencil behind his ear toasted me with his beer. "Tall, skinny, mostly legs, and a truly noble proboscis."

I opened my beer in his direction, but the spray didn't reach him. Smug, too-good-looking prick.

"Argh."

This from the swarthy one with the bandana whom I'd inadvertently doused. Argh, really? Then I got it. First thought: Hackers all. Second thought: WTF?

"Ah, that set his hair on fire." A freckled redhead raised his beer to me. Jumpsuit orange was not his color. An unkind thought I know, but I was still suffering from the proboscis crack.

"Pyrate," I nodded at bandana man. "And Pyro," to the redhead. "And Scribbler," to the nose critic with the pencil. "And…"

"Toast, as in you've been toasted."

YOU'VE BEEN TOASTED would be the last thing employees saw before their monitors went dark. I'd pictured a deep, arrogant voice delivering the news. The truth was squeaky and giggly, emanating from a chubby, acne-scarred hobbit.

I looked back at the court-holder, who was waving his hands above his head in that hook-em-horns gesture. "So, Bull," I said, "where are the others?"

The others were Shark, Moray, Cuda, and Snake. Six months ago an article had appeared on the Darknet naming the top ten hackers in the USA. The anonymous author had listed us alphabetically and described our greatest hits. Eight of ten saw it as celebrity and filled the chat rooms with testosterone. I saw it as notoriety and dropped out of sight as fast as I could. Snake disappeared as well. Then, about two months ago, one by one, the others vanished. It stood to reason that if six of us were here, the other four were close behind. First thought: What are the rules? Second thought: I understood how those assholes in black might have traced these loudmouths, but how had they found me?

"I don't know where they are." Bull quit his silly little dance and picked up his beer. "I showed up five weeks ago, on the beach, naked, lying next to a supplies container. Enough food, beer, and weed for me for a week, and two jumpsuits. I put on the one that fit, explored a little, made sure this really was an island, but mostly I waited. Six days later Pyro shows up. The next day a container appears on the beach with supplies for two and another jumpsuit."

"Been that iteration each week since," said Pyro.

"Except for the night we hid in the scrub and tried to see how they landed the supplies, thinking that might give us some ideas on how to sail off this island." Pyrate inhaled, beer in one hand, joint in another, bandana slowly working its way over one eye.

"Didn't work." Scribbler sighted down his pencil at Pyrate. "The supplies didn't arrive, so . . ."

"We decided to behave ourselves," Bull finished. "Stayed up here, away from their landing zone, and the supplies arrived the next night. We figure they have some drone with infrared tracking."

Bull obviously liked having the first and last word. Meanwhile Pyro busied himself rolling a joint and staring at Pyrate, who'd sailed away in place. Toast clutched his beer in his little hobbit hands and Scribbler watched us all with undisguised disdain.

"So." I fiddled with my bush hat, letting out the loopy tie so it wouldn't get caught on my face. "The idea is to wait until the gang's all here before we figure out what to do?"

"That's the plan," Bull acknowledged, "unless you have some objections."

First thought: Challenge me for leadership; fuck you. Second thought: Tilt your head in subservience, bide your time, play the long game.

Shrugging, I said, "Sounds good to me. Now what does a guy have to do to get another beer?" Scribbler had a can coming at me before I'd finished the sentence, like he could read my mind.

The next week went by quickly. I explored. The cliffs were a hundred feet above the breakers, offering a magnificent view of nothing but ocean. A fresh water stream fed a sandy-bottomed shallow pool a thousand yards or so from the beach. Inland were jungles and swamps and giant mangrove trees. The supplies container with my jumpsuit also included a tent, and I set up camp in the general vicinity of the others, off the beach, protected from the occasional rain and wind.

I played cards and chess competitively but made sure I seldom won. I was down thousands of dollars in a few days. The others played as if their ability to collect was just around the corner. They were evenly matched, gaining equally what I lost. Toast played only chess, at which he was a master, and clever enough to lose occasionally, which kept the others coming back. Scribbler only watched.

While we played, we speculated on who would fill the jumpsuit that had recently arrived. First thought: Someone about five-eight, broad in the chest like Bull, another weightlifter. Second thought: More testosterone games in paradise.

Our new addition arrived naked and sparkling wet from having washed the sand off her body. Conversation ceased abruptly when we recognized a female form marching toward us.

"Bull, get out her jumpsuit." Toast stood up.

We ignored him, and he sat down.

She stopped in front of us and pointed at Bull. "I'm Snake. Give me my jumpsuit and the rest of my geeky outfit. Jesus Christ, you look like an Australian penal colony for stoners."

We watched her dress in silence. The jumpsuit fit, if anything a little tight. Dark hair, dark eyes, and a body that would be gloriously Rubenesque in a few years. Bull tossed her a beer.

"Thanks, Bull."

He looked surprised, and then a little giddy that she would know his name. Snake popped the can in his direction, spraying his legs, then took a long drink and went around our little semi-circle calling each of us by name.

"Impressive," said Scribbler, rolling his pencil between his thumb and forefinger.

"Obvious," replied Snake. "That Top Ten Hacker bullshit that showed up six months ago knew about the DOD satellite I'd hijacked. Any idea how classified that was? Any guess at the resources needed to find out about that? Or all of the other hacks we did? It smelled of money and power, so I disappeared while the rest of you smash and grab idiots, Ibis excepted, strutted through cyberspace." She finished her beer in one draught. "Someone was hunting us and here most of us are, and you boys look like just what you call yourselves, props and all—like people growing to look like their pets."

"You don't look like a snake." Toast was in love.

"Exactly."

"If you're so fucking smart, how did you get caught?" Scribbler hadn't liked the bit about the props. His pencil had disappeared.

"After six months I ran out of the cash in my go-bag." She paused and watched as we shifted uncomfortably in wordless acknowledgement that none of us had ever thought of having a go-bag. "I had accounts in five different banks in five different names and had to hit the ATMs. Somehow they traced the funds through my offshore accounts into my domestic accounts. I figure my clients ratted me out. Once they had the accounts it was just a matter of hacking the real time information on my withdrawal location and the manpower to cover the territory. Only electronic trail out there for them to follow."

"And the fish boys?" asked Pyro.

"Dead," she said, motioning to Bull for another beer. "Shark, Moray, and Cuda, they were the sloppiest of all of you. Whatever this place is, they would have beaten us all here." She accepted the beer that Bull passed to her. "My guess—they were picked up quick, interrogated, and put to rest. What was learned from how they operated was used to build an algorithm that sped up leading to the rest of us, probably a variant on the old follow-the-money routine adjusted for our world." She swallowed half her beer. "Except for you, Ibis."

"Yeah, Ibis." Pyrate had pulled his bush hat down over his bandana. "Rumor has it that you only took payment in cash. Mostly in Boston, but sometimes in Providence or Worcester. Had a bunch of cutouts, chalk marks on dead drops, real Cold War spy stuff. How could they follow that money and find you? Hell, you haven't done anything in the last six months."

"No idea," I said. "None at all."

Snake glared at me. Scribbler looked away. They both knew I was lying, but I wasn't in the mood for sharing my bounce-around-foster-kid life. The foster mom who'd saved me was on an Alzheimer's ward in Brattleboro—no, life isn't fair—and to pay for her care I'd had to build her a stock portfolio in a hurry, based on the inside information I'd gotten for my clients. I couldn't imagine who could command the computing power and boots-on-the-ground resources necessary to find me through her, but it was my only electronic money trail.

Snake had described our merry band, me excepted, as "smash and grab idiots." They stole identities from the databases of major corporations or corrupted databases at the behest of well-heeled competitors or disgruntled employees with information to trade. Most recently they'd been breaching health care records, ferreting out secrets the rich and famous wouldn't want the world to know or CEOs wouldn't want their boards to know. Everywhere they went they left destruction in their wake.

Snake and I took great pains to cover our tracks. She made her money specializing in opposition research for political campaigns and conducting electronic "Watergates" into opposition plans. Leaving no trace was important in her world. The satellite hijack was probably just for fun, but no doubt pissed off some very important people in agencies that would be glad to hear she was off the board.

I worked for hypocritical, sanctimonious pricks who publicly decried the excesses of greed in our capital markets while paying me to scout through the secret files and correspondence of investment banks and their clients with regard to impending mergers and acquisitions. Nothing makes money like inside information.

Snake settled in and accomplished the obligatory "new guy" exploring. Our supplies arrived the following night. Sustenance for seven, no jumpsuit.

Whether dead, in jail, rotting in a hole living on insects, whatever, it looked like the fish boys wouldn't be joining us. A week later we were resupplied. Beer and dope for all, but someone had miscounted and shorted us on food.

"Derivative," snarled Snake after we'd parceled out short rations for the week.

"As in *Robinson Crusoe* or *Swiss Family Robinson*?" Toast hung on her every word.

"Exactly, Toast." She graced him with a smile.

That evening she suggested cards, playing for food to be paid now instead of money to be collected later. I declined, reflecting aloud on what a loser I had been. Scribbler said he hadn't played and wouldn't start now. The rest jumped in. Scribbler and I stood well away and watched the first deal.

"I'm sure the irony hasn't been lost on you, Ibis." Scribbler launched this out of the side of his mouth while looking down to roll a joint. "The introduction of a snake into our little Eden."

"Hmmmm." I had decided early on to treat everything Scribbler said as a rhetorical question. He was going to overwrite me anyway. It was his hacker MO.

"I enjoyed watching you and Snake trying to lose to each other at chess. She had your good-but-not-good-enough strategy figured out long before I did." He lit up, clearly enjoying himself.

I wrestled the joint out of his hand and took a hit. We watched Snake win the first hand.

"As for our smitten little Toast, I expect he found computers in middle school and his literary life became immediately truncated. *Swiss Family Robinson* indeed. So much literature to choose from, eh?" He turned to face me. "How long did you last among the Crimson?"

I handed him his joint back, but didn't want to.

Scribbler inhaled deeply and blew the smoke out his nose, framing his face in a translucent wreath. "Ibis: venerated in ancient Egypt, biblical symbol of fertility, and symbol of the Harvard Lampoon, complete with copper ibis atop 44 Bow Street, Cambridge, Massachusetts."

I walked away.

"I thought I recognized a fellow Harvard Yard-bird," he said to my back. "Lampooning us all, are you? Veneration and fertility a little over the top for someone who strives so hard to be underestimated, don't you think? Hubris, hubris. And you with that nose."

In the morning the asshole—he couldn't pass up that nose shot—and I pretended nothing had happened. Just the dope talking. Goes without saying, so we said nothing.

Snake had won food for two for the week. That night she shared it with us, got Bull drunk, and took him to her tent. He was a noisy fuck and became even more insufferable in the days that followed. Pyro and Pyrate came out of the closet and started sharing one tent, using the other to store their supplies. Scribbler, Toast, and I were left to our own devices. Fantasies of one's choice abounded. The next resupply had the usual amount of beer and marijuana, and someone had decided to throw in two cases of vodka. There was food for five.

We paid close attention to the division of food. That night Bull got right into the vodka, chasing it with beer, declaring he was making a meal of liquid bread. He and Snake stumbled off toward his tent. She'd matched him drink for drink. That girl liked her booze. As for the rest of us, we took a walk down the beach, so we wouldn't have to listen to him bellow.

By lunch the next day Bull hadn't made his presence known and we asked Snake if she'd seen him. She shrugged, laid his absence to a hangover—they slept in separate tents after sex—and gave a disgusted look at what water had done to a package of dehydrated peas.

By nightfall he still hadn't made an appearance. We looked in his tent. No Bull. The next morning we conducted a search and saw his body lying crooked on the rocks at the bottom of the cliffs.

"We should bury him." Toast was all broken up. Baffling, as Bull had bullied him without mercy.

"Good idea," said Scribbler. "You go on down there, brush that flock of gulls off him, and carry him to somewhere you can dig a grave."

That didn't happen.

By noon we were dividing up Bull's cache of food from his tent. I'm not sure whose idea that was, maybe mine; certainly we gathered up our respective shares with enthusiasm. By dinner, Bull seemed a faint memory. Snake manifested no sign that she was grieving and the following evening took me to her tent.

Toast snitted his jealousy. Scribbler nodded as if he'd known all along. Pyro and Pyrate toasted us with enthusiasm as we moved into the shadows.

She never stopped talking. Through it all, deep into post-coital bliss, she talked and talked. And she loved my nose. Nuzzle became her favorite verb. Grabbing my ears, running her fingers through my hair, she'd murmur, "Nuzzle, you son-of-a-bitch, nuzzle."

She was smart and beautiful and thought I was handsome and extolled the virtues of every part of me. Every man in her life had been a mistake until now. No need to go to your tent. Stay with me.

The next day Scribbler took me aside. "Watch your back, lover boy."

I picked up a shell and tossed it into the water.

"First the strong one and then the smart one. No fool, our girl Snake." He tossed his own shell toward the sea in a gesture of solidarity. "We all know Bull didn't like heights, wouldn't get near the edge of that cliff. Who had the power to lure him there?"

"Bullshit." Some accusations require a response.

"He probably did. All the way down." Scribbler laughed.

Later that day as we lay in Snake's tent, she warned me about Scribbler. "Watch out for our Cassius. I saw him walking the beach with you this morning."

"Cassius, as in the 'lean and hungry look . . . such men are dangerous' Cassius?"

"Bull was scared of heights, right? So he's up in the night with a full bladder and decides to take Ferdinand for a walk."

"Ferdinand?"

"That's what he called his dick. You guys all name your dicks something inane."

"Not all of us."

"And so there's Scribbler waiting, says he's seeking the same relief, and he challenges Bull to see who can whiz the farthest over the cliff. So Mr. Testosterone stifles his fear and edges up to the edge. There he is, not looking down, one hand on little Ferdinand and one on his hip, pissing for all he's worth, when Scribbler the Scrawny admits defeat and congratulates Bull with a hard, two-handed pat on the back."

"Why?" Little Ferdinand. I'd been glad to hear that. No competition for Moby there.

"Get rid of the strong one. Scribbler knows the food shortage isn't a mistake. We're being played with. Some kind of *Survivor, Lord of the Flies*, *Most Dangerous Game* derivative, combo-nonsense."

"But why? What's the benefit to watching a bunch of infrared dots blinking out?"

"I don't know." She took an affectionate swipe at my nose. "But between the two of us we can figure it out."

My last thought before the first nuzzle was that the boy and the girl had both survived in *Hunger Games.*

The night before the next scheduled supply drop, Snake's screaming woke me. Pyro and Pyrate's tent was engulfed in flames. They'd been their usual stoned selves when they'd left us after dinner. The stench of burning flesh was overwhelming. There was nothing we could do.

We sat on the beach until dawn, silent and suspicious. In the daylight, Scribbler discovered a charred, broken vodka bottle that had been smashed against a rock laid against the tent fly.

"Molotov cocktail. Nicely done." Scribbler looked directly at Snake. "My guess is, if we check their other tent, we'll find their vodka store gone for accelerant."

"She was with me," I said.

"She was outside screaming," Scribbler replied.

"The sounds of the flames woke me up." Snake grabbed my arm.

"And you, Toast?" I spun on the hobbit. "What do you think of this little toasting?"

"I think Scribbler found that bottle like he knew it was there," said Toast, choosing sides and receiving an appreciative smile from Snake.

We divided up their food and went our separate ways. The next night we were resupplied. More than enough booze and dope. Food for three.

"Bastards," Snake whispered to me. "They knew there were only four of us left."

That morning I began an extensive search for island food: bananas, pineapples, coconuts, plantains. I wanted to do that hunter-gatherer thing and beat my chest in victory in front of Snake. Toast must have had the same idea about finding food because I didn't see him that evening or any of the next day. Scribbler skulked about but didn't speak to us. He too disappeared for hours on end. Snake and I took turns standing watch at night.

Two days before the next resupply, while on another fruitless search for food, I found Toast's body on the edge of a mangrove swamp, his head caved in, the rock that was used tossed at his feet. When I got back to the beach Snake told me that Scribbler had disappeared, but she had a plan.

"Scribbler's wanted me since minute one. A girl knows."

Before I had time to think, I was lying in the high grass that bordered the freshwater pool, watching Snake, thigh-deep in the water, soaping her breasts.

"I've seen him stalking me here," she'd told me, as she pointed out where she wanted me to hide. "I'll get him in the water, take a hard shot at him, and you jump in, and we'll hold him under."

She delivered all this without emotion, like she was talking about writing code. I was tired and scared, and tired of being tired and scared, so I rushed off to do as I'd been told, on full autopilot. Scribbler appeared an hour later.

"Where's the boyfriend?" he asked.

"Flown away for good," Snake answered. "He couldn't stand the heat." She was sluicing the suds off her body and they were coiling in little circles between her legs. "You look like you could use a bath," she said.

He undressed slowly, turning to fold his jumpsuit neatly and place it on the bank, then turned back to face Snake. Obviously his little head had been thinking really hard.

"I guess I have saved the best for last." Snake giggled.

"Turn around," Scribbler said as he entered the water.

"That's how you like it?" Another giggle.

"Just making sure you don't have something sharp taped to your back."

Halfway through her turn she dropped the soap, bent over to retrieve it, and completed her pirouette. "Satisfied?"

"Not yet." Scribbler cupped her chin and brushed strands of wet hair from her face.

She took a soapy finger and, starting at his chin, traced a line down his chest, around each nipple, and continued down his centerline only to drop the soap again.

"Oops," she said.

Wrapping her hand around what Scribbler had brought to the party, she smiled at him, licked her lips, and bent over to pick up the soap, but instead she came up with a rock in her hand and struck him hard across the forehead. She must have placed the rock on the sandy bottom while I was hiding.

Stunned, blood flooding into his eyes, Scribbler made a grab for her, but she was slippery with soap. She hit him again on the left temple and he stumbled and turned and she hit him again. As he fell face forward she mounted him, holding his head in the water with one hand and using the rock with the other.

After what seemed like an eternity, Scribbler stopped struggling, but still she held his head under the water, talking to him all the time, like she had right from the beginning.

"Take that," she'd hissed, "and that, and that. Do you like me on top, Scribbler? Don't struggle, darling. It will be over soon. Just let go." Over and over again she'd whispered, "Just let go, darling, just let go."

I'd gotten up and rushed into the water at her first strike, but she hadn't needed my help; hearing her talk Scribbler through his dying started something very primal tearing at my gut. When she looked up from her kill, her mask dropped, or perhaps she hadn't had time to put it back on. She was the lioness; I was the antelope. First thought: Run. Second thought: Run faster, accompanied by the nagging realization that I hadn't being doing much thinking since I'd started getting laid.

Four days later I jumped from a tree, landed on her back, drove her face into the dirt, and bludgeoned her with a rock. She struggled beneath me, lashed backhand with her spear, but never said a word. Neither did I. When she finally gave up and let life go, I rolled off, vomited, then ran to the ocean and scrubbed her off me.

I'd watched her hunting me. She'd tossed the orange jumpsuit away just as I had and, like me, had camouflaged herself with green and brown mud. Unlike me, she had a spear fashioned from a tent pole. I was armed with pot and vodka, gathered up the day I'd run from the scene of Scribbler's dying, Snake's laughter in my ears.

I half-covered the vodka with leaves beneath the tree I'd picked out and started burning the marijuana. She followed her nose, scouted around for two long hours looking for a trap, then crept out of the underbrush spear in hand, still wary. Her weakness was booze and she'd probably run through what little was left. When she stooped to pick up the bottle, I struck. Scrubbed pink and raw, I sat on the beach and shivered in the heat, watched the sun go down, and passed out on the sand exhausted.

They came for me just before sunrise.

"Shit, it's him," the biggest one said, rolling me over, waking me up.

"Don't take it personally, Harold," their leader laughed. "The smart money was on Martha."

First thought: Martha. Unbelievable. Second thought: Tilt your head. Make it easy on yourself. I smiled as I felt the needle.

I came to at my desk, the three of them watching me shake off the drug. First thought: Alive. Home in Vermont. Second thought: Do anything to stay that way.

"I get it. I'll find something legit. Never breathe a word. Never." My voice cracked a little. Probably the drugs.

"Oh, Harold," she said, "that's not what we want at all. You are so naïve. But then, so were we." A black-gloved hand swiped at the dust on my keyboard. "I thought by ushering the best-of-the-best off to Rest-In-Peace I could significantly mitigate the hacking excesses that have been such a strain on capitalism. I pitched my business plan as the logical evolution of the traditional IT Help Desk and found several powerful people, in and out of government, eager to provide me with venture capital after I showed them my mechanism for their credible deniability.

"But then, after we sent the fish boys to sleep with the fishes and you and Martha went underground, dozens of newbies showed up, all wanting to take your places in the top ten." Reaching around me, she booted up my computer. "We soon realized our initial strategy would have us playing whack-a-hacker in perpetuity. So we did a mid-course correction, populated an island, and you know the rest."

I watched my computer come to life and instinctively reached for the keyboard.

"Good instinct, Harold." She put her hands on my shoulders, leaned over, and whispered in my ear. "What I want is for you to tell the others what's in store for them if they don't stop picking on the big guys. And be persuasive, Harold. If you aren't, we'll be back in a year or so and gather you up for our Tournament of Champions."

John Bubar spent thirty-six years as a pilot in military and commercial aviation. Retiring in 2006, he successfully squeezed a two-year writing program into six years, receiving his MFA degree from the University of New Hampshire in 2012. This is his fourth publication with Level Best Books. He is a two-time recipient of the Al Blanchard Award.

Acceptance Speech

Gary Braver

Thank you, President Ryan, and thank you, Alumni Association. First of all, I'd like to say how great it is to see some old friends and former professors after so many years. And hard to believe it's been a quarter of a century. It's also gratifying to see such a wonderful turnout for a 25th reunion!

Secondly, I am humbled to accept the Harold H. Clayborn Memorial Award and, I must add, with some dismay. Named after a young man who may have been the brightest guy in our graduating class, I would have assumed the recipient to be a CEO or captain of industry or an astronaut, not a just-plain-old high school science teacher. But thank you nonetheless for this high honor—and one that is personally meaningful.

As all of you fellow classmates out there well know, Hal Clayborn was brilliant—the kind of whiz kid who could take apart a TV set and reassemble the parts into an atom smasher. I'd take apart a TV set and end up with a pile of junk. You may well remember that Hal was the guy who left three-hour physics exams an hour early only to earn the highest grades in the class. The same guy who won full scholarships here and fellowships to physics grad school.

Because ours was the toughest department on the hill, we physics majors were a tightly knit group of young men and a few women—made so not just by a kind of tribal affinity but by mere survival. The work was constant and sometimes brutally challenging. And Hal was the envy of all of us—the guy every other guy wanted to be friends with and the bright, handsome charmer whom women flocked to. At the end of his freshman year, he earned an award for the highest grade point average. During his sophomore year, he was elected president of the local chapter of the American Physics Association. As a result, he was granted internships and summer employment that would have easily opened the doors to a fabulous career, and one full of high achievement. In his junior year, Hal was initiated into Sigma Pi Sigma, the national honor society recognizing outstanding achievement in physics.

But in spite of his high academic achievements, Hal Clayborn was no dullard. As some of you remember, he had a keen wit and was an inveterate practical joker. You'd be in your dorm room and a guy would show up at your door with half-a-dozen pizzas from Papa Gino's. Of course, you hadn't ordered them—but Hal did, using your name and room number. And while you were left with having to dole out a big fat check, down the hall Hal and a bunch of other guys were having a good laugh. But that was fine, and everybody piled into your room and whooped it up, chowing down on the pies.

Hal had a few dorm favorites for his boyish pranks. I won't mention names just to protect the innocent, as they say, but I'm thinking of one fellow in particular, also a physics major. I know he's not out there in the audience, so I take the liberty of saying that he was from a poor family. And although he was bright, he was no genius like Hal but had attended here on small scholarships and loans. Because even back then the cost of education was high, summer jobs were coveted since they paid well, particularly in high-tech companies. During our junior year, Hal sent this poor fellow a letter on company stationery, offering him a high paying summer job. The letter was from the company's Human Resources Office saying that he had been recommended for the opening by his professors. Thrilled to the core, the young man showed up at the HR office only to learn that nobody knew who he was or what he was talking about or why he was there. The word rapidly spread, and you can imagine the laughs that got across the campus.

As I said, Hal was brilliant—and deservedly won award after award throughout his four years here. He was also a class leader, president of this organization and that, serving on the student senate, captain of the lacrosse team, and one of the few students on the university's board of advisors for faculty recruitment. I hope he would forgive me, but I have a confession to make—probably not something to utter in front of President Ryan and other university officials and faculty. But as you all know, physics was and may still be the toughest major on campus. I can tell you that I wasn't alone in the struggle through some advanced courses, terribly afraid like so many others of failing and losing my scholarship aid. I don't know how to say this without saying it, but on a few exams we cheated. I know: hard to believe, and I'm red-faced with shame. But back then we didn't see what we did as moral backsliding but pure desperation matched by pure altruism on the part of Hal Clayborn.

Yes, Hal who, as I said, regularly left exams early only to ace them.

We had worked out a clever system for our three-hour midterms and finals where one of us would sit next to Hal only to copy his answers when the instructor wasn't looking and pass them down the line to the rest, clutched in toes or gummed to the bottoms of our shoes. This lasted for a few tests and, thankfully, we managed do well and pull up our GPAs.

But didn't I say that Hal was something of a practical joker? Well, he pulled a good one on us. The final in Advanced Thermodynamics was short answers derived from some pretty hairy calculations done on scratch paper. What Hal did was flash the wrong answers to the guy next to him who passed them down the line. Then just minutes before time was up, Hal scribbled down the correct answers on his own test. I can tell you that the bell curve for that exam was grossly lopsided with one 90-something grade and a spike around the 40 and 50 percent. And that was the end of that. But we were grateful to Hal for a hard lesson in honesty.

As you can imagine, Hal was a perfectionist who was hard on himself when on those rare occasions he messed up on a written test or lab experiment. When he did make an error, his favorite expression was, "I must be taking stupid pills." An innocent and cute phrase, I agree, but one that didn't feel so cute when *you* were on the receiving end trying to make sense out of Schrödinger wave equations. As I mentioned, Hal had a favorite fall guy for this expression as well as his practical jokes—a blue collar kid who was bright but who lacked confidence in himself and was something of a follower, who looked up to Hal in wonder at his high cerebral wattage, his rock-star good looks, and considerable charm. This fellow was the same hapless kid who got surprise pizzas in the middle of the night. In any case, his father was very demanding and wanted him to be a roofer like himself instead of going to college. But his mother valued education and insisted he be the first in their family to graduate from college. Luckily he managed to get a ride on loans and scholarships. He was also a pretty good musician who played lead guitar in his fraternity rock band. And at the time he was dating a lovely young woman named Wendy.

It's no news flash that most of us undergrads, especially the male techies, lacked the fashion gene. As I said, Hal was a very strikingly handsome young man who could have been a male model and who could look good in an outfit of trash bags. One night at a frat party, Hal laid eyes on Wendy and, like so many achievements, he wanted her for himself and put on a full-court press. In those days, fraternities were still a big deal, taking up the slack for resident students—a financial boon for the university, hurting then for dormitory space. So being Greek was a big deal that essentially forged the social life for those who belonged to a house. As many of you may recall, Hal was a big party animal who like so many of us enjoyed a beer or two or three . . . or ten.

While her date was busy jamming with the rest of the Frat Rat band, Hal cornered Wendy and turned on his charming best. Being a bona fide Alpha Male, he could pick the women he wanted. In fact, to use his words, he had "more notches on his gun than Billy the Kid." And even though Wendy was dating someone else, Hal secretly pursued her for weeks, doing what he could to win her over, sending her flowers and candy, stuffed animals and greetings cards. He even dropped her a note suggesting that her guitarist boyfriend was not the marrying kind—at least not to women.

Those of you who remember Wendy know that she was a pre-med major, highly intelligent, a first-rate student, and a kind and generous person. One might also say self-sacrificing. During her sophomore year, she helped start a local Food Bank. She volunteered at senior citizens' homes, she also was a nurses' aide at summer camps for underprivileged children. All this while taking rigorous courses in biochemistry and physiology. Wendy was also drop-dead gorgeous—a woman whom Hal thought would be a fitting match for himself. And although he did all he could to win her affection, Wendy just didn't light up to him, remaining at a polite distance. But he persisted so much that she eventually broke down out of sympathy, I assume, and conceded to go to a Pearl Jam concert. The performance was fifty miles out of town; and because of a snow storm, they were forced to overnight at a local hotel. Although Wendy was never one for letting herself drink too much or find herself in uncompromising situations, she apparently did that fateful night. Weeks later she discovered she was pregnant with Hal's child.

Back then, they didn't have a name for what had happened that night, nor laws against such. Nor did they do chemical tests on victims. Also at that time, women didn't report such occurrences for fear of being accused of bringing such things upon themselves. So Wendy said nothing, not even to her closest women friends. Hal denied it was his child and left her to fend for herself. At the time Wendy was only twenty-two and didn't want to become a mother on the threshold of graduating from college and entering medical school.

Yes, I hear the dismay in your murmurs.

But I stand before you because of Harold W. Claymore, whose tragic and untimely death put an end to a remarkable young man and sterling academic career mere months before his own graduation and entrance into a doctoral program here.

As I may have mentioned, Hal and I were lab partners. And as physics majors, we were required to do theses on original research. His was a project on lithium batteries, focusing on enhancing the energy density and, thus, the life of such batteries in critical medical devices including pacemakers. As you chemists out there know, a key ingredient in lithium batteries is an inorganic compound called thionyl chloride—a liquid which is explosive when mixed with water. With the intent of adding another colorless and odorless reagent, Hal unsuspectingly poured a container of distilled water into a beaker, setting off a violent explosion.

After twenty-five years, it is still not known how the container became mislabeled, but the accident ended Hal's life—a life that was full of high promise and, no doubt, inestimable benefits to humanity. Although we all knew the safety precautions, Hal was scrambling to complete one final test to wind up his thesis. Yes, he should not have been working alone that late night. And, yes, he should not have taken stimulants to keep him awake. But Hal was driven to succeed.

Were he at this podium, and it were me in that lab, he'd say I had taken one too many stupid pills.

We missed Hal at graduation. But were he here tonight, I'm sure he'd get a kick of my accepting this award in his name. As would Wendy Walsh, my former fiancée who a week after graduation sadly died on an abortionist's table. I accept this award in her name. Thank you."

Gary Braver is an award-winning, bestselling author of eight critically-acclaimed novels. His work has appeared in *The Boston Globe*, *The New York Times, Writer Magazine,* and Edgar®-winning *Thriller 2 Anthology.* As Gary Goshgarian, he is an English professor at Northeastern University and author of five college-writing textbooks. He holds a BS in physics from W.P.I. which recently honored him with the Robert H. Goddard Award for Lifetime Achievement.

The Fibonacci Sequence

Angela Gerst

To see a world in a grain of sand and a heaven in a wildflower
—William Blake

Rome, February 1948

Day One

Edna Bast's morning had gone wrong so quickly she half-believed some touchy Roman god had turned against her. On her way to the *caffe*, she'd tripped on the sidewalk and collided with a woman in furs who glared when Edna apologized. A sudden cloudburst had left her clammy. Now, sipping coffee at a window table with a view of the embassy, she couldn't stop shivering, from nerves more than cold. She reached for her cigarettes, and knocked over her cup. What on *earth* was she doing here? Of all the expatriates in Rome, why was an aspiring artist from Little Compton, Rhode Island stalking a Soviet agent?

It was her own damn fault. She'd allowed Arnold Remington, chief of a hush-hush department at the United States Embassy, to charm her into it.

They'd been chatting at the American Academy's New Year's Eve party, when out of the blue Remington blurted, "There's a spy at the embassy," at the same time maneuvering her into an alcove where the only head close enough to eavesdrop was Julius Caesar's, on its marble plinth.

"We need your help."

"My help? But—"

"Hear me out. James Feller joined us last July and a few months later the leaks started." Top-secret information about the nascent North Atlantic Treaty Organization, the address of an OSS safe house, and other secrets "too sensitive" for Remington to mention, though he did speak of Stalin and the Soviet Union at such horrific length Edna had pressed a hand to her cheek.

"We couldn't break his cover. Tapped his phone, intercepted his mail, followed him. He evaded us at every turn. But you, Miss Bast, he'd have no reason to suspect."

Remington was working steadily at the punch, a heady brew of cognac and champagne that Edna sipped slowly to make it last. One cup was her limit. "Feller hides by making a spectacle of himself. When in Rome—"

"Do as the Romans do. My grandfather lived and died by those words."

"Theodore Bast was a wise man. Our embassy is still in his debt." Remington paused, Edna suspected, to let the flattery sink in, but it touched her just the same. "As his granddaughter, you know the meaning of public service . . . so I hope you'll forgive my presumption in asking for your help." The hand he placed on her arm was warm, but Edna shivered under her party silks.

"Feller must be stopped, or democracy will die, and not only in Italy. Western civilization itself could be lost."

"And you really think I'm the one to stop him?"

"Who better than Theodore Bast's granddaughter?"

Remington's compliment, with its sparkle of the past and the punch, made his request sound like an assignment Edna could handle if she found her Bast family courage. "Is Mr. Feller here?" She cast her eyes around the crowded room. "What if he remembers me later?"

"He never parties and couldn't possibly know who you are."

People rarely noticed Edna, but she didn't mind. She knew she was plain; she dressed with an almost extravagant simplicity. Why bother to gild the daisy, as she put it to herself.

"Unlike your grandfather, Feller refuses to do as the Romans do. Siesta, for example. Rome shuts down for three hours smack in the middle of the day. Takes getting used to, but all of us at the embassy manage. Except Feller. He eats lunch in the Borghese gardens— outside in the damp and cold. Then he goes for walks."

"Everyone in Rome takes walks."

"Not during siesta. Feller pretends he's the naive American, parading his cultural ignorance. But mark my words, while Rome naps, Feller does his dirty work." Remington's deep-set eyes searched hers, and she felt a tug of attraction. "Miss Bast . . . Edna . . .we need you."

"But how would I recognize him?"

"Care to see a picture of my dog?"

"Dog" was a subterfuge, Edna knew. *Loose lips sink ships,* as true today as during the war. This opulent Academy event had attracted people from all over Rome: Italian dignitaries, embassy staff, film directors—Edna noticed Rossellini talking with Gore Vidal, a writer she'd never heard of until tonight. Even the Bast family lawyer, Giorgio Perlongo, had dropped by. Anyone here might be a secret agent.

Remington passed her a snapshot of a man in a suit. "My pooch Banjo." He winked. "With my wife."

Wife. Another subterfuge? No. A man like Remington, assured, circumspect, almost cruelly good-looking—Edna glanced at Julius Caesar—couldn't possibly be single. A fleeting disappointment stung her. She blamed the punch.

From the snapshot, James Feller looked about forty, balding, pinched nostrils, long upper lip, chubby chin. The rosebud in his lapel added a touch of elegance at odds with his slightly silly face.

"He could be anybody. I'll end up following the wrong man."

"Can't miss him. He always wears a boutonniere." Remington leaned in, his voice as soft as feathers against her ear. "Edna, please help us, you're the only one who can."

The only one. In a few hours, Edna and the year would both turn forty-eight. She was as old as the century, a coincidence that surely forged a link between her fate and the fate of nations. She couldn't possibly refuse.

Weeks later, in mid-February, Remington called and reminded her of her promise.

At noon, Angelus bells began to ring from every church in Rome. The *caffe* emptied. The sun came out. Across the street, embassy staffers trickled down the steps, and Edna spotted Feller's bright yellow boutonniere. He nodded to a guard and headed toward the Borghese gardens, a functionary with a briefcase who walked on the balls of his feet. Edna pocketed her cigarettes and the guidebook she carried as a ruse, and followed. Half a mile on, Feller turned into the park, but by the time Edna arrived he'd vanished. Was the surveillance game over before it began? Trying not to panic, she prowled among a confusion of paths, fountains, statues, pines.

Eventually she found him, seated on a corroded iron bench, reading a book while he ate his sandwich. She settled down at a distance and lit a cigarette. With her nose in her Baedeker, she hoped she looked like that other American archetype, the tourist in winter. When Feller finished his sandwich, he stowed the wrapper and his book in the briefcase; so silent was this corner of the park, Edna heard the locks click into place.

For a while, Feller leaned back and didn't move, and Edna enjoyed the irony that a man who ignored siesta might actually be dozing. She jotted her observations on the Baedeker's flyleaves. Tomorrow, she'd bring a sketchpad.

The locks snapped open again, and Edna watched, electrified, as Feller removed a Kodak with folding lens. Creeping from flowerbed to flowerbed, he took close-ups of plants that hadn't yet bloomed, while Edna lurked among the pines, following the sound of his shutter.

Two hours later Feller returned to the embassy, and Edna trudged home to the little palazzo she'd inherited from her grandfather. In the library, she transcribed her notes, using the elegant longhand she was secretly proud of. "After photographing seven flowerbeds," she wrote, "Feller strolled through the park. He stopped once to chat with an old man who rented boats . . ."

Edna dropped her pen.

The boatman.

Was he Feller's connection?

Her black market chicken was served at six, the time Edna preferred when she dined alone. She told the girl Flaviana she would retire early. "I won't need you again until breakfast. Go out and enjoy yourself."

Flaviana's *grazie* and smiles touched Edna, who remembered what it was to be young and in love. Thirty years ago her fiancé Henry had perished in the Great War, of influenza, days before Armistice. Flaviana herself was engaged to Luca, a hero of the resistance whose burning eyes reminded Edna of Veronese's "Count da Porto." Flaviana had shown Edna her engagement gift, a magnificent lace handkerchief that she'd pressed to her face while she spoke of Luca's wartime sufferings. After the Germans captured him, only thoughts of Flaviana's beauty had kept him alive.

Now recalling Flaviana's story, Edna grew pensive. No one, not even Henry, who once confessed that he loved her pilgrim soul, had ever called Edna beautiful.

What was beauty? Was Flaviana beautiful? Despite her unruly hair and sallow skin, the girl had a Botticelli elegance . . . tempered by the "architectural restraint" of a Piero. Edna smiled at language she'd heard only this morning in Professor Jordan Smith's seminar, which she was so lucky to attend. Despite her lack of qualifications, the lawyer Perlongo had arranged for her admission to lectures at the American Academy. Perlongo knew everybody, and perhaps the Bast name still meant something in Rome.

In her cavernous bed, Edna reviewed this new life of hers, which had taken such an unexpected turn. She burrowed under her blankets, her mind drifting downstream like an empty boat. Far off she thought she heard sounds, Flaviana entertaining Luca in the kitchen, or neighborhood cats slinking through the garden.

Day Two

Her grandfather's opera glasses enabled Edna to lag far behind Feller, and she was glad she'd thought to bring them. Apart from Feller's new boutonniere—three orange tulips—spying on Tuesday was exactly like spying on Monday: sandwich, photography, walks. She lost him once, in a maze of shrubbery, but before she could panic, his boutonniere glimmered through the evergreens. He was standing stock still, and Edna had the uneasy sense that he was watching her.

Back at the palazzo, she transcribed her field notes from the sketchpad that had given her cover: Edna Bast, artist-spy.

The rest of the afternoon she devoted to Professor Smith's lavishly illustrated book on Italian Renaissance art, which inspired her to take mental inventory of her grandfather's collections, still in storage. Throughout the war, the lawyer Perlongo had protected them and was now arranging their return. There are many ways to be brave, Edna thought: with guns, with pens, with loyalty and quiet resistance.

Later, instead of dining out, Edna retired early again, in part to keep warm. Without central heating, the palazzo was chilly, except the library, where she liked to transcribe her notes beside the fire Flaviana always lit well before Edna returned from shadowing Feller. At midnight by her radium dial clock she woke to the sound of voices, but when she crept out of bed to check, her heart racing, there was no one outside her window. Just a dream, she thought. Edna often heard music and saw colors in her dreams, the mark of an artist, Grandpa Teddy had told her once, and it was true that Edna dabbled in watercolors.

Day Three

"Within every work of art there lurks a hidden structure." Professor Smith inserted a slide and Piero's "Baptism of Christ" filled the screen.

"Like Leonardo, Piero was a mathematician, a musician, and probably an engineer." The professor beamed. "That's why we call these fellows Renaissance men."

For all his smiles, Edna felt that Smith's reverence touched on obsession. "Piero the mathematician organized this painting according to ratios known as the Fibonacci sequence, first described by a twelfth century scholar of that name. Zero, one, one, two, three, five, eight, and so on."

Out of her depth, Edna began to drift while Smith burned on about Fibonacci numbers, their progression, their beauty, how they underpinned Piero's art.

"The sequence, or code if you will, may be hidden, but we perceive it intuitively. Tree . . . angels . . ."

Smith's voice was a thousand buzzing flies. Let him dismantle Piero's painting and pick over the pieces. For Edna, the whole was always greater than the sum of its parts.

"Some say the universe itself is ordered on Fibonacci principles." Smith tapped his pointer impatiently while his helper fumbled with another slide. "Here we see the Andromeda galaxy—note the spiraling arms."

As the slides advanced from galaxies to cloud formations to ripples in a pond, the images held Edna spellbound. Once seen, the patterns, the inevitable symmetries, could not be unseen. What had Smith said? "Nature's own code." For her to decipher.

In the taxi to the *caffe*, she pored over pictures Smith had distributed at the end of his lecture—beehives, artichokes, starfish— but kept returning to the daisy, galaxies of seeds spiraling out from its core. *A universe in a daisy*. For a moment, Edna forgot espionage and remembered what had brought her to Rome. She had come to find beauty, and it was hiding in plain sight, everywhere.

The rest of the day passed like the others. To relieve the anxious boredom of following Feller, Edna tried quick-sketching clumps of early violets that grew wild all over the park. They nearly cost her the game. When she looked up, Feller had vanished. *I can't do this*, she thought. *I am not Mata Hari*.

But Feller reappeared, on a path that led to the street, and she shadowed him back to the embassy. On the walk home, she celebrated her relief by smoking a cigarette.

In the library while she transcribed the same old notes, an insight blazed straight from Professor Smith's lecture. She phoned Remington. "It's the flowers! Feller takes snapshots of flowerbeds. They're a code. A natural occurrence . . . something about Fibonacci ratios."

"Stellar work, Miss Bast!"

Remington's praise made her feel like a flower herself. "I couldn't stop to check, I was afraid I'd lose him, but there are so many varieties. And variables—petals, colors, seed patterns . . . Feller must be using them to communicate."

"I'll inform our code breakers. Continue your surveillance. Write down every flowerbed he photographs, and in what order. And Edna, be careful."

Day Four

On Thursday everything changed. Wearing yesterday's boutonniere, Feller left the embassy ten minutes early. In the park, without stopping for lunch, he trotted to the boat shack. Through her opera glasses, Edna watched him step into a skiff and paddle off. By the time she hurried down, he'd vanished around a bend in the stream.

"Where did he go?" she asked the boatman, who didn't understand her frantic Italian until she offered a handful of Chesterfields. Then, in his gruff dialect he told her that the stream flowed into a small lake near the tramline. The circuit took half an hour.

Maybe Feller's boat ride was habitual and meant nothing.

Thirty minutes passed, then fifty. Feller had been gone too long. Edna rushed back to the boatman. "Where is he?" she shouted.

A wary look crossed the old man's face, and only when Edna held out five hundred lire did he tell her that Feller had paid the day rate. If he chose, he could stay out *sul imbrunire*.

Until dusk.

Feller must have beached the boat and taken the tram to his contact. Edna stared at the water until its braided currents made her dizzy.

"Signora? You all right?"

Nothing was all right. Even if Feller hadn't spotted her, through sheer incompetence she'd let him escape. Not a single day had passed without slip-ups, but today she had failed utterly. On the long walk home she reached a decision. She was aborting her mission.

The sight of her little palazzo, its austere lines and pale stucco walls, lifted her depression. She clanged the colossal bronze bell, and then, too impatient to wait for Flaviana, dug under the topiary for the spare key. Before she so much as poured herself a sherry she would sit by the fire and write her final report.

But the library was as cold as the checkered-marble entrance hall. She rang for Flaviana, once, twice, then went looking for her.

"Flaviana?" Where was that girl? Why hadn't she lit the fire? "Flaviana!"

She listened, but heard only stillness. Moving quickly to the workrooms, she passed through the kitchen where a liqueur bottle sat on the table. Had the reliable Flaviana been drinking in the middle of the day? Hardly. She was probably washing sheets in the laundry and hadn't heard the bell.

But Flaviana was not in the laundry. She was in her bedroom off the pantry, on the floor beside Remington, their heads a mess of brains and blood.

Flaviana and Remington. Traces of gun smoke burned Edna's throat, and she slumped against the door to keep from falling.

Then she used the kitchen telephone.

Giorgio Perlongo arrived with Harry Greene, Remington's superior, and Edna stuttered out stories about Feller's espionage, the Fibonacci code, her own surveillance work, secrets Remington had sworn her not to tell.

Greene interrupted. "Fibonacci flowerbeds? Ridiculous. James Feller is a low level clerk. This was a lovers' ruse. Remington sent you on a wild goose chase so he could meet Flaviana here. And someone caught them out." He frowned at Edna, as if he suspected her.

From Perlongo, Edna learned that budget cuts had cost Flaviana her job as an embassy maid last summer. "Your palazzo needed a caretaker, and as Flaviana was known to be a hard-working intelligent girl, I hired her."

Budget cuts? More likely someone at the embassy discovered the affair and fired her. "How long were they . . .?"

"I have no knowledge," Perlongo said, in his precise lawyer's voice. "But after Remington's wife joined him from America, they must have used your palazzo. Until you arrived, late December, wasn't it?"

Something hardened inside Edna then. People she'd treated with kindness had betrayed her. *Et tu, Flaviana?* By stealing the palazzo for their trysts, the lovers had deceived not only Edna, but Remington's wife and Flaviana's fiancé. And they'd dishonored Edna's grandfather; Teddy Bast had cherished his Roman sanctuary.

One palazzo, two betrayers, three betrayed . . . the Fibonacci lecture snaked through Edna's mind and she couldn't drive it out. A shrewder woman would have grasped the truth long before the murders: civilization was not at risk. The fate of nations did not depend on little Edna Bast. Remington had played her for a fool.

Perlongo telephoned the police commissioner, and the matter was quietly resolved. Flaviana's Luca, well known as a jealous hothead, was arrested that afternoon.

Two people had been slaughtered in her home, and Edna was grateful when Perlongo insisted she stay with him for a few days. "My young sons and my mother share my apartment," he'd added, as if Edna needed assurances that this stocky widower's intentions were beyond reproach.

A few days became a week, and by the time Edna left, she and the Perlongos were using first names. "American style," Giorgio had said, rather impishly for him.

Back home, the murders haunted her, as did Luca, his cries of innocence. How odd that he would execute the lovers, a single bullet to the base of each skull. Wouldn't a hothead simply blast away? And the gun had not been found.

Without solid evidence of Luca's guilt, Edna could not stand by and let him be railroaded. Others had motive: A thief after the Bast collections. Or Remington's wife. Had she even been questioned?

Edna phoned Giorgio, and he agreed to arrange a private investigation. "But remember, dear Edna, almost always the obvious solution is the correct one."

It was the "almost" that plagued her. On the day of the murders, she remembered, Flaviana's room seemed disordered, as if the killer had done a hasty search, perhaps interrupted by Edna's clanging doorbell. If Flaviana had hidden something worth stealing—the motive for murder?—it had surely been found, if not by the murderer, then by the police.

But Flaviana was a clever girl. If she had something to hide—a big "if"—why not use the pantry or kitchen? They wouldn't take long to search. The bottle of *centerbe* Edna had noticed the day of the murders was still on the table. Tidy Flaviana stored liqueurs in the cupboard, so why had she left it out? Had she jammed something inside the bottle, with no time to put it away? Edna removed the cork and inhaled the aroma of bitter herbs. Then she held the bottle to the light and was disappointed to see only liqueur.

Returning the bottle to its shelf, she noticed that, shallow though it was, the cupboard might make a hidey-hole. She explored and, in a recess behind rows of glasses, unearthed a copybook filled with recipes.

But recipes belonged in the pantry.

Edna's hands shook under the weight of her find.

She held the book upside down, flapped the pages and finally, from inside its spine, teased out Flaviana's exquisite handkerchief.

Why hide a handkerchief?

Like a blind woman reading braille, she ran a finger over the lace. On each corner she felt, and then saw, tiny knots that looked newly embroidered. They varied in number: three, nine, seven, followed by spaces, more knots, more spaces. Were the knots random? Were they markers? Almost against her will, Edna looked for a Fibonacci progression. The knots must mean something.

She needed advice, but not Giorgio's. With his exacting mind he would pooh-pooh her suspicion that the handkerchief was connected to the murders. She didn't want him to think her foolish. Giorgio's good opinion, she realized, mattered to her.

The embassy man, Greene, maybe he could help. He knew Remington. He knew Flaviana. He knew a hoax from a mission. Even more than Giorgio, Harry Greene was a man who *knew*.

An aide put Edna's call through.

"Flaviana's handkerchief? Knots?" Greene chuckled. He'd stop at the palazzo on his way home for lunch and take a look, he told her, so very casually Edna suspected the knots did mean something, and that he would come sooner.

But when the bell clanged, the man at her door was James Feller. The hyacinth in his lapel exuded a sour reek, and without meaning to she stepped back. "Mr. Feller. I'm so embarrassed. Please accept my apology for . . ."

"Keeping an eye on me?" His brief smile assured her that he wasn't offended. "Harry sent me to pick up the," he hesitated, "your find."

"Yes, of course. Come in."

She left him in the library and hurried to the kitchen where her thoughts began to slow down and collide. Feller said he'd come for her "find," a hollow word. She'd given Greene specific details about the handkerchief, details Feller seemed unaware of. And if Greene had pretended to humor her, Feller was all business. Had Greene really sent him? All she knew was, James Feller, his twitchy smile, his hyacinth that stank of death, alarmed her.

She picked up the phone, and when she couldn't reach Greene, called Giorgio. "James Feller is here, and I'm nervous alone with him."

Giorgio told her he would come immediately. His office was a mile away, a twenty-minute walk, if he could manage the pace. This close to noon a taxi would take longer, Edna knew. Somehow she had to stall until Giorgio or Greene arrived: there were questions Feller needed to answer that she didn't know how to ask. She filled her cigarette case from a carton in the pantry, twisting a Chesterfield into her holder, hunting down the Ohio blue tips. Finally, she dawdled back to the library in a drift of smoke.

Feller was standing near a window. Winter light sharpened his face and laid his shadow on the floor. She decided to test him. "I must have left the codebook in my bedroom," she said. *Codebook, not handkerchief, and Feller didn't bat an eye.* The silence between them thickened. Did he sense he'd made a mistake?

His hand strayed to his lapel. "Understand that Remington and Flaviana were in it together. They cheated the Soviets and when the Soviets found out they executed them."

Edna lifted the ivory holder to her lips and inhaled to the pit of her lungs. "How do you know?"

"It's my job to know. I was brought in to find the leaks."

"You?"

He seemed offended by her surprise. "I'd been onto Remington for months."

"Were you aware I was following you?"

He grinned. "Miss Bast, you must never become a spy."

"Why did you play along?"

"To put Remington at ease while I gathered evidence. Now if you'll get the codebook, I'll be on my way."

She could almost believe him. But his eyes frightened her, their eerie brightness, wired for deceit. If Feller had been playing along, he wouldn't have ditched her in the Borghese gardens. And Greene wouldn't send a man he'd called "a low level clerk" and expect her to trust him. An operator at the embassy switchboard must have alerted Feller to her call, misunderstanding the heart of it.

Slowly, the truth sifted down. After all the twists, subterfuges, and lies Edna was back to square one. Feller, not Remington, was the spy. Flaviana had been *his* accomplice. They'd exploited Remington's passion for her, and whenever Remington let secrets slip, Flaviana passed them to Feller who sold them to the Soviets. There it was in a nutshell.

That deadly afternoon Feller must have paid Flaviana a surprise visit. He'd have wanted something in a hurry—the so-called codebook? In front of Remington, Flaviana may have tried to play dumb but Remington would've realized, too late, that he'd been their stooge. However it happened, Feller had murdered them.

It was almost noon. Where was Giorgio?

"Let's have a glass of sherry first, Mr. Feller. Or do you prefer grappa?"

He took a sharp step toward her, unbuttoned his jacket and let her see the gun holstered under his arm. "Just the codebook, Miss Bast."

His smile, she realized, was a tic. He was going to force her to give him her "find" and then kill her.

No. Teddy Bast would've gone down fighting. So would his granddaughter.

"Have a cigarette!" She lunged, jamming her red-hot Chesterfield straight into his eye. He howled and fumbled for his gun, but she snatched it out of the holster.

Far off a door crashed open. "Edna! Where are you?"

"Here, Giorgio!"

Pressing a hand to his bloody eye, Feller bolted to a window and tried to leap over the sill. Edna put a bullet in his thigh.

March 1948

Weeks after Edna had been what Harry Greene called "debriefed," she and Giorgio sat in her library drinking a *prosecco* Giorgio had brought back from a business trip to Venice. Edna's new housekeeper was a superb cook, and the *agnello arrosto*—lamb on the first day of spring was a Roman tradition—would soon be served in all its herbed and basted glory. If only Edna had an appetite. While Giorgio was away she'd caught a cold, and her elation at outsmarting Feller had faded.

"Greene didn't give much away," she said. Giorgio probably knew more than she about the entire affair but she needed to talk. "He did tell me Feller named names and admitted everything."

"How else to save his skin?"

"As Greene explained it, Flaviana wanted to eliminate Feller and deal directly with the Soviets. When Feller found out, he killed her and Remington."

Edna wandered to the fireplace, filled with tulips instead of flames on this warm evening. "There was no codebook, only Flaviana's handkerchief. The knots identified her bank safes. One for her assets, another for her secrets, including the name of a Soviet double agent planted by NATO." She swung around. "I feel like an idiot, harboring a spy under my roof and missing all the signs."

"Nonsense. You discovered the secrets of the handkerchief. You forced Feller's hand. Thanks to you, NATO's mission is safe."

The blood rushed to Edna's face. Perhaps the fate of nations *was* somehow bound up with hers, for this moment in time. Her time. One brief moment, blink and it's over. The Great War hadn't brought peace. Would NATO survive? She lived in Rome where an empire had fallen. Yet the city endured, blossoming around her.

Giorgio proposed a toast. "To you, my spy for all seasons."

"And you, a man I can count on." She studied her glass. "Look at the bubbles, Giorgio. They seem random, but they rise in a sequence. You just have to find the code." Fibonacci again, an incessant melody only she could hear.

"My beautiful Edna," Giorgio touched his glass to hers, "there is no code for *prosecco*. Or love."

A mix of emotions, fear, love, melancholy, unsettled her. She returned Giorgio's toast, and then lost herself in the randomness of wine.

Angela Gerst's "The Secret Life of Books" appeared in MWA's 2013 anthology, *The Mystery Box. A Crack In Everything* came out in 2011, Poisoned Pen Press. *In Harm's Way*, a work-in-progress, features an MIT dropout who parses the odds for her clients. "The Fibonacci Sequence" is second in a series set in post WWII cities around the world.

The Wedding Gift

Katherine Fast

2002 Toyota RAV4, license RW6—The crackle of the radio interrupted Officer Mannon's cataloging of the make, model, year, and license of every last vehicle that drove past his cruiser tucked in an alley off Main Street.

"Robbie, you there?"

Finally, a call, but probably just more busywork. "Officer Mannon, here."

"We've got a possible domestic at the Jamesons' place. Can you take it?"

"Affirmative." Although the ink was barely dry on Robbie's police academy certificate, he didn't appreciate Dispatch's familiarity. He was an officer of the law, not her grandson, for god's sake. Stuck out here in Nowhere, USA, population 7,215 on an absolutely dead night shift assignment.

He waited a few moments, but apparently Mrs. Lawson had signed off. He called back. "Ma'am, I'll need an address."

"Oh dear, I forget you're new to town. You go out the old Ridge Road a mile or so, past where the Dairy Queen used to be and then take a right on the second road, can't remember the name. Hold on a sec." Mrs. Lawson hollered, "Pete, can you give Robbie directions to the Jamesons'? I got another call coming in."

The Chief picked up. "The old Ridge Road is Route 20. From town, go west on 20 say, three miles. You'll see a dirt road on the right—it's called Jameson Road, but it isn't marked. Follow the road a ways and you'll see a big red barn on the right. Can't miss it."

"Any information on the situation, sir?"

"An elderly lady, Iva Tweedel, lives alone in a cottage across the road from the Jamesons. She said when the Jamesons returned from the Grange dance, she heard a lot of yelling and then a loud crash followed by a howl." He paused a second and then added, "Iva is a regular caller with a rather inventive imagination, but we have to follow up." He clicked off.

Sure, a red barn at midnight out some godforsaken back road. "Can't miss it," Robbie muttered. He flipped on the siren and strobes and spit gravel as the cruiser shot out of the alley.

"Choke it, Rob. It's a domestic, not a terrorist attack," the Chief's voice ordered over the radio.

Robbie gave the siren one last passive-aggressive whoop and sped out Route 20. He never got a chance to use all the toys. He passed fields and trees and fences and more fields. God, what do these people *do* out here? Churn butter and split logs? After five miles, he realized that he'd overshot the dirt road and had to double back. When he finally found the turnoff he was forced to a crawl as the cruiser jounced over deep ruts in the unpaved road.

The Chief was wrong. If it weren't for the moon, he would have missed the Jamesons' place completely. He turned into the driveway and pulled up behind a pickup parked half on and half off the drive with the driver's door hanging open. *2014 Ram 150 SLT 4X4.* Another car was parked in front of the pickup and a third beside the house.

Probably some redneck farmer had a few pops, came home half-cocked, fought with the wife, threw a few things. Although he knew domestics could turn nasty, especially when the cops showed up, he was a big, tough city kid. Nothing he couldn't handle. He cracked his knuckles, squared his shoulders and hitched his heavy equipment belt. Ready.

The air carried the scent of manure and hay from the barn behind the house. Not a sound but crickets, and no lights on in the big old farmhouse that loomed before him. He shuffled through newly fallen leaves to the truck. He put a light into the cab and peered inside. Empty.

"Bang!" An object ricocheted off the hood next to his head. Robbie dropped to a crouch and drew his gun, turning in a circular motion, searching the shadows for movement. A second acorn bounced off his head and fell at his feet. God, he was glad he was alone. He slowed his breathing until his heartbeat returned to normal.

Holstering his gun, he closed the door to the pickup and approached the house. No doorbell. Figures. He raised his hand to knock before he realized the door was open. "Graniston Police. This is Officer Mannon."

No answer. "Mr. Jameson?" He pushed the door open wide, entered and hugged the foyer wall in the dark. He felt behind him and hit a light switch. A dim overhead light illuminated a hallway with doors to the left and right and stairs to the second floor.

He called out one more time. He didn't want to startle anyone. At six foot four inches with the build of a linebacker, dressed in full police uniform he knew he intimidated people. No response. Evidently the "domestic disturbance" had petered out. Still, he needed to confirm all was safe.

He turned into the living room, winced and jumped aside to ward off a blow from a knight in full metal armor brandishing a lethal three-foot-long sword. He gasped and backed into something soft and furry. Turning, he looked into the glassy eyes of an enormous grizzly bear. *"Sheeit!"*

He flipped on a light. The place was a frickin' museum. A full-sized carousel horse stood in one corner with a man's jacket draped across the pommel of the saddle, and an upright piano occupied another. The room smelled musty with a hint of pipe tobacco and the sweet smell of marijuana. What kind of farmer smoked weed and had an armored knight and a stuffed grizzly in his living room?

He walked down the hallway and cracked open the next door. This time, he reached inside and turned on the overhead light before entering. Ceiling high bookshelves lined every wall space. Recliners, a wide-screen TV, papers on a small table. No people.

He returned to the hall and approached the dining room. A long wooden table dominated the center of the room. Two empty glasses with limes at the bottom sat on the table. He sniffed the closest glass. Gin.

Maybe it was just a lover's quarrel. A toke, a drink or four, some yelling and banging about. Kiss and make up. Could be upstairs in the sack as he wandered about their house. He smiled. Maybe one of them was a howler. His smile gave way to a frown. By now, even if he'd interrupted a love-in, someone should have responded to his multiple calls.

Again nothing was overturned or broken. No signs of a struggle. So what was the crash? And how could the old lady from across the street hear a crash from inside her house?

Family pictures lined the sideboard. Weddings, graduations, babies. Big family. A tall breakfront cabinet stuffed with china and glassware dominated the far wall. Interesting, the bottom cabinet door was open.

"Graniston Police. Anyone home?" he called as he entered the kitchen. Plates and glasses were stacked in the sink, and peanut butter and jelly and a gooey knife were on the counter. Maybe hubby didn't like his dinner, or they got the pot hungries.

A light tap on his shoulder sent him reeling. He spun around and reached for his weapon. A large tabby atop a cabinet jumped to the floor and dashed away. *Relax, man, relax.* Just a house full of weird crap and an angry couple. Who weren't anywhere to be found.

He felt a draft and followed the cat through a pantry and a mudroom to the back door. Wide open.

OK, the old lady across the road probably heard an argument and then the door slammed when one of them went outside to cool off. Except the door was wide open. Nothing made sense.

Robbie unhitched the mag light from his belt, stepped outside and was immediately accosted by the smell of chlorine. A pool. Gentleman farmer hippy freak with a pool. "Hello?" he called. Nothing.

He waved the light back and forth as he walked across a patio. On the deck, he spotted a pile of clothing. *Uh-oh!* Quickly he shone the light into the water. No one on the bottom. No floaters. He reminded himself to breathe. He poked the clothing with his boot. Adult duds, male and female. Pretty late in the season for swimming. He dipped his hand into the water. Heated. A little skinny-dipping at the end of the season? Playful couple.

He beamed the light around the deck and stopped a few feet from the back door where it picked up a glint of something. What the hell? He edged closer. Glass sparkled on the deck next to a large piece of slate. He skimmed his light across the back of the house. No broken windows and no glass in the back door.

He stooped to pick up a shard of glass. Heavy. Thick. Next to the glass he spotted a few dark spots on the deck. He knelt for a better look. Shiny. He touched one. Wet. Sticky. *Omigod, blood.* Something serious had gone down here. Heart pounding, his adrenaline surged.

Dropping to a defensive crouch, he shone the light around the perimeter, but couldn't see anything unusual. Slowly he followed the trail of blood around the pool past a table and chairs under a large umbrella. Past buckets of flowers. Past a lounge chair. Another lounge chair. A body.

"Holy crap!" Robbie took in a sharp breath. A large man lay splayed across the chair, not moving. Robbie inched forward. "Sir?" No response. He placed his finger on the man's neck. A pulse! He couldn't tell where all the blood was coming from. Turn him over? When was it you weren't supposed to touch a body?

He radioed and spoke with the Chief. "Man down, with a lot of blood. Can't tell how serious his injuries are. Big guy—maybe two-hundred-fifty pounds—white hair."

"Sounds like Mack Jameson."

Robbie's mental image of the couple instantly aged twenty years.

"Any sign of Mrs. Jameson?"

"Nothing so far, sir."

"The neighbor just called in again. Says she saw two people streaking across the pasture behind the house."

"*Two?* Was she sure?"

"Yeah. Iva sits on the porch in the dark with night vision goggles. She also said a white horse was running loose down the road. Keep your eye open for Mrs. Jameson, but be careful. I'll send backup and an ambulance."

Robbie signed off and checked Mr. Jameson again. Still breathing. God, the man reeked of alcohol. Robbie's mind raced with possibilities given the new information. Three players were involved. OK, so the husband returns home loaded, finds his wife with another man. They fight; he's injured. But no, the couple went to the dance together, and presumably returned together.

There were three cars. Maybe it wasn't a domestic at all. They return from the party and interrupt a burglary in progress. Mr. J battles with the thief and is injured. Still doesn't explain two figures running across the field. Unless . . . Robbie took a deep breath . . . the burglar heard his cruiser drive up to the house, knew his car was blocked, grabbed Mrs. J, and it's a hostage situation. Yeah, that's it.

Time was now a critical factor. The longer a person was missing or abducted, the lower the chance of recovering them alive. Nothing he could do for Mr. J, and the horse could find its own way home. He had to find Mrs. Jameson.

Robbie pushed open the back pool gate. If the old lady saw the abductor and Mrs. J running, they had to be on the other side of the house, otherwise the stockade fence around the pool would block her view.

Behind the house were fields, a paddock and the barn. With Mrs. Jameson slowing him down, the man's best bet was the barn.

To get there, he'd have to cross through the paddock. And the paddock gate was open. That explained the loose horse. From there it was a straight shot to the barn. There were two people out there, one of them was probably armed, and he was standing in the moonlight like a fool mulling over the situation.

He sprinted through the paddock to the front of the barn and pasted himself against the wood siding. He reached for a metal ring to pull aside the heavy barn door. *Wait.* Think. The barn would have a front and a back door. With him out front, the man could escape with Mrs. J and be halfway to nowhere by the time he entered. Better for him to cover the rear. Then when backup arrived, they'd be surrounded.

He fought his way through brambles to the rear door. Closed. They're still inside. He unclipped his radio, cupped his hand around the mike and whispered, "Hostage situation. Abductor with Mrs. Jameson in the barn. Suspect armed and dangerous. Rear door secured. Approach from the front." He clicked off.

He found the brass ring and hesitated. He'd really announce his presence when he hauled the door open. Nothing to be done about it. He couldn't help Mrs. J from outside. He turned off the light and clipped it to his belt to free his hands, grabbed the ring and pulled. The door didn't budge. He yanked, and the door moved and then settled back in place. He threw his full weight into it and was propelled sidewise with the door as it rumbled along a metal track and tossed him on his ass.

He crawled inside the barn and flattened against the siding. Moonlight shone through the doorway illuminating a tractor on heavy wood planking in the center. Stalls lined both sides, each with a Dutch door open at the top. Next to him, a mean-looking pitchfork guarded a tack room. He pushed the door open with his boot and crouched. All he heard was his own shallow breathing and the banging of his heart.

Couldn't see a damn thing. To secure the rear, he'd have to make sure the room was clear. With one hand on his weapon, he sprang to the side, grabbed his flashlight, and lit the room. Saddles and bridles, brushes and other equipment hung off pegs and filled shelves. He exhaled slowly, gripping the light with both hands to keep it from shaking, and returned to the barn proper.

Rustling. Or was it his imagination? Once again, he unsnapped his holster. Walking slowly, he checked each stall as he passed and then crossed the centerboards to the other side. In the middle, a wooden ladder led up to the hayloft. A whimper and a sharp whisper. *Not* his imagination.

The sound came from above. He shined the light upwards. Motes of dust and a wisp of hay wafted downward in the light. They were in the loft! They had to know he was below.

"You up there," he called in his best cop voice. "Come on down, now." What were the odds the man would surrender? Zero, if he hadn't done so by now.

He really, really didn't want to expose himself on a ladder. He'd be a sitting duck. He doused the light to conceal his position. If he were smart, he'd wait for backup.

Another whimper, and a high voice, "No!"

Mrs. J? His knees definitely did not want to climb those rungs. Not a sitting duck, a *chicken*. Show some grit; earn respect. Rescue Mrs. Jameson and catch her abductor. He wiped a sweaty palm on his uniform, and stared at the ladder. *Come on, man, move!*

He clipped the light to his belt, drew his gun and thumbed off the safety. He climbed upward with as much stealth as possible, left hand on the ladder, and in the right, his gun. At the top he sprang onto the loft floor gripping the gun before him with both hands and then ducked and rolled behind a hay bale.

Rustling. *But where?* He snapped on his light and rolled it to the side away from him. Pivoting slowly, he searched each portion of the loft.

"Police. Come out, hands over your head."

Nothing.

"One more chance. You're surrounded. Come out slowly, and no one will get hurt."

Movement to his right. He whipped to the side and aimed his gun at a mound of straw.

One tiny hand emerged, then another, followed by a small face with enormous eyes. "Don't shoot, mister, don't shoot!" whimpered a little boy staring into the barrel of the gun. Next to him another mound moved and rose, revealing a slightly taller child. Finally a third mound shook and a teenage boy stood, hands in the air.

Robbie lowered the gun. His knees gave way and he sank onto a bale of hay, heart pounding, sweat beading his forehead. *Jesus God,* he'd come that close to popping a little boy. "What the hell are you kids doing up here?"

"Sleeping," squeaked the littlest one.

The Chief pulled into the Jamesons' drive behind a Fire and Rescue vehicle and the backup cruiser, both with strobes flashing. As he jumped out of his car, two EMTs emerged from the stockade fence carrying a large form on a stretcher. The first EMT called out, "No hurry, Chief. Mr. Jameson has a nasty cut on his foot. Found him sleeping off a bender beside the pool." They loaded the inert form into the ambulance.

Moments later, two naked figures came out of the woods escorted by two backup police officers.

"Adam and Eve," muttered the Chief, trying to suppress a smile but mostly trying not to ogle the girl. Sally Kennedy, Graniston High's head cheerleader was a sight to behold in the buff. She and her boyfriend did their best to cover their privates, but there was plenty to see. They shivered in the night air, and Sally's hair dripped water down her ample front.

The Chief opened his mouth to ask a question, but a bobbing light by the barn distracted him. As the beam drew closer, he made out two shorter figures accompanied by one very tall one.

"Giddy up!" commanded a little fellow from his perch on Robbie's shoulders.

The taller of the other figures held the light, while the third peppered Robbie with questions. "Can I hold it? Is it real? Have you ever shot anyone?"

The Chief tilted his head to the side and swallowed another smile.

The tallest boy fumbled the light when he caught sight of Sally's fine rack. Couldn't blame the kid. The Chief addressed the first backup officer. "Give her your jacket and get 'em inside." He couldn't resist catching the rear view as they walked to the farmhouse. He sighed before speaking to Robbie. "Howdy, cowpoke. Who are those little dogies?"

"Grandchildren," mumbled Robbie.

"Help settle the boys inside," the Chief instructed the second officer. "But be careful. Don't let 'em get the drop on you."

Robbie scowled as the officer led the merry troupe away. Before he could explain the situation, a woman riding bareback astride a great white horse galloped into view. Her long silver hair flew behind her as they thundered up the drive and reined up a few feet from the Chief. "What's all the commotion, Chief?"

The Chief made a small bow. "A good evening to you, Mrs. Jameson." He nodded toward the ambulance. "Apparently Mack cut his foot on a piece of glass." He raised his eyebrows.

She glanced from the ambulance to the retreating couple and then to the officer escorting her grandchildren. "It's a long story," began Mrs. Jameson.

"The night is young," the Chief replied rocking back on his boots.

Mrs. J turned the horse, waved at Iva across the street and then rode to the barn.

The Chief and Robbie sat at the dining room table drinking coffee and listening to Mrs. Jameson's account of the evening's events. When she finished, the Chief leaned forward. "Let me recap so Officer Mannon here has all the detail he needs to write up the Police Log."

Cheeks ablaze, Robbie shifted in his chair and stared at the mug that he gripped with both hands. He stole a sideways glance at the Chief to see if he was smirking, but the older man maintained a first-class deadpan.

"When you and Mack came home early from your anniversary party because he'd tied one on, you surprised the babysitter and her boyfriend who'd smoked a joint and were skinny-dipping in the pool. You and Mack had a shouting match; you grabbed the punch bowl and smashed it on the back stoop. He slammed out the door, stepped on a piece of glass, and howled before staggering to the lounge chair where he passed out.

"The babysitter and boyfriend then streaked across the field, through the paddock leaving the gate open. The horse escaped and galloped down the road. The grandchildren, who were having a sleepover in the hayloft, supposedly under the supervision of the babysitter, were terrified by all the crashing and howling and burrowed under the hay. You took off down the road after the horse. Is that about right?"

Mrs. Jameson nodded.

"So, what's with the punch bowl?"

"Forty years ago today, Mack's aunt gave us a Waterford crystal punch bowl and twenty cups for a wedding present. It was an absolutely useless gift for a couple of hippies on a farm until one night I got so mad at Mack, I grabbed a cup and chucked it across the room. After that, whenever one of us got seriously pissed off, we'd grab a cup and smash it out back. Tonight I finally got to the punch bowl."

The Chief turned to Robbie. "You get all that, Rookie?"

Robbie scratched something on his notepad. "Yep." He showed the sheet to the Chief. Three words: "Perfect wedding gift."

Katherine Fast (aka Kat) enjoys writing, watercolor, handwriting analysis and working with her co-editors/publishers on Level Best Books. Her short stories have received awards in multiple venues. She and her husband live in Massachusetts with their dog Magnolia (Maggie Mae) and two kitties, Caddie and Crash.

Words Can Kill

Shelly Dickson Carr

Sebastian Merrick was the best playwright in Boston. Opening night reviews for his productions at the Huntington Theatre were so impressive and his reputation so exalted that he could ruin an aspiring playwright's career with one disparaging remark leaked to the press disguised as pithy commentary.

A Sebastian Merrick play always ended up at Lincoln Center or on Broadway. Scholarly and astute, with a plethora of Tony Awards, he was Boston's most eligible bachelor.

But could his luck last? Would the ever-fickle drama critics remain constant? Yes, Sebastian reasoned, as long as he continued to write plays with signature references to Diderot and Stendhal (whom most had never heard of) and Chekhov and Ibsen (whom most had).

So it was no surprise that the cultural elite in Boston admired Sebastian Merrick, or that Benedita Constanza adored him. Her homage was not singular among aspiring writers, only the most pronounced. When Sebastian married her, no one could explain it. He was an artistic Goliath; she, a literary neophyte.

Sebastian met Benedita at his ex-boyfriend's annual beach party at the Buzzard's Bay Yacht Club. Nelson (who liked to be called Nelly) was a world-renowned set designer who summered on Cape Cod. Benedita was the daughter of his caterer.

"Sebbie, darling," Nelson had said with trilling voice and punctuating hand gestures. "You must meet Ricco's daughter. Be nice, Seb. Ricco is a culinary genius. I can't afford to have you alienate the best chef on the planet. Benedita has aspirations to become a—" Nelson rolled his tongue around in his wide mouth with impish glee,

"—dramatist. Go over and talk to her. She's the shy little thing in the corner. Black curly hair. Skinny. Not unattractive, but totally out of her element. She's written a play or some such. Don't bare your teeth at her, Seb, or Ricco might poison the puff pastry."

Sebastian had rolled his eyes. There wasn't a party, outing, performance, or gala where he was not presented with a friend of a friend's play. He had fobbed off more wannabe writers than the Pied Piper's rats—and not by piping, but by stern looks of disapproval. His famous dragoon glare sent most newbie playwrights scampering.

Dressed all in black, Benedita Constanza had a row of tiny silver rings poking through her left eyebrow and a diamond chip sparkling in her nose.

"Good lord," Sebastian muttered under his breath. "Why do young people with artistic inclinations always have face piercings and the sartorial acumen of a slug? Must every would-be writer wear black?"

Nelson tugged him along by the elbow. "Ah! Ms. Constanza! This is Sebastian Merrick. You know, *the* playwright." And with that Nelson flitted away down the green expanse of lawn sloping to the beach, where Benedita's father was shucking oysters at the iced raw bar.

Sebastian turned a jaded eye on the girl. He resented the introduction, but begrudged the temerity of novice writers even more. If he tried until doomsday he would not be able to impress upon the proverbial amateur that the ability to write a halfway decent play eluded even writers of true genius.

Out of deference to Nelson, Sebastian did not glare at the girl, even though she was clutching a half-chewed pencil in one hand, a manuscript secured by a rubber band in the other. She must have sensed his annoyance because she blushed and stammered, "I—I can't believe it's you! I mean . . . well, you're . . . I mean," she continued to stammer. "I dreamed I'd meet you someday." Her large, cognac brown eyes, below their pierced brows, looked up at him with reverence.

What could he do but soften? And not because she recognized in him the virtuoso that he was, but because she let it be known by her voice, her look, her body language that talking to him was the crowning event in her young life. He would not only tolerate her, he told himself, but take enjoyment in her company.

They talked about his latest play, in its second season on Broadway. She told him she was attempting to transfer into the writing program at Emerson College in Boston. "But I'm . . . I'm . . ."

"Yes?" He glanced down at her.

"I'm struggling with the essay question . . . on . . . the . . . *um* . . . application," she said, hesitantly.

Sebastian's eyes narrowed. "What sort of essay question?"

"Can books be dangerous? Should books ever be banned? I need examples. Can literature . . . ever . . . be . . . harmful, Mr. Merrick?"

"Sebastian. You must call me Sebastian."

She bit her lip. "I—I can't come up with a good . . . answer. D— do you have any ideas?" She looked about to cry.

He opted for the Socratic method, after all she was a mere child. "What do you think? Can literature be inflammatory? And if so, what should society do about it?"

Her face suffused with a crimson wash. "No book should ever be banned. They tried to do that with Tom Sawyer, right? It's wrong. It's just wrong." Her lower lip jutted out in a semblance of fierce determination, as if ready to defend her pronouncement to the death. But a moment later that same lower lip was quivering with indecision. "I'm right, aren't I?"

Sebastian's eyes zeroed in on hers with razor-sharp focus. "What about Hitler's *Mein Kampf*, or a book that promotes child pornography? Or one that tries to incite racial hatred?"

She gasped. "Of course! I hadn't thought of that. That's it! That's the answer! We, as a society, c—can't allow books that hurt children. Why didn't I think of that?"

"And yet . . ." Sebastian said with avuncular flair, "who is to judge what book is bad or harmful? Who might society trust to arbitrate such moral disputes?"

She looked confused. "B—But child pornography? I think everyone can agree it's morally wrong, so—"

"*Really?* Shouldn't abhorrent ideas be challenged by better ones, not banned? Even you, Miss Constanza, might read a book that is full of bigotry, but be reasonably intelligent enough to analyze it, challenge its ideas, and articulate better ones."

The girl hastily scribbled down his words on the back of her manuscript.

Sebastian realized that though Benedita's thoughts and sensibilities were untrained, she was inordinately eager, with a desire to please that saved him from being bored at yet another of Nelson's obligatory beach parties. The fact that Benedita Constanza was petite and pretty, with slim hips and a pouty, pubescent mouth longing to be kissed, had little to do with his attraction, or so he told himself.

Three months later, she moved in with him. Not once had he asked to read her play, but when, at long last, she timidly offered it to him, he convinced himself that if her skill as a writer was banal (as surely it must be) he would merely persuade himself that beneath the immaturity of her style and improbability of her characterizations, was a glimmer of rare talent. But then he remembered the golden rule of any artistic relationship. *Never critique one's lover's art.* It would inexorably lead to the first of many tiffs, if not out and out guerrilla warfare. No. He couldn't risk it.

So he decided on a different course of action. He asked her to marry him. As his wife, she could give up her literary ambitions (as well as her facial piercings) and bask in the light of his own fame, or so he reasoned.

The *Huffington Post* made a great event of their nuptials: "August Playwright Marries Aspiring Young Writer with Curtain Call Worthy Wedding Vows." *The Boston Globe* showed sunset pictures with the caption: "Most Eligible Bachelor Exits Stage Right."

Secretly his inner circle of friends confessed surprise and even anguish by his choice. "What does he see in the girl? She's unpolished. A mere child. So young. So in love. Whatever was he thinking?"

Nelson, of course, drew out his claws: "It won't last. That timid little mouse of a girl hasn't got a tenth of Seb's intellect, his ardor, his erudition!" Hearing similar sentiments from other colleagues in the theater, Sebastian, who truly loved his new wife, set out to cultivate her mind and disprove the nasty gossip.

And never was a pupil more devoted, more captivated, more compliant. Benedita put her little manuscript and her application to Emerson College aside, as Sebastian advised, and plodded through the list of classics he deemed fit for her literary and artistic development. She attended the Boston Ballet, the Lyric Opera, the Symphony, and a cornucopia of modern and classical plays in Boston and New York.

When Sebastian instructed his wife to read Ibsen and lectured her on the merits of Hedda Gabler, she never yawned. She endured his deadly dull lectures because she loved him and believed in his wisdom.

Benedita did not know who Svengali was, nor would she have likened her husband to the fictional character if she had. And when she read George Bernard Shaw's *Pygmalion*, she patently ignored the play's similarities between Eliza Doolittle and herself.

But the day of reckoning came at last on a dreary afternoon in January when the wind began to whistle with a low, mocking moan, and the sky was one big gray snow cloud. Timidly, reverently, she presented Sebastian with a manuscript bound by two rubber bands.

"Sebbie, I've rewritten my script. Please, baby. I want you to read it."

Sebastian loathed being called baby, but allowed his wife to do so because it was a time in their marriage when he was most proud of her. She could recite dozens of his opinions on any number of plays, and he basked in the flowering of her intellect.

"You've rewritten your script—?" he couldn't help himself. "When? When could you possibly have had time? I've never so much as seen you on the computer . . . or even with a notepad."

"*Baaaabbbbyyy,*" she rolled her eyes playfully. "I write when you aren't looking. I steal a minute here and there. Ya' know. In the bathroom. On the subway. A little bit every night. And in the morning too. Haven't you noticed how early I get up? And sometimes I sit on the stairs outside your study and . . . well . . . noodle-doodle around with my story."

Noodle-doodle? Surely she hadn't used that phrase to describe the sacred act of writing?

"And it's *not* a play, Sebbie. It's a screenplay! I see it as a movie . . . or, like, maybe a TV pilot."

"Screenplay—" He almost choked. Being a playwright and being a screenwriter were two different animals. Any intellectually defunct idiot could write a screenplay. How many times had he told her so? Hollywood hacks were a dime a dozen, merely following a formulaic matrix using a character arc, plot arc, denouement arc, and out popped marketable drivel.

"Sweetheart, you know my views on—"

"Yes. Yes. But Sebbie, I'm a writer. And what I've written is a screenplay."

"Then I hardly think I'm the one to critique—"

"Sebbie, baby. I wrote it for you. It's just that I see it on the big screen, not a dusty little stage. It deserves a wider audience."

Was that the sound of his teeth gnashing? Sebastian wondered. Or just a roar in his head like a conch shell clamped painfully to his ear?

"Sebbie! You're always telling me that all good art comes from artistic struggle, and I've done all that. I've hit snags. I've gotten tangled up in knots. I've been stressed to the max. I've had my 'dark night of the soul,' as you call it. But I'm done struggling. I've nailed it. I want you to be proud of me."

How could he refuse her? And when a sad, slow tear zig-zagged down her cheek, he acquiesced. His wife was impetuous and he liked that, but for the first time in their relationship she was showing obstinacy, and he didn't like that.

Her lower lip quivered in a sort of extended pout. "Sebbie," she sighed. "If you want me to make it into a stage play, I will. I'll just change it into three acts."

Now he openly gawked. All this time she'd been agreeing with his critical assessments of plays and playwrights. But if she thought turning a screenplay into a dramatic production was just a snap of the fingers, an easy accomplishment like baking a three-layered cake, she'd surely learned nothing.

"Sweetness," he began, his voice as heavy as his heart. "Have you ever wondered why I'm not more prolific? Even with my pedigree in the theater? The magnitude of the task of writing a play takes careful planning. Dramatic construction is difficult. The use of metaphor and symbolism . . . the crescendos and denouements. To create a structurally sound play with beats, and scenes and acts, takes incredible hard work . . . years to perfect. Are you sure . . .?"

Again the hurt look, the pained expression in her cognac brown eyes.

"Let me have it then," he chortled. "We'll go into my study. I think the carpenters have finished the new bookshelves in the library alcove. We'll sit by the fire." Silently Sebastian was thinking: *Everything will be all right. Surely my wife has a soupçon of talent . . .*

a modicum of erudition? I'll nurture it, mold it . . . unsophisticated as it will surely be. But, oh! How I want to take her in my arms and tell her to put her literary ambitions on the shelf—the highest shelf in my study.

Then he floundered. He couldn't bring himself to step over the threshold into his study. It had been an easy task training his wife to appreciate the finer elevations of what constitutes dramatic art, but it would be another thing all together to critique her writing, that most personal and sacred wellspring that comes from the core of one's being. Benedita would resent him, grow to despise him.

But . . . if her screenplay has potential! If it shows the merest spark of creativity, surely I can work with her on it? We can spend months, even years, in happy revisions!

Benedita's voice wobbled when she thanked him. Her fingers trembled as she handed over her screenplay.

Please let it be good! Sebastian prayed. In his mind's eye he saw himself smiling, pleased with it. He'd laugh at all the right places, make his face express wonder. He could hear himself pronouncing it to be full of wit and brilliance.

But it was a foolish fancy. Sebastian had read only a handful of brilliant new plays (aside from his own) in his entire career, including playwrights such as Tom Stoppard—and all of these he had helped rewrite; slashing and cutting and adjusting the language until even the playwright knew it for what it was: *A Sebastian Merrick play.*

Surely he could do the same for his wife? Yes. He could make a masterpiece out of drivel if need be. But in his heart of hearts he hoped there would be something . . . a glimmer of talent, a spark of brilliance. Not much to ask from a woman who was writing under his name? For he could see clearly now the title page: Benedita Merrick. She had as easily dropped her maiden name and embraced his as she had discarded her facial piercings for the five-carat diamond he presented her at their betrothal.

He looked at his wife's expression, anxious and trusting. Throughout their short marriage, Sebastian never once regretted his decision. The uncultured girl of their honeymoon was now the woman who could quote Arthur Miller and Edward Albee and make references (if not inferences) to August Wilson, Lydia Diamond and Harold Pinter. Still, it was with a shuddering prickle of apprehension that Sebastian took the manuscript from her outstretched arms.

"Wait! Can I read it out loud to you?" she pleaded. "That way, I can hear my own words. Get a better feel for it."

And not see the embarrassment . . . or . . . er . . . triumph on my face? he thought bitterly.

"My darling girl!" he said with false enthusiasm. "Of course! Of course!"

She flushed and smiled. "It's good, Sebbie. I think you'll like it or I wouldn't show it to you."

"Darling, Benedita? What would you . . . do . . . if . . . I . . . didn't like it?" He raised an eyebrow.

His wife shrugged. "Write another."

Just like that? As if the Herculean effort to write a credible script were little more than noodling and doodling? But something in her posture, her voice, made him believe she might actually have pulled it off, written something deeply intriguing, magical even. *All right, let's do this!*

But then, with the timing of a second-string actor upstaging the lead, Benedita dropped yet another bomb. "I gave it to Nelson to read. He thinks it's extraordinary. Those were his exact words. And he wants to produce it. Or . . . what did he say? Find backers for it."

"Nelson? You showed it to Nelson? To Nelson before me? And produce it, you say? Nelson's not a producer. He's a glorified decorator. He started out as a *decorator.*"

"He's famous now, Sebbie. The best set designer on Broadway. And you know he hates when you tease him about being a glorified decorator."

"I don't tease him. I merely state the truth. He's a puffed up, stage draper. Not a producer."

"Nelson says it's so over-the-top sensational, he'll pass it around and find backers. He says I'm going to make a killing. *We're* going to make a killing."

Sebastian was so astounded, he opted for a short reprieve. "My darling! This calls for champagne! Right now. This instant. It's early, I know. But I feel the need to . . . to—"

"Celebrate!? Yes of course. But after . . . after . . . you'll let me read it to you?" She took hold of Sebastian and twirled him around the room and he followed her lead, a gesture uncommon for him. He was not, after all, a demonstrative man. Nor a dancer. But panic had taken hold of him.

When they raised yet a second glass of Dom Perignon, in a mock sort of toast, the suspense and Sebastian's high hopes for her screenplay seemed nearly as great as her own. But when he looked into his wife's guileless face, his hands were not quite steady.

In the library corner of his study, Benedita pulled up a chair close to his own, and after giving him a radiant smile filled with gratitude, she began to read, hesitant at first, and then with conviction.

Sebastian listened, his gaze fixed on Benedita's beautiful, round, pubescent mouth forming the words which tripped from her lips, happy and full of promise. After reading aloud for half an hour, amazement still gripped him. Could it be possible . . . ? When she first began to read, something of her excitement had caught hold of him, gripping him in its audacity. He had prayed that her writing might reveal, if not erudition, then untapped, raw talent . . . the promise of flair, of faculties to be cultivated. But this! This was beyond anything he had ever imagined.

He thought he'd be disappointed, but at no time in his heart of hearts did he actually believe he'd be totally flabbergasted! He was stunned that anyone, let alone his wife, could be capable of writing so badly.

The word atrocious would be too kind. It wasn't just her heavy-handed pacing, her clichéd characters, her it's-been-done-a-thousand-times-before plot, but her grammar, her syntax! There was nothing melodious or insightful about her writing, rather it was as if an elephant had tiptoed across a creaky floor while trying not to make any noise. It repulsed him. As he listened he felt more and more queasy until the pain in his stomach was worse than the flu. Like a carpenter's vice turned notch by painful notch ratcheting up the agony, he suffered silently, acutely. Even as she read with fervent conviction, the absurdity of her story, combined with the triviality of her characters, would be rendered utterly and laughably absurd by anyone with half an intellect.

He wanted to cry. He pitied her, pitied himself. He would rather sit through a dreary puppet show, night after relentless night, for all eternity than face the fact that his wife was a cretin. So when she closed the cover and said, "What do you think?" eyes brimming with hope so raw and optimistic it increased his suffering tenfold, he could only look at her weakly, stifle a groan, and take the cowardly way out.

"Read it again. From the beginning." He needed to postpone the pain.

"Girls just wanna be girls," she began in a clear, happy voice.

It was midnight when his suffering finally ended. Benedita leaned back in her chair with a look of smug satisfaction. No, not smug, he reasoned. Childish contentment. That was it. He'd married an intellectual child. Talent could be nurtured, molded like wet clay, hadn't he said so often enough? But this was his wife! Once word got out . . . once Nelson—*spiteful Nelson*— distributed the script . . . he, Sebastian Merrick, would be made a laughing stock. No, he mustn't say it, mustn't think it. But the words popped into his head unbidden like a fist yanking one's hair. He'd married a dim-witted nincompoop.

"My darling," he said. "There's something I want to show you."

Slowly Sebastian climbed the wooden library ladder to grasp a book on the topmost shelf. When she looked up at him adoringly, he called out: "Here it is. The answer to your question."

"What question?"

He took the heaviest tome he could find. "The essay question. When are books dangerous?" And with that he hurled it down at her. With the precision of a javelin thrower he threw volume after volume upon her crumpled body. Then slowly he climbed back down and, because the carpenters had not finished the book cabinet, toppled the entire thing over her prone, lifeless body. Stepping gingerly across the room to the phone on his antique desk, he dialed 9-1-1. "There's been an accident. A terrible accident." He pretended to sob.

When he hung up, he turned to the silent figure beneath the bookshelf. "An extreme example, my darling, showing how literature can be harmful, the written word can kill . . ."

Shelly Dickson Carr's grandfather, John Dickson Carr, was a Grand Master of "Golden Age" mysteries with two Edgar® awards. Ms. Carr's thriller *Ripped* won the Bill Fisher Gold Medal for Best First Book, two Benjamin Franklin Silver awards for Best New Voice and Best Mystery/Suspense in the 2013 Independent Book Publishers Association's awards.

Breakfast

Peggy McFarland

Judy removed the hash browns from the freezer and placed the bag against her swollen lip. The cold helped. She set the flame to low under the frying pan, then started the coffee brewing. Chuck sang from the shower. He was in a good mood, which was a relief. Of course, he'd already gotten rid of the bad mood. She'd better get his breakfast ready before he finished shaving. Anything could change Chuck's mood. She tore open the bag and shook out the potato shreds. For the rest of the morning, Judy hoped to avoid *anything*.

She placed the ceramic bowl on the counter, the one she'd gotten from Goodwill to replace the one Mom had handed down to Judy. Her knee wore the scar from a shard of that broken bowl.

Judy tapped an egg against the bowl, careful to break it clean, and opened the shell halves. A tiny woman slid out, landed on her feet in the bottom of the bowl. Judy had heard of half-formed chicks coming out of eggs, but a person? This one was alive. All Judy could do was stare.

The teensy woman's bright yellow smock draped over a bulging stomach. She was pregnant. And she looked just like Judy.

Envy and regret overwhelmed Judy. She wanted a child, but that was not in Chuck's life plan. And Chuck always got his way. She wasn't even sure if she could get pregnant again. Which was probably best.

The teensy woman stretched her arms, stretched her back, and then smiled at Judy. "Are you just going to stare, or help me out of here?"

Judy scrambled to get the woman out of the bowl, then gently placed her on the counter. Two-inch tall, Pregnant Judy walked over to the unopened newspaper and lifted a corner.

"Don't! Chuck reads the paper first," Judy said.

Pregnant Judy cocked her head towards the egg carton. "Shouldn't you be making breakfast?"

Yes. The shower had shut off.

Judy grabbed an egg, tapped it against the bowl. Another mini-Judy slid out, this one dressed in scrubs and wearing a stethoscope around her neck. She bent her knees and sprang, caught the edge of the bowl, and pulled herself up and over onto the counter. Dr. Judy waved before she hurried to give Pregnant Judy a quick exam.

The remaining ten eggs quivered in the carton. Judy cracked the next one, then the next, each egg opening to another version of Judy. The mini-Judy in a business suit wore glasses and a severe expression. She walked directly to the coffee pot, tapped her heels as Judy searched for a suitably-sized drinking vessel.

Trim-and-Fit Judy jogged laps around the drying rack while Artist Judy began shredding sales circulars from the accumulated mail pile. Model Judy posed in front of the microwave door while Hairdresser Judy used the reflection to fix their coifs.

Chauffeur Judy and Hippie Judy walked to where Chuck had left his keys and wallet. Foreman Judy joined them and gave instructions on how to lift the folded leather.

Judy wrinkled her nose, then coughed. Chef Judy pointed to the smoking frying pan. Judy hurried to shut off the flame.

"What the hell's going on in here!" Chuck appeared in the doorway, Downy-fresh towel wrapped around his growing gut, a fleck of bloody toilet paper stuck to his jawline. "Goddam smoke everywhere and it stinks! What stupid thing did you—what's all over the counter?"

Chuck took one step towards Judy, his hand rising, his face mottled with rage. Judy cowered, and saw Chef Judy beckoning. Hairdresser Judy and Model Judy raced along the counter-edge toward the stove. Fit Judy demonstrated a boxing jab.

Judy clenched her hand into a fist, pulled her elbow back. All by itself, her hand flew.

Chuck let out an *oof*, and bent over, clutching his stomach.

Oh my God, Oh my God! She'd never done that before. She

shook her hand, her knuckles tingling from where they'd hit the soft meat of Chuck. Should she hit him again, keep him bent over, or start begging for forgiveness?

Hairdresser Judy shouted, "Now!" The mini-Judies on the stove worked together and hoisted the frying pan handle. The pan toppled over the edge, then thumped against the back of Chuck's head.

Chuck moaned from the floor. He struggled to rise. Judy bit her lip, then grimaced at the sharp pain. He was going to be the maddest she'd ever seen him. If only she could keep him down there for a while.

Police Officer Judy dog-whistled. She flicked her head towards the toaster as Dr. Judy and Pregnant Judy nodded approval. Judy, trained to obey, yanked the appliance and threw it at Chuck. It bashed him in the exact spot that the frying pan had hit him. Chuck collapsed.

Judy blinked, waiting for Chuck to rise. She almost said *Honey?* but stopped herself. If he was okay, she could postpone the repercussions. If he wasn't, well, she could postpone those repercussions too.

A pleased *ahh* came from the counter. Judy turned. Artist Judy wiped her hands on her smock, then straightened, a self-satisfied smile on her face. All the versions of Judy joined the artist, admiring her handiwork.

Judy flung a greasy strand out of her eyes and inspected the torn bits of paper spread across the counter. *YoU caN Be YOurSeLf.*

Before her own thoughts stopped her, Judy grabbed the car keys, pulled bills out of Chuck's open wallet, and hurried to the door. She turned to thank the mini-Judies.

They'd disappeared.

Cracked shells and spreading whites littered the counter, as well as twelve, perfect, shimmering yolks.

Peggy McFarland's work in restaurants has inspired characters for her writing. Her stories have appeared in Level Best Books anthologies, *Uncle John's Bathroom Reader, Shroud Magazine,* and other on-line and print publications. She has also been a Derringer Award contender. She lives in Nashua, New Hampshire with her family and a neurotic dog.

Kill Switch

Chris Knopf

He was disappointed to see the big cutter slide into the lagoon. It was dusk, and the other boats anchored during the day had all sailed away. They probably thought it was still illegal to stay overnight, but the people who managed these things along the Connecticut shoreline had quietly lifted the ban a few months before. He'd counted on word getting out slowly, giving him time for some blessed privacy.

So far the theory worked. He was getting ready for his tenth solitary dinner in the cockpit, about to munch on his lousy cooking while admiring an unobstructed view of the surrounding marsh and the slowly darkening sky above.

The moment was hard-fought. It took three years of accumulated sick-time, personal days, unused vacation, etc., to scrape together a full month away from the job. That was the easy part. A full month away from his fiancée, Vivian, took the greater effort. He had to work through her stages of separation anxiety—disbelief, anger, cajoling, manipulation, more anger, outrage, pathos, and finally, the threat of leaving him. In the end, she hugged him and declared that she'd be there when he got back.

That was yet to be seen, though he had little doubt she meant what she said. Not because he was such an incredible catch. Vivian had already invested too much time and emotional energy in him to allow a brief pause in their inexorable march toward marriage to sidetrack her plans.

He sold electronic parts. Which made him a salesman, though he hated that description, a rare point of agreement between him and his company. They told his customers he wasn't a salesman, rather a business partner, a valued consultant, an ally, even a treasured confidant. His customers still saw him for what he truly was. A salesman.

He admired his fellow salesmen and women for their ability to smooth the transit of products the company made in China and Mexico into TV sets, computer hardware and mobile devices, also made abroad, for gadget-crazed North Americans. So it wasn't envy that consumed him. It was a sense of misidentification. I'm not a confidant or a salesman, dammit, he'd say to himself. I'm an inventor.

The cutter looked at least ten feet longer than his thirty-six-foot sloop. The headsails were furled and the mainsail roughly bunched along the boom. She moved slowly, tentatively, the bow swinging to and fro, and then aiming almost directly at his anchored boat. He stood in the cockpit, gripping the taut cable that secured the mast to steady himself.

The cutter drew too close for comfort, but then lurched off again, parallel to his hull, so he got his first look at the helmsperson, a woman with dirty blonde hair pulled into a ponytail, wearing short shorts and a tight white T-shirt. His disappointment eased a bit. He waved to her as she passed by.

She shouted something, but he was too far away to hear. He shook his head and pointed to his ear. She shouted again, but with even less effect, since her boat was now well off his starboard bow. She returned her attention to the helm and he stood and watched her circle.

This time she came dangerously close to the port side of his boat. Now he could hear her clearly.

"No anchor! What do I do?" she yelled.

"Come alongside. We'll raft," he yelled back, motioning with his hands to reinforce the concept. She gave him a quick thumbs-up.

There was little wind and the current was between ebb and flow, and thus not a factor, so it was foolishly easy for the woman to bring her boat up to the smaller sloop and for them to lash lines to each other's cleats, cushioning the interface with hastily deployed dock fenders.

It was a little unnerving, having a forty-six-foot custom yacht hard against his thirty-six-foot sloop, a valiant sailboat under most conditions, though now not so sure of herself. Nevertheless, he was certain his doughty old Danforth anchor could handle the extra load.

"What the heck happened?" he asked her.

"I'm an idiot, that's what happened," said the woman. "Dropped the hook and forgot to tie it off. Went to bed and the next day I'm halfway across the Sound. Bitter end just popped right out of the locker."

"Wow. I guess you're lucky."

"God looks after drunks and fools."

"Do you have a towing service?"

She shook her head.

"No problem, you're fine where you are," he said. "We can call the marina in the morning. They'll run you out a new anchor."

Her smile did more than the setting sun to light up the lagoon.

"You are *such* a doll," she said. "You have to come over for a drink. And scrumptious hors d'oeuvres. I'm a lousy sailor, but a great cook."

Her windblown hair fluttered around a face that reminded him of a popular celebrity, though he couldn't recall which one. Her body was even better, and he struggled to keep his eyes from drifting toward her straining T-shirt.

"Okay," he said. "Sure. Let me get cleaned up."

She stuck out her hand and he took it.

"Claudine DeCarlo."

"Roger Johnson."

After a brief shower, he took a foolishly long time selecting a fresh shirt and pair of shorts. As if clothing of any sort could compensate for his round, balding, insecure self. He was so enthralled by the impending social event that he'd nearly forgotten about Vivian. When thoughts of her returned, he felt a rough mixture of guilt, deflation and relief that she was back in Boston. That last feeling drove him up the companionway with a bottle of wine tucked under his arm.

Claudine was waiting in the cockpit of her boat. She wore a short summer dress made of fabric that draped agreeably over her pleasantly ill-concealed curves. She was barefoot and her hair was free of its ponytail. On the folding table were plates filled with cheese and prosciutto, olives and crackers. She offered him a gin and tonic.

"We can have the wine for dessert."

Comfortably ensconced with drinks and hors d'oeuvres, they engaged in the type of desultory small talk that usually made Roger feel so ill at ease, though strangely less so with this woman.

The conversation naturally turned to sailing, and Roger asked how long she'd been at it.

"It was my husband's enthusiasm. Sailed all his life. Very particular about how it was done."

She said that last part with a subtle bite.

"So not the laid back sailing teacher," said Roger.

"You'd only use the word 'laid' with Jason when referring to his administrative assistant."

"Oh," said Roger, suddenly attentive to the ice floating in his glass.

"I'm so sorry. TMI. It just popped out of me," said Claudine.

Roger gave an awkward wave of the hand.

"Of course. I understand. I mean, no problem here," he said, wishing he had said something different, not remotely knowing what that would be.

"I did divorce the son-of-a-bitch, by the way. Got the house and half the investment portfolio."

"And the boat?" he asked.

"And the boat."

"Good for you."

"This is probably a poor subject," she said, "happily involved as you must be. "

"Oh, you mean Vivian," he said, disappointed that he'd brought her up, until he realized he hadn't. "How did you know?"

"You haven't been flirting with me. Unattached men usually do," she said, looking at him through her long eyelashes.

He laughed.

"I have no idea how to flirt," he said.

"Well, there's a pity," she said.

Roger wondered if he should just thank her then and go back to his boat before she had chance to say what she really thought.

"So, Vivian must be quite a girl," she added.

He took longer than he should have to answer.

"When she's not railing at the world, she's a very sturdy person," he said, "with both feet firmly on the ground. I admire that, being more the dreamer type."

"What do you dream about?" she said.

"My inventions," he said, without hesitation. "She keeps telling me, 'be realistic.' She's probably right, but I keep thinking true success can't happen working for someone else, that you have to make your own success. Or, rather, make success you can own," he added, pleased with the turn of phrase.

"So tell me, what's your favorite invention," she said, before popping a wad of cheese and cracker into her mouth.

"Really? You want to know?"

"Of course I do."

"Okay, well, they're all related to sailing, and sailing safety. First, we have the *No Go Kill Switch*, which shuts off the auto helm and stops the engine if you fall in the water. You wear it on a lanyard around your neck, or just stick it in your pocket. For an extra charge, you also get the *Itty Bitty Beacon* with a GPS that sends a Mayday to the closest Coast Guard station. So don't ever drop it overboard. You'll have some explaining to do. Then one of my favorites, the *Totally Groundless 3D Shoal Detector*. Better than any depth finder, *Totally Groundless* not only spots the underwater hazard, it automatically steers the boat to safety, whether under power or sail."

Claudine clapped her hands together and lit up another of her 100-watt smiles.

"Well, that's marvelous. Those are delightful ideas. Where can I buy?"

Roger looked into his drink and swirled the ice.

"Nowhere yet. They're still on the drawing board, though I could have working prototypes in a year or two. But if those don't make it, others will. Edison would invent a hundred things for every one that actually got off the ground."

She leaned forward and gave his upper thigh a quick squeeze.

"That's the spirit," she said.

After that, words began to tumble out of Roger with such candor and verve, he scarcely believed it was him doing the talking. Claudine not only listened closely, she seemed to be fixed on his face, as if afraid a moment's inattention would rob her of priceless wisdom.

Roger told her how he'd tinkered with old radios and TV sets as a kid, and built go-carts with lawnmower engines and hydroplanes with salvaged outboards. How he couldn't afford college, but managed two years of technical school, which at least got him his sales job. That he inherited the sailboat from his grandfather, and how Vivian considered it a frivolous, unsustainable expense.

"You'll discover many things in marriage are unsustainable," she said.

"I guess you're right," he said, "but you have to give it a go. *I* have to give it a go, even though Vivian thinks I'm just a bullshit artist."

"Really?"

"Yeah, but how about you?" he asked, eager to change the subject.

So it was her turn to spill out her story, one of a promising theatrical career cut short when she married her husband, a financier who dragged her off to London, then Hong Kong, Singapore, Sydney, then back to New York where she could at least find acting jobs, though her husband's demands on her time—throwing dinner parties for business contacts, attending fundraisers and gallery openings, getting whisked off to some foreign capital at a moment's notice—took its toll.

"If they give you the part, they expect you to show up for all the performances," she said. "I passed up a lot of opportunities. Now I'm just an old broad."

"What, of thirty-five, maybe, tops?"

"Thirty-eight," she said, "but aren't you sweet."

If the conversation hadn't been so dizzying, he might have noticed a little sooner the effect of the gin and tonics. He stood up unsteadily and asked directions to the head.

She took him by the hand, led him down the companionway and showed him the guest head next to the rear berth.

"Mine is in the captain's suite in the bow. You should visit there sometime," she said, and he watched her glide off in that direction.

After using the head, he rushed back up to the cockpit before he had a chance to think about where else he might have wandered below. Claudine joined him soon after, and they talked for another few hours. Eventually, he confessed that, between his limited liquor capacity and the late hour, he was ready to cash it in.

She thanked him again, and before he could stumble back to his boat, she wrapped her arms around him and kissed him on the lips.

"You're a lifesaver, and a clever, clever man. I don't care if Vivian thinks you're full of BS."

It was harder to get to sleep that night than usual, but he eventually succeeded.

Out in the cockpit the next morning, fortified with aspirin and black coffee, he saw Claudine on the bow of her boat, wearing a scant bikini and spreading suntan lotion on her chest and down into her cleavage. She waved him over.

"I called the chancellery and they can get an anchor here this afternoon," she said. "I hope that doesn't mess up your plans."

"My plans are to stay right where I am, so no worries."

She looked pleased.

"We had quite a bit to drink last night," she said. "How're you feeling?"

"Wobbly."

She stood up.

"We need Mimosas," she said.

"We do?"

"Absolutely."

He got to watch her negotiate her way over the topside, through the standing rigging and down the companionway. Then he sat next to the windlass, a machine that cranks the anchor up and down. Curious as always, he opened the anchor locker and saw where the chain had come undone. He had the locker hatch closed well before Claudine came back on deck. She carried a towel over her shoulder and in each hand a clear plastic glass filled with yellow liquid.

"Hair of the dog, buddy," she said, making him clink after handing him the drink. "Nothing better."

It tasted rather good, he was pleased to note, having never actually consumed alcohol as a breakfast drink. She spread out the towel, which was big enough for both of them to sit on, though barely. It forced a fair amount of body contact, which Roger felt through his shoulder and thigh as a form of electrical current.

Claudine stretched out her legs and ran her hands across her shins, all the way to her ankles, and back.

"I like my feet," she said, wiggling her painted toes. "The rest of me might be falling apart, but my feet still look pretty good."

"There's nothing wrong with the rest of you," said Roger, "Trust me on that."

She said "Ahhh" the way you'd do over a puppy and leaned in to kiss him on the cheek, her hand resting on his thigh just south of the cuff of his khaki shorts.

"Keep saying things like that and you'll get to see it," she said.

"What?"

"The rest of me."

He told her that he'd like that very much, though right then he had to visit the head, a consequence of all the coffee and tasty Mimosas.

He started to apologize, but she cut him off.

"Everybody pees, Roger," she said.

He retraced her path over the cabin top and down into the boat, pausing briefly at the navigation table to flick on the GPS. By the time he was done in the head, the device had found their location and he was able to quickly run through a few menu options. Then he turned it off and went back topsides.

Claudine was now lying face down on the towel with her bikini top untied, the strings flung out to either side of her.

"You would be an even bigger doll if you put lotion on my back," she said.

It didn't take a lot of urging and he likely applied more than was entirely necessary.

"I know what happened to your anchor," he said, putting a generous wad of lotion in his hand.

She rolled up partially on her side so she could look at him. She held the bikini top to her chest.

"Really. That's wonderful. Save me from losing another one."

"All I need is a screwdriver to fix the problem."

"Well, then I'll get you one. I think I know where they are."

She reached behind her back and re-tied the bikini, and as she went to fetch the screwdriver, Roger opened the anchor locker again and looked over the piece of hardware he'd found that was meant to attach the anchor chain to the bulkhead. He dipped his head more deeply into the locker to study the chrome mounting plate.

That's why he didn't hear her approach until she spoke his name. He picked his head up out of the locker and saw her about ten feet away, wearing a sundress over her bikini and holding a small duffel bag in one hand and a long-barreled revolver in the other.

"The chain hardware didn't pop out," he said, his words fighting past the sudden lump in his throat. "It was unscrewed."

"Your phone," she said. "Toss it overboard."

He heard the splash as it hit the water.

"I checked the tracking on your GPS," he said. "It showed you went straight out into the Sound, floated around in about a hundred feet of water for a while, then motored straight back to shore and into this lagoon."

"I forgot that bodies float," she said. "The anchor was an improvisation, though it did pose a dilemma once I realized I needed the damn thing. I was so glad to see you here."

"There'll be other boats showing up soon."

"That's okay. By then you and this boat will be on the bottom of the lagoon. I opened a seacock in the engine compartment. It's like a fire hose."

"The mast will stick up."

"Doesn't matter. I'll be long gone. They'll never figure it out."

"You're taking my boat."

"Just to get to shore. I've got a car waiting. Quick trip to JFK, then that's that."

"I promise I won't say anything," he said. "I'll tell them your boat just drifted into the lagoon and I secured it."

"I wish I could believe you."

He continued to argue his case as she forced him over to his boat and directed him to raise the anchor, which he had to do by hand, since he could never afford a windlass.

She thanked him after his anchor was safely stowed in its mount below the pulpit. Then she told him to get back on her boat and undo the rafting lines. He did as she asked, loosening the lines until only the midship cleats were strung together.

Claudine kept the gun trained on him as she turned the key and started his boat's old diesel engine.

Roger stood holding the line until she moved the shift lever into forward and used the end of the gun to motion him to let go. A few feet of water opened up between the boats.

"Sorry, Roger," she said, pointing the gun at his head. "You won't believe me, but I really did like you. For real."

When he dove in the water he heard the bang of the gun, but didn't feel anything, assuming he was in shock or already dead. He swam underwater away from the hull of Claudine's boat as far as his legs and lungs would allow, then surfaced to see his own boat adrift on the gentle current, the diesel engine quiet as a corpse.

"It won't start again," he yelled to her. She lifted the gun and took aim. "And the Coast Guard is on the way," he added, pointing toward the horizon.

Claudine lowered the gun. She looked out past the channel into the Sound and saw the patrol cruiser racing toward the lagoon. She tossed the gun overboard. He swam closer.

"What have you done?" she said.

"I just jumped in the water. The *No Go Kill Switch* and *Itty Bitty Beacon* took it from there."

She shook her head, as if trying to free it of unnatural thoughts.

"You told me you were a year away from making prototypes, that you were only at the drawing stage," she said.

"Hiding things gets to be a habit for people like me."

"Vivian is right. You're nothing but a bullshit artist," she spat out.

He swam closer still, easily resisting the lagoon's languid current.

"Not an artist, Claudine," he said to her. "An inventor."

Chris Knopf has published thirteen mystery/thrillers. *Dead Anyway* earned the 2013 Nero Award and starred reviews from *Publishers Weekly, Booklist, Kirkus* and *Library Journal*. Knopf's Sam Acquillo series includes *Two Time,* one of thirteen mysteries listed in Marilyn Stasio's "Recommended Summer Reading" in *The New York Times Book Review. Cop Job*, Sam Acquillo Hamptons Mysteries Series #6, was released in September, 2015.

The Perfect Woman

Barbara Ross

April 24, 1947

Dearest Rose,

Today I met a man.

It was nuts at the office and Mr. Brownstein was even grouchier than usual. Tomorrow, one of our clients is selling his garment business. I typed and took dictation all morning until 12:45 when Mr. Brownstein barked, "Where's my sandwich?" I took the money out of petty cash, grabbed my jacket and handbag, and scurried out the door.

It was Thursday and that always means pastrami on rye, celery soda and potato chips from Metzger's. When the counterman handed me the change, I turned to leave and nearly knocked over the best-looking man I've ever seen.

"Lady, I'm sorry. You okay?" He put his hand on my arm to steady me and I could feel his strength. He wasn't tall, but was nicely built. He had a full head of hair the color of mahogany furniture when it's been well cared for, and kind brown eyes.

"My fault," I stuttered.

I took the sandwich back to Mr. Brownstein, who demanded to know what had taken so long, though I had been gone only the normal amount of time. He kept me until after nine, when all the documents were done for the closing. When he dismissed me, I took the subway, then the Hoboken ferry and walked home from the landing. I made a fried egg on toast and ate it in the dining room. How lovely it would be to have someone to share a meal with.

I hope you are happy, dear Rose, and though we are apart, I

believe we will be together soon.

Love,

Ingrid

April 27, 1947

Dearest Rose,

So much has happened since I last wrote to you.

I was determined to see the man from the deli again. I hadn't stopped thinking about him, even for a minute, and drifted off during Mr. Brownstein's dictation. Fortunately, he didn't notice. I'm just a pair of ears to hear and a pair of hands to type as far as he's concerned.

Though Mr. Brownstein's Friday lunch must come from Siegel's, I stopped at Metzger's on my way and bought myself a roast beef on rye, hoping against hope.

And there he was. The handsome man. As I worked up my courage to say hello, he greeted me. "It was nice running into you yesterday." He smiled, showing his perfect white teeth, which contrasted beautifully with his olive skin. "Johnny Bevilacqua."

"Ingrid Johansen." My mouth was so dry, I couldn't swallow.

"You work around here?"

I nodded, then found my voice. "Leo Brownstein, attorney-at-law. I'm his secretary."

"I work here, too, at Wolowitz's Wholesale Buttons & Notions. I travel for work, so I'm not in the city all the time." He hesitated. "Do you ever take in a picture show, Ingrid?"

My blush went so deep, my chest tingled. "I do."

"Would you like to meet me at Radio City tomorrow night? Seven o'clock show?"

"Seven o'clock," I squeaked. "I'll be there."

Mr. Brownstein yelled at me for being late back to the office, but even he couldn't bother me.

On Saturday, I took extra care with dressing and my hair. I rode the ferry from Hoboken and took the subway to Radio City. Johnny was waiting outside, smoking a cigarette. My heart leapt at the sight of him.

We saw *The Egg and I* which I thought was terribly funny. In the middle of the show, Johnny reached over and took my hand.

Afterward, we went for malteds. Johnny insisted on seeing me home, even though he had to come all the way to New Jersey and then turn around and go to back to Manhattan. He rooms on the Lower East Side with Ben Wolowitz, an old army buddy. Ben's the one who got Johnny the job as a salesman with his father's company.

On my front porch, Johnny gave me a kiss, then asked if I was on the telephone. "Party line," I told him, though he wouldn't have expected anything else.

"I'll call you tomorrow," he said.

And Rose, he did. We talked for hours and agreed to meet for lunch tomorrow. Mr. Brownstein won't like it, because I always eat at my desk, but I don't care.

I can feel the day we will be together coming. I hope it will be soon!

Love,
Ingrid

May 23, 1947
Dearest Rose,

It's been so long since I've written to you. Johnny has consumed my daytime thoughts and my evening company. I haven't been this happy since before Mother died.

We went out a few times after Radio City, but quickly settled on a routine where I make dinner here at the house. Eating out is expensive and I love to cook. He always gives me his ration book and cash to cover the cost of the meal. I'm so used to his company. When he's on the road selling Wolowitz's notions, the house seems as quiet as the grave.

He is thirty-five, ten years older than me, though that doesn't bother me a bit. Father was twelve years older than Mother and they were devoted.

While we eat dinner, Johnny tells me about his day, his funny customers and adventures. I tell him about life at Leo Brownstein's, though the truth is, there isn't much to tell. We spend the evenings reading the newspaper and listening to the radio, like an old married couple.

Though we are not an old married couple in one important

respect. Every night, Johnny goes home to Manhattan. This is getting harder and harder on both of us. We have had some kissing sessions that have gone quite far and left me breathless, but Johnny is always a gentleman. He stops when I ask him to. And then he goes home.

Oh, how I long for the day when he won't have to get back on the ferry.

And, oh, how I long for the day when I will see you at last.

Love,

Ingrid

June 18, 1947

Dearest Rose,

On Friday, Johnny told me he wouldn't be able to come to Sunday dinner because he had to travel to the Jersey Highlands for his nephew's birthday. It was the first time he'd mentioned his family, and it gave me a pang in my heart because a big Sunday dinner was all I ever dreamed of when I was on my own.

"You wouldn't like to go, would you?" he asked.

On Sunday he picked me up in Ben Wolowitz's car and we drove to the Highlands. His family's cottage is tiny, and cheek by jowl with the others around it. But when I got out of the car and turned around—the view! The skyline of Manhattan and the mouth of the Hudson. The Statue of Liberty and Ellis Island, where my grandparents passed through on the way to this magnificent country. Johnny's parents, too. It was cool for June, but I thought it was the most beautiful day I had ever seen.

Johnny's mother, Ella, is a small woman, dressed in black, a widow since before the war. His sister, who's called Gilly, was there and her husband Franco. Gilly's sharp-featured and elegant, with Johnny's same mahogany hair. I felt myself standing straighter just to be around her. Franco is huge. He works on the docks.

They have three children, Carter whose tenth birthday we were celebrating, and Neil who's seven and little Molly, not yet three. It made me so happy to see Johnny with his nephews, throwing a football and chasing them around the outside of the little cottage in a game of tag.

Afterward, I helped Mrs. Bevilacqua and Gilly clean up in the kitchen.

"Johansen," Mrs. Bevilacqua said. "I don't suppose you're Catholic?" Before I could answer, she said, "Never mind, never mind. You're the first girl he's brought around since before the war. I'm glad he's happy."

All the photos of Johnny and Gilly in the cottage include a third child. Johnny is the oldest and always stares boldly into the camera. Gilly is the seductress, looking slyly away. The little boy has Gilly's sharp features and Johnny's perfect teeth. He isn't ever mentioned.

On the way home, mellow from the excitement of the day, I asked Johnny about him.

"That's my brother Paul." His voice caught on the words, so I didn't press him. So many families have photos of someone who never made it home from the war.

At the house, Johnny walked me to the porch and kissed me goodnight. "I don't want you to go," I whispered. I had thought about it all the way home.

"Are you certain?"

"I am."

He wore a sheath, a rubber, he called it, to protect us. Later, he said, "That was your first time." I nodded, yes and he asked, "Why me?"

"Because I love you," I said.

"I love you, too," Johnny said. "You are the perfect woman." And then he wept.

I am sorry if I have made you uncomfortable with this tale, dear Rose, but I want us to be honest about our lives. I am so happy!

Love,

Ingrid

August 3, 1947

Dear Rose,

The summer has passed in a dream. When he's not on the road, Johnny spends every weeknight with me. His things have slowly migrated across the Hudson. Week by week, I find the suit he wore on Friday still hanging in the closet on Monday morning. The khakis and t-shirts he wears on the weekends in the laundry basket.

In the morning, unless Johnny has business somewhere else, we walk to the ferry together. I see the curtains twitch next door and I know my neighbor Mrs. MacDougall is watching. I hope she's concluded that Johnny and I have eloped.

We have gone every weekend to the Highlands, taking the train to Red Bank and the bus up the steep embankment, the highest point on the eastern seaboard. Gilly and Franco have rented a cottage nearby, and Johnny's mother's cottage is always filled with aunts and uncles, cousins and their children. It's like their entire neighborhood in Newark picked up and moved to the Highlands, block by block.

We swim in the ocean at Sandy Hook and laze on the beach. So many of Johnny's girl cousins are pregnant. They sit on the sand like beached whales and complain of the heat even when there's a cooling breeze. With the war over, there are babies everywhere. Babies and weddings. I long for both.

Johnny's family has embraced me. I help the women in the kitchen with all the cooking and cleanup, while the men sit on the porch smoking cigars, under the watchful eyes of the Twin Lights standing guard over New York harbor. The only difference between us and the other couples is that when we are in the Highlands, I sleep alone in the cottage's tiny guest room, while Johnny sleeps on the couch in the living room.

Johnny's brother Paul is never mentioned by any of these people, his father rarely. One day Mrs. Bevilacqua asked me to fetch her sewing kit from her bedroom. On her bureau there was a photo of her with the man who had to be her husband. They are standing in front of the cottage, smiling broadly and squinting into the sun. She looks almost the same as she does now, though instead of black, she wears bold stripes. I thought Johnny's father had died long ago, because he's so rarely spoken of, but from the car parked in the yard behind them, I can tell the photo was snapped not long before the war.

"When did your father die?" I asked Johnny on the long train ride home.

"1939."

"Why doesn't your family ever talk about him?"

"Because it makes us sad."

I understand, I think. Now that the war is over, no one wants to go looking for sadness. We've all had more than enough. But my own dear mother is never far from my mind. My father, too.

I long to ask Gilly for more information, but she has a way of controlling the conversation that doesn't invite confidences or prying questions.

Please take care of yourself, dear Rose. I believe the time when we'll be together is at hand.

Love,
Ingrid

September 3, 1947
Dear Rose,

Last night, on the last evening of summer, as she sat smoking on the back stoop after cleanup, Gilly said to me, "If you want my brother to marry you, you can't wait for him to ask. He isn't going to."

"Really?" The blood drained from my face. I was grateful she couldn't see me in the gathering dark. Would he, as my mother had so long ago warned me, not buy the cow now that he was getting the milk for free?

"He's not a believer in marriage," Gilly said.

"Why not?"

She stubbed out her cigarette on the stoop and threw it into the grass. "He thinks he has his reasons."

The bus ride and train ride home was long and tiring. I hadn't been careful enough and my pale skin was sunburned, which made me feel both feverish and shivery cold.

"Do you ever intend to marry me?" I asked as soon as Johnny had unlocked the door and we stepped into the dark foyer.

"Oh, Ingrid." He took both my hands in his. "I can't do that."

"Why ever not?"

He stepped into the living room without turning on the lights. I heard him drop into the sofa and pat the cushion beside him. "I can't marry you, Ingrid, because I can't give you what you want. I see the way you look at my cousins and their babies." His voice was hoarse in the darkness. "I can never have children. I should have said something long ago. I've let this go on far too long. I couldn't speak up because I love you so."

"What do you mean you can't have children? Did something happen in the war?" I knew from experience that everything worked down there. And if he couldn't have babies, why use the rubbers?

"No, no. I mean I won't have children. I don't want them. It isn't something I can do."

"What do you mean, you don't want them? I've seen you with Gilly's kids, and the cousins' kids on the beach. They adore you, and you can't tell me you don't love them."

"I do love my nephews and my niece. They exist in the world and there is nothing to do but love them. But I carry a disease in my genes, a disease that can't be allowed to go on."

"Gilly's children are perfectly healthy."

"We don't know that, yet. The disease shows itself when they're older. Besides, Carter was born before we knew my brother Paul was sick. And then, I think Gilly and Franco thought he needed brothers and sisters."

I was crying by then, sobbing into his chest. "But Gilly's children are perfectly fine. That isn't a reason. My own father died of leukemia when he was a young man. For all we know, I carry a bad gene, too. That's not a reason," I repeated.

"The Bevilacqua line stops with me," he said. "It stops here." Johnny hugged me tight. "I should leave now," he whispered. "I should leave now, so you can find a man who will give you everything you deserve."

"No, no," I begged. "Don't leave me. Why are you leaving me?"

"Because," he said, "you are the perfect woman. I don't deserve you."

I cried until I was sick, great convulsing sobs. In the end, Johnny agreed to stay. In a hushed voice, he asked me to think about what I wanted. He said if I could live without the prospect of children, he would marry me immediately, as soon as it could be arranged.

Rose, I am heartbroken. I don't know what to do or which way to turn. I value your advice as always.

Love,
Ingrid

September 23, 1947
Dear Rose,

I have not written in so long because I have been in agony. I cannot give up my Johnny. Because of him, I am never lonely, even on the days he is away for work. I have never had such comfort and happiness since Mother died.

But I cannot give up the dream of a child, either. As an only child, I imagined you long ago. I named you Rose for my mother. After I met Johnny, your hair changed from blonde to mahogany and you gained some of Gilly's glamour, but you were still my Rose.

I've tried to banish you from my imagination, but you've been with me more than half my life, and you held fast.

But I couldn't give up Johnny, either. I pressed him as much as I dared, but he wouldn't talk to me about Paul's dread disease. I would have asked Gilly, but with the cottage closed down for the season, we haven't seen each other very often, and then only around Mrs. Bevilacqua's kitchen table.

When I could stand it no longer, being pulled between the two things I wanted most in the world, I took action. I went into the bedside table Johnny has claimed as his own, and I pricked a pinhole in every one of the hated rubbers. I did it carefully, through the dark lettering on the packet, all the way through the rubber, but not through the package on the opposite side. It was a delicate operation. I had to throw three of the packages away, but I succeeded.

You will be coming soon, my Rose. I can feel it. I believe you are with me already.

Love,
Ingrid

October 27, 1947
Dear Rose,

I am pregnant!

I was joyous when I realized you were on your way, though I said nothing to anyone until the doctor confirmed it. I believed Johnny's objection to a child was to the abstract idea of one, but confronted by the reality, he would come to love a child as he loved me.

I was wrong.

Buoyed, by the doctor's report, I gave Johnny the happy news.

"But how?" He was dumbfounded.

I didn't confess. "I don't know," I said. "It's a miracle. Let's be happy."

But Johnny looked like he'd been punched in the gut. "You must get rid of it."

"No!"

His features softened. "I'll find you a doctor. I'll pay. I'll take care of you after."

"No," I insisted. "This is our miracle." I had begun to believe my own story. "This is all I've ever wanted."

He was unmoved by my joy. "I told you this could never happen."

"But why? Why? What did Paul die from?"

That did it. Johnny leapt up, shouting, spittle flying from his mouth. "Who told you Paul is dead? Paul's not dead. He's in Bellevue, locked up forever. He's a paranoid schizophrenic."

His words, and most of all, his anger, shook me, but I was undeterred. "Our baby will be fine," I insisted. "Don't be a coward. Be a man. Do right by me."

"I can't. It's me, or the child. If you keep this," he hesitated, trying to get out the word, "this baby, I am gone."

"I'm keeping her," I said.

And so he went.

Rose, I am devastated. But I am also joyous because you will soon be here!

Love,

Ingrid, your mother

December 1, 1947

Dear Rose,

Today, I was fired.

I knew it would come, of course. My waistline has been expanding, but Mr. Brownstein never notices me, so I thought I'd have more time. But then Mrs. Brownstein came into the office today. She's sharp as a tack. She took one look at me, the waistband of my skirt held together with a safety pin, went into Brownstein's office and closed the door. When he came out, he told me I was through, to gather my things and leave for good while they were at lunch.

I was so shocked, I didn't say anything to him, and while I put my possessions—a couple of books, a pair of galoshes, and my little plant, in a cardboard box—my hands shook and the room spun.

Mr. Brownstein keeps a loaded pistol in the back of a locked file cabinet drawer. "Just in case," he says, though he's never taken it out or used it. Before I left, I hid it in the bottom of my cardboard box. "Just in case."

I will find a way to keep us safe and happy, dear Rose.

Love,

Ingrid, your mother

January 13, 1948

Dear Rose,

I am utterly alone.

Until Christmas, I kept my spirits high. I took the little wooden candleholders, painted with angels and Father Christmases, out of the attic and set them on the mantel as my mother always did. I baked ginger cookies and dreamed of the day I would do this with you, my little Rose. I pictured you on Saint Lucia Day, clothed in a white robe, a crown of candles in your mahogany hair.

I believed Johnny would come.

I didn't think the loving, compassionate man who played with his nephews would leave me alone and pregnant at Christmas. I spent the last of my wages from Leo Brownstein on sausage and ricotta cheese. On Christmas Day I assembled a lasagna as I'd helped his mother do so many times over the summer. I put it in the oven and I waited.

The snow began gently. The weatherman on the radio had predicted flurries, so I didn't worry. But the flakes kept coming, and by mid-day, I couldn't see the other side of the street. What if Johnny was out there somewhere, trapped by the storm?

I telephoned his mother. The phone rang and rang. I called Gilly's house. Carter picked up. I could hear the sounds of a family party in the background. Oh, how I longed to attend. "Is your Uncle Johnny there?" I asked.

"Didn't come. Snow." Then Carter politely wished me a Merry

Christmas and hung up the phone.

By that time, I was panicked. Johnny was on his way! He was lying, buried in a snow bank at the end of the block. In desperation, I called Ben Wolowitz's number, prepared to beg him for help.

"Hullo. Bevilacqua here."

I threw down the phone receiver as if it were a snake. I tossed the precious pan of lasagna into the backyard and watched the snow bury it.

The Blizzard of '47, they're calling it, wiping away records set in the last century. The city streets are clogged with more than two feet of snow and drifts up to ten feet.

I had believed all along we would be fine. My mother left me the house. I thought I might take in typing or go out for dictation with you in a tiny basket to pay the rest of the bills. I see how ridiculous that was.

But most of all, I believed my Johnny would return to me. Now, I know he will not. I've picked up the phone to call him so many times, Mrs. Corrigan on the party line has taken to shouting at me, "Ingrid! Ingrid! Put down the telephone!"

Sometimes, I take the pistol out of my bedside table where I put it after I stole it from Mr. Brownstein. Its cold metal is such a comfort in my hands, to know there is another way out if I want it. Usually, that is enough, and I put it back in the drawer. But the day came when that wasn't enough, and I kept the pistol with me all day as I went about my chores. As the sun went down, it was still in my hands, and I sat in my father's chair, turning it over and over.

Today was Hilarymas, the first day after the blizzard the coalman's truck could make it up the street. I gave him the last of my savings for a quarter bin of coal. I put the angels and the Father Christmas candleholders back in the attic. I never want to see them again.

I am despairing, Rose. Only your occasional quickening in my womb keeps me from harming us.

Love,

Ingrid, your mother

February 26, 1948

Dear Rose,

I called Johnny. "I have a gun," I said. "I'm going to use it to end my life and your baby's. You never wanted her anyway."

"Oh my God. Ingrid, don't. Don't do anything. I'll be there as fast as I can."

It seemed like an eternity until he pounded on the door. I let him in, but the gun never left my hands. When he came through the door, I aimed it at my head. "You have one last chance to do right by me. There's nothing wrong with our baby. She won't be sick like Paul."

Johnny voice was a low hiss. "I found him, Ingrid. I found Paul swinging an axe at my mother. My father was already dead, his face gone." Johnny sobbed, gasping for breath. "My mother had taken a blow to the arm. I was the one who subdued him and called the police. I didn't know whether to restrain him or stop her bleeding. There was blood everywhere. I rode with him in the ambulance, Ingrid. I went to his trial and testified against him." He looked at me, eyes pleading.

I realized then Johnny would never, ever marry me and be a father to you, dear Rose. "I can't do this alone." I steadied the gun. "I was crazy. I never should have put those pin pricks in the rubbers."

"Ingrid, please. Stop!"

"I was crazy then, but I'm not crazy now." Johnny lunged toward me and I pressed the trigger. There was a horrific bang and the world went black . . .

February 27, 1948

Dear Rose,

I was too tired to finish our story yesterday, so I'll do it now. I'm in the hospital. The moment I awoke, I knew I'd lost you. You weren't inside me, and you were too little to survive on your own.

A kindly police detective told me Johnny deflected the shot from my temple, but it punctured my womb. The bullet lodged in your tiny skull. You saved my life.

The nurse said when I was unconscious, I called out, "Rose! Rose!" "Your gentleman friend said that was your mother."

This is the last time I will write to you, dear Rose. For my sanity, I must let you go, but I know you await me in heaven, should I ever be able to earn my way there.

Today a doctor with grey in his hair and concern in his eyes came and sat at my bedside. "You know you've lost your baby," he said in a kindly voice. "But there's more. We've had to remove your womb. You are barren. I'm sorry."

He left me alone then, to mourn as I could, though the truth was I was still too numb to cry.

Johnny showed up in the evening, with flowers and a ring. "We'll marry," he said. "There's no longer anything keeping us apart. I've always loved you."

Johnny saved my life by grabbing the gun, but why did you have to die? But I love him, more than ever. And now, he is perhaps the only man who will have me. "Yes," I said. "I'll marry you."

Johnny came to my bedside, put an arm around my shoulders and kissed my lips. "At last," he said, "you really are my perfect woman."

Love,

Ingrid. May you and God forgive me, my dear Rose

Barbara Ross is the author of the Maine Clambake Mysteries, *Clammed Up, Boiled Over, Musseled Out* and *Fogged Inn* (coming February, 2016). *Clammed Up* was nominated for an Agatha Award for Best Contemporary Novel and was a finalist for the Maine Literary Award for Crime Fiction. *Red Dawn* is her final volume as a co-editor/co-publisher at Level Best Books.

www.maineclambakemysteries.com

Brotherhood

Gerald Elias

Dimsky clammed up like a Mafia witness as soon as the waitress arrived. He seemed to have aged a year for every month since I had last seen him, and he exhibited worrisome signs of distraction. An unshaved patch of whiskers, more white than black, colonized his left jaw. In the corner of his mouth, residue of some white ointment stretched into a strand when he spoke, making it seem as if his mouth would snap shut if he opened it too wide. As the waitress poured our coffee and served our pastries—a cruller for him, an éclair for me—Dimsky fidgeted impatiently with a packet of nondairy creamer as if it were rosary beads.

Once the waitress left, he tore open the packet and, oddly lacking his usual dexterity, absently spilled most of its contents onto the table. What managed to find its way into the cup floated on the surface like a gray-brown scum. Dimsky took an exploratory sip without even bothering to stir it.

"So when Maestro breezes by me for another bow," he resumed, "he gives me this look with his eyes popping out and silently mouths some words. He looks like a fish out of water, gasping for air. 'What?' I ask him. He mouths them again. I make out what he's saying: 'In my office.' That was not a good sign."

"You said before that he had a big smile on his face."

"The smile's for the audience. The eyes were for me."

"If looks could kill?"

"Kiss of death. I'm wondering what gives. Last concert of the season. I'd played okay. And it's not like it's the first time I've ever played Beethoven Nine. So what's to discuss?"

"I gather this is not standard protocol for conductors."

"Only when something bad is about to happen. I needed to assess the implications of his 'invitation.'"

"Of course. You needed to pull yourself together."

"So I take my sweet time hauling my bass down to the basement. The guys are emptying their lockers since we're off for a month. They can't wait to get the hell out of there, and I'm feeling the same way, but I have to act the opposite. I take my time changing out of my monkey suit into street clothes. Everyone's gone by the time I go up to the third floor."

"Postponing the inevitable?" I offer.

"I don't want anyone seeing me paying a visit to Maestro."

"Dimsky! Your cruller!" I gesture to his cup. He hasn't noticed that the cruller he dunked into his coffee has become saturated beyond its ability to remain intact. Half of it is now floating sludge. He gazes at it as if fascinated, then casually gaffs it with two fingers, depositing it on the white paper placemat. A brown stain spreads like time-lapse mold growing in a petri dish, but Dimsky seems not to notice. Not wanting to offend him, I pretend not to, either.

"Why wouldn't you want anyone seeing you go to the conductor's room? I would think it would be considered an honor."

"Word's out he's got spies in the orchestra. I don't want anyone to think I'm ratting on anyone."

"Isn't that a little paranoid?"

Dimsky looks at me as if I were as naïve as Neville Chamberlain.

"You tell me. I knock on Maestro's dressing room door. 'Come in, come in,' he says. Very welcoming. He's sitting at his desk. On the wall behind him are his action photos."

I give Dimsky a questioning look.

"You know," he says, making windmill gestures in the air. "Rehearsing the Berlin Philharmonic with a sweater tied around his neck. Stepping off a prop plane with Rostropovich. Holding his opened eyeglasses in one hand and looking heavenward as if he's in the midst of a profound thought. You know. The usual!"

"But at least you say he was welcoming," I reply, hoping to sound encouraging.

"Yeah, or so it seemed, sitting there with his Beethoven score. He closes it with a sigh, like I've interrupted him studying it, but we just finished playing the damned thing and he's already taken a shower and changed, so I think he's putting on a show.

"Maestro stands up and leans over the desk and shakes my hand. You know how everyone thinks he's such a towering figure?"

"He's not?"

"No! He could hardly reach over his desk. He's just a little old French slug in a red bow tie. Hardly over five feet. Guys in the orchestra call him 'L'escargot.' Sometimes just Les, for short."

"Geez. I never would've guessed. How do you account for the illusion?"

"Musical presence. The force of Maestro's personality."

"Sometimes you just have to tip your hat," I say.

"Yes. I have to confess, Maestro had that *je ne sais quoi.*" Dimsky almost sounds defeated making the admission and seems to shrink even more into himself.

"Is he great?" I ask.

"Not as great as he thought he was. Few of them are. But good. Very good."

"Why do you keep calling him Maestro, by the way?" I ask. "He does have a name."

It was as if I had poked a snake with a stick.

Dimsky snaps back, "I don't want to jinx things. Okay?"

"Okay. Just asking." I raise my hands in surrender, reducing Dimsky's boil to a simmer.

"Are you going to let me finish my story, or what?"

Other customers look at us. Dimsky glowers back until they lower their gazes and return to their own conversations.

"Sorry," I say. "Go ahead. I'll shut up."

When Dimsky resumes, his voice is subdued.

"'Have a seat,' Maestro says. So I sit. He pats the score. 'You know,' he says, putting his hand on his heart, 'that was one of the most momentous performances of the Ninth I've ever conducted.'

"Who am I to disagree? So I nod thoughtfully and make some clucking sounds. Maestro goes on to tell me how profound a piece this is. How we're all brothers. How humanity must all join together under Beethoven's vision of universal brotherhood. As if he's the first one to have discovered this."

"Beethoven?"

"No. Les."

"And meanwhile you're wondering, 'What the hell is this all about?'"

"Don't rush me. I'm getting there. Maestro says, 'Dimsky, you've been principal bass player of the orchestra for twenty-six years.' Twenty-eight, I correct him. He gives me the look again."

"He doesn't like being corrected?"

"What conductor does? But then he starts telling me how my leadership and experience have been so invaluable to the orchestra and to him personally. He gives me this leery, sideways smile like the proud father whose son has just gotten his first lay."

"And you're thinking, is he setting you up?" I ask, starting to catch on. Who would have guessed playing in an orchestra would be such a snake pit?

"Yes. That's what I'm thinking. But where the hell is he going with this? I'm wondering. Then he tells me why he 'invited' me to meet with him, 'before I go up to my sanctuary in Maine,' he says, with a faraway look. 'I must prepare for next season. Alone. Alone with my scores and the vastness of *la mer.* It allows me to study, to contemplate, and to *imagine!*' He goes into more detail than I want to know about what a lavish place he has overlooking the Atlantic, and how it's all worth it even if it did cost him an arm and a leg."

"Poor guy."

"'But I am wasting your precious time,' Maestro says. 'Let us get down to the brass tacks. The last chair of the bass section has been vacant for two years,' he reminds me, as if I needed reminding. It's my own damn section, and he knows shit about bass playing, yet he's nixed the finalists at the last three auditions over everyone's objections. 'Two years,' he repeats, and raises two fingers to make sure I know what two means. So now I'm thinking Maestro has some cockamamie scheme to fill the vacancy over the vacation and wants me to be a *collaborateur* so he doesn't have to eat crow. I act respectful and ask how I might be of service, but I'm thinking, 'Okay, get ready, it's coming.'"

"The classic setup."

"He says, 'But first, I must share my vision for the orchestra with you.' As if his vision's a big secret that hasn't been a tape loop for the last four years. 'I want to nurture the artistry! I want us to blossom into the greatest orchestra in the world!' And how he wants to tour and record all the Mahler symphonies and about the sound he's been trying to create since day one and . . . you know, the whole nine yards. Again I ask how I might be of help.

"He tells me he wants whoever sits on last chair to not only be a strong player but also one who has experience, knows the repertoire inside out. Has great listening skills. Gets along well with his colleagues."

"That seems reasonable. Isn't that what everyone always wants?"

"Of course," Dimsky says. "But I figure I'll humor him. I ask, 'Maestro, do you have someone in mind?'

"'Yes,' he says.

"'Who?' I ask."

Dimsky points his half cruller at me, I suppose to dramatize the moment.

"'You, Dimsky! You!' that bastard says, with his bastard smile."

Shades of O. Henry!

"What?" I say, dumbfounded. "But—"

"Yeah. Well, that totally catches me off guard, too, but I try not to betray my shock. I keep my eyes fixed on Maestro's, but I'm out cold on my feet, trying to think. I must not have said anything for a long time, or maybe my stare made him uncomfortable, because it's Maestro who finally breaks the silence.

"'Well?' he says. 'What do you say?'

"I felt like I was sinking and needed to tread water so I wouldn't drown. 'Let me get this straight,' I say. 'After twenty-eight years of being the principal bass player of this orchestra, which you just said I've led with distinction, you want me to go from first chair to last chair?'

"'Exactly!' Maestro says. 'And that way we can get a new, young principal player'—he emphasized the word *young*—'who will be better than anyone we could ever hope to hire for the last chair. And you can mentor the new principal until he gets his wings under him."

"Wings under him?"

"His words, not mine," Dimsky says. "Maestro folds his hands like he's single-handedly wrapped up the Middle East situation, but I can tell he's a little nervous, too, because he keeps wriggling his fingers. He says, 'I think it is an inspired solution. Do you not agree?'"

"And you're probably thinking, 'What a son of a bitch,'" I say supportively. "The humiliation! And to ask you to babysit your own replacement! After all you've done for the orchestra!"

"And for *him*! I had his back even when some of my confreres had less than savory things to say about him.

"I say, 'Maestro, I don't understand. Why are you doing this? And why now?'

"Maestro puts his hands on the Beethoven and gazes down at it like some kind of Hindu hocus-pocus from which he's divining profound esoteric wisdom. Then he looks up at me and lets out a big sigh, and says, 'Let me be honest with you, Dimsky. You're not the player you were twenty years ago.' And then, like it had been the devil who had dragged the words out of him against his will, he bangs his fist on Beethoven Ninth."

"What an actor!"

"One of the best. But that's what wakes me up! Like a hypnotist clicking his fingers, it gets me out of my trance.

"'What are you talking about?' I say. *'You weren't here twenty years ago!* You've been here four years, and I can show you the rave reviews of all the solos I've had in that time.'

"It must've made him nervous to have someone fight back for once, because he stands up and starts pacing. I get up, too, and I don't know why, but I follow him around and around his desk. It's like a two-man conga line. I can tell he's getting worried because he's moving faster and faster, but my legs are longer so I have no difficulty keeping pace.

"I feel like I'm on a roll. 'Besides,' I say, 'what if I don't accept your *generous* offer? There's nothing in our contract that gives you arbitrary authority to reseat musicians.'

"'Yes, you have a choice,' Maestro says, and suddenly stops in his tracks. I almost run him over. His head is about even with my chest so he looks up into my face. 'Here is your choice: last chair or no chair. If you decline your new position, I am prepared to offer you a nice severance package. If you choose this option, my secretary has typed up the letter for you to sign.'"

"The swine!" I say.

"He thought he had me, but I know our contract. 'You can't fire me now, the last night of the season,' I say. 'March first was the deadline.' I figured I had him there. But again he's one step ahead of me.

"'You want to fight?' Maestro says. 'You want to sue? Go ahead, but if that's what you want, you lose your severance package.'"

"Sounds like he had you over a barrel."

Dimsky's body sagged. He gazed blankly at his half-empty coffee cup with its dregs of cruller, and the soppy mess on his place mat, as if they were burned-out vestiges of a ruined kingdom.

"To tell the truth, I kind of gave up at that point."

Dimsky fell back in his chair. He was sinking. Dimsky was totally dedicated to music. It had cost him his marriage to a wonderful woman who tried to understand but ultimately couldn't accept being a lifelong second fiddle. I sense that is what's on Dimsky's mind. As a friend, I feel this is the crucial moment for me to help him rally.

"You can file a grievance! Certainly your colleagues will back you up!"

Dimsky can tell what's behind my words, and he gives me a half smile.

"Most of them. But some of the others, they're malleable, if you know what I mean. They'll fall apart. Like my cruller."

"Worried about losing their own jobs?" I ask.

"Like that."

Dimsky sighs, closing the parentheses.

"So I ask Maestro if I can have overnight to think about it, but like I said he's figured it all out. He reminds me he's off to Maine where he turns off his phone and will be unreachable for a month. I have to decide immediately or I lose everything.

"I sit back down and try to see the rest of my life in one minute. My two choices: groveling on last chair with audiences thinking, 'He used to be good.' And for how many more years? Until I've finished babysitting? Until I shrivel away behind my bass? I couldn't take that. But resigning with my tail between my legs?"

"The lady or the tiger."

"One would think."

There's a lull. Dimsky closes his eyes. Could he have fallen asleep? I'm about to call his name when he opens them. There's a gleam that hadn't been there before.

"But!" he says.

If nothing else, Dimsky always could tell a story.

"Yes?" I ask.

"There was a third choice!"

Dimsky pulls his chair closer to the table. He speaks to me in little more than a whisper, but he's animated now.

"'Maestro,' I say, 'if your Beethoven Ninth was my last performance, what better way to go out? Would you honor me by coming down to the basement to see me off? I'll sign the letter there.'

"You couldn't imagine more relief on someone's face if he'd been given an enema after a month of eating rice. 'I am only too happy to oblige,' Maestro says. I think getting rid of me was what he really had in mind all along, and you can tell he's forcing himself not to laugh out loud.

"Maestro packs his Beethoven Ninth and some other scores with his concert dress in a little carry-on suitcase. We take the elevator down."

"I gather everyone's long gone," I say.

"I already told you that," Dimsky says. "Don't make me lose my train."

I apologize.

"I ask Maestro if he would be kind enough to autograph the inside of my bass case and then I'll sign the letter. I can tell he's in a hurry, but his vanity prevails. I take my bass out and he takes his pen out of his pocket and hands me his carry-on. While he's signing—"

"How's everything?" the waitress asks, smiling, appearing out of the ether.

Dimsky blinks at her. It takes him several moments to reconnect with his surroundings.

"What difference does it make?" he yells at her. The waitress admirably manages to freeze her smile but beats a hasty retreat, assuring us if we need anything to just let her know.

I reach out to Dimsky and put my hand on his arm to calm him down. He seems to have lost his train, so I remind him.

"Maestro is in the process of signing your case," I say.

"Oh, yes," Dimsky says, and suddenly a dam seems to break. A calm comes over him. He's the old Dimsky I've known for all these years.

"Yes," he continues. "I clobber him over the head with his

suitcase and knock him out. I push him into the case, throw in the letter, and snap it closed."

"Just like that?" Dimsky always was a problem solver.

"Just like that. I leave the hall by the security entrance. It's the only way out. I wave goodbye to Chloe, who's on duty."

"That couldn't have been easy, with you schlepping your case and Maestro's luggage."

"Bass cases these days are on wheels, like his suitcase. And everyone had been emptying their lockers, so I didn't look out of the ordinary."

"So no problem with the guard?"

"Just one little glitch. She asks me, 'Have you seen Maestro? Everyone else is gone.'"

"That would've given me a heart attack," I say. "How did you respond?"

"I pat my case and say, 'Yeah, he's right in here.'

"She laughs and says, 'If only! He must've gone out with the chorus.'

"'I guess,' I say. 'See you next month.' And then I went home."

"What about your bass?" I ask.

Dimsky acts perturbed, like I'm trying to poke holes in his unbelievable tale.

"What do you mean, 'What about your bass?'"

"Well, you took your bass out of the case and you won't be back for a month. Won't that make people suspicious? And how are you going to practice?"

"You don't know much about orchestras, do you?"

I admit my ignorance and request enlightenment.

"A lot of bass players have two instruments," Dimsky explains, "one at home and one at the hall. That way they don't have to lug it back and forth twice a day. Saves on wear and tear, both on the instrument and on the human. I left mine next to a half dozen others. No one will be the wiser."

"Well, I guess you covered all your basses," I quip.

"You're not taking my situation very seriously."

"My apologies. So what did you end up doing with Maestro?" I ask.

"That was the hard part. I really hadn't thought everything out."

"He hardly gave you the chance."

"Obviously, I had to kill him. Otherwise, knocking him over the head would have been superfluous."

"Obviously."

"So I did."

I manage to refrain from saying, "Les is no more," for fear of irritating my friend further. But I look into Dimsky's eyes, and a chill goes through me. I'm beginning to think Dimsky is serious.

"How?" I ask instead.

"Let's just say he didn't suffer. But as you can imagine, I can't keep him in my apartment very long. I have to get rid of him. At first, I thought about doing something poetic, like burying him in my bass case at the old Granary Burying Ground, maybe next to Paul Revere, or slipping it into Boston Harbor, but . . ."

Dimsky shrugs. I take a guess.

"Why waste a good case?"

"Exactly. So ultimately I decide on practicality over poetry."

"And?"

"When no one was looking, I fed him to the hyenas at the Franklin Park Zoo."

I look into Dimsky's eyes. There's no indication of insanity, but what signs should I be looking for?

"Why not the zoo in Stoneham?" I ask. "It's closer."

"The farther away, the less suspicion. Besides, there are no hyenas at Stone Zoo."

Dimsky has done his homework well. But still I probe for the clue that will shatter the tale.

"How did you get Maestro through the bars?"

"Piece by piece."

"But certainly you've got to be worried. What if the authorities find his remains?"

"Hyenas eat everything. Bones and all. I read up on that. And don't forget, no one even knows he's missing. They all think he's holed up in Maine communing with God. Or vice versa. It'll be weeks before anyone starts worrying. But even if they do, who's going to look for a missing conductor in month-old hyena poop?"

I couldn't argue with that.

The waitress arrives, warily, to clear plates and give us the bill.

After she leaves, I thank Dimsky for confiding in me.

"Hey, what're friends for? We're like brothers," he says. I reach for the bill, but Dimsky is faster.

"It's on me," he says. "Besides, how do you know if it's true?"

"What do you mean?" I ask.

"Well, I could have made the whole thing up. It could simply be a figment of my warped imagination."

"I suppose we'll know in a month," I say.

"More or less."

We get up to leave. Dimsky empties his pockets of cash and leaves a huge tip for the waitress.

"So what do you do now?" I ask.

"What else? Get ready for next season. I've got that big solo in Mahler First right out of the gate."

"What'll happen at the first rehearsal?"

"If Maestro doesn't show up, the assistant conductor will be there to cover. Part of the job description."

"Is he any good?"

"If not, I have an extra case."

Gerald Elias, internationally acclaimed musician, is author of the award-winning Daniel Jacobus mystery series that shines an eerie spotlight on dark corners of the classical music world. An award winner of the 2014 Al Blanchard contest, his provocative essays and short fiction, ranging from broncos to Berlioz, grace many online and prestigious publications, including *Ellery Queen, Sherlock Holmes,* and Level Best anthologies. www.geraldelias.com

Singed

Dorothy Cannell

B other, blast, b . . . mothballs!"

This outburst from Major Arthur Bollinger, a burly man on the shady side of middle-age, was uttered in a roar consistent with having single-handedly lost a world war. One that should have been winnable with a couple of shots from a water pistol. Chagrin of the deepest order seeped through every syllable. Had there been a minefield propitiously laid out before him he would have charged on to it, embracing the prospect of being blown to smithereens.

Regrettably no such out presented itself. It was a summer afternoon and he was seated at a bridge table at Cloisters, the gracious home of the Misses Hyacinth and Primrose Tramwell, glaring at the remaining card in his hand. Ace of spades! If played when should have—different story. Now tossed down he saw it trumped, as he'd known would happen, by the two of hearts. Oh, for a bayonet in the back! His ruddy face worked. His bushy eyebrows converged over his nose. His moustache looked ready to fly off his face and hit the wall a dozen feet away. Down three tricks doubled, giving Primrose Tramwell and Sir Hugo Everard 800 points. He, the seasoned, much decorated soldier, blenched at meeting his partner's gaze.

"Apologize, Hyacinth! Should never have taken us to six hearts. Ought to have left us at the four level in your clubs. Deserve to be court-marshaled!"

What should have been a mumble erupted due to his harried state of mind into another roar awakening Minerva, the sisters' beloved dog, an ugly yellowed-eyed creature of ignoble ancestry with enough teeth for a pack of wolves. Fortunately before she could lunge from her velvet-cushioned basket (circa 1830 as befitted the room's ambience) and produce the death Major Bollinger had hoped for, Hyacinth Tramwell stayed her with a look. One that owed much to the grim visage of a great-great-great grandfather whose portrait hung above the mantelpiece. Legend had it that this incarnation had been banished on multiple occasions to the attic only to return under its own power to the place he had selected for its placement when still possessed of earthly limbs.

As was said in the village of Flaxby Meade, the Tramwells past and present could never be described as wishy-washy. Hyacinth's appearance certainly ridiculed such a possibility. Her eyes were as black as her hair which, given her sixty-plus years, appeared not merely questionable but blatantly dishonest. Her attire was always idiosyncratic. On this occasion it comprised a badly knitted jaundiced yellow dress coupled with assorted draperies that might once have hung at bordello windows. Not an ensemble to compliment her sallow complexion.

Through the years many persons had quailed under her jetty stare, including at aged three a fearsome nanny who had departed at dead of night by means of a knotted sheet rope tied to a balcony railing. But the look she gave Major Bollinger was not venomous, reducing him to an empty regimental uniform, but filled with kindly concern. Dangling earrings suggestive of piratical treasure trove swung at her neck as she leaned towards him.

"My dear Arthur, do not distress yourself. It's been clear from the moment we sat down to play that you have something exceedingly troublesome on your mind."

"Not in love with no hope of return, old boy?" Sir Hugo Everard suggested in an attempt at lightness. "Confirmed bachelors can take that sort of stuff hard."

"Oh, do not tease him," responded Primrose Tramwell in her habitually fluttery voice. She was the younger of the sisters by three years but had gallantly allowed her hair to turn from brown to silver. Or perhaps she'd realized how well it would suit her sky blue eyes, petal soft skin, and rosebud mouth. Her clothing was of the ruffles and frills sort, the one disparity a large Mickey Mouse wristwatch. "I agree with Hyacinth, Hugo, that our dear friend arrived in a state of anxiety—courageously borne, but which prevented the meagerest of concentration on so trivial an activity as bridge."

"Graciously said considering your passion for the game," replied Sir Hugo, "but I don't doubt you are in the right of the matter. The prowess you and Hyacinth have demonstrated these past years as private detectives would never permit me to dismiss your observations without discussion."

"So gratifying," fluted Primrose.

"Indeed!" Hyacinth's bright orange mouth stretched to a smile. In addition to be being a friend of longstanding, Sir Hugo was the Chief Constable of the county causing The Flower Detectives' paths to cross professionally with his on several occasions.

"Well, there is a matter . . ." The Major paused to clear his throat.

"And you shall tell us all," inserted Hyacinth, "but before beginning I think we should seat ourselves more comfortably." The four had barely settled themselves on a pair of facing sofas when the door from the hall opened and Butler, the butler, stepped into the room. He was a short, neatly built man of uncertain age with the imperious bearing and inscrutable facial expression considered requisite to his position. In only one way did he not fulfill the image. He was shoeless, although it had to be said that his socks were impeccable, ironed to a nicety. This eccentricity resulted from Butler having been engaged in the burglary trade before entering Hyacinth and Primrose's service. Far from holding this against him they were wont to say his ability to move silently made for the ideally unobtrusive employee. Not only around the house, but also when assisting in their detective work by slipping unseen into an establishment in search of evidence and departing undiscovered.

He now addressed his employers. "You was about to ring for tea, Madams?" His clairvoyance on such household matters was one of his most valuable assets.

"We were," Hyacinth told him, "but whatever is the matter with you? Why is your nose twitching?" This was an exaggeration. His nostrils had flared almost imperceptibly.

"I prefer not to say, Madam, it not being my place."

"Do not be tiresome, Butler. Give voice to what disturbs you."

His features displayed stoicism worthy of a martyr tied to the stake. "Very well, Madam, at your insistence and with the hope of not giving offence I admit an aversion to the odor, however faint, of camphor."

When he had padded from the room Hyacinth glanced at her sister who nodded. Major Bollinger appeared too deeply sunk in thought to have heard or seen what had just passed, but Sir Hugo raised an enquiring eyebrow.

Primrose tinkled a laugh at him. "Neither Hyacinth nor I have taken to dabbing it on our wrist or behind the ears, so let us listen to dear Arthur's account of what is troubling him. Very possibly there is nothing we can do to lighten the load, but it so often helps—does it not—to unburden oneself?"

"What?" The Major shook himself alert. "Good of the three of you to be interested. It's my sister Madeleine. Maddy as she's always been called. Suits, seeing she's always been a little off kilter. As a young woman she joined one of those religions that don't allow for doctors. Medical intervention of any sort strictly forbidden. Goes against the will of God. Pray yourself out of what ails you. That's the way of it. Bunk I call it, for all I'm a church-going man. But until recently her nuttiness didn't present problems that would've made me feel obliged to try talking sense into her. Maddy's always been healthy as a horse, apart from having no sense of smell these past twenty-odd years. Don't know how that came about, but not the sort of thing to kill you."

Hyacinth contemplated this information before saying that if she remembered correctly his sister had remained single and lived in Walton-In-The Fields. This was a hamlet no more than ten miles from Flaxby Meade.

"That's right. At Pond House. Rambling old place, off the beaten track, and going to ruin because she's never been willing to shell out the money to have it put to rights." Major Bollinger sighed. "As I've said, she's always been an odd duck."

"Tell us how she is currently," Primrose urged gently.

"Yes do, old chap." This encouragement came from Sir Hugo. "What has changed? Do you fear your sister, after a lifetime of rude health, is now seriously, even dangerously, ill?"

Major Bollinger tugged at his moustache. "Have been worried about her for months. But when I saw her today, having invited myself to lunch, I was shocked by her physical and mental deterioration.

I'd been away, you see, on a fortnight's holiday. Maybe it was that absence from seeing her even in so short a time that brought the reality of her condition home to me. Never on the plump side, she was reduced practically to a skeleton, trouble breathing, dizzy spells—would have tripped and fallen several times if I or Virginia had not been standing close enough to catch hold of her."

"Virginia?" His three listeners enquired in unison.

"Maddy's companion."

"Of many years?" Hyacinth asked.

"Coming up for two, I think. They met at a religious convening— or whatever the group terms its gatherings."

Butler drifted into the room as if on a current of air, deposited a laden silver tray on the table between the sofas and vanished. Hyacinth did the honors with the teapot, milk jug and sugar bowl, but no one eagerly eyed the plates of sandwiches, scones and fruitcake. It was clear what interested them was Major Bollinger's narrative.

"Virginia was a new convert," he continued, "eager for guidance and Maddy from the sound of it fell all over herself providing it. She'd never been one for making friends. Didn't want them. Adamant she preferred her own company. No more than a grudging affection for me. But when it came to Virginia she was like . . . like a moth drawn to a flame."

"Ah!" Primrose inclined her silvery head.

"Powerful personality, Virginia! But not in a dominating sort of way. I'd say vibrant best describes her. Filled with enthusiasm for life. Amazed me how she managed to bring Maddy out of what had seemed to me a lifeless existence. Off they'd go together, tramping through the woods, rowing on the pond, cycling to surrounding villages."

"How long before she moved into your sister's home?" Sir Hugo enquired.

"Matter of a few weeks."

"Did they go in for entertaining?"

"No. A case of being sufficient unto themselves, although can't say Virginia was unwelcoming when I made the occasional visit."

"I don't think you mentioned her surname," remarked Hyacinth.

"Jones."

"Yes," Primrose nodded, "I thought it would be something of the sort suited to persons who prey upon others."

The Major looked embarrassed. "Hope I haven't been so ungentlemanly as to make such a suggestion."

"Oh, my dear Arthur. You may not wish to acknowledge even inwardly the suspicion that your sister's failing health is the result of a wicked woman's plotting. And it must be handed to Virginia that she has been very clever. The motive of course being money. When you spoke of Maddy allowing her home to fall into ruin, there was the implication that she could well afford to maintain it. How well-off is she?"

"Rich. Very." Major Bollinger gave one of his nervous tugs at his moustache. "She inherited several million pounds from a great aunt."

"And would we be correct," said Hyacinth, "in assuming that while still of good health in mind and body Maddy made a will leaving almost if not all of what she was possessed to Virginia?"

"Yes."

"Anything to you?"

"I've no idea, but no reason she should. I'm comfortably placed. Don't see how you can be so sure that Maddy's failing health can be laid at Virginia's door. She's a few years older than me—nearing seventy. A good many people may be living into far greater old age, but not all are so fortunate. Besides, by what means could Virginia achieve so dreadful an objective? Poison? An autopsy would presumably reveal its presence in the body."

Hyacinth agreed. "But considering its nature the likely conclusion would be accidental death."

"Nature?"

"You gave us the hint."

"He did?" Sir Hugo's brow furrowed. "When?"

"With his exclamation after misplaying that last hand. Remember? 'Bother, blast, b . . . mothballs.' Understandable, Major, that you caught yourself before uttering a word you'd view as unsuited to female ears. But why not cricket or golf balls for instance? The answer is obvious. You had been to Pond House before coming here and had smelled the odor of mothballs emanating from your sister. And it jarred your mind. This is summer. Was she wearing wool?"

"No. I suppose," the Major shook his head, "it must have niggled at my subconscious. And something stirred when Butler admitted to scenting a whiff of camphor. Must have got onto my clothing when I hugged Maddy goodbye. Not usually demonstrative but she looked so dreadful."

"Then," said Primrose, "there was your describing her as being drawn to Virginia like a moth to flame. Let us hope your sister comes out of this with only her wings singed."

"I stand amazed," voiced Sir Hugo, "I had no idea mothballs could be so hazardous to one's health."

"Indeed, yes! I remember reading about the effects in some medical publication. Large quantities in a closed space, over a considerable period of time. I imagine Virginia secreted them around Maddy's bedroom and made sure that when the poor woman was asleep at night or resting during the day the door was shut. The symptoms of weight loss, respiratory problems and dizziness are classic. Amongst others. There can be damage to the liver, skin, and even more distressing, to the central nervous system. She may no longer have been capable of rational thought. What made her the ideal candidate for this means of disposal was her having, as you told us, no sense of smell and beliefs that ensured she would not seek medical care."

Sir Hugo had rarely looked grimmer. "How long for the end to be reached?"

"I don't know," replied Primrose.

"Somehow," Hyacinth's orange mouth tightened, "I think Virginia will not be inclined to wait. There'll be an accident. My thought is by her drowning in the pond for which the house is named. So easy to believe she wandered out of the house, experienced a dizzy turn, and fell in with no one around to rescue her. You, my poor Arthur, will I am sure be asked at the inquest to attest to those spells. Further questioning will reveal that you had always known her to be odd, making it appear likeliest that she was responsible for the placement of those mothballs out of an excessive desire to protect her woolens."

"What is to be done?" Major Bollinger rose to his feet.

"You must return immediately to Pond House and force a confrontation with Virginia. It has to be hoped that the prospect of her plan to make herself a rich woman will cause her to lose control and launch an attack on you. A risky proposition, but you will take

Butler with you, he slipping in unnoticed and standing at the ready to rescue you in the nick of time."

Sir Hugo was also on his feet. "I will arrange to have a policeman waiting outside ready to break in if matters do not go well. Let's hope this effort won't come too late."

"I'm optimistic," said Hyacinth, "and I suggest, Arthur, that when your sister recovers you encourage her to play bridge. It is a game that teaches one to read people with better clarity."

"True," chimed in Primrose. She was about to add that it could also on occasion bring about the urge to murder, but decided an attempt to lighten the mood in this way would be unsuitable. The Major had the air of a soldier relishing the prospect of going into battle. It wouldn't do to deflate his confidence by inserting the idea that after that badly misplayed hand she and Hyacinth wouldn't be unduly distressed if he didn't survive his confrontation with Virginia, relieving them of the impoliteness of not inviting him to make up a foursome again. Such a dear man! Certainly no such thought had played any part in the advice they had given him. True, their friend the vicar's wife had been taking lessons and was very eager to start playing . . .

Dorothy Cannell was born in Nottingham, England, and came to the U.S. in 1963. She married Julian Cannell, and lived in Peoria, Illinois, from 1965 to 2004. They then moved to Maine where they reside with their dog Teddy and two cats. They have four children, Warren, Jason, and Rachael, who live in central Illinois, and Shana, who resides in Missouri. Among them, there are ten grandchildren.

Hero

Vy Kava

It was a black night, no stars, no moon, just the headlights of a Pontiac barreling down the street. It screeched to a halt and its driver bolted out of the car and ran towards the Mitchell house. He sprinted down its long driveway, leaped over the front steps and with his right foot kicked the front door open. Inside, he darted from room to room screaming, "FIRE! FIRE! GET OUT!"

The house timbers screamed as fire consumed them.

He found her half alive on the second floor bedroom. He threw her over his shoulder and dashed down the stairs.

Once outside, she grabbed his arm, "My babies. My twin boys."

Yellow flames billowed from the bedroom windows. Darkness and black smoke surrounded him. He dropped to his knees and crawled to the kids' bedroom. His lungs were burning.

He found one underneath the bed.

"Where is your brother?" he yelled.

No answer.

"Where did he go?"

Still no answer.

With one child in tow, he crawled through the room till he reached the closet; crouched in the back was the second boy. With a child under each arm, he bolted down the stairs as hot ashes rained on them.

Someone grabbed the children from his arms, patted his shoulder. He felt lucky, all had survived.

He needed air, needed to leave. Once in his car, he told himself that the next time he torched a house, he'd better get the address right.

Vy Kava is a certified public accountant who lives in Glastonbury, Connecticut. This marks her second appearance in a Level Best Books anthology. She has received numerous honorable mentions in the *Alfred Hitchcock Mystery Magazine.* In 2014, she was one of finalists in the Golden Donut short story contest sponsored by the Police Writers Academy. Currently she is working on her first novel.

Old Doc Sloan

Alan D. McWhirter

Back in the thirties (the nineteen thirties), during the Depression (the twentieth-century Depression), Doc Sloan was a saint of the poor and pregnant. He delivered an untold number of children and never billed families. Old Doc Sloan is a Waterbury legend. Doc died a half century ago, back in the sixties.

It's said by some that for his kindness a higher power granted him a partial stay until the last of those he birthed at no charge was ready to pass over with him. A few claim to have sighted the old doc, lugging his black leather bag through the frigid snow on a winter's night or the toxic fog of an early spring thaw. I've never believed all that nonsense. Then again, I've never believed in much of anything to speak of.

My name's Joe Chandler. I used to be a New Haven cop. Now I'm a private investigator. I've been divorced three times. Four times, if you count a nasty breakup with the New Haven PD. The Department filed for divorce, claiming irreconcilable differences. They were probably right.

I started in early at Murphy's, the bar across from The Horse on the east end of the Waterbury green. The Brass City, or what's left of it, exists in the no-man's land between Boston and New York. No-man's land is inhabited by a number of clans. There's the Red Sox clan and the Yankee clan. In keeping with Waterbury's position in the universe, I had three Manhattans and a brace of Boston Beer chasers. There are other clans in Waterbury too. Clans of a different ilk that fight over turf and what they call "respect" and sometimes women.

When I gave up my stool, Millie, the waitress, asked if I needed a hand getting home. Millie's a looker, if you know what I mean. For a moment, I imagined Millie seeing me home and staying the night. She volunteered Leonard, the clean-up man, to make sure I got where I was going. I declined her offer. A spring-melt fog descended over downtown. All I needed to do was lean towards the middle of the green whenever I stumbled into a piece of Main Street which borders the green on both sides.

Halfway down the green, near the Civil War monument, at the confluence of all the frost-heaved and root-erupted sidewalks, an old man carrying a black-leather bag stood directly in my way. I got within thirty yards and he turned away and beat a path toward the end of the green. Well-fortified from Murphy's, I abandoned the few good instincts I had left and followed. I kept trying to close the gap to get a better look. I never gained an inch.

The old man led me west from the green and turned right at Willow. A hundred yards up the hill, he climbed the steps at Brandolini's Funeral Home. All the funeral homes are on the west side of Willow, across from Grove, where the pimps, drug dealers and prostitutes own the night. I've never read tea leaves well enough to figure out the connection. The old man paused on the top step at Brandolini's. The door opened, he passed inside and the door closed behind him.

I swear the doorman opened the door for the old man. The doorman swore he didn't and said no one carrying a black bag had come in all evening. A thorough scan of the premises found no sign of the bagman.

I hate wakes. The only things I hate worse than wakes are funerals. I don't go to the wakes of people I've known all my life. Now some guy I never met had seduced me into Brandolini's parlor. I didn't even know whose wake it was. I didn't bother to sign the guest book or express phony written condolences.

An easel by the parlor door was covered in pics of a female from the time she was a young girl until she reached her mid-twenties. Keen detective instincts and the sign in bold letters told me her name was Libby Shepherd. Figuring I'd come to Brandolini's for some reason other than free beer, I took a peek in the open casket. Maybe someone had substituted a mannequin or a body double.

The elderly die by the dozens in Waterbury these days. But Libby Shepherd wasn't one of them. Even in death she was a creature I would have liked to have met before her transformation. There were no injuries to indicate an auto accident or other good cause for an early demise.

The usual receiving line was assembled to the right of the casket. Grieving parents, a sister and brother perhaps, or a sister and brother-in-law. Then a white-haired lady, probably more than eighty; a grandmother of the deceased.

Little doubt the reception committee had seen me standing by the casket and wondered what my connection was to Libby. I was too gutless to just disappear out the door, too polite to try and explain and, despite my visit to Murphy's, smart enough not to open my mouth and let the fumes of confession add insult to the mourners' grief. I worked my way down the line, nodded as I encountered each of the assembled, and nodded again every time I got a "thank you for coming." Until I got to Grandma.

I nodded and Grandma nodded back. Then she gave me one of those please-help-me looks I've been a sucker for all my life. She curled her finger at me to come close. I leaned in where Grannie could whisper and only I could hear.

"Mr. Chandler." *I hadn't told anyone my name.* "Please find whoever caused my granddaughter's death. Her soul won't rest in peace unless you do. Nor will mine." Grandma went on, "*He* told me you would help."

Before I could ask the "who told you" question, Grandma pressed into my hand the string of rosary beads she'd worked over all night and I was unceremoniously nudged down the line where I nodded some more to the lesser of the grieving.

Having survived the official mourners, I took myself to the back of the room and held down a chair where I could observe the rest of the comings and goings and not have to breathe on anybody. I wondered whether Millie had read my lascivious thoughts and spiked my last shot with some hallucinogenic to avoid walking me home.

Ten of nine, just before closing, a fog-colored trench coat came in out of the misted night and passed by the table that held the guestbook. The young man filling out the coat didn't sign in. The only people who do that are intoxicated private investigators who don't know the deceased and people who do but don't want their attendance recorded.

The young man stood frozen in the doorway to the parlor for almost a minute. He was just short of six foot, mid-twenties, a dash of red to his hair and clearly Hispanic. His eyes never left the casket. A tear escaped down his cheek. Then, drawn by an irresistible magnet, he slipped forward and knelt by Libby Shepherd's casket. Unseen by all except my trained eye, he dropped a miniature rose near her pale and lifeless hand. Then he struggled to his feet and left by the back door without passing through the reception line. Naturally, I followed.

I battled the wake of mist he left on his way down Willow, followed him across West Main and into the resurrected dive on the corner. Chato's has had a dozen names since I was a kid. But it's always been a bar. Only the last two incarnations have been Hispanic. The last time I'd been inside it had been called O'Reilly's. I was as out of place in Chato's as a white cracker at a black revival meeting in the North End. The patrons probably figured me for a cop. It's easier to lose the pension than the image.

The trench coat sat alone in a back corner. His chest barely supported his chin. He didn't look like he wanted company. So I joined him. I brought along a second of what he already had in front of him. "Tequila straight up," according to the barkeep.

The first hadn't been touched. I placed my offering on the table and pushed it in his direction. He looked up. The tear he'd dropped in the parlor wasn't the only one he'd given up.

I'm not much for small talk, so I got to the point. "How do you know Libby Shepherd?" I asked.

"Who the hell are you?"

"Joe Chandler."

"A cop?"

"Once upon a time," I said. "Now I'm just Joe Chandler."

I played my card face-up with all the confidence of a gambler showing a pair of aces—

Joe Chandler, Private Investigator
Thorough, Confidential, Discreet, Unconventional.

He seemed less than impressed, gave it a harsh look and left it on the table.

"And who are you?" I asked.

"If you're not a cop, it's none of your business."

"I've been asked to investigate Libby Shepherd's death."

"By who?"

If I told him "Grannie and some guy with a black bag" I might have scared him off and lost any cred I had. "That fits into the confidential part," I replied and pointed at the card.

He picked up the card, read it quickly and put it back face down. I pushed my offering of tequila closer. He pushed it back.

"I quit drugs three years ago," he said. "I've been off the booze I substituted for it for eight months."

"So what's the shot in front of you?"

"Chato thought I needed it. Said it was on the house."

I glanced at my spurned offering and put it to good use.

Persistence or stubbornness is one of my faulty virtues. "What does Chato call you?"

He delivered a penetrating look. "On the street they call me 'Cobra.' What do you want?"

"How did you know Libby?"

Maybe it was phrasing the question in the past tense that made a difference. I could tell he didn't want to say. Then again, maybe he did.

"She was my girlfriend."

"Back up the street you didn't give her family a glance."

"Her family don't know about Libby and me. They don't need to know Libby had a lover who was a gang member, drug addict and alcoholic. Spare them."

I'm good with some secrets. "How did you meet Libby?" I asked.

"Met her at AA."

"Libby needed AA?"

"God no! Libby never touched the stuff. She had a girlfriend with a suspended license who couldn't get to AA on her own. Libby gave her a ride to meetings. In the hallway, outside the meeting, we got talking. She invited me for coffee and things just took off and then got out of hand and . . . Neither of us meant for things to happen the way they did . . . and then she got pregnant." There was a very pregnant pause.

"How pregnant?" I asked.

"Four months pregnant. She hid it from everyone. Her family was clueless, though Libby thought her grandmother had it figured out. Libby wouldn't consider an abortion or hear of giving the child up for adoption. We were talking about how to explain me and the baby to her family. Then she was murdered."

It was the first time anyone mentioned murder. Must have slipped Grandma's mind.

"You sure it was murder?"

"Libby was shot in the stomach and left to rot in an alley off South Main Street."

Through the lifting fog of Murphy's finest, I recalled the headline from the *Waterbury Republican American* three days earlier, "Girl Found Dead in South End." I'd figured it was another Hispanic girl who overdosed close to home. The brief article hadn't provided a name or cause of death.

"How do you know she was shot in the stomach?"

"One of my friends found her and called 9-1-1. He told me about it the next day. I . . . I didn't know it was Libby until I got to the AA meeting the next night and . . . then found her obit in the paper."

"Have you talked to the police?"

"They don't know I was a part of Libby's world any more than Libby's family. But they'll figure it out, won't they? AA don't keep secrets as well as they claim."

I was beginning to like Cobra. It's a dangerous thing to begin liking prime suspects. Bad habit of mine.

"You'll be the number one target when the cops find out about you," I said. "You were in a tight spot and one way out would have been to do away with Libby. Just give them your name, rank and —"

"Go fuck yourself, dick head! I didn't kill Libby! I'd never hurt Libby! She meant everything to me. Libby convinced me to start

Criminal Justice at Naugatuck Community College. *Me*, in criminal justice?"

"Easy. Easy. Just remember Chandler's Rules when talking to the cops. Rule One—If you don't talk, you might walk."

Curiosity must have gotten the better of Cobra.

"And Rule Two?" he asked.

"Rules Two through Five are the same as Rule One."

Cobra gave me a strange look. "Who are you giving me advice?" he remarked. "Like I said, go fuck yourself. Libby was an angel. I don't shoot angels."

"Only devils?"

He thought a moment. "Yeah, now and again. And only when I have to."

Cobra and I were in many ways reflections in a mirror.

"You have any enemies that might relish getting even for something by harming your girlfriend?"

"A few. But nobody knew I was seeing Libby. Nobody."

"Looks like somebody did," I said.

Cobra was ready to leave.

"Is there a number I can get you at?" I asked.

"Seriously? You want my cell number? Why? So the cops can find me sooner than later?"

"They'll find you one way or another."

"Whose side are you on, Chandler?"

"Libby Shepherd's. I could use your help."

"I'll give it some thought." Cobra pocketed my card. "Sure you're not a cop?"

"I'm not a cop."

"Smell like one."

"Can't help that. The stench wears off slowly."

He pulled the pen from my shirt pocket and scribbled a number on an unused napkin.

"That was too easy," I said. "Why?"

"So you can call me when you find the son-of-a-bitch who killed Libby. Then I can . . ."

"Then you can what?"

Cobra pushed the untouched tequila in my direction and left. I tossed it down. No sense wasting good medicine.

The next morning, in a page eight footnote, the *Republican* identified the girl found in the South End alley as Elizabeth Shepherd of upscale Bunker Hill. Said she was shot. There was nothing else.

I dropped in at Police Headquarters on East Main and paid Lt. Brad Gooch a visit. There was a Captain back in New Haven who patted me on the back and told me I did the "right thing"—then told internal affairs I didn't. Gooch was recently up for Captain but got passed over. Probably too honest to make Captain.

"You want to know about Libby Shepherd?" he asked.

"Yeah."

"How'd you get involved?"

"I'm on retainer."

"By who?"

"You wouldn't believe me."

"Try me, Chandler. Confessions are good for the soul."

"You gonna read me my rights first?"

"You don't have any."

"Then my questions first," I said.

"I could book you for obstruction of justice."

"Then you'd read me my rights and I'd take your advice and shut up."

Gooch thought a moment. "What do you want to know?"

"According to the morning rag, Libby Shepherd was shot to death. But no details?"

"Once, in the stomach, at close range. She died of . . . complications."

"I understand she was pregnant," I said.

Gooch gave me a sharp look. "No one knows that, Chandler, not even her family yet. How well did you know Libby Shepherd?"

"Met her at her wake last night."

"That's a relief. I'd hate to think you were running around knocking up god-fearing Waterbury girls at your age."

"Got a motive?" I asked. "Robbery?"

"Looks like a personal thing. She still had her wallet, her credit cards, her cell phone and thirty dollars in her jeans. No one in the family can figure what she was doing in the South End. We're tracking her cell records. Should have them by tomorrow."

"She have any enemies?"

"She worked as a dental assistant up on Chase Parkway. But I assume those tortured by the dentist would have gone after him and not her."

"Any recent boyfriends?"

Gooch's reply dripped in sarcasm. "Obviously! The only one the family could identify was a Howard Horowitz. Talked to Country Club Howie myself. Guy says he got dumped seven months ago. Claims he didn't get past second base before the breakup. Insists the girl was the wait-until-the-wedding type."

"Was he okay with it?"

"The not getting any, or the breakup?"

"Both."

"Frustrated with the first. Not too happy with the breakup either."

"Poor Howie," I said. "Wait till he reads some new guy knocked her up."

"Horowitz said he suspected there was another guy. But he couldn't figure out what any rival could have over him. He planned to become a dentist."

"Did you check Howie out?"

"I haven't gone stupid just because I didn't make Captain. Howie played golf all afternoon with three doctors and then hobnobbed at a wedding in Poughkeepsie all evening. Dozens of witnesses."

"Does that eliminate him?"

"That, and the fact that Libby Shepherd was found in a dead-end South End alley, not on the third tee at Western Hills. Now, who got you involved?"

It was time to fess up.

"Old Doc Sloan . . . I think . . . maybe . . ."

"You mean the freakin' ghost? You been spending too much time at Murphy's." *Maybe Gooch was right.* "Hope he gave you a decent retainer."

I put my hand in my pocket and fingered Grannie Shepherd's rosary beads. "Enough," I said.

What's with Waterbury PD? Even when you confess they won't believe you.

I told Gooch about the guy Libby met at the AA meetings. They were going to catch up with him anyway.

"Where'd you find him?"

"In a bar."

"Figures. Ever try AA yourself?"

"I get my counseling at Murphy's."

"Probably why you're seeing ghosts. What's the boyfriend's name?"

"Goes by the street name of Cobra."

"Hispanic guy? Five-ten? About twenty-five?"

"Yeah. Know him?"

"Maybe . . . maybe not."

I headed down East Main. Looked for the man with the black bag along the route. It was too sunny and too early in the day. I hadn't dropped by Murphy's yet. Stopped at the green to remedy the oversight.

Just before six, the local news on the HD screen above Millie's blonde curls started a "Breaking News" rant. According to the never-let-the-truth-get-in-the-way-of-a-good-story news anchor, Waterbury police had "taken into custody" a person-of-interest in the shooting death of Libby Shepherd. I wondered if Cobra remembered my hard-earned advice.

The next morning I found Gooch in his office.

"You again? What do you want this time, Chandler?"

"Anything from Libby Shepherd's cell phone?"

"Not yet. Anything else?"

"I'm looking for Cobra."

"You mean Francisco Herrera? He's gone home. He didn't feel like talking and I had nothing to hold him on, just like the last time."

"The last time?"

"Three arrests, no convictions. Last arrest was for manslaughter. Not enough evidence to make it murder or pin it to him. Herrera's a member of the Latin Kings. Last year some creep from a splinter group raped his sister, trying to gain 'respect' if you buy that crap. Same creep ended up on a slab at the morgue. All of South Main and

Baldwin Street suffered a massive brain freeze. Victim must have been a real popular guy."

"Must have been. Many visitors at the morgue to pay their respects?"

"None I can recall. By the way, Cobra figures you fingered him. I'd stay out of the South End. It might prove hazardous to your health."

A little after noon I got a cell call. The voice was young, Hispanic and female. I secured the number, though likely it came from a phone that couldn't be traced.

"I hear you askin' about Cobra and that white bitch."

"And if I am, you got answers?"

"Maybe. What's it worth to you?"

"Depends what you have."

"Seven tonight, meet me on the corner of East Liberty and South Main. Park where the house burn down two blocks closer to the center of the city."

"How will I know you?"

"You won't. I'll know you."

I don't take Gooch's advice often. Didn't this time either. I packed my gun and half an hour before my appointment went calling on the South End. I didn't park in the recommended lot. Didn't have a car to park there. I drifted down South Main asking for Cobra. Nobody ever heard of Cobra. Tried his cell number four times. The last try it rang right behind me.

"Looking for me?" he asked.

"You weren't answering your phone."

"I recognized your number. Thanks for the police referral."

"Sounds like it went well. Gooch got nothing from you, I hear."

"I followed a strange man's advice. So? You know who killed Libby?"

"No."

"Then what are you doing here?"

Before I could answer a Hispanic girl, maybe eighteen, came

around the corner and stared us down. She looked a little surprised. She had a pistol drawn and aimed at my chest.

"Welcome to my town, Mr. Detective. Turn left at the next alley. When we get there, Paco, you frisk him and take his gun."

We walked twenty feet, turned left and walked another fifty feet down a foul-smelling alley. It looked like other alleys I've taken a wrong turn into. Lots of alleys look alike. But this one had the smell of recent death in it. Maybe the alley where they found Libby Shepherd.

I'd been set up. But something told me Cobra wasn't in on the plan. Sometimes I'm right. Still Cobra lifted my weapon and took two steps back behind me. "Maria, drop the gun!" he said.

"Go fuck yourself, Paco. I found the big-shot detective's card in your wallet. Same place I found the picture of your fancy white whore and her cell number."

"My wallet?"

"I always at your house since I was a kid. You always drop your wallet in the same place when you come home. Paco, why you chase Bunker Hill pussy when you can have South End pussy for the asking?"

Cobra didn't have an answer, at least one he wanted to share.

Maria looked at me. "What's so fuckin' hot 'bout Bunker Hill pussy?"

I didn't have an answer either. Growing up near Hamilton Park, I'd always been partial to the East Mountain variety.

"Why were you in my wallet, Maria?"

"I need her name and number."

"Why?"

"So I can arrange a meet. She no good for you, Paco."

I glanced over my shoulder. I didn't like the expression on Cobra's face.

"You killed Libby?" he asked.

"You mean that white whore? Somebody got to. The Bunker Hill bitch seducing you away from your own. Your sister told me the girl got herself pregnant and blaming you for it."

"She didn't get herself pregnant, Maria. I got her pregnant."

"What a shame. Well I got her un-pregnant. Your sister told me you were thinking of marrying the whore. What do you think her father say if he knew about you and the Kings? Someone had to fix things. You lost your mind. I did it for you, Cobra."

Maria had a gun pointed at my chest. Cobra had another pointed at my back. I didn't like the way the conversation was going and I was dead in the middle.

Cobra's face turned to steel. "Put down the gun, Maria."

"No."

"Maria, put it down."

"I can't, Paco. It's too late," Maria looked at me. "Mr. Detective knows too much." Maria raised the barrel until it looked me in the eye. The shot went off. And she dropped like a sack of potatoes. I checked for a pulse. There was none.

Cobra stood three feet away, as immobile as the body at my feet. The barrel of my gun was still pointed at the corpse. For an hour-long minute neither of us said a word.

"She a former girlfriend?" I asked.

"Maria? Not really. She had a crush on me growing up. Didn't know she still had it. Always over at my house."

"Did you ever . . .?"

"Once, when she was fourteen, I think. But that was part of her acceptance with The Kings. She was a good friend of my little sister."

"The one you got even for?"

Cobra finally looked at me rather than the corpse. "You looking for a confession, too?"

"I hear it's good for the soul," I said.

"Been told that recently," Cobra replied. "Still don't buy it."

When I started out in New Haven I knew what "justice" was. I had a clear sense of Right and Wrong. The truth's got a whole lot murkier with time. And I learned that Brass City justice is different from the New Haven PD kind.

"Give me the gun, Cobra"

"Why?"

"It'll be tougher for the cops to prove possession without a permit if they don't find you holding a smoking gun and standing over a dead body. And if they show up with weapons drawn, I wouldn't want mine to go off accidentally." Cobra gave it some thought. "It's my gun," I added. "I've got the explaining to do. The way I see it, you saved my life. It's near the same as self-defense."

"I saved your life?" Cobra said. "Or did I kill Maria for taking Libby and my unborn child away from me?"

I didn't know the answer. Maybe Cobra didn't either.

"Why don't you let Gooch ask the questions and me provide the answers."

In some parts of the Brass City a single gunshot will unleash the cavalry. On South Main one shot doesn't cause a stir. Just someone getting rid of the rats. I had to call Gooch myself to scare up a posse.

A week later, after the prosecutor gave up the chase, I went looking for Cobra. Figured I wouldn't find him in the bar. Hung outside the clandestine AA meeting. He didn't show there either. Figured he didn't want to be found until a day later when Grandma came into Murphy's with a new friend.

"She insisted on an escort," Cobra said.

Grandma smiled. Maybe for the first time since her granddaughter's death. "I had to say thank you, Mr. Chandler. And I wanted to give you this."

She tried to push three Franklins into my hand.

"Grandma, I can't accept this. You paid me the first time we met."

"What a pair, Mr. Chandler; you . . . you and Doc Sloan, I mean. You know, Doctor Sloan brought me into this world and never sent my poor parents a bill."

I wasn't surprised.

Before he gave Grandma an escort back home, Cobra asked, "Tell me, Chandler, does anyone ever manage to escape their past?"

I was the wrong one to ask.

Grandma and Cobra left and I ordered a stiff one. Millie said it was on the house. She said an old man had been in earlier and paid the tab.

"About five-six, white hair and a black satchel?" I asked.

"That's the guy," she replied. "Freaked me out. Said you'd done a 'bang-up' job. Paid for one stiff drink. Then he handed me something to give you. I put it under the bar and when I looked up he was gone."

Millie reached beneath the bar and pulled out a bottle of Epsom salts. "Old man said it's still the best remedy for hangovers."

Old Timers swear there are hundreds of ghosts in the Brass City. I wouldn't know. I've only laid my eyes on one of them.

Alan D. McWhirter is a retired criminal defense trial attorney whose prior works of short fiction have appeared in Level Best anthologies, 2009 and 2010. He is building his dream model railroad and tending his roses and vegetables with passion. A member of the Connecticut Soccer Hall of Fame, he lives with his wife and dogs in Cheshire, Connecticut.

High Crimes and Slick Demeanors

Susan Oleksiw

Anita Ray pulled open the closet doors, and ran her finger along the low shelf, checking for dust. The wooden hangers, evenly spaced across the bar, pointed uniformly to the back. She closed the doors and turned to examine the rest of the room. Guest room number seven had to be perfect—new sheets, not merely cleaned and pressed, but newly purchased; two new pillows, one for each bed; a new table cloth, not merely an old sheet cut to size and hemmed; a new television, though not a flat screen (even Anita had her limits); a new telephone; and fresh flowers. A small table for *puja* was placed against the wall beneath the window, where it would receive the first rays of the morning sun—the perfect spot for morning worship. And that was just the beginning.

Anita looked carefully at the ceiling and corners, searching out any missed cobwebs. There were no pallis, or lizards, hanging about—she saw fewer of them every year—but not more spiders as a result. She walked to the door opening onto the small balcony and shook the curtains: they hung neatly, freshly ironed without a single crease or wrinkle. She went out onto the balcony to check the two chairs and small table, inspected the glass in the windows and door, and noted the balcony flooring had been swept and swabbed.

Below on the beach, a number of tourists stared up at the sky, searching for the satellite the tour guide promised would appear. World Space Week in Kerala drew an enthusiastic crowd of sky watchers. Later in the week this group would tour the Vikram Sarabhai Space Centre, just up the coast. Anita closed the balcony door, gave the room one final look, and returned to the registration desk.

"I only hope I haven't missed anything," Anita said to Auntie Meena. The younger woman hopped up onto a stool. "Mr. Dayamani is so particular that any little thing can set him off."

"When is he due?" Auntie Meena looked up at the clock as she spoke. "Hotel Delite cannot come to a halt every year to honor his arrival."

Anita laughed. "He arrives at four next morning. Joseph will collect him at the airport."

"Have you shifted Madam Colleen?"

"She objected a little, but I offered her a reduction in the room rate and she was sweetness itself," Anita said. "She is now in room two."

"And the Bergers?" Meena counted on her fingers, trying to keep track of each guest.

"I explained that Mr. Dayamani was prone to complaining about children when he saw them even if he never heard them. So though the two Berger children are extremely well-behaved—to which Mr. Berger nodded and Mrs. Berger said Danke several times—I thought it would be best for them to move. They now have one very large room, also at a reduced rate."

"You are knowing, Anita, that some hotels refuse certain people." Meena tried to say this subtly, but she was not good at it, and she looked like a B actress trying to be sly.

"We may be driven to that," Anita agreed. "The sisters are in their usual room, and no bother at all."

"And how is Mr. Walters?" Meena smiled at the mere thought of the man. "He is so nice and accommodating. No troubling at all. And what room have we given him?"

"He is in room number four," Anita said. "Those two men belong on opposite sites of the hotel if not opposite sides of the resort."

At 6:30 the following morning Auntie Meena banged on the door to Anita's small flat over the garage. Most Indian workers were up and ready for the day at this hour—children had bathed and gone off for their first tutorials before school, and workers lined up for buses. But Hotel Delite was still relatively quiet, with kitchen workers arriving and firing up the stove, preparing the Kerala breakfast of the day, on this morning *puris* to go with *bhaji*, potato curry. Anita opened the door to see her aunt looking haggard.

"It's Mr. Dayamani, isn't it?" Anita said.

"Buzzing and buzzing and buzzing. It is something about the mattress." Meena leaned against the doorjamb. "He is here not even three hours and already I am defeated. What to do?" The guest must have caught her unawares because she was not dressed to meet anyone. She had hastily tied up her hair and wore an old sari.

"I'll go," Anita said, and finished dressing.

Mr. Dayamani stood in the doorway to his room, his arms folded across his chest, glaring at Anita as she crossed the hall. He was about to launch into his complaint when the two French sisters emerged from their room and directed a warm greeting to him. His response could only be described as desperation masked by arrogance. Holy men, and Mr. Dayamani was considered one of the greatest, disliked contact in any language with foreign women. Anita turned his attention to his complaint.

The matter was the mattress, which he insisted was the same one he'd had last year. He hadn't liked it last year and he didn't like it this year. Since there were two beds in the room Anita thought about asking him why he hadn't moved to the second bed, but knew it would be futile. She went in search of a new mattress. A few minutes later, Anita showed Mr. Dayamani the tag testifying to the newness of the mattress and by seven-thirty all was settled. Anita thanked Mr. Dayamani for bringing this oversight to their attention.

"Who is that man?" Mr. Dayamani stiffened at the sight of another guest crossing the hallway to the stairs. Anita nodded good morning to Mr. Walters. "Another guest, from the States," she explained.

Mr. Dayamani harrumphed and closed the door.

"Why do we put up with him?" Auntie Meena said in the privacy of the hotel office.

"Because he is a famous divine, and even IT millionaires consult him." Anita reached for the tray of coffee.

"Surely they must tire of him." Auntie Meena sagged in her chair. "Any meeting revolving around that man must be torture—even Kali herself would seem less terrifying."

Mr. Walters, on the other hand, was a different story. He took a small table in the upstairs dining room and stared out the window while he waited for someone to bring him a menu. He didn't shout, snap his fingers, glare at anyone. He waited with a half-expectant smile on his face, as though worried he might have shown up in the wrong place at the wrong time.

"Ah, *puris*. I do like *puris*," he told the waiter. "That's for me." He handed over the menu. "And coffee. A pot, if you please."

"Good morning, Mr. Walters." Greeting this guest was a pleasure and Anita let the conversation wander.

"A new book you are on?" Anita saw the small notebook beside his water glass.

"Just started it." He patted the notebook and gave her the smile of a child excited by a secret he could now share. "It will be slow going for a while but I'll get through it."

"Yes, you always do, isn't it?"

"I think I'll take a few short trips to get into the feel of the story. I'm writing about an American family traveling while they sort out family problems. You know, maybe a love spat in front of Meenakshi Temple," he said, his thick black eyebrows wiggling. Anita smiled though privately she thought it sounded like an unimaginative soap opera (which raised the question, was there any other kind?).

"He's writing another book," Anita said when she found Auntie Meena in the office.

"I do wish he'd send us a copy of his earlier ones." Auntie Meena put down her pen. "It is always good to showcase important guests, isn't it?"

"I don't think he wants to be showcased," Anita said. "Besides, his work may not be any good."

"Who are you to say this? You have not seen his books." Meena was nothing if not loyal to her guests.

"I have seen a page. He tore up a page last year and left it in the waste basket," Anita said. "I put it together with cellotape. It was ordinary—some sort of family argument. I think it is the sort of thing he writes."

"Perhaps he would like to know his fans appreciate him," Meena said, still hoping to discover a star in their personal firmament.

"I think he comes here because it is quiet and he can write."

Meena grew thoughtful. "Perhaps I should ask the temple to lower the volume on the morning music. I could also ask the mosque to lower the evening music."

"You could also learn Punjabi and become a North Indian."

"Anita! The things you say!" Poor Meena looked so shocked that Anita reached over and gently put two fingers under her aunt's chin and lifted it, closing her gaping mouth.

At ten o'clock that evening, as the guard drew the metal gate into place and the cook wandered off home, Auntie Meena sprawled in a chair wiping her face with the end of her sari. "Three times just since tea he has called. Three times. He may be a divine but so difficult."

"He is very unhappy this year," Anita said.

"Unhappy!" Meena sat up and nearly shouted. "Unhappy!"

Anita took a final check of the registration desk and waved to Sanjay, the inside night guard, who was spreading out a blanket on the floor in the parlor. He might sleep but any unusual noise would have him up and ready. Outside his cousin watched over the parking lot, the lane, and the rocks in front of the hotel.

"We can only do what we can do," Anita said, pulling up a chair. "This is his karma, his life, to be so unsettled and unhappy wherever he goes."

"He is a madman this year," Meena said. "He has been to the kitchen three times to inspect, certain that a problem with the food was there. No problem was found. He insisted on interviewing cook."

"Oh, not good," Anita murmured.

"Cook is understanding. For now."

"Has Mr. Dayamani eaten this evening?"

"Eaten and retired." Meena covered her face with the end of her sari, and then looked up at Anita. "But tomorrow! Tomorrow he wants to empty the hotel of guests and inspect it. He feels interference with his work and he must be able to intuit without interference for his meetings. It is the reason he has come."

"Perhaps we should give him the names of companies in Mumbai and he can improve his clientele—bigger city, more money." Anita smiled, but Meena looked grim.

"How can I tell eleven people to leave the hotel at one time and stand in the hot sun in the lane while one guest walks through the building to satisfy his mental state? If he does not drive me mad tonight, surely he will do so tomorrow."

At precisely 10:08, much to Anita's amazement, Hotel Delite was empty except for staff and Mr. Dayamani. Anita wasn't quite sure how it happened, but it did. The Bergers went to the beach, Mr. Walters went off in a taxi to see the sights, Colleen went shopping with a new friend, the elderly British couple went off with a guide to help them on the steep slopes to the beach, and the French sisters went in search of a tailor. Anita hurried to tell Auntie Meena, and the two women knocked on Mr. Dayamani's door.

The divine, famous for steering new companies into lucrative business deals by a combination of astrology and pure intuition, merely arched an eyebrow when told the hotel was empty of guests. He looked at both women, waved his hands for them to move away from the door, and stepped into the hallway. He closed his eyes and appeared to meditate.

"We begin," he said, turning to his right. The trio went from room to room. The Bergers' room was neat and tidy. The clothes were hung up, the beds made, water glasses in a row, and a bright red teddy bear sitting on one chair. Anita smiled. The Bergers were regular guests and she enjoyed watching their children grow. This was probably the last year for the teddy.

At Mr. Walters's room, the divine seemed to breathe roughly and looked around, taking a quick few steps into the room before Anita could stop him. Breaking every rule, she reached for his elbow and he stopped, gave a half turn, and closed his eyes to meditate. "This room should be cleaned," he said as he returned to the hall.

Mr. Dayamani went on in this way. He suggested that Colleen's room belonged to a confused woman and the furniture should be rearranged, the British couple's room had once hosted a dead body (Meena glared at Anita, who glared right back), and the French ladies were keeping secrets from each other. That sounded a bit prosaic to Anita, but by this time she didn't care what he said as long as he finished his tour before anyone returned and found the front gate locked.

"I must take rest now." Mr. Dayamani returned to his room and closed the door.

"Why do I allow this, this man to come into my hotel?" Auntie Meena fanned herself with a newspaper and paced the small office. "It is not worth it, not worth it."

"You may be right," Anita said. She had found the whole incident curious. "But his clients do pay you enough to cover all sorts of additional expenses and he continues to prefer this hotel to all others."

"Perhaps that will change," Meena said. "I am glad to have business from returning guests, but perhaps it is time to tell him and his patrons there are other places to stay, many of them closer to Technopark, with more stars." Meena paused. "How many stars do we have?"

"Unofficially, two, I think."

"Is it enough?"

"It is enough."

"I shall order the changes he has directed, including the cleaning of Mr. Walters's room, which was thoroughly cleaned top to bottom this week only, and it is fully cleaned every day it is occupied." Meena looked disgusted.

"And the French sisters? You will tell them to be more honest?" Anita grinned.

By late afternoon the various changes, to the extent possible, had been carried out. If she had been confused, as Mr. Dayamani intuited, before she left Hotel Delite, Madam Colleen must have been doubly so when she returned and found her furniture rearranged. The other guests didn't seem to notice the small changes insisted upon, and Auntie Meena allowed herself the luxury of hoping the worst was over.

"Do you not think there is something peculiar about Mr. Dayamani this year?" Anita turned around to face Auntie Meena.

"He is always peculiar."

"I mean especially peculiar."

"What are you thinking, Anita?"

But Anita left the desk without answering. She went in search of the maidservant who cleaned rooms this morning. "Did you find paper in the wastebasket in any of the rooms?"

The maidservant looked puzzled, but said yes, she found a few scraps in Mr. Walters's room. She opened the plastic bag containing debris and fished out a clump of balled-up sheets of paper. In the pantry Anita spread out the paper on a table and smoothed out the creases. The sheets were torn in half only once, so there was little repair work to be done. She could read the pages easily enough.

"What are you doing?" Auntie Meena came up behind Anita and read over her shoulder. "Oooh! What have you here?" Meena moved in closer. "It is exciting, this, isn't it?" She nudged Anita aside and continued reading. "Ooh, this is very fine. Look here, the love of the little kitty and here the love for his mother. This character must be the hero, isn't it?"

"Auntie Meena, you read far too many bad romances."

"Reading cannot always be edifying, Anita. Sometimes a little something for the foolish heart is wise." Meena turned the page over and read the next fragment.

"If I thought you'd like it so much, I would have shown you the page he tore up last year."

"Eh? What are you talking about?" Meena asked.

"It is almost the same words on the pages he tore up last year." Anita shook her head. "He is writing the same story."

"Ooh! It must be very popular!" Meena said.

The following morning a large white Mercedes Benz rolled down Lighthouse Road and into the parking lot. Anita announced its arrival to Mr. Dayamani, who descended the staircase like Egyptian royalty, looking straight ahead, his arms crossed over his chest holding a scroll.

"He has gone, Anita, he has gone." Meena braced both hands against the counter and closed her eyes. "Peace of mind for four hours. Shiva has blessed me." She lifted her head. "Anita? Anita?"

As the white car drove up the lane Anita climbed the stairs, a heavy brass key in her hand. She opened the door to Mr. Dayamani's room. She noted the table for puja pushed up against an inside wall, the bed carefully made, and clothes hung in the closet. She studied the suitcase stored on the lower shelf of the table. It was not locked. She studied the zipper tabs on the sides and top; she examined visually the stack of books sitting on the bedside table, and then took out a pair of tweezers. She examined visually the door to the small refrigerator. She locked the room and returned to the office, where she found Meena pouring herself a cup of milky tea.

"I am indulging because rare is the moment of peace."

"It won't last, Auntie." Anita lifted the pot, felt it half full, and poured herself a cup.

"Oh no! Really, Anita. You are unkind." The tea sloshed in the saucer as she picked up the cup.

"Let us consider the evidence," Anita said.

"Evidence for what?" Meena groaned. "No, Anita, please do not find trouble."

"Evidence of ill doings, Auntie. This divine, who reads the horoscopes to ensure successful business deals, moves the puja table away from the morning sun." She did not mention that he left a newspaper covering the offerings.

"Anita, this is quibbling." Meena reached for a thin digestive biscuit.

"And he places small hairs on every zipper tag to reveal if anyone opens any part of his suitcase. His stack of books contains many new titles, but none look even to be opened. His clothing is exactly the same as last year's, but no more worn."

"It is cold in America," Meena said.

"He lives in Florida." Anita pressed her lips together.

"Anita, please, you are giving me a headache."

"One book is in French. It is in the old style," Anita explained. "The pages are uncut."

"Old style, new style. Does it matter?"

"Yes, Auntie Meena, I think it does." She frowned. "The French sisters greeted him and he looked shocked. But he did not even answer them in French with a simple *Bonjour*, just to be polite as he usually does with others."

The following morning Anita rose early and left the hotel before the staff had even started breakfast, leaving Auntie Meena to cope on her own. Six hours later, Anita strolled down Lighthouse Road.

"Thank god you have come," Auntie Meena said, dragging herself out of the office.

"Do not worry, Auntie. Soon all will be well." Anita gave her a cheerful smile and began humming on her way to the dining room. Anita was not surprised to find Mr. Walters happily ensconced at his usual table by a window, craning his neck to get a better look at the young people diving into waves and body surfing to shore.

"Good afternoon, Mr. Walters," Anita said. "Is your writing going well?"

Mr. Walters smiled up at her, his usually vacant and soon-to-be-elderly face even more vacuous than usual. "It is so lovely here. I may finish my book early."

"How exciting for you," Anita said, and asked him about his plans for the next few days. She suggested he add a visit to a new museum to his itinerary, and perhaps a side trip along a canal. His eyebrows lifted and he seemed taken with the idea. "The views from the last lagoon are truly uplifting," she assured him.

The following morning Anita listened to Auntie Meena bemoan the efforts she had to make the night before to find a boatman to carry Mr. Walters down the old canals on the other side of the city.

"I don't know where it will end," Auntie Meena complained.

"At the old boat club," Anita said.

"Sometimes you are far too literal," Meena said, and marched off to complain to the cook, who knew to be sympathetic.

At three o'clock the following afternoon, three members of the CID in uniforms and two others in mufti marched into the hotel. From her place in the office Anita could see Auntie Meena wobbling and hurried out to steady her.

"Sars, you are wanting?" Auntie Meena said. Behind her Anita smiled.

"Ah, you have come to search rooms, isn't it?" Anita said.

"What?" Auntie Meena said, shocked and confused. "For what reason?"

"You are looking for evidence, isn't it?" Anita smiled. "Come." She led the way up the stairs, the master keys in her hand. "Which room are you wanting first?" When the men stopped and glanced at each other, Anita waited.

"I am the one who sent Mr. Walters on the boat ride down the canal and called your office that he would arrive there," she said. "And I am also the one who called the company at Technopark and suggested a closer look at Mr. Dayamani's shirt pockets before he left the complex."

She waited while the men tried not to look at each other.

"The two men have stayed here over several years, but they are professing not to know each other. Such frauds." She smiled again and led the way to Mr. Walters's room and unlocked the door. "You will find small notebooks in the lining of his suitcases. And then we are looking in Mr. Dayamani's room." She relaxed in the hallway while the men searched, and then unlocked the door to the divine's room. She pointed out the hairs on the suitcase, the books in French, and the various items of clothing that showed little wear from year to year. And then she left them to conduct their searches alone.

Anita found her aunt in the office gasping for air and waving a magazine futilely in front of her. Anita flipped on the overhead fan and called for cold water.

"I am confused, Anita, very confused."

"As you were meant to be," Anita said.

"And you are not?"

"Not anymore."

"Tell me. I must know the truth."

"It is simple. Mr. Dayamani is not a divine. He is a swindler."

"This is not new, Anita. But even such a one can bring others to faith."

"Perhaps, but his swindle is not to persuade others to follow a spiritual path. He offers divine guidance to the CEOs of new important companies, scientific companies, and while he is there, gaining trust and friendship, he filches little bits of information—photos and discs and scraps of paper, little things. And these he hides in his books, which he carries with him as he departs. No one would suspect a divine with a book. And a disk on its side is so thin as to be just another part of a spine in a book. Uncut pages in a book are envelopes for holding scraps of paper." She paused. "I wondered why he was so distressed when the sisters greeted him in French."

"He is not holy?"

Anita shook her head. "And Mr. Walters is not a writer."

"But I read the bits from his story—the kitten and the narrator's Mom. It was so sweet and tender."

"The kitten is a sarcastic reference to the kitty that a group of priests and amateur Indian scientists sent up in a rocket back in 1959. I don't remember—I wasn't alive then—but you were."

Auntie Meena gasped. "Oh, yes! The men who build the rockets for temple festivals built one for a cat and sent it up and the cat came back to earth in a parachute. Oh! The wonder of it!" She blinked. "So the cat is not in the story? But his Mom?"

"Mom is the nickname for the glorious rocket we have only just sent to Mars," Anita said.

"Oh!" Meena fell back in her seat, her face a sheet of dismay. "The scientists call the rocket Mother?"

Anita stifled a laugh. "No, Auntie. The letters MOM are an acronym. In 2013 India sent a rocket to Mars. We did this on our very first try and for low cost. Have you not heard about the unmanned orbiter Mangalyaan, the name for the Mars Orbiter Mission? The scientists call it MOM, or Mom, as it was in Mr. Walters's notes. This is a very important accomplishment for a country like ours, and other countries want to know how we did it," Anita said. "So they send their spies. I don't know who Mr. Dayamani works for or who Mr. Walters works for, but the CID will find out."

"They are spies? Here in Hotel Delite?"

Anita gave her aunt a sad look. "Yes, it is so. Mr. Dayamani is spying on business and Mr. Walters is spying on Mr. Dayamani." At just that moment, three pairs of shoes clumped down the stairs and across the hall.

"We have left guards," one man said. "Both foreigners are in custody, as you may have surmised. They will not be returning."

"Oh!" Auntie Meena clapped a hand over her mouth.

Anita knew exactly what she was thinking—two rooms not paid for, numerous meals not paid for, other guests disrupted, possibly a reputation in tatters. Meena began to tear up as she watched the government officials leave the hotel. "But, Anita, if you are knowing these men are spies, why are you sending Mr. Walters on this boat trip? The canal leads directly to the lagoon below the Vikram Sarabhai Space Centre. Here is the site of India's first rocket launching." Auntie Meena stared at her, wide-eyed.

"It is my little joke," Anita said.

"I cannot believe Mr. Walters is a fake!" Meena said. "I am using very best cutlery for him. And the crockery with the band of pink flowers instead of the plain white ones. To give him beauty so he will be inspired to write his wonderful stories!" Meena grew visibly upset. "He should not deceive people like me. I would buy his books."

"Yes, Auntie, and where he is going he will have all the time he needs to write one especially for you."

We know you will take the very best care of Tom.

Susan Oleksiw writes the Anita Ray series (*When Krishna Calls*, 2016) and the Mellingham series featuring Chief Joe Silva (*Last Call for Justice*, 2012). Her short stories have also appeared in *Alfred Hitchcock Mystery Magazine*. Susan compiled *A Reader's Guide to the Classic British Mystery* (G.K. Hall, 1988), and co-edited *The Oxford Companion to Crime and Mystery Writing* (1999).

Paradise Lost

Margaret Press

Saturday night. I've elbowed my way toward the bar when it dawns on me I'm standing behind the woman who killed my brother. I'm in a dive called the Paradise Lost near the Swampscott-Lynn line. A dark, unholy place. I'm here because my son's at a sleepover tonight and I, a single mom, am very much in need of a night out. And particularly because it's the anniversary of my brother Sheridan's death. This was his favorite hangout.

At this moment the only thing standing between me and my glass of chardonnay is Doreen Mitchell, formerly a nurse, engaged last year to my brother, and recently acquitted of his murder. Crucial evidence was tossed out before the trial, and she—well, she was very, very good. So was her lawyer.

Now, granted, I do not mourn my brother's demise. Some folks need killing. In fact, I came close to taking care of it myself. Sheridan was a heartless SOB. A familial trait, which works well for improving our odds of survival, until we push someone too far. Sheridan often pushed me too far.

The only thing my brother ever did for me was to send me a generous supply of a tasteless, odorless powder so that I could put our very sick grandfather out of his misery. Which I obligingly did. Granddad's death last winter—shortly after Sheridan's own demise—was painless, and a godsend. Now as the only kin and sole heir I have a small starter house in a neighborhood where my eight-year-old son can grow up safely—Asa, who lights up even the darkest corners of this barely working working-mom's world. Life has turned around for us. To pay down my debts I'm selling my brother's stuff on eBay. Except his 42" hi-def plasma TV which I've given to Asa. My overjoyed son is in paradise and I am on the road to redemption.

Doreen is handed a glass of something red. There are no empty stools at the bar so she slips off in search of a spot. I order a chardonnay and then, glass in hand and out of curiosity, I trail after her. We're both from Salem—what brings her to Swampscott to drink? Probably to escape the notoriety from the Salem trial. No escaping me, however. I followed the proceedings closely and know her pretty damn well by now. Doreen Mitchell put Sheridan out of *our* misery. Shot him dead. Now she's in the Paradise Lost looking for a place to settle her recently-saved ass.

She finds a table farthest from the TV. As I approach she turns, but doesn't recognize me, her former future sister-in-law. The advantage of not being too close with family. I ask if the seat next to her is taken. She nods me into it.

"I'm Rhode," I say after the requisite comments on the blizzard and her vermillion Land's End ski jacket. I watch her face. There's no change in her expression. Either Sheridan never mentioned me to her by name, or she's too self-absorbed to remember. At her trial I would have been only one face in the crowd. I leave well enough alone.

We chat. Doreen is a well-put-together redhead in her thirties, wildly overdressed for this bar. To warm her up I ask for the name of her hairdresser. By the time we get through our first round of drinks I also have the name of a good plumber. And the number of her awesome lawyer.

We seem to have much in common. I wonder if my brother chose her because he saw in her a kindred spirit. Doreen is totally *What's in it for me?* Nothing wrong with that. She would've fit right in with our family. But Sheridan was a cheating bastard, and Doreen, too, was pushed too far.

The irony does not escape me: If I weren't from a family of psychopaths, if I could feel anything about my brother's death, I'd probably want to be avenging him. But here we sit amiably together—a couple of murderers—just like regular people, as nice as can be.

"Do you come here often?" I ask.

"I used to, with my fiancé," she says wistfully. "Every Saturday night. He passed a year ago today." Damn if she isn't tearing up. Did

I say she was good? I see why she's here in this dive on this night. She's marking the occasion, too.

"Oh I'm so sorry," I murmur.

Turns out she's recently moved. Well, she was locked up for the past year, but she doesn't mention that.

"I'm having to get settled in a new place. Alone. Putting the pieces of my life back together. What an ordeal! Address changes, unpacking, waiting a full day for the cable guy, and then—on top of everything my TV broke down!"

"Shame."

"I think it happened during the move. It's just the last straw. I expected to be married by now. I was registered at Macy's!"

We're on our third round of drinks. I'm feeling a rare tinge of something akin to sympathy. I shake my head and mouth more condolences. I wonder if Sheridan really would have gone through with this wedding. Hard to believe. It occurs to me that he probably chose this establishment far from Salem and the possibility of running into his other girlfriends. Everyone's anonymous here. Everyone's eyes are on the loud game above our heads, or they're crying in their drinks. It's a neighborhood dive bar. But not Sheridan's neighborhood. And not Doreen's.

"But I may have a solution," she continues, tapping the rim of her glass.

"To . . ." I come back.

"My broken TV. I'm hunting down my fiancé's family. He had a TV of mine. It was a lovely one. I'm sure they'll be understanding about it."

I nearly choke on my wine.

"Really?" My blood turns to ice. "You think they'll give it to you?"

She smiles. "I have the receipt. I loaned it to him when I got my new one—the one that didn't survive the move."

"Wow. Well, good luck with that." Any shred of sympathy gone, gone, gone.

We natter a bit longer, then I rise and pull on my jacket. My dull brown Salvation Army jacket. "We should do this again sometime," I say.

"I'm here every Saturday," she tosses back.

This just isn't right. It's not enough she kills my brother? She has to steal our TV too? Putting back the pieces of her life? I can see the look on my son's face now. Heartbreaker. What about *his* pieces.

The following Saturday should be my turn for the sleepover, but I call the mom of Asa's friend Jeremy and swap nights, explaining I need to take care of something. Family business. I drop Asa off and head down Paradise Road to our bar.

Doreen Mitchell is seated at a corner table near the restrooms. I pick up my glass of chardonnay at the bar and join her. "Hi there! It's Doreen, right?"

"I didn't quite get your name last week," she says. Did she figure out we talked for over an hour and *I* never came up as a topic?

I mull for a nanosecond. If she's been hunting down Sheridan's executor, my unusual name will be a tip-off. "Rose," I say instead.

We talk some more about her, since we can never get enough of Doreen. When we've drained our glasses I offer to fetch the next round. "Cab, right?" I ask. I weave my way back to the bar. In my left pocket is a neatly folded up cocktail napkin I've brought from home. Five minutes later I negotiate the return trip through the jostling crowd and carefully place our glasses on the table.

"How's that TV project going? Any luck with the family yet?"

Doreen's touching up her lipstick. "Still hunting them down. But I'm not worried."

"Really! You're pretty sure they'll just hand it over to you based on that receipt?"

A sly smile crawls onto her face. "I have something they'll find more interesting." She drops her lipstick into her purse and reaches toward her glass. "Very, very interesting."

I suddenly react. In the next split second I manage to knock her glass off the table before her fingers can close around the stem. Cabernet sauvignon splashes her Land's End jacket and cascades to the floor.

"Oh shit!" I yell. "I am sooooo sorry, Doreen!"

I make a beeline for the Ladies Room and return with a pile of paper towels. She grabs some and dabs angrily at her jacket.

"Lucky about the color, huh?" I offer lamely, mopping up the table with the remaining towels. She doesn't reply. I leave her to her distress and go back to the bar for another glass of cab.

Doreen has my attention now. After she calms down and I offer to pay her cleaning bill, I lead us back to the subject. "You were about to say . . ."

"Where was I? Oh—so, I know how Sheridan's grandfather died."

I stare at her. My mouth goes dry.

"Sheridan asked me for help. His grandfather was in a lot of pain and wanted to end his life. I told Sheridan what to get. He ordered it, and then he sent it to his sister. I saw his email with instructions to her. Actually I saved a copy. And I saved the shipping order."

She leans forward, winks, and whispers: "I'm a nurse. Guess I know my poisons." *Was* a nurse. Would Salem Hospital have taken her back? But I digress.

"Wow." I process this. "Wow. So you've known this for a year? Why bring it up now?"

"I didn't need a TV until now. What was in it for me?"

I make a third visit to the Paradise Lost the following Saturday, once again imposing on Jeremy's mom. The unrelenting snow has made finding a parking spot a challenge. I pull up onto a snow bank and stomp into the bar. Doreen's in her usual corner looking impervious to the ravages of winter.

"I'll buy tonight, honey." Doreen rises after I've settled in. She slides her way toward the bar.

I work my arms out of my snow-pelted jacket and turn around to see Doreen negotiating the obstacle course back to our table. She's juggling two glasses in one hand and a basket of popcorn in the other. A burly man is in her way, shouting at the hockey game blaring above our heads. Over the din Doreen calls out to me: "Here, Rhode, grab the wine!"

I was no longer Rose.

I take the glasses from her and set them down on the table. She slides in opposite me and pushes the popcorn in my direction. I pull my hands into my lap and look across at her.

"How long have you known?" I ask.

She takes a long sip of her cab. "I thought I remembered you in the courtroom. When you knocked over my wine I figured it out. Sheridan sent you plenty of his fairy dust, didn't he."

We're both uncharacteristically silent for a time. I look up at the game. "So what do you really want, Doreen."

"I just need a good TV."

"You're such an expert on poisons—why did you shoot my brother? Wouldn't poison have been easier?" I need leverage. This is not looking to end well.

"You forget—I didn't kill him. As I testified—either he shot himself out of unbearable guilt, or that other woman did it, in a jealous rage."

That 'other' woman, whom by the way Doreen also tried to kill, did not live to testify. Despite surviving the attack, she died two months later in a freak car accident. Doreen was blessed with exceptional talent or extraordinary luck. My hat's off to Sheridan for his choice in women.

I look forlornly at my wine. "Would you like to try my chardonnay?" I ask.

She grins. "No thanks, honey, I'm good." She helps herself to popcorn, so after a minute, I decide it's safe to do so, too. But I steer clear of the wine.

"It doesn't sound like you have any real evidence against me," I try. "And I have all of Sheridan's files. Some not-so-nice things about you, too." I've been busy this past week combing through his effects.

"I'm not looking to get you convicted of anything. I happen to believe you did the right thing for your grandfather. Poor man. But I could make life difficult for you for a while—and for your son."

"You are an evil woman." I am indignant. Revenge may not be a useful quality. But self-preservation most certainly is. And protecting my child. What will happen to his coveted sleepovers if rumors course through Salem that his mom might be a killer? Would Jeremy's mom allow Jeremy to go to Asa's house after that? Not bloody likely. "Evil," I repeat.

She drains her cabernet in response. "'Better to reign in Hell than serve in Heaven.'" Then she looks at my untouched glass and laughs. "I wouldn't poison your chardonnay, Rhode. We were nearly sisters-in-law, for heaven's sake!"

So I guess I count this as a draw. I could get Asa a Play Station. And Doreen and I could both live to see another day. We arrange the handover of the TV for next Wednesday. I pull myself up and reach for my defeated-looking jacket. We each have knowledge. We each have tasted the fruit.

"Honey—you're really not drinking your wine?" she calls after me.

Family is everything. But I'm not going to push it.

Margaret Press, Salem-based author of mystery/true crime novels, stories, and essays, continues her sagas of an oddly-functional family of psychopaths and the constellation of characters whose lives they touch. "Paradise Lost" is the fifth to appear in the Level Best Books anthologies. "Family Plot," uncovering the deadly perils of family history, won the Al Blanchard Award in 2008.
www.margaretpress.com.

Hope It Fits

Dale T. Phillips

Louis Petronelli took the silk blouse he had just purchased and carefully placed the tissue-paper-wrapped package in the shopping bag he held in his other hand. The bag's twine handle cut into his fingers a little, because it was so heavy. *But then, a .32 automatic with a full clip will weigh a bag down,* he thought.

"Girlfriend or wife?" The saleswoman's voice cut into his thought process.

He looked up. "I beg your pardon?"

"The blouse. Is it for your girlfriend, or your wife?" She smiled.

"Who do you think it should go to?" He grinned back at her.

"Oh, you're a naughty one. Make it to your wife, then. She deserves something for putting up with a bad boy like you."

"So, one gift for the girlfriend, and one for the wife. And you think my wife deserves the blouse. I guess the girlfriend should get the other surprise, then."

"You've got good taste, at least in blouses. Especially for a man. Come on back sometime, if you get tired of the girlfriend."

Louis smiled again. He had a good smile; it was one of the things women liked him for. "Maybe I'll do that."

"See you around, then."

Louis left the store, pondering the question of where to go first. Home, or over to Sheila's? He supposed he should go home, start there. He had a problem, and he had a solution. One wife, one girlfriend; one of them had to go. It was that simple. But which?

Louis drove the Lexus at a leisurely pace. He certainly didn't want to get stopped for a traffic infraction and have some nosy policeman find a loaded gun in his bag. He didn't even have a permit to carry one. And considering what he planned to do, it would be rather inconvenient to be discovered at this stage. Plus, he enjoyed driving the luxury car, and had time to think about his dilemma.

He drove home, into the neighborhood of huge, expensive McMansions, each more ostentatiously garish than the last. His was not the biggest, or the worst. Mavis had made him buy the place. He would have preferred being in the city, with so much to do, and such easy access to temptation. Here, one had to watch one's step, for prying eyes could discover what needed to remain secret.

He pulled into the expanse of driveway, and deliberately parked with one tire over the edge of a flowerbed. That kind of thing drove Mavis absolutely batshit-crazy. He would shrug and claim it was an accident, a careless action, when he had meticulously thought it out well in advance. She, of course, would retaliate by rearranging his treasured record collection. He had a precise system of what should go where, and she could wreck the whole thing with a dozen "accidentally-misplaced" albums. That was okay, he expected it. As long as she didn't put her greasy, greedy fingers on the vinyl itself. That was too much.

As he went inside, he wondered what tone to take. Apologetic? Angry? Disaffected? He supposed it depended a lot on her mood.

"I'm home," he announced. There was no response, but he hadn't expected one. She wouldn't come out to greet him, either. Those days were long gone. He figured that she supposed herself in the catbird seat, and didn't have to care. Divorcing her would be far too expensive, and she damn well knew it. Louis had built his fortune carefully, and over time, and would not countenance handing it over to her and a team of lawyers. But a person could put up with only so much, and today would decide how it was all going to go from here on.

She was in the living room, gazing out the back window to the vast expanse of flower gardens, groomed and manicured to museum-like quality.

"I got you a surprise," Louis said.

"Well, aren't you just full of surprises?" Her tone was as flat and hard as the marble counters in the kitchen.

Louis cocked his head. "Ah. Let me guess. You re-hired that

private detective?"

"You make it too damn easy for him to earn his money. Sheila, isn't it?"

"It is. Would you like me to get rid of her?"

"Why bother? There'll be another, soon enough."

"There doesn't have to be."

She turned to look at him. "I do believe you're half serious."

"What if we tried again?"

"Tried what? Pretending we don't hate each other?"

"Hate is a strong emotion," Louis said, his voice grave. "That means there's still something alive."

"Baby, those ashes burned cold a long time ago. With that first little lemon tart you sampled."

"You had your revenge." He shook his head and smiled a sad remembering. "Tennis pro, wasn't it? How sad."

"Boris *was* rather athletic," she said. "Like your dancer."

"At least I kept it outside our circle. Not like you, though, trying to go through my board members and business partners."

"Hit you where it hurt, didn't it? Right in the old pocketbook."

"True. You never understood how hard it is to make money. Never having worked for it."

"Oh, I worked for it, all right."

"I don't mean on your back."

Her face stiffened, then she smiled, a bitter slash across her face. "Set that one up for you, didn't I?"

Louis shrugged. "Sorry, you did. Reflex. So can we chalk everything up as even across the board, and move forward together?"

"There you go again, trying for a win-win. It's what makes you so good at business."

"Thank you."

"But it doesn't work with people. We've got memories, emotions. Every damn time we hurt each other, we kept score. You say you're willing to call it a draw. Damn decent of you, I'm sure. You've got your latest little number all waiting for you in that apartment you paid for, and you want to sweet-talk me while you're thinking about how soon you can leave and be with her."

"I told you, that can change."

"Tired of her already? You're getting jaded, my dear."

"Look, you hired the detective, even though you knew just what he'd find. So something in you cares a little. Maybe that's enough. I'll tell Sheila it's over. And I won't replace her if you say so."

"What would we do?" There seemed to be a longing in her voice, or maybe he just imagined it.

"What about a cruise?"

"The one we never took? Because you were too busy making all that money?"

"Sure, how about it?"

"The two of us, trapped on a boat, in a little cabin, for a couple of weeks? We'd kill each other."

Louis grimaced. She was right, damn it. "What about somewhere else, then? If we get tired of a place, we can move on."

"It sounds a lot like running away, Louis. But our past will go along with us."

"It doesn't have to. We can make a fresh start."

"My God, you almost make me believe it. And wouldn't that shock the hell out of all the people we know?"

He smiled. "It would, at that."

"And if I don't go with you, are you going to take your little friend?"

Louis sighed. "Forget her. I told you, she'll be gone."

"Our detective friend said she seems pretty smitten."

"She says she cares for me."

"At least for your money."

"Then that's something the two of you have in common," he said.

Her face twitched, not in amusement. "Don't I deserve something, for all I've put up with, all these years?"

"Look around you. I earned all this, and it's what you said you wanted."

"What I wanted was to be happy."

"You could have chosen that at any time," Louis said. "We each have a little something missing, and we tried to fill ourselves with other things."

"Didn't work."

"I guess not. But we can rewrite the ending, you know."

"Ride off into the sunset, like we're twenty-five and have our whole lives ahead of us? I don't think so. You're a businessman.

What are the odds?"

"Forget the odds. Just say you'll try."

"I don't know, Louis, maybe you're sincere, maybe not. After all the lies between us, I don't know what to believe."

"I'm standing right here, telling you it can be how we want it. What other choices are there?"

"One of us could always hire a hit man." She laughed, short and bitter.

"That's not funny."

"Why? Rather do it yourself? Oh, get that look off your face. I was only joking."

"And I've never been more serious."

"And I want to know why you waited so damn long. Even so much as five years ago, we'd either be in bed at this point, or laughing on our way to the airport. But now . . ."

"If we had it once, we can have it again."

"Tell me something, Louis. If you had to do it all over again, knowing what you know now, would you?"

He took a moment too long in answering. "Of course."

"Ah," she said. She didn't say anything more.

"What are you thinking?"

"I'm thinking of our wedding. And what a long time ago that was."

He shifted from foot to foot, waiting to see if she would say anything more. He wanted a clear indication that the scales had tipped one way or the other. But she stood like one of her garden statues, silent and opaque. He grew restless, as always, and his foot nudged the bag. He looked down at it. He picked it up and reached inside, feeling the rustling tissue paper, and then the checkered handle of the gun. His fingers played over both. She was like Schrodinger's cat, both alive and dead at the same time. He was tired of waiting.

"Time for my surprise," he said. "I hope it fits." His hand found his choice and pulled it forth, as she turned to look at him.

Dale T. Phillips is the author of four novels, over fifty short stories, story collections, poetry, and a non-fiction career book. He's appeared on stage, television, and in an independent feature film, *Throg*. He co-wrote and acted in a short political satire film. He competed on *Jeopardy* and *Think Twice*, and lost in spectacular fashion on both.

Last Mango in Paradise

Lucy Burdette

Even after Mrs. Silpat was poisoned to death in her Key West conch cottage, the mah jongg players would not eschew refreshments. Or so insisted my geriatric houseboat-mate, Miss Gloria. If anything, she added, the shock was likely to render the ladies ravenous.

The tragedy had unfolded the week before when Miss Gloria went to pick up her friend for their regular game. Mrs. Silpat had not been her favorite friend—she wasn't loyal. She put herself first in any situation. And anything she baked ended up tasting like sawdust or old chicken fat. All that aside, years of clacking tiles together, chatting about families scattered to the winds, and exchanging recipes, meant something important in Miss Gloria's book.

Miss Gloria had knocked loudly several times on Mrs. Silpat's door and finally went in without an invitation. When she found the woman collapsed in her kitchen, by all appearances dead, her first call was to me—a food critic, not a cop.

"I'm too shook up to think," she'd said.

"Hang up and call 911 right away. I'm not in the police department, remember?" I told her gently. "I'll take a cab over ASAP so I can drive you home."

By the time the pink cab dropped me off in the narrow one-way street in front of Mrs. Silpat's eyebrow-style house with gingerbread trim, two police cars with their lights flashing flanked Miss Gloria's old Buick. A fire department EMT van had nosed into her driveway. I hurried onto the porch but was instantly repelled by a cop in polyester blue.

"My roommate's inside," I said. "She found her friend—"

He held up a paw the size of an oven mitt. "You need to wait out here."

As I settled into a wood rocker, an enormous fluffy cat the color of salted caramel leaped onto the porch and wound in figure eights around my legs. Miss Gloria burst out of the house; the screen door slammed behind her.

"I'm sprung, at least for the time being. Let's scram before they change their minds."

The words sounded tough from an old lady who'd just lost a friend, but I could see the tremble in her lower lip. The big cat approached Miss Gloria and meowed.

"Oh, Mango," said Miss Gloria, tears filling her eyes. She leaned over to ruffle the tufts of fur behind his ears. "I'll have to let Miriam know he's here. She lives nearby and she loves cats and I bet she'll want to take him in, poor guy. And oh lordy, the other girls will be wondering if I up and croaked. Anytime I'm a little late, they think I've been called to the great beyond." She whipped out her cell phone and began texting the news of the cancellation of the game and more importantly, Mrs. Silpat's death.

Since the young cop had moved to his cruiser to take a call, I ducked my head into the living room to see if any of the officers checking out the home were cops that I knew. "Hello?"

"No one allowed in here, miss," said another young guy who looked vaguely familiar. "It's a crime scene." He strode up to the screen door, blocking my view of the chaos in the kitchen, just past the living room. I caught a glimpse of the EMTs on the floor next to an inert figure, a decimated buffet of lifesaving equipment spread out around them.

"I'm taking my roommate home, if that's okay?" I flashed a helpful smile. "Need anything else from her?"

"We'll be in touch," he said gruffly, waving us off.

"Those cops wouldn't tell me anything," Miss Gloria said indignantly after she'd hung up with her friends, "even though I might be the person with the best clues about why she died."

"She wasn't a young woman," I said, looping my arm around her shoulders to give her a comforting squeeze. "What makes you think she didn't die of natural causes?"

"She was healthy as a workhorse," said Miss Gloria, rapping

her diminutive fist on her chest. "She bragged to us only last week about her latest physical. Her cholesterol numbers were perfect and her blood pressure was that of a thirty-year-old. There was nothing wrong with her except for her attitude."

Once we were safely aboard our houseboat and I'd settled Miss Gloria on the deck with a cup of tea and a sliver of pineapple upside down cake, I asked her to tell me the story again, from soup to nuts.

"She didn't answer when I knocked. That never happens—she's always early—even out on the porch tapping her foot if I'm a minute late. Since the screen was unlocked, I went in. And there she was on floor, splayed out like a rag doll, with the most awful expression on her face. And half a cookie clutched in her fingers."

I took her hand and stroked it. "So then you called me, and the police, and waited outside?"

She nodded. Then her gaze flickered away from my face. "Well, not exactly. I did what you would do—poke around for possible clues until they got there," she admitted. "But I didn't touch anything. And I didn't notice anything out of place."

How could I scold her? I, too, was born inquisitive. "Close your eyes and picture the scene and tell me what you saw," I suggested.

"Everything was tidy. She was a little anal," Miss Gloria said, her eyes squeezed tight. They flew open. "Although there was a box of peanut butter cookies open on the counter."

"Like the cookie in her hand," I said. "From the grocery store? Would that be unusual?"

"Not from the grocery store," said Miss Gloria. "From a bakery."

I couldn't help flashing on a death I stumbled into two years before. The murder weapon was a poisoned key lime pie delivered by a bakery, and a woman died as a result. "Can you remember the name of the bakery?"

She wiggled her fingers, and Sparky, her black cat, jumped onto her lap. "Almost like a homemade logo," she said. "Something like Paradise Treats with little palm trees drawn on it, too." She grimaced and buried her knobby fingers in the cat's fur. "But her face looked awful— contorted and blue."

When the next week rolled around, along with the date for the mah jongg group, the police department still had no solid leads on Mrs. Silpat's death. As far as we'd been informed anyway.

"Why don't you come with me to the game?" Miss Gloria suggested. "You could pretend you want to learn but meanwhile, listen in. Maybe one of the girls knows something about Mrs. Silpat's enemies but she doesn't know she knows it. But we can tease it out of her and crack the case."

For a moment I considered demanding that she leave the talking to me. But last time I extracted that kind of a promise, it only seemed to egg her on.

The mah jongg ladies had been meeting for years beside the pool of a condominium complex, which overlooked the harbor where the cruise ships docked. They sat in the shade with the palm trees rustling, and played and ate and chatted. The number of tables the players occupied went up and down with the flux of the women's lives and health. This morning, with Mrs. Silpat gone, their number was four.

Miss Gloria introduced me around. "You know Mrs. Dubisson from our marina."

I nodded hello at my housemate's best friend.

"And this is Mrs. Phyllis Gagner—"

"Phyllis, please," said a cheery woman in a yellow sweater.

"Phyllis," Miss Gloria amended. "And this is Mrs. Miriam Reddington."

"Pleased to meet you," she said, though she did not offer to have me call her by her first name. "Gloria talks about you all the time."

I was dispatched to arrange the snacks on a side table—the ladies had brought deviled eggs, finger sandwiches—both tuna salad and ham—brownies iced with ganache, and ginger cookies. The players began to set out ivory-colored tiles, patterned with green, red, and black designs, on a green felt tablecloth that was pilled in the center from years of play.

"There are no partners in this game," explained Mrs. Reddington, "so you aren't going to disappoint anyone if you fail. If you make an error you have only yourself to blame. Kind of like life."

"Honestly, there's a certain amount of luck in the tiles that you draw," said Phyllis. "The important thing is to have fun."

The four women reviewed the rules of the game. The terms

rolled over me: the Charleston, breaking the wall, the bams, the dots, the east and the west. For some minutes, they concentrated on their tiles. The palms around the pool deck whispered, and I could hear the whine of the Disney cruise ship's engine in the background, occasionally broken by the notes of the ship's signature tune, "When You Wish Upon a Star."

"Since you ruined my hand, I'll take both jokers," said Mrs. Dubisson to Miss Gloria. Ten minutes later, Mrs. Dubisson had won the round.

"It's a little like playing poker in Vegas," said Miss Gloria, as she swept her tiles into the center pile. "You have to sell your story. Sometimes it doesn't matter what tiles you have, as long as you're confident in your play. You have to be willing to take risks, too."

Phyllis added, "By now we know each other pretty well. So we keep an eye on the tells." She pointed across the table. "Both Miriam Reddington and Mrs. Silpat tap their tiles on the rack—or tapped in Mrs. Silpat's case—when they have a good hand. And they play those good hands aggressively."

Mrs. Reddington grinned and tipped her chin. "Don't give all our gambling secrets away," she said with a snort of laughter.

"You can be the best player in the world," said Miss Gloria, "but if your emotions take over, you go on tilt. You can start to lose a lot and you get anxious, and then you can't stay on an even keel. That's a terrible feeling."

"Speaking of terrible feelings, is there anything new on Mrs. Silpat's death?" Phyllis asked. "I have to admit I miss her, even if she was a grump lately."

"Believe it or not," said Miss Gloria, "the police department has not chosen to keep me informed."

The other three women cackled with laughter.

"But Hayley and I suspect the killer delivered the poison in the form of peanut butter cookies," Miss Gloria explained. "Maybe with a little something extra to hide the flavor."

"For example, they could have spiced up the cookies with Chinese hot sauce," I said.

The other women made faces. "Really?" asked Mrs. Reddington.

"I know," said my geriatric houseboat-mate, "it sounds a little disgusting. Chili sauce in cookies? But Hayley made them once and it gave a little bite to the sweetness that made them taste even more delicious than they would have been. Just the right kick."

"And enough off to disguise the taste of something in the dough that shouldn't have been there," I said, nodding.

"How is your Evinrude getting along?" asked Mrs. Dubisson. "I do love that cat."

"For a feline born and raised in New Jersey, he's adapted so well to living on a houseboat," said Miss Gloria. "And he loves my Sparky."

"What color is he?" Mrs. Reddington asked, her voice full of longing.

"Gray tiger," I said. "Do you have a cat?"

"I did. He disappeared a few months ago. I still miss him. Shall we have a bite before the next round?"

The ladies moved to the snack table, chirping and chattering as they loaded their plates.

"I'm glad you brought brownies rather than peanut butter cookies," said Mrs. Dubisson. "Do you suppose Mrs. Silpat's death might've been related to a love triangle gone sour?"

I looked at her in astonishment. "A love triangle? At her age?"

"You young people all think the same way—that young is beautiful," said Mrs. Reddington. "But old can be beautiful too. Our wrinkles are like the lines in a tree stump. They tell the story of a lot of years. Did you see the article including Rupert Murdoch in the *New York Times Style* section? It was all about sexy men. He's old as the hills, but he still collects young women and publicity."

"It helps that he is filthy rich," said Mrs. Dubisson. "That's always good for sex appeal."

"I'm pretty sure that Mrs. Silpat had a new boyfriend," said Phyllis, "so maybe your triangle theory has some merit."

"In fact, the police were in his apartment only yesterday taking fingerprints. I'm quite sure they will find the murderer's prints among them—all they have to do is match the prints to the bakery box," said Miss Gloria. "And they are also in the process of analyzing the handwriting on the box."

"I thought you said the cops weren't telling you anything?" said Phyllis.

Miss Gloria winked. "I have my ways," she said. And then she held up the score pad that sat on the table.

Suddenly Mrs. Miriam Reddington sank to a folding chair and began to weep. "You got me," she said, but then added defiantly: "That old battle-ax, she deserved to die."

"It was really you?" Phyllis asked. "But how?"

"Just like Hayley guessed—you put hot sauce in the cookies to disguise the poison, right?" Miss Gloria asked.

Mrs. Reddington smirked a little. "She was so addicted to her sweets, she'd eat anything."

"Tell us why," I said. "You must have had a good reason."

She wiped her eyes and looked directly at me. "To a young girl such as yourself, the company of an old man might not sound like much. But Howard was a real gentleman. He complimented me if my earrings matched my sweater—"

"Like the time you wore those miniature Teddy bears," Miss Gloria said, and her friend nodded. "They were awfully cute."

"He noticed things. He noticed me." Mrs. Reddington's eyes shimmered with tears that had yet to be shed and I had to believe she loved him. Loved him—none of this Agape love the universe stuff. She loved this old man.

"So about the cat . . ." Miss Gloria's words trailed off.

"That was the last straw," Mrs. Reddington said, her face turning ruddy with fury. "It was one thing to steal the old man out from under me. He was like an overripe mango when you get right down to it—a dime a dozen this time of year. But the cat? What kind of woman puts cans of the best cat food out on her deck to lure him over? What kind of person allows someone else's pet to nap in her house during the day? Then she had the nerve to put him out the back door if I asked if she'd seen him."

I stood up and took my cell phone from my pocket, then put my hand on her shoulder. "I'm going to need to call the police."

Fifteen minutes later, they trooped onto the patio and led Mrs. Reddington away.

"How in the world did you know she was the killer?" asked Mrs. Dubisson.

"The clues began to stack up," said Miss Gloria. "It didn't strike me immediately, but I thought I recognized the orange cat on Mrs. Silpat's porch. And we all know she stole Howard's attentions. And then the writing on the box of peanut butter cookies. It looked so familiar." She waved the mah jongg score pad, containing all of their scrawls going back several years.

"When the cat deserted her for Mrs. Silpat, she went on emotional tilt," I said.

"The whole thing is so very sad," said Phyllis. "We've lost two friends."

"And two players," said Miss Gloria.

The ladies turned to look at me. "Hayley, were you paying enough attention when we explained the rules to take her place?"

Lucy Burdette (aka Roberta Isleib) is the author of fourteen mysteries, including *Fatal Reservations*, the latest in the Key West series featuring food critic Hayley Snow. Her books and stories have been short-listed for Agatha, Anthony, and Macavity awards. She's a past president of Sisters in Crime. www.lucyburdette.com

The First Wife

Christine Eskilson

When the obituary caught Charlotte's eye she read it twice, the second time very slowly. *Susannah Butler, 42, unexpectedly, at home in Providence.* The accompanying picture showed a smiling, wind-swept blonde against a backdrop of sailboats. Honors graduate of Smith College with a successful career in digital marketing. *Survived by her beloved parents, Dr. and Mrs. William Perkins, of Jamestown, Rhode Island. Services are private.* The obituary also mentioned Susannah's brother, who died many years ago as a teenager, but contained no reference to Jack.

Jack Butler, the man who had once been engaged to Charlotte, but who had married Susannah.

Maybe that's how obituaries handled divorces, Charlotte mused. Just pretend that the marriage never existed. Her cat pounced on the newspaper when she went to the kitchen to pour another cup of French roast. Not that she needed it; her heart already was racing. She hadn't seen Jack in well over fifteen years. Would Susannah's death bring him back?

Coffee mug in hand, she paused by the mirror in the hall to examine the faint lines around her mouth, and the thick streak of grey in her dark curls. She'd told herself the streak was dramatic when it first appeared, but now she remembered how Jack had loved the inky black color of her hair.

Back in the living room, she put down her coffee and opened the laptop. It took her all of ten seconds to find him. She'd successfully resisted for years, even on those late nights with only a bottle of Merlot for company, but there was no need for restraint now. His New

York law firm's website came up first; Jack was a partner specializing in white-collar criminal defense. The headshot with his bio showed eyes as blue as she remembered, staring at her from the screen. As if it had a mind of its own, the cursor hovered over the CONTACT JACK BUTLER link. Should she do it? Wasn't this exactly what she'd been waiting for?

Still perched on the newspaper, the cat yowled for breakfast as Charlotte clicked on the link to pop up an email and began to type.

Over the next few days she incessantly checked Gmail on her laptop, her iPad, her computer at work and her cell. Ann Taylor was having a seasonal sale, one of her library books was overdue, her high school class was planning a twenty-fifth reunion dinner (was she really already that old?), but no reply from Jack.

Charlotte reread her email to him in the Sent box multiple times. Maybe she'd made a mistake sending something so personal to his work, but she thought she'd struck the right tone, compassionate and kind, an old friend reaching out from across the years, no pressure to respond.

Then, finally, an email from JButler appeared. *Charlotte, I was surprised and pleased to hear from you. Susannah's death came as a great shock to me as well although, as you may already know, our marriage ended a few years ago.* Jack's email continued to tell her that he would be in Rhode Island the following week to pay his respects to his former in-laws and if she would consider a drink with him on his way back to New York he would be very grateful. She immediately wrote back to accept.

On the day of the scheduled drink Charlotte left work early and spent a good two hours debating what to wear. Jack would remember her as a vibrant twenty-something, crammed with Susannah in a one-bedroom walk-up in the East Village where a claw foot bathtub absurdly divided the kitchen and living room. She wore tight jeans and tighter t-shirts then as she made the audition rounds of any play that even remotely qualified as off-Broadway. Although she still felt toned and strong from years of swimming and tennis, extra pounds and her job as director (aka glorified fundraiser) of a local educational nonprofit had led her to more comfortable and conservative garb. She finally decided on black—narrow black pants and black shell, topped with a flowing sheer black blouse that skimmed her body to the hips.

Then, afraid Jack would think she was in mourning, she added a chunky silver necklace and matching earrings.

He already was at the restaurant when she arrived, sitting at a small table near the back and frowning at his iPhone. She'd agonized over the venue, too, finally settling on a quiet place in Federal Hill that was cozy but not overtly romantic and where the manager wouldn't mind if they simply had a glass of wine.

She knew from the bio picture that he hadn't changed much over the years, but she'd forgotten the way his quick smile sent a rush of blood to her cheeks. He put the iPhone in his pocket and stood up as she made her way to the table.

"Charlotte!" he exclaimed, giving her a quick hug. She'd also forgotten how easily she fit into his arms. "You don't know how good it is to see you. You're looking very well."

"Thank you, Jack. I'm glad you could stop by. How are Susannah's parents?"

"They're taking it pretty hard as you can imagine," he replied as they both took their seats. Jack called over the waiter and ordered two glasses of Merlot.

"I hope you don't mind," he said. "I remember you liked it."

She felt herself blushing again and hoped that the restaurant's subdued lighting concealed it.

After the wine arrived he took a long swallow and set the glass back down, gazing at her intently. "I'm sorry it's been years since we've been in touch, Charlotte. And I'm sorry it took something like this to make it happen."

"I wasn't in any shape to see you for a long time," she answered and was gratified to see him wince.

Although at the time it had shredded her heart, in retrospect she could have seen it coming. While Charlotte was consumed with acting classes, auditions and odd jobs to supplement the money she'd saved for this grand New York experiment, as her parents called it, Jack, the college boyfriend she planned to marry, and Susannah, her childhood friend, spent more and more time together in the tiny apartment. Jack was taking some time off before law school working as a paralegal on Wall Street and Susannah picked up occasional waitressing stints when the money from her monthly trust fund checks ran low.

One day she came home unexpectedly early to find the two of

them sitting together on the sofa, Susannah in one of Charlotte's favorite sweaters. Although they were not even touching, the air of intimacy between them was overpowering. She didn't know what hurt most—the flicker of annoyance in Jack's eyes when she walked in or the smug smile on Susannah's face.

She left her engagement ring on the end table and didn't look back.

"Did you ever run into Susannah after she moved back to Providence?" Jack asked. "I guess she was only living here a few months before the accident."

"I didn't keep in touch with her either," Charlotte replied and noted a second wince. "Was that what happened? Was it an accident? The obituary didn't say."

Jack nodded. "One of those flukes that could have happened to anybody. She slipped on something spilled on her kitchen floor and fell the wrong way—hit her head on the countertop. They didn't find her until the next day."

The perils of living alone, Charlotte thought but didn't say. She experienced those perils every day.

With her assent, Jack ordered two more glasses of wine. "Maybe we should have gotten a bottle," he observed.

"But you have to go back tonight, don't you?" Charlotte asked.

He shrugged. "My morning meeting cancelled so I have a little more flexibility. Do you have dinner plans or do you mind if I order something to eat? I'm starving."

They shared a calamari appetizer and ordered pasta and salad. The conversation came easily. He told her about his law practice and the 1920s cottage on Long Island Sound that he spent every spare weekend fixing up. He seemed genuinely interested in her strategic plan to increase the nonprofit's visibility, and she made him laugh telling him about the street cat she had smuggled home from a trip to Istanbul last year. The Jack sitting across the table was very much like the Jack Charlotte had fallen in love with the first week of college. The Jack before Susannah.

After the waiter cleared their plates, Jack reached out to clasp her hand. She looked down at his long fingers covering hers and then looked back up at him again.

"Charlotte," he said, his voice catching a little, "I want you to know I'm so sorry about what happened. Susannah and I handled it very poorly. We both loved you, you know."

"It was many moons ago, Jack," she said lightly but didn't take her hand away.

Jack gave her hand a final squeeze and called for the check just as the waiter approached to offer dessert or coffee. "I'd love to keep talking but we don't have to stay here," he said. "I'm going to need a shot of caffeine, though, if I'm going to drive back to the cottage tonight."

Although his words were exactly what Charlotte had hoped for, not wanting to appear too eager she hesitated before making the offer. "I can do coffee at my place," she finally said.

Jack followed her Honda in his rental car to Wayland Square. She signaled him to take the space in front of her building and then parked up the street. She felt a quiver of excitement as she walked toward his lanky figure, standing with his hands in the pockets of his trench coat, that easy smile never far from his lips.

They paused for a few moments under the street lamp until he broke the silence. "Shall we go in?"

"Yes, of course." She fumbled in her purse for her keys, glad for an activity to keep her eyes away from his while she mentally reviewed the state of her condo. Were the yellow tulips she bought on the way home from work still brightening the table in the front window? Had she closed the door on her clothes-strewn bedroom? Were the candles and wine within easy reach but not appearing as the centerpiece on her mantle?

She unlocked the heavy front door and led him to the staircase in the foyer. "I'm afraid I'm on the top floor. It's four flights up," she warned. "This used to be an old schoolhouse before it converted to condos."

The dimly lit stairs were narrow and steep so they climbed in single file. Charlotte led the way, very conscious of his deliberate footsteps behind her. The flush in her cheeks from earlier in the restaurant seemed to be spreading through her body. They had almost reached her floor when Jack chuckled. "I'm getting a flashback to that apartment of yours in the Village. Do you have a tub in the kitchen in this place, too?"

She reached the landing and turned back to him with a smile.

Without thinking, she said, "Of course not. And Susannah didn't have one, either."

Once the words were out of her mouth she wanted to snatch them back. Jack stopped on the staircase, one step below her, with a puzzled expression. "I thought you hadn't seen Susannah since New York."

Charlotte froze at the top of the stairs, searching for an explanation. She'd come across an ad for Susannah's marketing firm and realized Susannah was back in Providence. She could tell him that. At least it was true.

"It was strictly business," Charlotte said. "I told you about the strategic plan. I thought she might help me."

He didn't move up the stairs to join her on the landing. "But you know what her kitchen looked like."

Charlotte thought back to the cool early Sunday morning two weeks ago when she appeared at Susannah's back door with a box of muffins from an East Side bakery. The narrow street was lined with cars so she'd had to park the Honda three blocks away. Susannah had been surprised but appeared pleased to see her and readily let her in. Susannah brewed a large pot of coffee and poured a pitcher of juice. They'd sat at her kitchen table, talking about everything but Jack, until Charlotte finally, simply asked the question she'd carried for the last eighteen years.

"Why, Susannah?"

Susannah stood next to the stone countertop in her stocking-feet, her lovely face turned to the window overlooking her pocket-sized garden. "Because he was yours, I guess."

The words sounded as insubstantial and fleeting as the crocuses scattered in Susannah's tiny lawn. "That's all?" Charlotte had demanded, her voice rising. "That's all you have to say?"

"I don't know what you want from me, Charlotte," Susannah said. "It was a long time ago. Jack and I aren't even together anymore. You can have him back if you want."

Charlotte felt a burning sensation behind her eyes and a buzzing noise sounded in her ears. Susannah's face blurred against the window. Charlotte stood up roughly from the table, knocking the coffee and juice onto the floor. The liquid spread across the mottled green ceramic tiles as she moved toward Susannah.

Charlotte shook off the memory as Jack asked, "Did you see Susannah?" The blue eyes were no longer puzzled but now narrowed in suspicion.

"I—I need to explain something," she started to say but Jack shook his head and held up one hand.

"Listen Charlotte, I'm a lawyer but I don't represent you. I don't think you should tell me anything. I can give you some referrals for someone to talk to." He turned his body away from her. "I have at least a couple of hours drive ahead of me. I'll grab some coffee on the road."

"No, wait, please." She stepped back onto the staircase but he didn't even turn around. He was leaving her again, leaving her again because of Susannah.

Charlotte took a deep breath and planted her legs firmly on the stair tread, her arms outstretched toward his back. "I'm sorry, Jack," she whispered, "but I can't let you go."

And then she pushed.

Christine Eskilson received honorable mentions in the 2012 Al Blanchard Short Crime Fiction Contest and the 2012 Women's National Book Association First Annual Writing Contest. Her stories have appeared in *Blood Moon* (Level Best Books, 2013), *Rogue Wave* (Level Best Books, 2015)*,* the *Bethlehem Writers Roundtable* (September, 2014), and *Creatures of Habitat* (Main Street Rag, 2015).

Fool Proof

Bruce Robert Coffin

Billy Firkin knelt quietly in the dark, steadying himself with his hands, as the container rocked from side to side. The claustrophobic feeling was bad but the odor was far worse. His feet slipped on the barrel's slick bottom. *Three more miles to freedom.*

Billy had professed his innocence from the start, lying to his attorney, denying any involvement in the murder of his unfaithful girlfriend Tina and her new beau, even after the cops found his bloody shoes in the trash. Lying had always been second nature, and he was extremely convincing. As a young boy, he'd displayed an innate ability to manipulate others. His mother had cautioned friends, "That boy has the face of an angel. Just remember to check his pockets before you go."

His string of successful cons ended abruptly the day a Portland jury, comprised of his so-called peers, spent less than two hours deliberating his fate. "Guilty," they'd said.

During his sentencing, Justice Stratham, rebuked him. "Anyone capable of inflicting as much pain and suffering as you did on that poor couple deserves to die. You sir, are an abomination to mankind. Were it within my purview, I'd sentence you to death."

Billy caught a lucky break by committing his crime in a state devoid of capital punishment. Stratham sentenced him to life without the possibility of parole. He was shackled and carted off to the Maine State Prison in Thomaston, eleven months ago, in the summer of '61.

On the eve of his planned escape, he'd barely slept a wink. The excitement and promise of the coming day were nearly intolerable. All he could think about was rising early and dressing for breakfast, but he'd forced himself to wait, having learned the value of patience.

"A successful scam artist has to have patience," his father once told him. "Takes time to gain a person's confidence, son. You gotta earn their trust, slowly. But once you get it, you can do anything, anything at all."

Everything had to appear status quo. The last thing he needed was for his cellmate to start asking questions or, worse still, some nosy bull like Jeeter smelling a rat. Bull was convict-speak for prison guard.

The seeds of his plan had been sown during his first month inside. One afternoon he'd been out in the recreation yard smoking a cigarette, when he saw his cousin, second cousin actually and only by marriage, driving a flatbed truck through the prison gates. Cousin Frank was employed by Milo Trucking, a company the State of Maine contracted to remove prison refuse.

Armed bulls, carrying rifles, removed Frank from the truck while they searched the cab, the payload, and the undercarriage using mirrors. After they had finished, Frank drove around to the rear of the chow hall. Billy noted that the back of the Dodge was loaded with both red and white fifty-five gallon drums, the same white drums that the kitchen detail used to depose of the waste grease from the fryolators. Discreetly, he continued to monitor the event until finally the truck reappeared. When Frank reached the main gate, the bulls repeated their search. They searched everything, everything except the barrels. It was on that very afternoon that he began to plan his escape.

The first step was getting assigned to the kitchen detail, but it hadn't been easy. Prison trustees were required to stay out of trouble for their first six months, no fights, no bad disciplinary reports, and no contraband. Several times he'd turned the other cheek, when what he really wanted was to drive a homemade shiv through the guts of another convict. Six excruciatingly long months of, "yes boss, no boss, thank you boss," until finally his request had been approved. He'd spent the remaining months meticulously planning each and every aspect, even conducting research by reading books from the prison library.

The cost of putting his plan into action had only been six cartons of cigarettes for Mel, the head of the kitchen detail, and a promise of four thousand dollars to Cousin Frank. Billy didn't actually have four thousand dollars "hidden away from a scam," but Frank didn't know that and had readily agreed to help.

Like all of his best schemes, this one was simple. With Mel's help, Billy planned to seal himself inside one of the waste containers. The barrel in question would only contain a small quantity of grease, allowing plenty of room for him and making the overall weight seem about right, should anyone become suspicious.

The truck lurched over a pothole, slamming Billy's head against the inside of the barrel. *Dammit all to hell, Frank. Take it easy, wouldya.* The pavement smoothed. He resumed his shallow breathing.

He'd waited until the other inmates began to rise and prepare for their morning duties, before sliding out of his own bunk. Silently, he dressed in his prison gray shirt, blue cargo pants and black shoes. He shaved, brushed his hair and teeth, everything as normal. He stood waiting by the cell door as the bull appeared.

"Morning, Firkin," Barrett had said.

As bulls went, Barrett was a good one. He'd been professional and pleasant since the day Billy first arrived. The same could not be said of all the bulls.

Barrett's boss Jeeter, a horse's ass of the highest order, was small in stature but big on bullying. Being a bully was Jeeter's favorite past-time, frequently caving-in some convict's skull with the hardwood club he carried. He'd even named the club, carving Mabel into the side of it. Billy didn't know if "little man's syndrome" was a real malady or not, but if so, old Jeeter the Bull was in the advanced stages. Rumor had it that he was also king of the swirlies, the name given to Jeeter's practice of taking a con's toothbrush and swirling it around inside the toilet bowl, before replacing it undetected. As far as Billy was concerned, having Barrett on duty today rather than Jeeter only meant that the god of good fortune was smiling down upon him once more.

"Morning, boss," Billy replied, needing every ounce of his self-control not to push past Barrett and run down the hall shouting, "I'm free, I'm free." He studied the bull's face for any indication that his excitement had been detected, but saw nothing. Billy was escorted down the corridor to the other detailees. The entire group then walked to the kitchen, where they prepared the day's first meal.

Breakfast was always served at seven o'clock sharp. Members of the kitchen detail ate first, at quarter till. This morning's meal had consisted of chipped beef and gravy on toast, scrambled eggs, canned peaches and of course black coffee. Billy despised chipped beef and gravy, or what the inmates fondly referred to as "shit on a shingle," but today was his stepping out day and he ate a double helping that tasted more like the ambrosia his grandma Josephine used to make. Viewpoint is everything and Billy had come to believe that his cup would soon runneth over.

Following breakfast, under the watchful eye of the bulls, the kitchen crew cleaned up. Dishes, utensils, and cookware were scrubbed, dining tables cleared, and floors were swept and mopped. The cycle began anew as they prepared for the noontime meal. Billy worked quietly alongside the others, not wanting to draw any attention to himself, no matter how slight. He'd just finished mopping the chow hall when Jeeter appeared.

"Well, well, well, what do we have here?" Jeeter asked with a sneer.

Billy's heart skipped a beat. Not having seen Jeeter until that very moment, he'd foolishly assumed the bull wasn't working. The other inmates, grateful that Jeeter wasn't targeting them, stopped to watch.

"Just cleaning up, boss," Billy said.

"Just cleaning up, boss," Jeeter said, mocking him in falsetto. "Think you got it all, convict?"

Billy nodded in the affirmative.

"You sure?"

"Yes, boss."

Billy knew what was coming, having witnessed this sadistic game before, but was powerless to stop it. Jeeter hooked his highly polished black military boot under the bucket upending it, sending a wave of dirty water cascading across the previously clean concrete floor.

"Oops," Jeeter said. "Looks like you missed some after all. You'd best clean that up, convict."

"Yes, boss."

Jeeter laughed then walked away, spinning Mabel and whistling a happy tune.

Billy hated Jeeter. Sometimes he'd daydream about slicing the bull's throat, giving him that nice below-the-chin grin. The same grin he'd denied carving into the throats of Tina and her boyfriend.

Two-thirty couldn't come soon enough.

Another pothole jarred the Dodge violently. Billy's barrel bounced up, momentarily losing contact with the bed of the truck, then landed hard, nearly tipping over. He struggled to maintain both his balance and his composure. His legs were beginning to cramp from being bent so long. *Only a couple more miles.* He closed his eyes, repositioned his legs and resumed his shallow breathing.

Twenty minutes, according to the prison library book about Harry Houdini, is the amount of time an average sized person can survive, if sealed in a fifty-five gallon drum, before running out of air. Houdini had been handcuffed, sealed in a metal barrel, and then submerged in ten feet of water. Twenty minutes later, he escaped. Afterward, when asked how he had been able to continue breathing for so long, Houdini explained that he took shallow breaths and willed himself to remain calm. Billy practiced shallow breathing every night before falling asleep.

Billy's brother Darryl came to see him at the prison once a month. Darryl was also very adept at getting people to do what he wanted, although he used a gun and had done time for armed robbery. It was during one of these visits that Darryl agreed to help his brother. The two men were very careful when discussing the details of the plan as the bulls were always watching, but not always listening.

Darryl lived in Portland, over seventy miles south of the prison, and wasn't all that familiar with Thomaston. Billy asked his brother to reconnoiter the surrounding area for anything abandoned with a loading dock. The only additional requirement was that it needed to be within close proximity to the prison, as Billy would only have a limited supply of oxygen.

Darryl located an abandoned warehouse exactly 3.1 miles from the prison, according to his odometer. It couldn't be seen from the road, had no guards, and no gate. What it did have was a cement platform, perfect for offloading a barrel.

Billy, who'd always been good with numbers, calculated that it would take seven or eight minutes, depending upon traffic, for Frank to reach the warehouse after leaving the prison. He knew that the bulls only spent two to three minutes conducting the exit search, leaving him nine minutes. Nine minutes for Frank to load the barrel onto the truck, drive to the prison gate, then roll the barrel off the truck and onto the platform at the warehouse. If everything went according to plan, he'd have a window of four and a half minutes. Two hundred and seventy seconds were all that stood between glorious freedom and death by suffocation.

During the months that followed, Billy had Darryl go over the plan with Cousin Frank repeatedly until he was confident that both men had it memorized.

Mel, the kitchen chief, was a friend to Billy. He'd taken him under his wing immediately upon joining the detail. Because of Mel, Billy always got plenty to eat and was only rarely assigned to P and P duty, convict speak for pots and pans detail, considered the nastiest of all kitchen work. The slop sinks were deep, making it tough on the back, and the water was scalding. When Billy first broached the subject of trying to escape, Mel's eyes sparkled with excitement. It had actually been Mel's idea to mark Billy's container.

"It should be something ironic," Mel said. "A big F.U. to the bulls."

Billy liked the idea initially, but worried that it might be foolhardy. He couldn't risk anything that might be detected during the exit search. In the end, he'd instructed Mel to mark a large letter B on the lid of the barrel. The marking would enable Frank to know which of the barrels to offload at the warehouse.

The temperature inside the container was rising quickly. Billy was just beginning to feel the first prickles of fear. He willed them away like swatting at flies. *Nothing to worry about. Everything was proceeding exactly as he'd planned. Less than a mile now. Shallow breathing.*

Lunch was uneventful. The menu had consisted of tuna salad, stale bread, soup, and fries. Billy's stomach was in knots, partially because of his earlier run-in with Jeeter but mostly because the hour of his escape was nearly at hand. He wasn't hungry but he'd forced himself to eat, it was a necessary part of the ruse. It wouldn't do to have one of the bulls notice he wasn't eating, especially Jeeter.

All of the remaining details had been worked out during Darryl's last visit. Billy told him to pick up a sandwich then park out behind the warehouse. If anyone inquired why he was there, he'd simply say he was eating his lunch. Billy instructed him to hang back as the barrel was unloaded, waiting until Frank drove off before making his approach.

"How will Frank know which barrel to unload?" Billy asked, testing his brother.

"He'll know because there will be a big letter B written on the top, in black marker."

"What do you do as soon as he drives off?"

"I high-tail it to the loading dock, pry off the lid and get you the hell outta there."

"What else?"

"I'm to bring you a change of clothes and a trash bag for the stuff you'll be wearing."

They'd been over the plan again and again, until Billy was confident that everyone knew exactly what to do. Frank knew to be at the warehouse by two forty-five. If he hadn't made it by then, he would scrap the plan and get Billy out of the barrel. Billy promised that Frank would get his money either way. Greed is the best insurance.

At two-twenty, Billy and Mel were working in the kitchen along with several other inmates. Mel was cleaning out the fry-o-lators while Billy assisted. The rest of the crew had begun to prep for supper. Billy could hear several of the bulls laughing about something, just beyond the kitchen door. At two twenty-five, Billy and Mel moved into the back room. They were standing at the loading dock doors when Jeeter walked into the kitchen and began hassling one of the workers.

"Dammit," Billy whispered. "Not now."

"Stay here," Mel said wiping hands on his apron. "I'll take care of this."

Billy waited nervously, beside an open barrel. A loud crash came from the adjoining room.

"Why don't you watch what the hell you're doing, convict!" Jeeter yelled. "Clean that mess up."

Mel hastily returned through the doorway, just as the truck was backing up to the loading platform.

"Now," Mel said. "Let's go, we've only got a second."

Billy climbed into the barrel and crouched down just as he had practiced. "Wish me luck."

Mel picked up the lid and looked down at Billy one last time. "See you on the other side."

Then there was only darkness.

All of his senses were dampened by the enclosure. It was like being blind. He was aware of movement and heard the muffled banging of other barrels being loaded onto the truck, but aside from those things he was effectively cut off from the outside world. After a minute or so he felt the truck begin moving toward the main gate, toward freedom.

He knew the bulls would realize he was missing by supper time, he only hoped they wouldn't notice beforehand. His only regret was not being around to see the look on their faces. If all went according to plan, he and Darryl would be across the state line into New Hampshire by the time the inmates sat down to eat.

Billy knew they were close. Frank had made an unmistakable right-hand turn. Judging by the way his barrel was bouncing, they were now traveling on the dirt drive which led to the warehouse. The air had become noticeably thinner. He felt lightheaded. Concentration was more difficult and the leg cramps were almost unbearable. *Just a little longer.* The truck came to a stop.

Darryl was parked exactly where he was supposed to be when the blue Dodge came into view. He checked his watch, two forty-six. They'd done it. He threw the rest of his half eaten sub out the window and turned the key. Nothing but a click. "Shit!" *This can't be happening. Not now.* He'd forgotten about the Merc's temperamental starter. He knew it had a bad spot but it hadn't acted up for some time. He turned the key in the ignition again. This time he heard a loud screech. "Come on. Come on." He watched anxiously as Frank backed the truck into position and got out.

As Frank wrestled with the barrel, he tried the key a third time. "Come on baby." The engine roared to life. He let out a sigh of relief. Frank got back in the cab and began driving away. Darryl shifted into drive and sped toward the loading dock. He jumped out of the car, pry tool in hand, and hopped onto the concrete platform where a single white barrel stood. On the lid in black marker was a big letter B. "I gotcha, Bill," he said as he pried off the lid.

Frank was one happy camper. "I'm rich!" he yelled out the window to a passing car. "God damn, I'm rich! Four thousand buckaroos." He reached down and cranked up the volume on the AM radio and began to sing along with Elvis. "Let's rock, everybody let's rock."

Billy wasn't sure if the lack of oxygen was muddling his thoughts or if the truck really was moving again. *It couldn't be. They'd stopped and Frank had moved his barrel. He was positive. What if he only moved your barrel to get at another one? What if he unloaded the wrong barrel? No, it couldn't be. The barrel was clearly marked.* But muddled thoughts or no, they were definitely moving again. As if to punctuate this thought, his barrel bounced up and down on the flatbed. He opened his mouth to scream but couldn't draw any air into his lungs. Panic set in, and unlike the little flies of fear he'd shooed away earlier these were huge and had sharp teeth. He beat on the inside of the drum with his fists, but his arms grew heavy and the pounding ceased. With his last bit of strength, he pushed his entire body up against the lid.

Darryl stared dumbfounded into the open barrel. It was full to the top with foul-smelling brownish lard. He checked the lid again confirming the letter B. He checked his watch, two-fifty. His brother Billy had been locked in a barrel, some other barrel, for twenty minutes. In desperation he drove his arm into the grease hoping to feel his brother's head but felt nothing.

He leapt off of the loading dock and back into his car. He floored the accelerator. Spinning tires threw gravel everywhere. *I've got to catch up with Frank.* He locked the brakes. In a cloud of dust the Mercury skidded to a stop at the main road. Darryl looked both ways. Frank's truck was nowhere in sight. They'd never discussed where he was headed after unloading the barrel. It wasn't part of the plan. Darryl figured he had a fifty-fifty chance at guessing correctly. He spun the steering wheel hard left and screeched out onto the pavement.

Darryl guessed wrong.

The two men stood out on the loading dock, enjoying the warm afternoon sun and smoking cigarettes. One wore a greasy white apron over his inmate clothing, the other a spotless prison guard uniform.

"Well, I guess he'll think twice before he murders the nephew of a bull again," Mel said.

The guard took a long drag off what remained of his cigarette before dropping it onto the loading platform and twisting it under his highly polished boot. "I'm sure you're right," Barrett said with a chuckle. "I'm sure you're right."

An award-winning artist and retired police detective sergeant, **Bruce Robert Coffin** has penned a number of short stories along with his first novel, *The Reaping*. He resides in Maine with his wife. "Foolproof" is his first published story.

No Aura

Annelisa Johnson Wagner

W e're out of eggs!" Sharon called from the kitchen.
"What's that?" asked Carl. He flicked the mute button on the
TV remote in the den.

"We're out of eggs!" Sharon yelled. "I'm in the middle of making
this cake and I need two eggs."

"I had scrambled eggs for supper last night while you were out
with your lady friends," answered Carl. He sank deeper into his La-Z
Boy, hoping to hide from Sharon's wrath. "I used the last two."

After forty-two years of marriage, Carl could picture his wife
in the kitchen, hands on hips, lips like a taut string, glaring into the
refrigerator at the place where eggs were supposed to be but weren't.

Sharon emerged from the kitchen and assumed an offensive
position in the doorway, arms crossed tightly across her chest, a
deflector shield. "Well, you're not supposed to take the last two of
anything," she declared. "Unless you replace them first."

Carl squinted up at her, trying to assess how mad she really was.
Her eyes drilled into his. Yes, sir, she was pissed.

"Well, goodness, it's not like I planned it," said Carl. He rubbed
his temples. He had a headache and this discussion about eggs wasn't
helping any. He hauled himself up out of the recliner. "Just sit tight.
I'll go get some."

"Well, you better hurry up," Sharon ordered. "I already mixed
the wet with the dry and I don't want the batter to lose its oomph."

"Yeah, yeah, yeah," muttered Carl. He grabbed his Red Sox
baseball cap, patted his pockets to check for his wallet and keys, and
headed out the screen porch. He resentfully stepped over the Sunday

Portsmouth Herald that he had hoped to relax and read before Sharon had her hissy fit. Carl pulled the cap's visor down low over his eyes so the needles of the May morning sun glinting on the silver Honda wouldn't make his head throb even more.

Poppy wanted to take advantage of this warm Sunday and she was toasting the end of college classes with her first iced coffee of the season. She sat in the sun in the brick courtyard of a café in Portsmouth. Ivy climbed the brick wall next to her, each five-pointed leaf turning to face the morning sunshine. The small patio was crowded with students basking in the sun while cramming for final exams. If Poppy concentrated, she could almost pretend the traffic noise on Market Street behind her was the sound of a woodland stream.

There was nothing Poppy could do, however, about the kaleidoscope of colors that assaulted her eyes. Poppy saw auras. Always had. Big pulsating bands of color surrounded all the people she encountered. It didn't matter if they were strangers or friends. The prisms were constant. Even when she slept, Poppy dreamed auras around the people who stalked her private nightscapes. She could hold up her own hands and marvel at the play of colors that emanated from them.

As a kid, Poppy thought everyone saw colors. When she was five, she happened to mention to her mother that the mailman had a bubble of her favorite colors around him (light blue with twinges of pink around the edges), her mother refuted this and told her she was being silly. Mr. Johnson was just Mr. Johnson and he had no colors around him, her mother insisted, blue, pink, polka-dotted, or otherwise. Poppy should hush up, eat her breakfast, and mind her own business.

When Poppy grew older, she began to associate colors with various characteristics. She worried about an old lady she had seen on the corner. Her aura reminded Poppy of the brown spots on the flesh of sliced avocados and this meant her health was failing. She knew she should steer clear of the man shopping in the bookstore whose aura flashed spikes of dark green. He was loaded with resentment and anger and should be avoided. Poppy could tell that her best friend was lying when her typically pink aura was stained with clots of gray.

People in groups were especially problematic. When two people were together in close conversation, their separate auras blended in a hypnotic way and Poppy felt like a voyeur, privy to aspects of the couple's relationship she shouldn't know. If there was tension, their auras flashed like a warning, the red lights of an ambulance suddenly coming up behind you on the highway. Poppy wished she didn't know so much about the people around her. She wanted to live behind an opaque window so that she could look out at the dull edges of people rather than confront their chromatic flashes.

When she was a teenager, Poppy accepted the fact that the colors were not going away. When she made peace with this, she was better able to let the auras settle into the background so that she could focus on her teacher, conversations with friends, or her list when she shopped in a crowded grocery store. The colors never dimmed but she learned to focus on faces and not the shimmering halos.

Poppy propped open her Intro to Econ textbook and relaxed her mind, letting everyone's colors bleed quietly into the background.

Carl sat behind the steering wheel of the car in his driveway, concentrating on taking deep breaths. It felt like a bird was trapped in his chest, a sensation of fluttering wings. Tiredness rolled over him like a sluggish wave.

"Must be coming down with something," Carl muttered. "I better get these goddamned eggs so I can get home and get to bed." He fumbled with the keys, nearly dropping them into the space between the seat and the center console. He started the car, tapping the fingers of his right hand against the steering wheel to wake them up and dispel the tingling. He popped the car into reverse and backed down the driveway into the street.

Poppy sipped her coffee and chewed on the ice. This was a habit her mother had detested.

"You'll break your teeth," her mother had warned, "and then where will you be?"

"I'd be right here with broken teeth," Poppy had replied, trying to be funny.

Her mother obviously hadn't appreciated Poppy's humor any more than she had appreciated Poppy's knack for seeing colors. Poppy watched her mother's aura turn from the bland color of a Band-Aid to the clouded color of a blood orange.

"Don't be fresh," her mother had said and she had given Poppy a swat.

"You'll break your teeth doing that," a voice behind Poppy intoned.

Poppy turned. Was someone channeling her mother right now? An attractive guy, seemingly her age with a UNH t-shirt and a mop of curly brown hair, sat at the table adjacent to hers.

"Chewing ice," the man continued. "It'll ruin your teeth. I used to chew ice and then I read it was because of an iron deficiency. Like when dogs eat dirt."

Poppy sucked in her breath sharply. No aura. This man had no aura. No glimmers of color floated along this man's edges. His contour stayed put, a definite line separating him from the background. She stared, trying to make sense of what she wasn't seeing. Some people had narrow bands of color if they were masking emotions, but this guy had nothing.

"Sorry," Poppy stammered. "I—I didn't think I was that loud." She refocused. Maybe an aura hadn't emerged yet because she hadn't quite tuned in.

"Oh, no problem," said the man. He pushed his floppy curly bangs away from his gray-blue eyes. "But you should look into the iron thing. It might make a difference."

"Yeah, right, I'll have to check into that," said Poppy. She turned back to her econ book. Her mind raced. A breeze ruffled the ivy leaves and they all seemed to face her.

"An iron skillet," the man said.

"What?" asked Poppy, turning back, willing there to be a glow, for there to be something. Nothing. She couldn't make herself understand. Heaviness saturated the air around her and Poppy labored to draw in a breath of air as thick as cotton batting. The courtyard wall next to her seemed to sway closer, the ivy leaning in.

"Yup," said the man. "I started to cook in a cast iron skillet and that was the end of my iron deficiency and my ice crunching."

"Um, I'm happy for you," said Poppy, hoping that this would end the discussion with this man with no aura. Instead, the man turned his chair as though to join her.

"I'm Sam," the man said, reaching out his hand to her. Poppy watched his hand grasp hers. Her aura pulsed as orange as a monarch butterfly's wing. Where Sam's thumb and fingers touched hers, she noticed that her orange glow was tamped down or more accurately, it seemed that her aura was being absorbed into his lack of one. Her hand felt cold.

Poppy had to concentrate on breathing and couldn't focus at all on what order of words could stream from her mouth. She withdrew her hand and scraped her chair back, away from Sam.

"I'm Poppy," she murmured.

Sam smiled, a friendly, easy-going, wide grin, but Poppy could only see the void around him. It was like looking into a dark pit, where no light could travel.

Carl had planned to head to Newington to the market where he and Sharon did most of their shopping. They preferred to buy food that was organic. Two minutes down his street, Carl gave up on this idea. He'd stop at the Cumberland Farms in Portsmouth even if their chickens were stuffed into miniscule wire cages and forced to lay eggs at gunpoint. He didn't have the energy to drive the extra mile to the market. Sharon would just have to make do with Cumby eggs, despite the hens being fed genetically modified corn laced with antibiotics.

Carl's eyes weren't quite working right. "What the hell?" he thought. He'd lose focus and both sides of the street would shuffle together in a disjointed way in front of the car. "Pull over, you damned fool," Sharon would have protested, had she been riding shotgun. Glad she wasn't here to nag at him, Carl rubbed his bleary eyes and shook his head. His eyes cleared and he was confident that he could make it two more blocks, park at Cumby's, wait for the spell to pass, buy the goddamned eggs, and go home to bed.

"So, come here often?" Sam chuckled. "I've always wanted to use that line and it seems appropriate."

Poppy forced a smile, but it probably looked more like she had tasted something gone bad. She continued to open herself up to him, scanning for a glimmer of something, anything. Her stomach churned and her head swam from the effort of looking for something that wasn't there. Was he a zombie, a representative of the non-dead right here in Portsmouth? Was he an alien?

"Is something wrong?" asked Sam. He leaned closer and Poppy could tell from his eyes that he was genuinely concerned.

Poppy's brain would not allow her to form words. She felt as though she was spinning, falling. She pushed away from the patio table, her iced coffee tipping over onto her econ book. Ice cubes spun crazily across the table's surface and a cascade of coffee dumped onto her jeans. Her stomach roiled and she knew that she was going to be sick. She felt her aura being sucked into Sam's void. Repulsed, Poppy staggered backward, her left hand raking through the ivy leaves that covered the courtyard wall. Her other hand covered her mouth, choking back vomit.

Sam, she saw, was standing now, too. "Oh, my God! Are you going to faint?" he asked, taking a step toward Poppy and reaching out to her.

Poppy gasped. Sam's outline was drawing inward. His edges were becoming less distinct and Poppy saw that his core was becoming darker. She turned toward the wall and clutched the ivy with two hands, hoping the flimsy vines would help hold her up. Her nausea overtook her, she bowed her head, her stomach heaved, and she threw up against the brick wall.

Jumbled thoughts and a lightening bolt of panic raced through Carl's brain. He struggled to grasp the steering wheel with his left hand. His right arm had become an old dishrag hanging limply at his side. His left hand had to do all the work to hold the car on an even keel. His eyes crossed and he felt as though he was plummeting through a long tunnel. All lines of perspective ended in a dot ahead of him, but even this dot wouldn't stay put. He needed to stop, stop now, but his right foot wouldn't move off the gas. His left foot jabbed ineffectively at the brakes. Carl sagged sideways and slumped over in his seat. The tunnel ended abruptly as Carl's car jumped the curb and careened onto the sidewalk.

Poppy turned at the sound of twisting metal and frantic screams. A silver streak, a car she realized, was impossibly on the sidewalk and then in the courtyard and then was plowing toward her table, only feet away. Sam had heard the warning cries and had seen the car. Poppy watched as he tried to step aside, but his feet became tangled in chair and table legs. Trapped, he faced the car hurtling toward him, his arms outstretched, his eyes wide, his mouth agape. Poppy's horror cut through her as she watched the thin eggshell of Sam's dark core implode. With a sickening crunch, the car slammed into Sam head on, his body crushed at the waist between the brick wall of the courtyard and the car's front end. The car's engine raced and its tires spun. Even now, the driver must be continuing to step on the gas as though he were on a mission, unwilling to admit defeat.

Poppy collapsed four feet away. One man rushed to the accordion that was once a car, yanked opened the driver's side door, gingerly reached over the prone driver, and turned off the engine. Others, from the front passenger's side, attempted to attend to the driver. Two men carefully approached Sam. They held his hands and spoke softly to him. A third pulled off his sweatshirt and placed it under Sam's head as he slumped forward onto the hood of the car. Poppy's econ textbook lay open against the windshield, its pages fluttering like Buddhist prayer flags. Several witnesses paced around, gripping their cell phones, frantically trying to convey the sharp shards of the scene to a 9-1-1 operator. The witnesses' auras were tight and close as they all tried to make sense of the trauma.

Two women approached Poppy and kneeled on either side of her. Their auras cast a soft buttery light. Poppy leaned back against the brick wall of the courtyard. The ivy leaves trembled in the light breeze.

"Oh, my God!" whispered one of the women. "You were there. You were right there. Are you okay?" She placed her hand on Poppy's shoulder and Poppy was thankful for the warm contact.

"That was so close!" the other woman gasped. "One more second and you would have been hit, too. Do you know him?" she asked.

"Sam," Poppy managed to say. "That's all I know." But Poppy

also knew that she and Sam were like two magnets, their south poles aligned, her repulsion saving her from the car's insane trajectory. Poppy unclenched her fists and crumpled ivy leaves fell onto the bricks of the courtyard and skittered away in the warm May breeze.

Annelisa Johnson Wagner grew up in northern New Hampshire but now lives in southern Maine. She misses the White Mountains but appreciates the rocky coast. She is a middle school teacher and a member of Writers on Words, a writing group. This is her first fiction publication, but she has also completed a novel and continues to hone her writing.

Nice Guy

Kate Flora

Donnie Parker had had a thing for Linda Lyle, Linda Osborne as she was now, since the day back in high school when she'd dropped her mittens rushing for the bus. He'd scooped them up and run after her, handing them over shyly at the bus door and she'd looked at him with those warm brown eyes, smiled her wonderful smile, and said, "Oh, Donnie, you're so sweet."

There's a country western song that goes, "You had me from hello . . ." She'd had him for sure.

Not that he'd done anything about it, then or later. She was dating Bud Osborne, and Osborne was a big deal. Quarterback on the football team. Student council president. He'd had the hottest truck in the high school parking lot, bought brand new. Bud Osborne was good-looking in a magazine-ad way. All the girls wanted to go out with him, while Donnie was scrawny and blemished. Donnie was good at fixing things, a shop major, and tongue-tied around girls. Some of the wilder ones had bummed cigarettes off him in eighth grade, but otherwise, girls didn't know he existed.

He'd got his growth late. At thirty-five, he was taller than Bud. Bud outweighed him by a good sixty pounds of beer weight, though, weight Bud pushed around to get what he wanted at the price he wanted, never mind who got hurt or was it fair. Bud had the biggest truck, biggest house, biggest boat, biggest ATV, biggest snowmobile and darn near the biggest mouth in the county. And, till just recently, the prettiest wife.

Donnie darn near fell off his chair over at Smokey Joe's when he heard Jeanine, the waitress, telling a guy down the counter that

Linda had left Bud. Just up and took their two kids and moved home. When Jeanine swung by to refill his coffee and tell him they'd got an outlet back in the kitchen needed looking at, he held her a minute to get the story.

"You say Linda's gone and left Bud? Why'd she do that?"

"Guess she couldn't stand him no more. I dunno. Can't be easy living with a big-mouth like Bud."

"That's it? She left him 'cuz of his big mouth?"

Jeanine just shrugged, leaving Donnie with the feeling she knew more than she was telling. He got that feeling from women pretty often. "Why?" she said. "You thinkin' of askin' her out?"

It had never occurred to him. He'd thought about Linda thousands of times. Savored those chance meetings on the street, at Shaw's, or in the bank. She'd always smile that same slow smile like she was glad to see him and say, "Hey, Donnie, how ya doin'?" Over the years, lines had started by her eyes, but that just made them sweeter. She still had kind of a springy bounce when she walked, like the cheerleader she'd been.

He'd conjured her up as he showered, imagining her in there with him. Late nights, sometimes, watching the smoke curling from his cigarette, he'd have imaginary conversations with her. Conversations and other things. Last time he'd seen Linda, she'd looked different. Sadder and slower, like the bounce was slipping away. But they were all getting older, so he hadn't thought much about it.

He put three bucks down and slid off his stool. "Maybe I will," he said.

As Jeanine swung her pot toward another empty cup, she gave him a hard look. "You do," she said, "you gotta go real easy." She looked like she was gonna say more but she just poured old Tom Welks some coffee and disappeared into the kitchen.

"Like I'd be any other way." He banged out the door. He hated it when people went all secretive like you were supposed to pry things out of 'em.

Coming back that afternoon from a job, he saw Linda's white Volvo turning in at the gas station. He flicked on his blinker and pulled up to the pump behind her. She was wearing faded blue jeans and a blue fleece top, her blonde hair in a ponytail. He watched her struggle with the gas cap, twisting with one hand, then both, her ass in the tight jeans firm as a girl's. When she gave up, pounding on the side of the car, he went up to her.

"Hey," he said. "Let me do that."

The knuckles on the hand she raised to swipe at her tears were scraped raw. "It was just too tight. Bud always does that. I've asked him a million times not to."

Donnie undid the cap and lifted the hose. "What kind you want?"

"Cheap," she said. "I'm gonna have to start learning to live cheaper."

"Yeah," he said, fitting the hose into the tank and starting the gas. "I heard you left Bud."

"That's a small town for ya," she said. "People know things about you almost as soon as you know 'em yourself."

He bit his lip, thinking about his conversation with Jeanine, then turned back to Linda, pushing the words out before his nerve failed. "I know it's probably too soon, but would you . . . uh . . . maybe . . . like to go out some time or something?"

He thought his knees would give out or he'd choke on the words, make a jerk of himself. He stared down at the nozzle, cold in his hands, more than half expecting she'd laugh. The hose jerked and was still. He waited a few seconds, pulled it out slowly, shaking the last drops off the end, then carefully replaced her gas cap. Not too tight.

"It's been a while," she said finally. "I'm not sure I'm ready."

"There's no rush. I've just, you know, always liked you. It doesn't have to be fancy. Burgers at Smokey's or somethin'."

She flipped her head, the thick honey ponytail switching. "Given how nosy this town is, maybe we should just go for a walk in the woods. But it's hunting season, and wouldn't that just be my luck, I'd leave Buddy, go for a walk, and get shot?"

"Bow hunting season," he said. "Not too many people go bow hunting."

She flicked the ponytail. "Buddy does. Some of the idiots who work for him do. I'm surprised one of 'em hasn't shot another by now, way they all tank up before they go."

"There's no hunting on Sundays."

"No *legal* hunting. You think that stops those jerks?"

She reached for her car door, then turned back toward him, givin' him that smile. "Friday, then. Smokey Joe's. Burgers and beer. If my mom can babysit the boys. Buddy Junior's old enough to leave in charge but he picks on Joey and they're both of 'em upset about the move. Missing their rooms and their stuff." She sighed. "I shoulda made Buddy move but I just had to get out." Her eyes did that crinkling-up thing. "Call me and I'll let you know."

Boy howdy, Donnie thought. Was this really happening? He gassed up the van and headed off to Mrs. Sibley's. She'd left a message on his machine there were ghosts in the overhead lights. He was an electrician, not an exorcist, but he thought he could fix her problem.

Mrs. Sibley followed him around, chatting at him, trying to keep him from getting done quick and getting out of there. She was lonely, he knew, so he tried to give her the time, but everywhere he went to put his foot down there was a cat, and her place smelled like a litter box, no matter that she had a houseful of nice antiques. He had a place like this, he'd take care of it.

Donnie liked taking care of things. He kept his few good pieces of furniture polished, had a couple nice pictures he'd got at yard sales, even had some plants.

Now, when he looked around his place, he tried seeing it through Linda's eyes. He'd bring her there, she'd look, what would she think?

"Womanish," was how his brother Len put it. But that was when Len was looking in the refrigerator for more beer and Donnie'd only had the one. He'd tripped over enough of their parents' empties, growing up. Now he bought small and drank careful. You couldn't do good electrical work if your hands shook. Len nearly always had the shakes and he was two years younger.

He'd asked her on Monday. He gave it two days and then called her mother's, his trembling, callused hands nearly missing the numbers as he punched them in. Linda's mother was a church lady, a stiff, upright woman with rigid gray hair. Most women around town wore stretchy pants or jeans and sweatshirts, but he'd never seen Linda's mother when she wasn't wearing a dress. Her "hello" was friendly enough 'til he asked for Linda. Then he got an edgy, "Who's calling?"

"It's Donnie Parker, Mrs. Lyle," he stammered, feeling about sixteen.

"You aren't calling for Bud, are you?"

Now he understood. Buddy must of gotten some other guys to call Linda for him because she wasn't taking his calls. "No, ma'am, I'm not."

"You wait a minute," she said. "I'll see if she can come to the phone."

He could hear indistinct voices, then Linda said, "Sorry 'bout that. Buddy was calling about every ten minutes so I stopped taking his calls. Now he gets his guys to do it. I guess I've spoken with just about everyone on his crew. Told 'em to stop botherin' me. He just doesn't get it that I've left him. But hey . . . I don't guess you called to hear about that."

He heard a crash. A child's cry. "Buddy Junior," she called, "Haven't I told you no hitting?"

The boy's reply was rude and distinct. "Daddy says sometimes you gotta hit people to keep 'em in line."

Her voice came back on the line, fast and flustered. "Smokey's. Friday. Seven. I'll meet you there." She hung up.

Friday after work, Donnie spent a long time in the shower, trying to get himself calmed down, but he shouldn't have bothered. He was still jumping in his skin when he pulled the truck into Smokey's lot and wished he hadn't of worn this blue shirt where the sweat stains showed, even if a girl had once said it made his eyes look real blue. He quick scanned the lot, looking for her Volvo. No sign of it yet, which was okay. He preferred to be first. Get them a good table, maybe a beer to help calm him down, then watch people's faces when she walked in and sat with him.

She was a good fifteen minutes late, hurrying toward him in a pretty skirt and a low-cut white sweater, the tops of her breasts just peeking out. He didn't have to look around to know she turned every head in the place. When Jeanine came for their order, he ordered a beer and Linda asked for a Cosmo. He didn't know what that was, but when it came, it was pink and girly and seemed to make her happy.

He had another beer. She had another Cosmo, and then he had a burger, like always, and she had a salad with chicken. Fridays and Saturdays there was a band, and she said she'd like to dance. He liked the look on her face when she found out he was a good dancer, surprised first, then flushing pink with pleasure, like she'd been given a treat. Most guys, she said, couldn't or wouldn't dance, at least not with their wives. He knew she meant Buddy, who was known to show up at Elks Lodge dances over in Augusta without her, making an ass of himself with any woman in the room.

Dancing made him hot, so he had another beer, then excused himself to go to the men's room, hating to leave her alone. He expected he'd come back to find her dancing with someone else. Instead, he found Buddy, half in the bag, his face flushed and twisted. There was a red mark on Linda's arm.

Donnie pulled an empty chair over from the next table and sat down, leaning in so he was between them. "Bud, what did you do to her?"

"What goes on between me and my wife ain't your business."

"Maybe what goes on between you and my date is."

"Date?" Buddy's red eyes narrowed. "Date? Linda's my wife, Donnie. She can't go on dates. Bitch's just using you to stir me up. She don't even like you. She thinks you're pitiful, the way you moon after her."

"Buddy, I never . . ."

Ignoring her, Buddy said, "Excuse me, dreamer, but we're out of here." He grabbed his wife's arm, giving it a jerk that hauled her halfway onto the table, dragging the front of her sweater through the dregs of her salad.

When she tried to pull her arm loose, Buddy tightened his grip. "I just love it when you squirm, honey."

The way he was holding her treated both men to the sight of her breasts spilling out of her sweater, turning her face pink with embarrassment. "Cute, honey," Buddy said, "I like your tits with lettuce stuck on."

"Buddy, I have left you." Her voice was low and furious. "You don't tell me what to do anymore. Now let go. Everyone's staring."

Buddy released her with a shove that sent her sprawling back into her chair, shoved his own chair back and grabbed her arm again, jerking her toward the door.

She dug her heels in, resisting. "Donnie, goddammit," she said, "aren't you going to do anything?"

He took his mug of beer from the table, tossed the contents into Buddy's eyes, and when Buddy'd let go of Linda to paw at his face, he swung the empty mug into Buddy's nose. Surprised as all hell, Buddy sat on the floor, cursing and threatening as blood poured through his fingers. Donnie dropped two twenties on the table, grabbed Linda's coat, and followed her out the door.

She was standing by the Volvo, picking bits of salad off her sweater with shaking hands, the silver of her tears illuminated by the light on a nearby pole.

"I brought your coat," he said, holding it open for her.

"Dammit. Dammit. Dammit. Ouch!" She kicked the tire hard, then swung her boot back and forth, wincing. "I can't stay around here, Donnie. He's always gonna be like this. Coupla days ago, he tried to drag me out of the market. Yesterday, he showed up when I was getting Joey at school. Every time, he grabs me and tries to make me go with him, like I'm his property."

She snatched the handkerchief he held out and buried her face in it. "Jeanine says to get a restraining order to make him stay away. I've got my lawyer workin' on it, but Buddy won't pay any attention. He doesn't think the law applies to him."

"He will if he has to go to jail."

"Yeah. Big if. Who are the deputies around here? Bill Packard and Stevie Sawyer and even the one woman they got, that's Ruthie LaPlante. We went to school with all of 'em, and they everyone think Buddy is a real good guy."

He put his arms around her and pulled her close, patting her awkwardly as she cried. When she looked up, her eyes swimming with tears, he bent and kissed her. Starting out gentle, like he meant to be, but the feeling of those soft, quivering lips and seeing her breasts pushing up out of her sweater loosened the lid on fifteen years of longing.

Next thing he knew, he was crushed against her lips, one hand cupping her ass while the other had found the softness of her breast, squeezing, caressing and then plunging down inside her sweater. He held her against him as she struggled to get away, hot with the rush of feeling her breast in his hand.

The stinging slap jerked him back. "Donnie, stop it, dammit. Stop. What are you doing?"

She twisted out of his grasp and backed away, her face twisted with shock and fury. "I thought you were better than this, Donnie

Parker. I thought you were a nice guy."

Her voice was a harsh whisper. "I am so sick of being grabbed and held and mauled. Being treated like property instead of like a person." She pushed up her coat sleeve and held out her arm. "Look at this."

Her arm from wrist to above the elbow was black and blue. "This isn't from tonight, Donnie. It's what Buddy always does. Like he said in there, I am *his* wife and he thinks he's got the right." She pulled her sleeve down and leaned back against the car, her eyes closed. "I had to leave before he killed me. And now you're doing it, too. Like I invite it. Like I deserve it."

If he'd had a gun, he would of shot himself, right then and there.

"Linda." His voice was a wretched croak. Fifteen years he'd dreamed of this moment, then he'd acted like a horny sixteen-year-old and blown it big time. Jesus. He *should* shoot himself. "Linda, listen. I'm so goddamned sorry. I never meant. You know I think the world of you . . ."

"And you've got such a nice way of showing it. First Buddy, now you. What? Do I wear a sign or something that says cheap woman deserves to be treated badly?" Her voice staggered to a stop, choked by tears. "Is something wrong with me?"

"God, no, Linda. I think you're great."

"Great at what, Donnie? I try to be a good wife, a good mother. A good person. And what? My husband beats the crap out of me every chance he gets, and when I leave him, the first guy I go out with treats me like a whore. What am I supposed to think?"

Well, he deserved that.

"I feel all funny inside," she said. "Like I'm broken or something."

That hurt so bad she might as well have stuck a screwdriver in his gut. "You got no reason to believe me, but I'm sorrier than I've ever been in my life about anything," he said. "I never meant for anything like this to happen."

She was silent a while, staring off into the dark. "I don't know what to do."

"For starters," he said, looking back toward Smokey's door, surprised Buddy hadn't appeared yet, "you'd better get out of here before he comes looking for you."

"Good idea." She stared up at him, the skin under her eyes dark from smudged mascara. She looked weary and discouraged. "He's gonna come looking for you, too, Donnie."

He shrugged. "I can handle Buddy."

"That's what I used to think."

He got in the van, disgusted with himself, knowing she thought he was no better than Buddy. On the way home he bought a pint of bourbon, then sat in the dark, smoking and drinking, until the sweet hot fumes finally drove her stricken face away. As he slipped into nightmares, he heard the crash of breaking glass.

When early sun pierced his bruised eyes, he staggered up. Someone had pounded roofing nails into his head. It tasted like he'd eaten roadkill. On the way to the bathroom, he looked out. The van's windshield was smashed.

He grabbed a fistful of aspirin, then called the Sheriff's Patrol, his insurance agent, and the mobile glass guy. Linda was right. The deputy who showed was Stevie Sawyer, who shrugged his slope shoulders, fingered the albino stubble on his chin, and allowed that a man might get irked if someone tried to date his wife.

"She's left him," had no effect on the deputy. Trouble with 'local law enforcement' was the word 'local.' Donnie figured getting angrier would only hurt his head. "Gotta do a report for the insurance," he said.

Saturday mornings he only worked on emergencies, but there were always emergencies, or things people thought were emergencies, like the outlet that had been hinky all week needed to be fixed right now because they wanted to watch TV and the plug kept sliding out. Or a lightbulb had broken off in a socket and the homeowner was afraid it might leak electricity and burn the house down. People had some weird ideas about electricity.

By 1:30, he was home and had turned the ringer off so the machine could take messages without bothering him. Figuring an afternoon in the woods, away from people and the reflection of his own ugly mug, would be good, he put on his Bean boots and his jacket and went out to the workshop to get his bow hunting gear. As though killing something would make him feel better.

It looked like someone had been in his shed. Things were stirred around. Not so most people would notice, but Donnie was precise. Precise enough to see that some of his arrows were missing.

He was a good shot like he was a good dancer, enjoying the smoothly working rhythms of his body, but he rarely loosed an arrow at anything but the hay bale targets out in his back orchard. He spent some time out there, pretending they were all Buddy Osborne. Then he shouldered his gear and headed into the woods.

It takes skill to move quietly through the woods in the fall. Leaves rustle and mask fallen branches and sticks snap like rifle shots and crackle like popcorn. Learning to move quietly was one of the few good things he'd got from his dad. Mostly he'd learned about staying out of the way, about the desperate lot of a gentle woman married to a violent man. Seen her lost to bitterness and drink as well.

He probably knew a lot more about Linda's situation than she gave him credit for. Not that it mattered now. He didn't expect she'd ever look at him again.

A sound off to his right made him pause, holding his breath as he peered through the sun-dappled trunks. A man in camouflage was coming up a parallel path about a hundred yards away. Donnie's binoculars showed a beefy, balding figure with a rusty little beard. Red Schofield. One of the morons who worked for Osborne. He slid behind a thick tree trunk, keeping the glasses up. If Red was there, his brother Skip probably was, too, and Skunk Wheeler, so stupid he made the Schofield brothers look smart, a plumber's assistant who'd never made the connection between plumbing and cleanliness.

Skunk never figured out that deer could probly smell him, too. Donnie could almost smell him from here. If the morons were out, did that mean Buddy was? He fingered the taut bowstring. Thought of his new arrowheads as he shifted to look farther up and down the trail. No sign of Buddy. Quietly, he set down his bow and slid off the quiver. Pulling out a camouflage bandana, he wiped down each arrow and straightened, checking the trail again.

Off to his right, between him and the path, movement led him to a small figure in camo, crouching, like him, to watch the hunters. Had one of them brought along a child? He lifted his bow and used the sight, which sometimes gave him better focus. The crouching figure wore a greenish watch cap. Peeking out the back was a long strand of honey-colored hair, and a bottom that didn't belong to any twelve-year-old boy. Propped against a tree trunk, almost invisible against the bark, was a bow.

Men's voices drew him back to the path, and Buddy Osborne's fat gut heaving as he lumbered up to meet the others, a shiny, high-tech crossbow cradled in his arms. Deer for miles around must have been shivering in terror. Osborne raised the bow and panned it across his three grinning pals. His face was a mess, nose swollen and red, the piggy eyes nearly lost in puffy flesh.

Their loud voices echoing through the silent woods told Donnie they'd been drinking. Bow hunting was hard. You had to get close to your deer to be sure of a clean kill. Now these jerks were making sure that they would see no deer and neither would anyone else who might be around.

They spread out until all but Osborne had disappeared into the woods. Donnie faded back into thicker brush to watch. When he looked again, the small figure was gone.

Now Osborne was coming his way, snuffling like a pig through his damaged nose, snapping sticks under his heavy feet, holding his bow half ready, stopping periodically to raise the bow and peer through the sight, looking for all the world like one of Tolkien's grotesque orcs. Snort, snuffle, stomp. Snort. Snuffle. Stop.

Then, more quickly than Donnie would have thought possible, Osborne had jerked in surprise, whipped out an arrow, fitted it to the bow, and let it fly toward where the small camo-clad figure had been. There was a rustle and a thud. Osborne grinned.

Donnie thought his heart had stopped. He notched his own arrow and aimed. "Osborne, you fat fuck, that's your own goddamned wife you're shooting at."

Osborne's second arrow came flying at him, tearing through his jacket and slicing along his ribs.

"And that's her goddamned lover I'm shooting at," Osborne yelled. Donnie's arrow reached him seconds later, burying itself in Osborne's chest.

Osborne stared at Donnie in surprise. He dropped his fancy new bow, clutched at his chest as he fell to his knees like a character in an old Western, then slowly toppled forward onto his face, his swollen nose plowing a furrow in the decaying leaves.

Donnie stood by the fallen body, stunned almost into immobility by the sight of the fallen man, collapsed in the final indignity of death, his ass in the air and his nose in the dirt. Donnie used a foot to flip Osborne, pulling his own jacket tight to keep his blood from dripping onto the body. A second arrow protruded from the man's chest. Another of his, but he'd only shot one. Using his bandana, he jerked the arrows out and shot two of Buddy's own into the man's chest.

Feet crashed through the brush. Red's voice calling, "Bud? Buddy? Hey, Buddy, where you at?"

He grabbed a handful of Buddy's arrows and began walking quietly toward Linda.

She was propped against a tree, jacket open and her shirt rolled up. The shaft of an arrow protruded from her pale flesh. She gave him the ghost of her usual smile. "Hey, Donnie. How's it goin'?"

"He shot you."

"Yeah. He did. Always said he'd kill me if I ever tried to leave him."

"Buddy's dead."

"Dead? You mean I actually hit him?"

"Someone did."

She looked away.

"I just gotta stir things up a bit, make these guys think maybe they did it."

She closed her eyes. "Think it'll do any good?"

"Worth a try." He raised his bow, using the sight to spot the morons, who were circling now, calling for Buddy.

"You're such a thoughtful man," she sighed.

"We've gotta get you to a hospital."

"No. Take me home," she whispered. "It's just down the road. I'll call from there. Tell 'em Buddy did it and then took off."

"You're so smart," he said, "maybe you know what kind of arrows the morons are usin'?"

Her lashes rested wearily on her cheeks. "Same as Buddy and me. They're always losing theirs, having to borrow from him, so he keeps a whole stash of 'em around."

The same kind as hers *should* have been. A different kind from his.

"I'll just be a minute."

He slipped through the trees toward the spot where Buddy lay, sending more of Buddy's arrows in the direction of the morons.

As their voices rose in protest, he mimicked Buddy's voice. "I'm gonna shoot all you jackasses," and shot off one more arrow. As the answering arrows whistled toward him, he slipped into the trees.

He carried her through the noisy woods and the slanting afternoon sun, up onto her back porch, and into the kitchen. Striving not to jar her or bump the arrow.

"This wasn't how I'd planned it," she said.

"No," he said. "I don't guess it was." He didn't know her plan—whether he was supposed to kill Buddy or Buddy was supposed to kill him. Or if it was just supposed to look like he'd killed Buddy. Maybe, if she lived, she'd tell him.

Gently, he laid her down on the floor, dialed 9-1-1, and handed her the phone. When she was done, she let the phone drop. "Buddy's really dead?"

"Yeah."

"I do it?" Her voice was light as a butterfly.

"Probly not. You want your bow and stuff in here with you or somewheres else?"

She tilted her head toward a doorway. "Mudroom closet's good. Maybe . . ." A pause while she found some breath. " . . . the hat, too."

He swung her gear onto his shoulder and plucked the hat off her head. She looked older now, and tired. Still beautiful. She'd said she used to think she could handle Buddy. Had she also believed she could handle him? Was he just supposed to be collateral damage? Whatever it took to leave Buddy?

He saw his thoughts reflected in her eyes. "Hell if I know," she whispered. "Seems like Buddy always wins."

"He only wins if you die."

He put her things in the closet, using his bandana to keep from leaving prints. Searched the floor for bloodspots he might have made, wiping his tracks as he backed toward the door.

"You'd best be getting home, Donnie," she said. "You don't wanna be found here."

Grimacing, she closed her eyes, resting her head against the cupboard. "Thanks for helpin'," she whispered, as he was closing the slider. "You're such a nice guy."

Kate Flora is the author of fourteen books. *Death Dealer* was an Agatha and Anthony nominee. *And Grant You Peace* won the 2015 Maine Literary Award. Flora also writes the Thea Kozak series. She's a former Maine assistant attorney general, a founder of Level Best Books, and was international president of Sisters in Crime. She teaches at Grub Street in Boston.

"Hello?"

Rae Padilla Francoeur

I was closing in on Magallaway's rocky summit when I heard Susan scream.

"Charlie's collapsed!"

Charlie was Susan's dad. He was a fit sixty-five-year-old, though the past year had worn him down. Today promised to be even harder for both father and daughter—and not just because of this hellacious hike.

Hearing Susan's screams snapped me into overdrive. I'd been hanging back, bringing up the rear as I thought about my dead friend, Alyssa, whose ashes we were about to disperse. Each of us—Susan, Charlie, Howard, and I—had a sealed baggie of Alyssa's ashes at the bottom of our daypacks. Her father, sister, husband and I wanted to bring her back to her favorite spot on earth and let her go one last time.

We slogged through a torturous year to get to this one-year anniversary of Alyssa's passing. Her death by hypothermia was, according to the country prosecutor, a most cruel murder. The trial, thankfully behind us, was polarizing. Finally, we had the bandwidth to think about Alyssa, her ashes, and what she would have wanted.

Now her father was in trouble. Another 200 yards and I'd be there to help. I could hear Susan's excited voice but I didn't dare rush. The granite was icy and a misstep now could be catastrophic. It was 4,238 feet straight down and everybody knew Coot Trail was a proven killer. I pushed and panted my way upward, hoping and praying Charlie was going to be okay.

Though it was only fifteen degrees when we started out this

morning, it took less than five minutes to strip down to our base layers. It might be mid-December but climbing uphill with lunch, ashes, and water on my back was hard work. In no time hikers overheat and dehydrate. If they aren't dressed properly, hypothermia is a real threat. Charlie wasn't the first to collapse on this heart-pumper of a hike. Look what happened to Alyssa.

I heard Susan's cries clearly now. I was almost there. I resorted to hands and knees, and scrambled to the top. There lay Charlie, clumped in a heap on his back. Susan and Howard knelt on either side of him.

"Susan, how's your dad?" I called. I was breathless and could barely get the words out so I repeated myself. "How's Charlie?"

"I think he fainted," Susan said as I knelt beside her. "One minute he was fine, the next he just slumped to the ground." She tucked his parka around him and straightened his legs.

Howard had his hand on Charlie's neck, feeling for a pulse.

This must be like déjà vu for Howard. Alyssa's husband had been found innocent of her murder just last week. As a posthumous gift to my oldest and dearest friend, I swallowed my discomfort and my doubts and took on the job of Howard's defense attorney. Pro bono. It was the least I could do for my friend, even if Charlie and Susan weren't keen on the idea. They, too, had their doubts about Howard. The prosecutor claimed Howard let Alyssa freeze to death. She died on December 15th in a fierce snow squall right here on Magallaway's summit.

We all knew Howard's story was suspicious and, on top of that, we thought he was a jerk. In Howard's world, it was all Howard all the time. But Alyssa never complained. We shared a law practice and it was her nature to take on tough cases involving the down-and-out. Howard, a sporting goods store manager down in Colebrook, wasn't exactly a loser on paper but that's how he looked. Only the most compassionate among us would bother to give Howard a second glance. Alyssa was a saint.

Even she needed a release valve.

No one knew Magallaway better than she did. This mountain was her touchstone and her inspiration. "It lifts me to God," she used to say. She hiked the Coot Trail with strength, grace, and ease at least once a week till the snow got too deep. Somehow she got surprised and disoriented by the squall, called Howard, and asked him to come up with her parka and some water. Or so Howard said.

Alyssa blindsided by a storm? Never. Of course the police suspected Howard.

He said he got to the top but couldn't find her anywhere. By then, the squall had turned to a blizzard. He called me because I'm a volunteer EMT.

"There's nothing I can do. I can't find Alyssa anywhere." He was frantic.

I asked him where he was.

"On top of Magallaway. But I can't stay here any longer. I'll freeze to death."

We found her body later that night, fetal, frozen in plain view beside the fire tower. By then the snow had let up and Howard was home in bed.

The jury was sympathetic. Howard was inconsolable. And New Hampshire's northernmost mountain, like Mount Washington, was benevolent one minute, hostile the next. You never knew. Risk loomed at every turn in the North Country and people up here got it.

I took Charlie's pulse and made sure he stayed covered. I raised his feet and loosened his boots. Howard and Susan scooted back a tad and let me work.

"I think he's okay," I said.

We sat silently, Charlie's hands in ours, as we heard a raven's ragged squawk echo over the Connecticut River Valley, all the way to Maine, Canada and Vermont. We were at the top of world.

Nobody spoke for a long minute.

Then Charlie stirred. "Good," said Howard. "He's got a strong pulse."

"But we need to get him down. Fast," I said. "He's in danger of hypothermia at this point."

"Howard," I said, "call an EMT. Call Pete, he's the one with the sled."

But Howard held to his crouch, pulling Charlie's jacket tighter around him.

"Let's get Pete up here," I said. "We don't want Charlie to have to try and get down on his own. It's too icy."

Howard wasn't moving. What was up with him?

"Hey. Help me out here. This could be serious." My patience with Howard had long since run out.

"Lost my phone on the way up." Howard looked nervous, agitated.

"Are you okay?" He'd been through hell. Maybe this was just the last straw. First his wife. Now his father-in-law. I finished taking off Charlie's boots so I could warm his feet.

"Howard?" Now Susan was looking at him. "Howard, what the hell?" Susan was angry.

"Here's my phone. Pete's number is right there on the screen. Call him." Her tone was oddly hostile.

Up here, everybody has emergency numbers in their contacts. Things go wrong. Your foot wedges between two rocks in an icy river in mid-cast. The trout gets away but you're stuck. Or your snowmobile runs out of gas. Or, unexpected childbirth, like what happened to Sally Jacobsen when picking blueberries at Third Connecticut Lake. North of the 45th parallel, the cell towers looked like giant white pines. The pols, dignitaries, foreign princes and celebrities who hunted and fished here had to have their cells, their WiFi and their 472 channels of television.

"Susan," I snapped. "Stop this. You make the call."

"I tried."

"Try again."

"No signal." Susan was still staring at Howard.

"What do you mean, no signal?" It was as if somebody'd knocked the wind out of me. No signal?

I thought back to the trial, how Alyssa was caught in the blizzard and how Howard claimed that she called him for help. By the time he'd arrived, she had gone missing in the whiteout. All she had on was a long-sleeved T-shirt and jeans. Howard said she hadn't dressed for bad weather. He related all this on his phone from the top of Magallaway.

Charlie stirred, squeezed my hands, opened his eyes.

Hallelujah.

"Hey there, Charlie," I said. "How you doin'?" I squeezed back.

"What the hell?" Charlie looked around. "What happened?"

"You fainted," said Susan. "But you're okay, now, Dad."

"Something's wrong," he said.

"What's wrong," I said, "is we can't call for help."

"There's no service up here," said Susan, looking over at Howard, who was now standing.

Howard straightened. Locked eyes with me.

"Come on, Howard," I said. "Let's see you call for help, like you said Alyssa did that day."

Howard shrugged. "So she didn't make the call. So what?"

"So . . ." We seemed to be searching for the problem. It was there, but we just couldn't quite put our finger on it.

"So," I pressed, "how did you know where she was? How did you know to come here? And, as the prosecution asked you, how come this experienced woodswoman wore nothing more than a T-shirt in sub-freezing conditions?"

Howard shrugged. "She could have died anywhere. I gave her a choice."

Charlie, who'd managed to get to his feet, faced Howard. "You miserable worm. You killed my little girl. We loved you like a son."

"Spare me."

"I'll see you in civil court. You'll wish you were dead by the time I get through with you."

Howard smiled and jerked his head north. "There's more than one path down this mountain. That way," he pointed off to his right, "takes me into Canada. I've got a hunting camp there and a stash. Had it for years. I'm set for life, old man."

But just as he spoke, a blast of wind nearly knocked the lot of us off our feet. Predatory black clouds, looming all day, swept in like the beating wings of the raven. In seconds, Magallaway was wrapped in a ferocious gale.

And in that instant, Howard made his move. I watched as he disappeared down a little-used spur off the Coot Trail. Gone in a flash. The spur he'd taken veered east, a tough plunge into Maine thickets too dense for moose. There would be no cabin, no stash, no rescue squad in that direction. Disoriented, he'd taken the wrong path.

"Funny how things turn out," Charlie shouted, leaning toward

Susan and me so we could hear him over the winds on the wide-open top of this amazing mountain on this auspicious day. "He's about to find out firsthand what Alyssa went through."

We pulled the ashes from our daypacks and stepped closer still, tightening our circle. One at a time, we released Alyssa's ashes.

We looked up in wonder. Ashes, snow and icy fog swirled and lifted to the heavens, where all matter mingled and realigned, anew.

Read **Rae Padilla Francoeur's** memoir, *Free Fall: A Late-in-Life Love Affair* and her weekly book reviews published by *GateHouse Media*. She's a journalist and editor who's managed both newspapers and magazines. She writes fiction and nonfiction, and runs New Arts Collaborative, an arts/culture/tourism marketing business. She blogs at www.FreeFallRae.blogspot.com.

The Wrinkle Curse

Ruth M. McCarty

Beatrice Flanagan stood naked in front of the full-length mirror attached to the back of her bedroom door. Her body sagged and drooped in all the expected places for a seventy-five-year-old. Beatrice could live with the body; it was her face that concerned her the most.

She'd been a smoker for nearly fifty years and each cigarette had carved a crevice in her once beautiful skin. Smoking had seemed so sexy then. So Lauren Bacall. She raised her liver-spotted hands to her face. Even without her glasses, she could see the destruction her lifestyle had etched. Her mother had warned her about smoking, and gardening without a hat and gloves. Silly old woman, she'd thought then. Can't she see how beautiful my tan is?

Now, she thought, they could make a pocketbook out of me.

After she dressed, Beatrice sat at her kitchen table with a cup of tea and an untouched slice of toast. She tried to smooth out the wrinkled piece of paper she'd just retrieved from her kitchen wastebasket. Could she do it?

Two weeks earlier she'd been sitting in the air-conditioned shopping mall watching people and killing time until she'd have to head back home to watch her favorite soap opera.

"Beatrice, don't you recognize me?" the smiling young woman standing before her shouted.

I'm not deaf, Beatrice thought as she scrutinized the woman. She prided herself on her memory, especially for faces, but she honestly didn't recognize the woman. Except for her teeth. Somehow, she recognized her smile, which didn't make sense.

"Beatrice, it's me, Lilly."

"Lilly who?" Beatrice had asked.

The woman calling herself Lilly let out a deep-chested laugh that Beatrice would have recognized anywhere. "But, it can't be," she'd said. "You look like you're thirty-five!"

The woman sat beside her. She must be dreaming! Lilly was her age. The sounds of children crying and mothers talking echoed around her bench. She could smell the pretzels cooking at Auntie Anne's kiosk and the garlic from the pizza restaurant across the food court. She pinched her arm. No, she really was wide awake.

"It's a miracle," Lilly whispered.

"How?" Beatrice searched Lilly's face for telltale signs of a face-lift but couldn't find anything. No stitches. No redness. No bruises. She even looked behind Lilly's ears. Nothing. "This can't be. I just saw you at bingo on Monday night. No offense, but you looked every bit of your seventy-five years and then some."

Lilly just smiled. "This is only day three! By Friday, I'll look like I'm eighteen. Beatrice, it's a miracle!"

"Where can I buy it?" she'd begged.

"I can give you a name and a phone number. But Beatrice, it's going to cost you a lot of money."

"How much?"

"Remember, there's no anesthesia, no cutting, no bruises, no pain."

"How much?"

"Fifty thousand dollars."

Beatrice nearly fell off her bench. She couldn't afford that kind of money. She'd have to use all her life savings. "But, Lilly, how did you find out about this wrinkle cure?"

"My cousin from Brooklyn. She called every day to tell me about how much younger she looked. She even sent pictures, but they were lost in the mail. But the poor thing, she slipped and fell onto the sub-way's third rail on the fifth day of the wrinkle cure. She never even had the chance to enjoy her new looks."

On Friday evening, Beatrice dialed Lilly's number. She had to see the results! Lilly had said she would look like an eighteen-year-old, but when Lilly's daughter had answered the phone, Beatrice knew right away that she'd been crying.

"Haven't you heard? My mother died this afternoon. A car accident. She went right through the windshield."

At the wake on Monday, Beatrice had hoped to get a close-up look at Lilly's face, but the casket was closed due to her injuries. Poor Lilly, she thought. She didn't get to enjoy her miracle cure.

Now, two weeks later Beatrice retrieved the name and number and placed the call. A low raspy voice with a Hungarian accent answered, "Madam Mariska."

"Lilly gave me your number," Beatrice said into the phone. "I want to buy your wrinkle cure."

She waited for an eternity before the woman solemnly answered. "You know the cost. Ya?"

"Yes," Beatrice answered.

They arranged to meet in the park across from the bank where Beatrice, against the manager's wishes, had requested a treasurer's check in the amount of fifty thousand dollars, payable to cash.

It was only ten o'clock in the morning and the temperature had reached nearly eighty degrees. While she waited, Beatrice closed her eyes and raised her face to the sun god for probably the last time. She opened them as a young woman sat down next to her.

"Madam Mariska?" she asked.

"Ya."

She recognized the raspy voice from the phone. The woman was beautiful. She had light olive skin that glowed from within and shiny, waist-length black hair.

"May I ask you how old you are?" Beatrice whispered.

"Ninety-one, last month."

"But that's impossible!" Madam Mariska looked twenty, tops. "Can you tell me what's in the cream?"

Mariska shook her head. "It is a secret passed down from my ancestors. We are gypsies. We cannot stay in one area too long because people would wonder why we never age. We ask for the *small fee* to keep traveling around the world, so everyone thinks we are a new generation when we return."

Beatrice hadn't thought about that. What would she tell her friends? She could sell her house in Durham and keep on the move. She could meet new people, make new friends. She smiled, and with her wrinkled hands took the check out of her pocketbook.

Madam Mariska pulled a small tube from her sleeve.

Beatrice balked at the size. "But, it's so small."

Mariska gave her a sullen look. "Okay, if you do not want it, someone else will."

"No." Beatrice grabbed for it and handed over the check. "I want it."

"It's only enough for your face and your hands."

Beatrice looked down at the tiny tube. When she looked up, Madam Mariska was turning the corner. Beatrice thought she moved pretty fast for a ninety-one-year-old.

That night, Beatrice squeezed what she thought was one fifth of the tube into her palm. She meticulously applied the cream, first around her eyes, then over the deep lines around her mouth. She applied a dab on her cheeks and forehead. Then she rubbed the remainder onto her hands. Carefully, she made sure she had covered each liver spot.

The next morning she reached for her glasses and the mirror she'd put on her nightstand. Her heart did a back flip as she noticed the lines on her lips had improved. She burst into tears. It had worked. She looked at least ten years younger. She looked at the hand holding the mirror. The spots had faded! She jumped from the bed, showered, and dressed, then headed to the mall to do some shopping. She was going to need a much younger wardrobe to go along with her face.

Tuesday night she rubbed the miracle cream into her face and hands. On Wednesday morning, she couldn't contain her excitement at the change. It worked! It was worth every penny of the fifty thousand dollars. She felt like a new woman.

That night, she hailed a cab. Dressed in black pants and a brand new purple silk blouse, she walked up to the bar at the Holiday Inn and ordered a very dry martini. She looked into the mirror behind the bar and raised the glass to the beautiful woman looking back at her. She drained the glass, and laughed out loud as a fine-looking man sat down beside her and asked if he could buy her another. "No," she smiled. "I've got places to go and things to do."

On Thursday, she packed her new clothes into her suitcase. She had priced her house to sell and the first person her realtor brought to see it gave her a ten-thousand-dollar deposit. Now she had spending money. "I've been transferred to the West Coast," she'd told the realtor. "I'll open a bank account once I'm settled so the proceeds can be wire transferred."

When he said, "Funny, you don't look like a Beatrice," she just laughed.

On Friday, her fifth day, she cried. Her face was beautiful. Not a wrinkle, not even the hint of a worry line. And her hands! They were like a baby's. Not a liver spot. Not even a freckle, and the veins had tightened so she could hardly see them. She turned them over, looked at her palms. Not a line. She looked closer.

Not even a lifeline.

She picked up her suitcase and headed to the airport.

Ruth M. McCarty's short mysteries have appeared in Level Best anthologies and in *Over My Dead Body! The Mystery Magazine*. She won the 2009 Derringer for Best Flash Story for "No Flowers for Stacey" published in *Deadfall: Crime Stories by New England Writers*. She is former editor at Level Best Books, a past president of the New England chapter of Sisters in Crime, and a member of Mystery Writers of America. www.ruthmccarty.com

Lawyers, Drugs and Money

Alan Vogel

How do you discover your wife is cheating on you? Is it a fully formed belief that strikes from out of the blue, a sort of gestalt? Is it through a projection of your own infidelities, if indeed you have been unfaithful, which compel you to believe that she too has been with another? Or is it a mounting of the evidence, a gathering of the little things that eventually gain weight and convert suspicion into certainty. Or perhaps it is simply when she tells you, when she looks in your eyes and says, "I am having an affair."

Which brings me to my wife Anne. How did I find out she was, shall we say, involved? Our relationship, to my way of thinking, was deep and trusting. We liked each other, showed one another real affection. We'd been married for fifteen years, weren't overly possessive, and neither gave the other cause to feel jealous, ignored, or pushed aside. We were open and honest. In light of what happened I obviously need to add that I believed all those things to be true.

We had no children. This was our choice and when Anne turned forty she did so without regret. Last year when I turned fifty, like her, I didn't succumb to late life parenting urges as so many men seem to these days.

Have I ever been with another woman while with Anne? If I had, but she didn't know, it wouldn't have had anything to do with Anne's infidelity. But it could certainly color my perceptions of why she did what she did, and because of that I will confess that, no, I have never cheated on Anne.

So, what was it? How did I know? How did she give herself away? Certainly not by any of the well worn clichés. I'll leave it at a sudden glance away, a sentence begun, but only that. I simply followed the crumbs she'd dropped . . . all the way to Richard's house. Maybe Anne mentioned his name in passing, maybe not. As I said, the facts surrounding this affair were simply so slippery and innocuous, that his name just . . . was. A name I somehow knew.

I've neglected to say that at the time all this happened, my high earning years were behind me. I was still making rain, but rain is subjective in the practice of law, and my partners, for whatever reasons, put enough pressure on me that to this day I'm not quite certain whether I was forced out or left voluntarily. The entire experience soured me on the practice. I suppose I was burned out anyway and by the time I learned about Anne I really wasn't doing much more than some court-appointed criminal, juvenile, and domestic cases, which were satisfying, but the pay was minimal and quite delayed.

Anne never complained. As luck would have it, her gallery was taking off, so as my ship was slowly sliding into port, hers was happily gliding into lucrative new waters. In hindsight, it was inevitable there was a change of pressure within the family unit.

Day after day my thoughts circled in an unending loop. Did Richard bring anything to the table other than sex? I needed to confront him, pay him a visit and find out firsthand. No Glock automatic, no irate husband out for blood and justice or at the very least a leveraged position in a divorce. I simply wanted to know exactly what was what, and I wasn't prepared to confront Anne. Richard struck me as the proper vector for my curiosity, and yes, I admit, my anger.

I stood, thinking all this over when I noticed Anne's cell phone on the kitchen table. An odd place, as it was normally in her purse or attached to her ear. A green text bubble was centered on the screen.

"Tonight? Usual place?" It read. And the name: Richard Stone.

It was as if this man and I were in the same room, and I picked up her phone without hesitation.

"Where are you?" I texted.

"Home from 2:00 to 4:00. The usual place?"

"I want to talk to you. Now."

"Why?"

"About the affair you're having with my wife."

"Who is this?"

"Take a guess, asshole."

I googled Richard Stone and got an address in a working class neighborhood on the Norwalk border. I was surprised. It was not what I'd consider Anne territory. She was definitely more of a tony Westport woman.

I had no idea what I'd say and kept my mind blank while I drove, and after I parked in front of his house, and while I walked up the front walk. Right until I was ready to knock on Richard's door. It was in that moment when I felt the hurt, the deep betrayal and sadness overwhelm me. Like a wave.

I knocked harshly, with the authority of the Stasi at 4:00 AM. The knock that cannot be ignored. When he answered, and I assumed it was Richard who answered, he looked at me with a puzzled look. As if he hadn't expected me.

I said, "My name is Max," and I could tell from his expression that he knew exactly who I was.

He smiled. "Come in," he said pulling the door open, letting it swing wide on its own, as if he had nothing in the world to hide. "I'm Richard," he said, and offered me his hand. I took it because as angry as I felt, a refusal would have diminished me.

We stood pretty much eye to eye, though he was a bit taller, with the lean body type of a runner and long straight dark hair, parted in the middle, falling to his shoulders. I thought about hitting him, in his face, no words, no warning. But if that sort of thing is going to happen it has to be instantaneous, and the moment passed in the time it took to think it.

"You know why I'm here," I said straight off. I had no interest in dancing.

He nodded that he did, turned and walked into the room, gesturing me to follow by raising his hand in a modified "wagon's ho" gesture.

He sat on a couch with a rectangular coffee table in front of it. The table's surface was covered with pills and scales and large pharmaceutical bottles. Clearly he'd brought me into the room in order to see the very thing most people would chose to hide. If he'd wanted to throw me off balance he'd done a damn good job of it.

"Sit," he said, gesturing at an armchair to the side of the couch. Looking around I noted that the room was bare but for these three pieces of furniture: the couch, the table, the chair, all curiously old-fashioned colonial.

He tossed me a large white bottle which I instinctively caught. I looked at the label:

500 Percocet; Generic Name acetaminophen/oxycodone; Strength(s) 325 mg-10 mg

There were five more bottles on the table. Next to them an equal number of jars labeled Oxycontin 80mg.

"You're a lawyer, huh?" It wasn't really a question. And it completely ignored the fact that he'd thrown me an illegal bottle of narcotics, which I, for some reason, held onto.

"You know I am," I said.

"But you're not making a whole lot of money these days. Are you? What's up with that?"

"None of your damn business." My voice tightening with each word.

A friendly smile. "Sorry man, didn't mean nothing by it, really. I didn't." He dropped the pill cutter and picked up one of the bottles. "Brand, baby blue. Hard to get these babies even with a prescription on account of the insurance companies. It's a generic world, my friend, a generic world."

I was completely turned around. I came to confront the man who was having an affair with my wife and somehow he both disarmed and insulted me, then seemed intent on engaging me in pharmaceutical policy.

"I'm sorry," he said while still looking down at the bottles and the scale.

I stared at him. "About?"

"About me and your wife. It's wrong and it's not something I've ever done."

"And I'm supposed to say what to this?"

He shrugged. "I have no idea. I just wish it never happened. And it's over. I promise. It's over."

"Just like that," I said.

He looked up. "Yes. That's what she said. Your wife. Anne. That it's over. I suppose in a way I was glad. I'm too weak to have ended it." He stopped. Then added, "I promise, man." He raised his hand a bit, reminded me of a schoolboy.

"How long? I asked.

"Not long. We met, then ran into each other a few times. I was absolutely blindsided by the intensity of the attraction. I hadn't felt anything like it in a long time. Years, decades. So, you go with it, you know? What else you gonna do? You get what I'm talking about?" He didn't wait for a reply. His thoughts were not in the room. "We had a drink. Then met for another. And again. Everything, for me at least, got ratcheted up. But sex. Twice. Only twice."

"And I should believe this," I said.

"You can believe whatever you want. But I can tell you that what I'm saying is the truth and that you don't have to make yourself crazy unless that's what you need to do. Your wife is wonderful and she's yours. Believe me. She is yours." He gave out a short laugh. "Wish she wasn't. Wish she would run away with me. But what I wish doesn't matter cause she won't. Like I said, she is yours. I was a fling, that's all."

He stood up and walked out of the room. I sat where I was, holding the bottle and thinking about what he'd said. The manner in which this entire meeting had unfolded was confusing and my emotions were mixed. I wanted to hate this guy Richard but I couldn't. I wanted to believe him, but I didn't. Yet I did believe the substance of what he'd said, because I believe if something did happen between Anne and another man the way he claimed it happened and the way he claimed it ended felt right to me.

I began to think about how I'd use what I'd learned with Ann. Whether to let the entire affair drift away into the ether or confront and forgive her in one simple narrative. For a moment I thought about hurting her emotionally before putting it behind us. The only thing I knew for certain was that it would be put in the past, that I wouldn't let a single incident destroy our relationship.

When I think back on this episode I have no idea why I didn't wonder where Richard Stone had gone, or how long it'd been since he'd left. What stands out in my memory is what happened next. The sounds, the shouting, the violent immediacy of the police with their guns and their blue windbreaker jackets and their cursing and their demanding that I get down on the ground, that I show my hands, that I shut the fuck up, repeating it over and over like a cop mantra. I did what they said, confused and angry, hoping not to be shot dead in

Richard Stone's house.

My arms were pulled behind me with a force which should have dislocated my shoulders. I was barraged with questions. Every time I spoke they yelled at me, told me not to be a smart ass, yet at the same time they urged me to talk and explain myself, purge myself of my obvious guilt. They'd somehow ascertained I was a lawyer, yet continued to tell me how much better things would go for me if I talked to them. This reinforced my belief that either they watched too much television or simply just shouted what the guy next to them shouted, like dogs who bark simply because the other dogs are barking.

I ignored it all and did what the situation demanded. I said I wanted an attorney and nothing more, ignoring all their reasons why I should tell them what they wanted to know. I ignored them because, as an attorney, I knew I should ignore them, that answering them would do me no good, TV cops be damned. And because of the contempt in their voices and what I learned about their case from their questions. What was I doing in this house? How long had I been selling drugs, who was my supplier, and on and on. Suddenly fidelity wasn't the question. The question was why had I been set up? And by whom?

No reason to go through all the details. Too painful. Bottom line—I took the deal because the evidence against me was too strong and the time I could have gotten had I rolled the dice with a jury was simply too much to consider. The house was part of a sting and Richard Stone, a detective, set me up. Truth be told, I have no idea if that was even his real name. I have no idea why he set me up. Or what exactly Anne knew about any of it. But I do know that he set me up as a dealer of stolen prescription drugs. And this Richard Stone must have had a lot of juice. He got a supplier who was already in prison to testify that he'd sold me large lots of drugs on a number of occasions and two mid-level dealers (one currently working on the third of a seven-year stint, the other on the first of a nickel) to testify that they'd bought pills from me. Immunity and sentence reduction can work wonders.

You'd think I'd be confident a jury would see through this ruse.

But I'd learned early in my career that juries act from a sort of ersatz group logic that may or may not have much or indeed anything to do with the law. So I ended up taking the offer of three to five years in state prison. And disbarment. My wife was conspicuously absent during my ordeal. Bail was higher than it should have been, but it's the luck of the draw when it comes to which judge hears your bail reduction motion and luck was not on my side. On the positive side I had long-standing ties to the community, I was not a flight risk, and I'd immediately surrendered my passport. But the prosecution argued that the fact I didn't have children or living parents, let alone a significant place in the legal community belied my argument of ties to the community and my career slide provided additional motivation to leave the area. The result was that I spent the pre-trial months in the county lockup. Anne visited me twice. Once to tell me she loved me. The second to tell me it was too painful for her to see me anymore.

How well do you know your wife?

I was able to survive in prison, something I didn't think I'd be able to do the day I walked in and a thick metal door closed behind me before a similar one opened in front. It was loud and bright, and I was trapped and frightened. I came in on a Thursday and on Friday I figured if ever there was a time for religion, this was it, and I attended Friday night Shabbat services. A very good move. Not to stereotype, but many of the Jewish inmates were former professionals; attorneys, doctors, accountants—a Jewish mother's wet dream. I was immediately taken in and introduced around.

Turns out we know about the Aryan Brotherhood, the Black and Latino gangs, but we hear very little about the Jewish inmates. Some of the lawyers and accountants had prior relationships with the Italian mob as well as some of the more financially sophisticated gang members. As a result, these guys were, for the most part, able to protect the other Jewish inmates through a web of favors owed, friendships formed over the years, and current services rendered.

Over the next year I established myself as one of the go-to prison lawyers. Most jailhouse lawyers were amateurs who spent their days in the law library pouring over statutes and case law for themselves and other inmates. I was a bone fide, experienced litigation attorney. Also, aside from my affiliation with the "Jewish Brotherhood," I was an old man given the prison demographic, so they called me Pops and for the most part I didn't have to worry about a shiv between my ribs, or any of the aggressive sexual behavior we hear so much about.

One day an old timer named Morey, Americanized from Moritz, walked up to me in the yard. He looked like the kind of aging synagogue regular able to read the Torah at the speed of light, having memorized large sections of it. And he was, in fact, that man. He was also doing life without parole for murder. Seems he killed his business partner, a young guy just out of school who tried to push Morey out the business he'd started. Morey once mentioned that his life might be ruined, but at least he wasn't moldering somewhere in the swamps of Jersey. That in the end one of them was going to end up there, and Morey was glad it wasn't him. Would he rather be free? I believe that goes without saying, but we play the hand we're dealt in this life. Every con knows this. Those that don't lose everything, including their minds.

He gestured me off to the side. " Kid," he said, "you got a bum deal."

"No kidding," I said. "Tell me one guy in this place doesn't feel the same way."

He shook his head, like I wasn't getting the point. "I don't think you know exactly what it was happened to you."

"And you're going to tell me?"

"If you like."

I nodded.

"Seems the cop, and maybe your wife set you up, figuring you'd get clipped in jail, a nice Jewish boy like you. Bound to happen. Right?"

"She's my wife. An affair, that's one thing. What you're talking about? Very different. No way my wife would do this to me."

"Maybe it wasn't her, just the cop. Or maybe both of them. Doesn't really matter, does it, kid? But you had plenty of life insurance, right? She knew about it, and so her cop friend knew about it. He probably engineered the whole thing. Maybe he figured when the life insurance money dropped in her lap, what was she going to do, give it back? Who knows?"

I said nothing, filled with disgust and crushed by a suffocating sense of betrayal.

"But you survived. Because you're protected," Morey continued, "And so now things have been taken a step further."

"How?"

"Suffice to say your days on this beautiful earth are numbered in the single digits."

I was numb. How could my world, already upside down, continue to invert, implode, and perhaps worse, how could a lifetime of belief reveal itself as nothing more than delusion?   .

"Why would he do this?" I asked. Then added in a whisper, "Or them? Why would they do this? It's too elaborate."

Morey just shook his head. "Why? Because it's clean. Because people get murdered in prison all the time. And their killers are on the inside which is a very convenient alibi for the guy on the outside who sets it up."

His logic was solid. Didn't make me feel any better, but it made sense.

"So," Morey asked. "What do you want to do?"

"Do?"

"I understand. You're in shock. But you're also in prison where men who don't act decisively die. You have a choice."

"I have a choice?" My voice was flat. Words for their own sake.

"Yes. You get the inmate who's been paid to clip you to talk to the guy who's paying him. He should tell that guy you'll pay them more if he kills the cop. More money for both of them if the cop dies than if you do. It's business is all it is. Like anything else. He can also do your wife. I mean what kind of woman . . ."

"My wife?"

"Sure. Money's not an issue here. She's got life insurance also, right? Don't worry, you pay us when you get out. We know you're good for it, boychick."

My wife, I thought.

How well can you know another person? How well, in fact, do you know yourself?

Alan Vogel, a former Connecticut attorney, currently lives and writes in Northampton, Massachusetts. He was the host of the radio show "Lit103.3; fiction for the ears" on WXOJ-FM. The show featured fiction readings, excerpts, and talk about publishing and writing. He was also the co-host of "Swimming with Sharks," a somewhat humorous, yet informative, show about the law.

The Demise of My Wives

Gin Mackey

Sometimes the muse just didn't visit. Balling up another piece of paper filled with words that wouldn't work, I lobbed it into the wastebasket. An easy two points.

All that practice.

Visit? Hell, some days I wondered if she even knew where I lived anymore. Sighing, I got up, went to the bathroom to pee, made more coffee. Three in the morning. Yawning, I walked back into the room that served as my office. A man sat at my worktable. I sucked in breath, stopped short.

He looked at me, calm. "It's okay, Frank. Come on in."

"Who are you?" It wasn't the muse.

"A friend." He smiled.

"My friends usually knock."

His smile evaporated. "Sit down. Or else."

I wanted to say, "Is that a threat?" In fact, I'd always wanted to say that, I'd just never had the opportunity. But there was a gun on the table, so I thought it was implied. Nuance is something I'm working on in my writing. Never been good at it.

I sat. "Take anything you want. I'm a writer. I don't have much."

"You have what I want."

"Which is?"

"I want a story."

I opened a file drawer. "Here, I got a bunch. Any particular kind? Mystery, thriller, sci-fi? Published? Unpublished?" I took out a handful.

"No, I want you to write me a story."

Must have been the look of total bafflement on my face that made him continue.

"My wife's been pissin' me off. I mean royally. Not once. Not twice. On a real regular basis." He gave me a "Women!" look. "I'm good at some things, but not especially, um . . ."

"Creative."

"Yeah, and you're a writer, so I figured you would be."

I glanced at the stories now strewn across the table. Seemed like a fair assumption. But I was glad he hadn't asked how many I'd published. I'd hate to disillusion him. I took in what he was saying. "Oh. So you mean you want me to write a story about something bad happening to your wife?"

"Real bad."

"Like her demise?"

He looked at me, eyes narrowing.

"You want her dead?"

His eyes widened. "O' course. I wan' her as demised as she can get."

"Too bad you don't have two wives you want me to write about."

"Why?"

"The title. It could be, 'The Demise of My Wives.'"

He barked a laugh. "Ooh, I like that. It practically rhymes. I knew I came to the right guy. Hey, throw in my ex-wife. I've never been too fond of her, even when I was married to her."

"Great. You want it macabre?"

"Huh?"

"You know, gruesome. Lots of blood and guts and so forth?"

"Heck, yeah. Lots of that, and with cool ways of doin' 'em in."

"Sure. No problem." I pulled my chair to my computer, opened a new document, and typed in the title at the top of the page. "When do you need it?"

"Right now."

"Now?"

"Yeah. You write it while I wait. I got *The Globe*." He unfolded the Boston paper, scanned the front page.

"But I—"

"What?" He slapped the paper down on his knees.

"Usually I take some time to come up with an idea—"

"You got the idea. I gave it to ya already."

"Right, but usually I write a first draft, then take some time to think about it, revise it, think about it some more, tinker with it—"

"So how long does it usually take?"

"It varies. A week. A month."

"What? For one stinkin' story? Nah, that won't work. You gotta do it now." He picked up the paper. "I look at the obits first. You want I should read a couple out loud? Maybe it'll inspire you?"

"Sure, okay."

He flipped the paper open and folded it back. "Here we go. Let's see, the first dead guy died of an intracranial hemorrhage. Gee, that's too bad. But it does bupkus for us, if ya know what I'm sayin'. Next one's a heart attack. So what else is new? They got a picture. A big fat guy. Wouldn't ya think he woulda seen it comin'? Wow, another brain hemorrhage. That's kinda weird, almost like it's goin' around, you know what I'm sayin'? Cancer. Cancer. Another cancer." He looked up at me. "Story you're writin' would be totally boring if all it was about was just waiting for 'em to croak from cancer."

He took another look at the paper. "Here's a suicide. A lotta that lately, I've noticed. Now here's two little kids, twins. Ohmigod, they drowned in their own pool. Where the heck were the parents? They shoulda been watchin' 'em. Look at this, it's heartbreakin'." A pained expression on his face, he handed me the paper, pointed at the picture. "Is this helping you at all?" he asked, "'cause it's makin' me very sad. Maybe I should turn to the police blotter. Might be more what we're lookin' for."

I closed the paper and handed it back to him. "That's okay."

"I'm Brucie by the way." He extended his hand.

"Brucie?" Shaking his hand, I struggled to suppress a surprised snicker.

"Yeah, that's my name. You wanna see my birth certificate?" he snarled.

"No, it . . . it just doesn't seem to fit."

He rolled his eyes. "I get that all the time. You're the writer. If it makes you feel better, come up with another name. Anything you want." He snapped the paper open and started to read.

What if this was a test? If I didn't come up with a name he liked, he could get really annoyed. Well, he was annoyed already, but he could get more annoyed. Start to really dislike me. When you disliked someone, you started to dislike everything about them. He'd start to question my creativity. And be less inclined to like the story I was writing. That wouldn't be good. Hmm. A name. It should be manly without being a caricature. Joey was definitely out.

Brucie stopped reading, glanced at his watch, glanced at me, started to read again.

Right. The clock was ticking. The story. The story. I needed to concentrate on the story. I glanced at him, glanced at the gun, but the glance turned into a look and then I couldn't tear my eyes away. The more I looked at it, the bigger it seemed. The gun started to glisten.

I started to glisten.

I turned to my keyboard and began writing. I wrote my butt off. Apparently the muse had shown up. I just hadn't expected her to be a guy with a gun who wanted a story. Whatever the reason, I got in the zone, totally into the story. The ideas just kept coming, and I kept typing as fast as I could hit the keys. It was like a movie in my head. I could picture the wives, see all the horrible things happening to them. Brucie had said to go for the gruesome, and I didn't want to disappoint him. The next thing I knew, he was shaking my arm.

"How you doing?" he asked.

It was six in the morning. The story needed a little editing, but I wasn't sure he'd notice. I printed out the pages, handed the story to him.

"Hey, by the way," he said, "I'm just curious. Didja come up with another name for me?"

I'd been so busy writing, I hadn't consciously thought about the name thing. But apparently my mind had been at work on it. I heard myself say, "Your name's Brucie, right? I just changed it up a little, to Bruise Z."

His eyes widened in surprise. "Like Ice T?"

"Ice T. Jay Z. Yeah, like that." I swallowed, watched him consider it, try it on.

"Bruise Z," he said. Then slowly, with menace, "Bruise Z." He nodded. "I like it."

Whew. "Sure beats Brucie." I giggled. I should have just shut up, because he didn't think it was funny. What can I say? I was nervous. He gave me the hairy eyeball, then got interested in the story.

I watched him as he read. He plodded through the first page, looked up at me, read a little more, sat up, started reading faster. At one point he laughed, "Oh, that part on page five, with all the flying body parts, that's really good. See, I never woulda thought of that." He kept flipping pages, reading now as if I wasn't there.

He finished it, put it down. I smiled. I knew he liked it. And I knew it was really good.

"Just one more thing," he said.

"What?"

He picked up the gun. "Now you gotta demise 'em."

Gin Mackey spent years writing for Fortune 500 corporations before finding her passion: writing fiction. Her short story "Swimming Lessons" appeared in the anthology *Fish or Cut Bait.* Gin lives on the coast of Maine, where she's hard at work on her novel *Disappear Our Dead,* featuring Abby Tiernan, a grieving widow turned home funeral guide. Visit Gin at www.ginmackey.com.

Druid Hill

Cheryl Marceau

Verity Warren was painfully reminded, with every jolt of the coach, that she was traveling to a remote corner of the Massachusetts Bay Colony.

Her arduous journey ended at last at the Conant farm on a warm June afternoon.

She hadn't seen her young cousin Mary since her wedding to Roger Conant, when Mary and Roger left for their home on the frontier. Mary's invitation a fortnight ago had been cryptic and urgent, pleading with Verity to come to them but giving no reason. Verity could not deny a kinswoman in need. Neither could she deny her powerful curiosity.

She conjured a thousand stories behind Mary's invitation, all of them dire, so it was with relief that she greeted her cousin at last. Mary's figure had filled out since her wedding and she appeared healthy and strong, none the worse for frontier life. Her ruddy cheeks and hearty laugh had once reminded Verity of her own dear father, eldest brother to Mary's father. Mary still looked like her uncle, but her laughter was not in evidence now.

As soon as they welcomed her into their rustic one-room house, Mary exchanged a guilty glance with her husband. "You are the answer to our prayers, cousin."

The three sat at the table that evening, eating their supper of salted cod, boiled potatoes, and asparagus from the kitchen garden.

"I've waited long enough to ask," Verity said. "Why did you

summon me?"

"We've not yet been blessed with a child. Twice I felt life quicken inside me, but it came to naught each time. Last autumn I carried a child to term, but the life was gone from her before she was delivered." Mary rubbed her rounded belly. "As you have surely guessed by now, I am in a family way again. My confinement will come in four or five months' time. I can't bear to lose another child."

"It isn't right my good wife should have suffered so," Roger said. "There's no finer woman in Massachusetts Bay." He swigged ale from his tankard. "The minister says it's God's will, but I think not."

"Cousin," Mary said, "I'll speak more plainly. Some say we're cursed, that there can be no other explanation. If that be so, I beg you to end it."

"You shouldn't repeat that gossip," Roger said.

"I have no power over evil. Surely you know that." Verity peered into Mary's face, hoping to see comprehension. "I'm a midwife and a healer. That's all."

"Why can I not have a child, when there are women of little virtue, who have no such difficulty? Why have I been singled out? I do as the Bible says, never have I broken a commandment, yet others who are not troubled by such scruples are blessed while I have been cursed." Mary burst into tears. "You've worked your powers before. You must make this right!"

Verity wrapped Mary in a warm embrace, desiring to comfort her and at the same time to make her see reason. The only powers Verity possessed were learning and medicine. She doubted there was a midwife here on the frontier with half her own experience or skill. If Mary were to have a healthy baby, no local midwife would suffice.

The next morning, Verity walked to the village. If she were going to live with her cousin for several months, she would want to know her new neighbors. She strolled about the township, paying her respects, chatting with passersby who greeted her in the street, and pausing in the shops to admire the wares.

Verity saved her most important call for last, stopping at the parsonage to pay her respects to the minister.

Reverend Ward welcomed her. "Mrs. Conant is fortunate that

you came, Mrs. Warren. She has had a difficult time. I believed she must have harbored sinful thoughts, for the Lord to punish her so, but perhaps she has atoned and will now be well."

"My cousin is no sinner, Mr. Ward." Verity paused, while a young woman brought in a tea tray and served them both. She's too old to be his daughter, Verity thought, guessing the young minister's age, and I think she is not his wife. The woman hovered for a moment.

"Thank you, Miss Emerson," said Ward, dismissing her. The servant nodded and left the room.

Verity heard her retreating footsteps, but from the sound, suspected the servant did not go far. "As I was saying, sir, my cousin has neither done nor thought anything sinful in her life."

"That may be," said the minister. "We will know in the fullness of time, will we not?"

Verity thought about nothing but her conversation with Reverend Ward as she made her way back to the farm, trying one argument after another to rebut his smug piety. She heard heavy footfalls on the sun-baked dirt road just as she reached the Conants' front step.

"Mistress!"

In the next instant, the minister's servant stood before her, flushed and breathing heavily from her exertion.

"It's Druid Hill you'll be wanting."

"Why? What is there?" Verity asked

"They say . . . no, perhaps you should see for yourself." She gave directions best understood by someone who had spent a lifetime in the area. Before Verity had time to ask more, the young woman was already walking back to the village.

Verity determined at once to set out for Druid Hill. The rough directions proved more difficult to follow even than she'd imagined. I'm certain I've seen that tree once already, she thought, trying to get her bearings but unable to tell the direction of the sun for the high canopy of leaves. All the while she imagined what she might see when she finally found the place. The name conjured images from stories her father had told when she was a young girl. He once showed her pictures in a book, of a stone circle in Salisbury said to have been sacred to the Druids. He told terrible tales of pagan rites in that circle.

Finally, as Verity began to fear she was truly lost in the wood, she realized she had found the last landmark described by the servant. With great curiosity, and more than a little apprehension, she arrived at Druid Hill.

She spied a circle of standing stones as she crested the hill, and caught sight of an enormous stone slab. In the warm sunshine of a summer afternoon, the place seemed quite peaceful. Oak trees grew here, sacred to the Druids according to the old lore. Of course, there are oaks everywhere, she told herself, this means nothing. Yet she didn't recall seeing them elsewhere.

Verity could imagine the hilltop a lovely place to build a cottage and a small garden, quiet and calm, away from the intrusions of village life. She circled around the stone pillars first, admiring the views of distant hills through the trees, before turning toward the stone slab. She could see something atop it, but couldn't make out what it was.

A tremor of fear ran through her as she got near enough to see well.

It was a hare, slit down the center and splayed open, its lifeblood drained out and congealed on the stone.

Perhaps, she thought, as she inched nearer to inspect the hare, there is evil here after all.

Roger greeted her when she returned to the farm at last, and handed her a tankard of cider, cool from the cellar. "Have you had a profitable day?"

"I walked about the village," she said, "and paid my respects to Reverend Ward. And I went to Druid Hill."

Mary sat on the back step, hulling strawberries. At the mention of Druid Hill she paled and dropped her knife. "You should not have gone. You may have caused more harm than you know!"

"Mary is right," Roger said, becoming agitated. "Could you not see it was evil?"

Verity hesitated. If she told them about the hare, Roger would be certain to keep her from returning, and she was determined to return. She'd been shaken by the sight, but now that she was over the shock, she wanted to explore further. "It's a fine place to view the countryside," she said. "I found it quite pleasant."

"I'm curious about the stones on Druid Hill."

Verity waited until after supper that night, when she and Mary were cleaning up, to revisit the subject. Roger had gone to tend to the animals. "Someone must have taken some trouble to place them there, especially the monstrous slab."

Mary shook her head. "You cannot leave well enough alone, can you?"

"Don't you want to know more? It is a wondrous mysterious place."

"If it be the work of Druids, better that we not speak of them. If it be others, what does it matter if we know? Perhaps native people put them there. We have no need to go up that hill, and no need to care what is at the top."

Verity wondered at Mary's attitude. Why was she not curious? "Who in these parts can tell me more about it?"

Roger returned in time for the last of their conversation. "About what?"

"Cousin Warren and I were talking about the farm. She asked how we came to own it." Mary shot a look at Verity that commanded silence.

"It's a fine piece of land. It was wilderness when my father's people came here. It took all the strength they had to clear enough land for crops. It will go to my children someday." He looked with great longing at his wife.

Verity spoke with honest appreciation for the work that had been done and what a good farmer Roger was. She wondered all the while how she could learn more about Druid Hill. The name called to mind unspeakable images from a dark past. It would not have been given casually.

She told Mary and Roger she was weary from her rambles that day, and was going up to sleep in the loft where she would not be in their way. They bade her a good night's rest and left the house.

It would be time for the evening milking, Verity thought. She crept back down the ladder and peered through a chink in the kitchen door, to be sure they were out of view.

Satisfied, she made her way from the house to the lane. They would not be looking for her to reappear from the loft until morning.

Verity reached the path through the trees and thence to the stone circle, almost at once looking for the sacrificial hare, as she'd come to think of the animal.

The evening light angled through the trees. Sunset would not come for an hour or more. She had some time to explore before total darkness.

The stone slab was perched on a base of smaller stones, atop a hollow in the ground that looked like a cellar. She wondered if it had once been a home site, now turned to a different purpose. Her instinct told her the servant was right, that this site was the key to Mary's tribulations. Someone or something wanted folk to stay away from Druid Hill, which only fueled her conviction that she must learn its secret. She hoped she was not acting out of foolish pride, destined for a fall.

A ray of light fell precisely on the stone monolith at the center of the ring of standing stones. It was as the Druids would have planned it, Verity realized, remembering how well they were said to track the movement of the sun and stars. She also remembered terrifying stories of blood sacrifice.

As the sky darkened, Verity heard scrambling in the oak trees and the underbrush on the hill below. Her heart raced. It's likely hare or deer, she thought. It grew darker, and each new noise startled her. She continued to tell herself it was woodland animals, fearing all the while that it was Druids come for their horrific rites. Pulling the hem of her skirt to her knees, the better to clamber through the bushes, she found a hiding spot behind one of the wider standing stones off to one side of the circle. It was far enough from the slab and from the solstice stone, as she had come to think of it, that she felt she had a chance of remaining undetected.

In the next moments, she heard hushed voices. This time she could not mistake the human sound. She compressed her small figure as tightly as she could, praying she could not be seen.

As the last hint of light disappeared from the sky, and a crescent moon appeared on the eastern horizon, Verity spied a handful of cloaked figures emerge from the woods, scurrying like prey towards the stone slab. There they vanished, seemingly going into the earth itself.

Verity trembled. There was something unwholesome about these folk, with their furtive looks, their hasty movement, their faces hidden.

An eerie chant rose from beneath the slab. Verity peered around the stone where she still hid, and in the dark she saw a faint flicker from a candle or lamp. She faced a choice—bide in this spot, and learn what sort of sorcery was plotted, or escape and get help. She weighed the likelihood that she could get back to the path unnoticed, then down the hill without making noises in the dark that would give her away.

Her blood thudded in her ears. For one of the few times in her life, she was uncertain what to do. She listened intently to mysterious foreign-sounding incantations. The air cooled and Verity felt her muscles cramp from being in one position too long.

At last the chants stopped. The silence was even more frightening. Once more she heard movement through the woods. She guessed that the mysterious figures were returning from whence they had come. The moon was a fine crescent of silver that gave off little light. Verity reasoned that the dark night would hide her as well as them. If she were careful, she could follow them down the hill at a distance and escape.

She picked her way around the outside of the circle, keeping the stones on her left, until she reached the spot where she had emerged from the woods and onto the hilltop. This was where the figures had descended, seemingly into the earth itself, beneath the stone slab that was now within her reach. She wanted desperately to see what lay beneath the stone, but all was in darkness.

It was quiet down the hill. Verity feared being lost in these unfamiliar woods, but as long as she could glimpse the moon, she would manage. She rooted on the ground around her, and found a dead branch to serve as a walking stick. Thus armed, she set off down the hill. For the first time in hours, she felt the familiar stir of adventure and freedom that came to her on solitary nighttime walks.

From behind her, a hand seized her arm. Another hand clapped across her mouth.

"Shhhh, quiet," the stranger whispered.

Verity writhed and bucked, trying to get free of the fierce grip on her arm and the large calloused hand on her face.

"I'll hold you all the rougher if you're not still."

She strained to place the voice, wondering if it was someone she had seen or spoken with in the village. She couldn't tell if it were man or woman

"You must forget you saw or heard anything."

Verity nodded.

"I know who you are. You'll regret it if you say a word. Wait until the moon sets before you leave." She was spun back to face the stones. "Don't look down the hill when I leave, and don't speak. Return to the house where you are staying. If you say anything about this, to anyone at all, harm will come to the people in that house. Will you be silent if I let you loose?"

Verity nodded again. She'd stopped breathing as the figure held her, and nearly collapsed as she heard the rustle of leaves on the forest floor where the figure descended.

As she waited for the moon to set, she returned to the stone slab. The scent of extinguished candles as well as something pungent and unfamiliar drifted toward her. What terrible deed had taken place, and how could she keep it to herself? Good folk did not gather in a place like this and hide their deeds by cover of night.

The moon had dipped beyond the western horizon by the time Verity returned to the farm. She removed her shoes before she sneaked into the house, and tiptoed across the floor to the loft ladder.

"Good morning, cousin. You're up early. Are you rested?"

Verity started at the sound of Roger's voice. She wondered if he'd been awake and had seen her come in. She tried to think of an excuse if he asked why she was tiptoeing, shoes in hand.

"Very much so, thank you," Verity said.

"Then you can come to Sabbath meeting with us after all."

Verity's adventure on Druid Hill made her forget today was the

Sabbath. She was desperately in need of sleep. Now she would be forced to sit awake through the full day of services, risking the stocks if she nodded off.

How can I avoid Sabbath services? she thought. Mary was so pious, she would not heed excuses. And the villagers would take notice if Verity were absent. Change had long since come to Verity's village of Avebury, so near the influences of Boston and Cambridge, and her fellow townspeople were more lenient in their churchgoing. Out here on the frontier, people adhered to the old ways. Anyone who failed in his or her religious duty could be whipped, expelled, or worst of all, tried and punished as a heretic.

"Is it really the Sabbath already? Travel has made me forgetful. Is there time for me to wash my face?"

"You have time." He tilted his head to the door, suggesting that Mary was outside using the necessary.

Verity poured water from a large pitcher into a crockery bowl, and splashed her face. The cool water helped to revive her a little.

Roger shook out his and Mary's cloaks, preparing to go to meeting. Though it was June, the meetinghouse could still be chilly and damp. Something fluttered to the ground. Roger bent over, but Verity was closer and picked it up.

Verity noted that it was an oak leaf. There were no oak trees on the farm. She'd seen maples, elm, beech, sumac, and a stand of birches along the lane near the house. The only oaks were on Druid Hill. She held it up.

Roger looked at the leaf, then about the room, seeming to avoid her gaze. "We'll have to set out soon or we'll be late."

"Where did this come—" Suddenly Verity was held in a firm grip, a knife at her throat.

"Do not scream." It was the whispered voice in the woods. Verity's mind raced. "I did not ask you here to ruin our lives. Why were you so intent on going where you should not go?"

Verity realized with a shock who it must be. "Mary! It was you on Druid Hill, at the pagan rites. Is your Christian piety only a masquerade?"

"I worship the same God as you," Mary answered. Verity felt her trembling.

"Are you denying you are a Druid?"

"My wife is no pagan," Roger said, rushing to defend Mary. "She is as you know her to be, a pious woman." He looked sad and defeated.

"Which of you sacrificed the hare? What evil rituals were you practicing under the stone?" Verity asked.

The grip on Verity's arm tightened. "It was no evil ritual," Mary said. "The hare was meant to frighten you. We were going to cook it for supper, but Roger heard you talking with the minister's servant about Druid Hill. He went by a different path and put the hare on the stone. We thought you would be frightened away."

"But what of the people hiding themselves, and chanting strange words?"

Tears trickled down Roger's face. "It was innocent, I swear. Nothing evil happened."

"The strange words, as you call them, were Latin," Mary said. "We were celebrating the Mass."

"The *Roman* Mass?"

"It was not a Black Mass, if that is your meaning, cousin." She spoke defiantly, no longer trembling. "I am no witch. It was the holy sacrament of the Mass."

Mary was a Papist, a Roman Catholic. A heretic.

"But the curse—" Verity started.

"If I'd told you only that I've failed to deliver a healthy child, would you have stayed?" Mary said. "For all I know there may be a curse. I know of no other explanation for our woes."

"Your faith—it's against the law of this colony." Verity was terrified for her cousin. She could as well have been a Druid, for all the magistrates would care. "You could be hanged!"

"I knew it was wrong," Roger said, "but she was so determined to practice her mother's faith that I hadn't the will to make her stop."

"My mother was a good woman, as was her mother before her. They were willing to risk persecution for their faith. That did not make them sinners."

"I always feared Mary would be found out, and we would be destroyed," Roger said. "I never thought it would be at your hands, who was to have saved us." He wiped his eyes with his shirtsleeve. "Give us time to leave on our own, before you give the alarm. I don't know where we'll go or how we'll survive, but we're as good as dead if we're discovered."

Verity thought about her cousin and the child inside her, and of her own dear father. Mary reminded her so of him.

"Wash your face, Roger," Verity said. "Mary, let me loose. We must hurry if we have any hope of getting to Sabbath services on time. It wouldn't do to start idle gossip, not with that child on the way."

Cheryl Marceau is a human resources executive at a technology company in the Boston area. "Druid Hill" is her fifth short story to appear in Level Best Books' anthologies. She is also working on a mystery novel featuring colonial midwife Verity Warren. She and her husband live in the real-life Avebury, Massachusetts, which local folk know by another name.

Call Off the Search

Stef Donati

S avannah paused the image. In this rain scene—scene 49, her notes said—the handbag was beige, not the mauve it had been in the restaurant. Compared to Harry Potter's ever-changing seat location during term feast, or Dorothy's long-short-long pigtails in Oz, this continuity blunder would have netted scant attention from film buffs. But Savannah still wondered: The actors, the prop crew, even her boss . . . were they pulling these goofs on purpose? Testing the newbie?

If they were, she was passing. All day, she'd stayed in this screening room, playing and pausing and replaying yesterday's shooting scenes. Every frame. And this handbag's color was the lone continuity error. For once, only one. She was as certain of that as she was about Earl.

She pocketed her flash drive, all ready for tomorrow's meeting with the A.D. Months from now, when this film hit theaters, the closing credits would name her: *Savannah Sutton, Continuity Assistant.* A flicker of fame.

And Earl would be with her. Earl, who did pull goofs on her, but tenderly. Like the time he'd told her the Bluegrass Bonanza was sold out, before brandishing tickets on the day of the first show. Or when he'd "taken" a job downcounty, on the one-month anniversary of their first date, only to surprise her with *pad thai* from the best— okay, the only—Asian restaurant in town. The same restaurant where, last night, he'd proposed.

God, life was so good now.

She locked up, hurried down creaky stairs into fading daylight. Her rusting Forester squatted alone in the lot, her nothing-to-prove co-workers already long gone.

Halfway to the Forester, she heard a yell. "Don't marry him!"

Running toward her was a tall man, a redhead, his curls and jean jacket as jarring as his words. She squinted. Familiar, but from where?

"You *are* Savannah Sutton, yes?" He slowed, wheezing. "Yes, you are."

She squeezed her car key as the man stopped altogether, an arm's reach away. Whoever he was, she'd scratch out his eyes if she had to.

She cleared her throat. "Who I am, and my private life, they're hardly—"

"No coyness, Savannah; there's no time." Even the raspy voice was familiar. The lean frame and pudgy chin. "You marry Earl Mason, it'll be the mistake of your life."

A prankster, this guy, some co-roofer of Earl's. Had to be. Hell, this whole warning might be Earl's latest prank, his best since that "sold-out" Bluegrass Bonanza. A prank. Except this man was standing too close, soaking in every inch of her.

And Earl, her Earl, would never want her afraid.

"Answer fast," she said, drawing her cell. "Why shouldn't I marry Earl?"

The moment the man reached into his jacket, she punched a '9' and a '1'.

A pickup rumbled down the street, scraping a tire on a chuckhole.

"Time's up," she said, ready to stab the next digit.

"No!" The man lunged for her, then pulled back. "Before you call anyone, hear me out. Please, Savannah." His tremble reminded her of herself, in that screening last week, when she'd pointed out the error even her boss had missed—"If the attic's so old, shouldn't there be some dust?"

With a sigh reeking of onions, the man withdrew from his jacket a battered manila envelope. "My guess is, Savannah . . . and I'm sorry for this . . . you'll react first by cursing me. Screaming. But you'll thank me later, for warning you. Now, where can we talk?"

Nowhere. She tried saying it. *This conversation is over.*

But battling a breeze she was only now noticing, the man slit open his envelope, pried free a small stack of photos. The headshot on top was a young woman with curls as auburn as his own, plus a smile. His fingers stayed at the photo's edges, letting that smile radiate untouched.

Savannah stared. Knew she was doing it, but couldn't stop. It had been, what, three years since she'd seen this woman's face? Followed the frenzy about her disappearance and eventual washing-up onto the Cuyahoga?

And this man . . . Savannah stepped backward . . . he'd been part of that story. That's where she'd seen—

Rustling. Three more photos surged forth, the corpse-to-be morphing into a teenaged ballerina, then a gap-toothed middle-schooler, finally a laughing bride. Whose groom, laughing beside her, was . . .

No.

Yes. Earl. A younger Earl, no goatee, but Earl all the same. Alongside this doomed woman.

"Elizabeth Fenshaw."

"I remember," Savannah managed. "From the news."

"'Betsy,' we called her. She was my kid sister." The man nodded, as if to confirm his own claim. "And this man, the man you plan to marry . . . was her husband."

Her killer, he meant. Who'd fled as police blitzed the airwaves all the way from Sandusky to here. *The husband, the fugitive, is six foot one with a slight limp.*

Like Earl.

And hazel eyes. Like Earl.

Savannah teetered. Dammit, detail was her job. Spotting the slightest change in place settings as a dinner scene progressed.

"This joke's in lousy taste," she told this man, "and it's stupid besides. I remember those newscasts. The husband's name wasn't even Earl." She thought hard. "It was Edward. Edward Something."

"Mayhew." A tone of condescension, as if she were the one being stupid. "Edward Mayhew, Earl Mason. Same initials, Savannah; fugitives often keep them."

"Not this time." She jabbed at the wedding photo. "*This* guy might be guilty, but he's not my fiancé. No goatee. And the hair is too red."

Although hair could be colored, and goatees could be grown.

"Look closer, Savannah. The hawk nose, the big ears."

She'd looked too closely already, but she looked again. This couldn't be Earl. It *couldn't.*

"You're in shock. But you're a good woman, and—"

"How would you know that?"

The man shuffled the photos, leaving the ballerina—young Elizabeth Fenshaw—Betsy—on top. "I've been in town a while, watching you. If you were a bitch, Savannah . . . if you knew he'd killed my sister and were staying with him anyway . . . I wouldn't be here. I'd just let the police hunt him down, or try to, after he does to you what he did to her."

Focus, thought Savannah. This is your life, your career. Is this man really that poor woman's brother, now three years older? The mourner who'd wept on the news, begging the cameras to deliver Edward Mayhew back home, preferably dead?

"But you do deserve warning," he was saying. "So I'm taking this risk."

Risk?

"That you'll warn *him.* About me. In which case, best outcome, he'll run—and I'll have wasted three years tracking him down." A gust scattered the fallen leaves by the curb. "Worst outcome, he'll kill me."

"Or kill us both," Savannah said, flinching, "since now I know, too."

Was she really saying this? Believing it?

A motorcyclist roared past, then an aging Civic. Nobody slowed, nobody stopped. She wanted to kick those leaves into a pile, as she and Earl sometimes did, the whoosh and crackle blending with joy and laughter.

"I've bet on your courage, Savannah, and your respect for his victim. Let's tell the police. Together."

Craig, she remembered. This grieving brother was named Craig. Not so lean as three years ago, but the same person. No scam artist, no continuity errors here. No hope for denying this nightmare.

"You're still in shock," he whispered, "so take a few minutes. The police station can wait."

She wrestled forth media-memories. Elizabeth Fenshaw . . . her husband had been a guitarist. Like Earl. In a rock band, not bluegrass, but a guitarist. Before ever existing, could Earl have once been that monster?

People talked all the time of becoming someone new. Hell, she herself used to ache to flee this town, with its oblivious happy families and its shuttered stores, the laundromat with half its machines forever "Out of Service," the church she'd always attended alone, the only semi-young single parishioner. Thinking next month she'd turn happy, or next year. And just when she'd begun settling, on neither escaping nor changing her life, along had come Earl with his pensive gaze and periwinkle-blue shirt—and, yes, his big ears, same as in this photo—sneaking peeks at her from the next booth at The No Finer Diner, two misfits near midnight, peeked so many times that she'd thought *Hey, stranger, just talk to me. Even a perv would be better than nothing.* Slowly he'd risen, shyly he'd smiled, asking her in that stutter, "M-Miss, it's g-getting crowded in, in, in here. Folks are w-waiting for t-t-tables. Maybe we c-could share a, a, a booth?"

The diner hadn't been crowded at all.

His glance downward. As if her rejecting him would crush his world, as if she, Savannah Sutton, could wield such power. His long handshake as he said, with no stutter this time, "My name's Edward."

No. *Earl,* he'd said. *Earl.* How could she so botch this memory of their first meeting? How could he, so smoothly, have forged a new life?

Earl. Whatever crime Edward Mayhew had done, her Earl was a man who grew vegetables, labored deep into the night to perfect a guitar solo, and at three different gigs had shouted "I luh, luh, love you, Savannah!" from the stage. Her Earl not only accepted but cherished her meager curves and prematurely graying hair, her habit of over-explaining the set-up when telling a joke.

She shrank from the photo being again waved in her face. But she made herself imagine Earl killing this woman. Imagine, much earlier, his romancing her, stroking these curls and curves Savannah could only long for.

What does he see in me?

"I was wrong," said Craig Fenshaw, "about how you'd react. I'm impressed; you haven't screamed once."

She raged at the awe in his tone. Had he also presumed, from his spying, that he grasped even a little what it was like to be her, to have *been* her all those years, starved for human touch? Savannah Sutton, the thickest-thighed swimmer at the rec center, whose best friend was her cat and whose too-keen eye had eroded any enjoyment of movies, any immersion in make-believe. Until Earl. Earl, who after one spring and summer of dating, had glowed at her promise to, yes, marry him.

Could that be the prank? Saying he loved her, letting her strum his Gibson, assuring her she was playing it well?

"The police, Savannah. We need to tell them. You're his fiancée; you can affirm who he is, who he *was*."

And if she didn't? Would this man harm her? Leave her to her conscience? The skylight grew pink. No cars at all now. This time, when Craig Fenshaw reached out, she took his hand. The guy had lost a sister; Savannah could survive simply being lonely again.

With a hunger that startled her, she seized his photos, examined each one, burning their entirety into her heart.

"I had nightmares, you know. At the time."

He gaped. Really, this surprised him, her having once cared so much? About a bride her own age who'd gone missing, and who weeks later washed up dead, strangle-marks on her throat?

"I'm sorry, Savannah. But turn him in, and you'll be safe."

She clawed for hope. That she'd missed something, and this man was some imposter, a madman. No victim's brother at all.

Returning the photos, she studied his face. "Details," she demanded. "About Betsy."

"You don't want to hear."

"With all the newscasts I watched, all the nights I prayed for her? Yes, I do. Give me her middle name. Her birthday, her hobbies."

"Is this a challenge?"

"You can't, can you?"

His whole body tightened. "You're wrong there, Savannah. But my stating those won't prove a thing."

No, it wouldn't. Any scammer could have unearthed such simple data. Authentic or not, this grieving brother . . . if she defied him, would he let her live? Let Earl live?

"That news coverage, it left so much out." He clenched his fists. Delaying himself, she guessed. With his long hunt nearly ended, how would he fill his days?

"For instance, the story she wrote, when she was seven or so.

With drawings and everything. About a soldier who'd gone off to war, away from his wife, for a very long time." A smile. Or a smirk? "When the soldier-husband came home, safe and sound, the wife hugged him and kissed him—c-i-s-s,' Betsy spelled it—and said 'Darling, I have a surprise!' and presented him . . . it was Christmas . . . presented him with five babies." The fists unclenched. "The news never mentioned that, or how as an adult Betsy got into bluegrass— *his* bluegrass, your beloved goddamn Earl's—or how she worked two different jobs waiting tables while he played in that lame-ass band night after night. The news never mentioned, the world never learned, how any time he got stiffed on some gig, my sister was the one who fought for him."

"That's not enough."

This man, this Craig Fenshaw, frowned.

"Not nearly!" Too harsh. Gentler: "I'm just saying, you can't be sure. That it was Earl . . . her husband . . . who committed . . . who caused . . ."

"Murdered, Savannah."

How must it feel? To lose a sister that way, to seethe in fury all this time . . . how much sleep had this man lost, how many hours had he sacrificed, chasing justice?

"If you're right," she said, "and my fiancé's living a lie . . . tell me about him. His life with her."

In the dusk she edged closer, craving some hint of deceit.

"I admit, at first Ed—Earl—seemed good for my sister. But . . ." Somewhere, a horn bleated. "But he changed. He—"

"Did he stutter?"

"What?" A bobble of the photos. "Of course he stuttered."

Of course. Of course everything. Forget movies. Shouldn't there be continuity in *life*? She choked her keys. The longer he stayed Earl, the worse she would hurt if he stopped.

Darkness. She staggered toward her Forester, letting Craig Fenshaw follow. Her vehicle, and not his. If he even had one, it was nowhere near this lot.

"So you'll do this?" he asked, sounding almost disappointed. "Tell the police?"

"Isn't that what you want?"

His nod came slowly. "It is. It's just . . . I mean, I've waited so long for this, getting him sent to prison. Now here I am thinking better of him. For finding a woman so decent."

"Wasn't your sister decent?"

"Oh . . . very. It's just, well, I'm sorry for the pain I'm causing." Savannah's eyes shut. "Don't be."

She leaned forward, creaking the springs of her couch. *Our* couch, she corrected herself, now that he lived with her.

The anchorman donned a grave look. "Our lead story tonight: This morning, in the Muskingum River, a body was found. The deceased has been identified as forty-year-old Craig Fenshaw, of . . ."

"D-damn!" A voice, her fiancé, her Earl, beside her. As real as last night. "You, you know who th-that man is, honey? Was? B-B-Betsy's . . ."

"Shhh, baby. I know."

"The, the M-Muskingum River. Why? I mean, I mean, C-Craig never swam, never f-fished. How, how did h-he end up there?"

Savannah's mouth opened. But despite Earl's gaze on her, and this question she'd spent a whole night and day bracing for, no words came. Until, without quivering, she said, "Some people, baby, just have bad luck."

He clasped her shoulder, stroked her eyelids, her too-close-together eyebrows. "S-some people," he whispered. "B-but not, not, not us."

So *Earl* of him, not prodding her to confess. Just holding her, cradling her, as she wept. Happy tears, mostly. From the very first time they'd made love, when he'd trusted her with his secret, she'd ached to comprehend. Fully. To share in the shame and the flashbacks, the fear of discovery.

Now she could.

Stef Donati hosts a radio show in Vermont, loves most forms of music, and roots in vain for Cleveland sports teams.

Devious Doings in Dallas

Sanford Emerson

Frenchy Plourde had a reputation as a wicked dink, so it was no real surprise that he had a nasty, pissed-off expression on what was left of his face that January morning when I found him frozen to the floor of his cabin. Most of his 300 or so neighbors in Dallas Plantation, Maine, weren't too upset when they heard about his passing, as they'd all of them borne the brunt of his lewd, crude and rude behavior for years. The majority of those I talked to later, though, thought it was just damn sad the way Frenchy's mangy, three-legged dog was found curled up next to his master's body. Before he too froze to death, poor starving Sumbitch had gnawed off his master's right ear.

In a weak moment a while back I sort of volunteered to be the Plantation's constable, which explains how I got involved in this whole mess to begin with. You see I retired about ten years ago from the Coast Guard and settled into an old hunting camp on the side of Saddleback Mountain that I inherited from an old shipmate who died of cirrhosis. What I did in the Coasties was mostly maritime law enforcement—think SWAT on a speedboat. I retired as a Chief Gunner's Mate on a fast cutter. We did a whole bunch of drug enforcement and I personally sank a couple of cigarette boats. It's really awesome what a Ma Deuce with armor piercing ammo can do to a boat's engine block! Anyway, when I let some of that slip one day to the checkout clerk at the IGA in Rangeley, the next town over, she told her boss, who told the Dallas Plantation clerk's husband. He told her and it turned out our Board of Assessors needed someone to post legal notices, serve tax lien papers and just generally be "the guy in town who does stuff." No badge, no gun, and "for God's sake, no arresting people" was the job description they gave me. It doesn't pay much, but I don't have to do much either and the extra income helps covers my tab at Sally's. It did take me a little while, though, to figure out that the reason that I, the flatlander, was asked to take the job, which had been vacant for years, was that nobody else in town wanted it.

Anyway, that's why Shorty Devereaux came banging on my door on one of the coldest mornings since "eighteen-hundred-and-froze-to-death." Shorty's job is to plow and sand the twenty-three-and-a-half miles of public roads that make up the plantation. The good citizens assembled on the Budget Committee have repeatedly declined to put a radio in his truck and he's given up trying to figure out how a cell phone works, so when he noticed that Frenchy hadn't dug out his outhouse for a week, which is lazy, even for Frenchy, he drove over to my place.

"You're the constable. You should go check on him," Shorty said.

"Why don't you call the sheriff, or the staties?" I said, looking past him at the thermometer on the old maple tree in my yard. It was below zero, but the lower end of the scale was obscured by an icicle, so I couldn't see it.

"They won't think it's important enough. Besides, they won't come up here anymore since Frenchie shot at them two years ago. They're all scared of him!" Shorty actually whined. "I'm not going in there, either. The last time I hit his mail box with the plow he told me he'd shove a grenade up my butt the next time I came near his property."

"He'll probably do the same to me. Why should I go?" I said, feeling a little sick to my stomach and whiny myself.

"Because that's what we pay you for." Shorty snorted.

I knew he was going to say that.

The deputy sheriff they sent up looked to be just about as old as my daughter. Even so she didn't flinch when the wind banged the door shut behind us as we stepped into Frenchy's cabin. I'd held the door and politely let her go in first. She'd been nice enough to me so far, considering I was technically a civilian with no real police standing, despite the title.

Most of Frenchy was still sitting upright on the floor in front of the open wood stove. His head was cranked around sharply to the left as if he was looking at the front door. He had a filthy rag wrapped around his left hand and an unlit Lucifer match in his right. The stove itself held a full charge of kindling and birch wood blocks, probably from Fletcher's wood turning mill over to New Vineyard. The cold half-light from the two filthy windows did a real poor job of illuminating the powerless cabin, so we both pointed our flashlight beams into all the corners. She was probably looking for clues. I was watching out for porcupines.

The place was almost empty, just a few open shelves with some canned goods scattered around, a dumped-over tin of loose tobacco and couple of old plastic five-gallon water buckets also frozen to the floor in the near corner. A half full bag of blocks sat by the door and a few bundles of dry "vegetation" were draped off the rafters. There was also a faintly familiar smell that I imagined would be a lot stronger once the place warmed up.

"Just you been in here?" she asked.

"Think so," I said. "The path to the road was just one boot wide, but there was a dusting of snow over it. Didn't see any tracks."

"Snowed up here last night, right?"

"Just enough to justify a couple of hours overtime for Shorty Devereaux," I said.

"Did you touch or move anything?" she asked, pulling a pen out of the breast pocket of her tan parka and a thin spiral notebook out of her hip pocket. Her nametag read "Wilma Brackett" and she was a "slick arm," having no service hash marks sewed to her left sleeve.

"No, I didn't have to," I told her. "It was pretty obvious after a second or two that there wasn't anything I was going to be able to do for him."

She nodded, peering at the body. "So this is the famous Frenchy Plourde. Did you know him?"

"Frenchy?" I said. "Everybody knew him. Didn't you?"

"Never had the pleasure," she said with the hint of a smile. "I was at the Police Academy when he took a shot at my boss. They probably should have shot him but my dad tackled him instead."

She's actually kinda pretty.

"He got out of the Correctional Center in Windham about six months ago," she went on as I collected myself mentally. "He did a year for Reckless Conduct for shooting at the sheriff and he is, uh, *was* on probation. I called his probation officer on the way up. Sounds like he didn't have many friends."

"Looks like his only real friend went with him," I said, nodding at Sumbitch's body.

"Poor thing." She sighed. Looking back at me she asked, "OK, what's the first thing you saw when you walked in?"

"Just his face at first," I said. "He looked like he was mad enough to spit at me until I realized he was dead."

"What else?"

"Saw the dog, obviously. And that . . ." I pointed at a pile of stuff by the back wall that was probably the bed.

"Could've done with a housekeeper," she said. "He's got something of a reputation as a poacher. Do you know what else he does, uh, *did*?" She actually blushed and grinned.

Mister man, a boy could get used to that fairly quick.

"Drink and fight, mostly. Probably some of that, too," I said, pointing to the hanging gardens. "I think he gets SSDI for drugs, but that's just a rumor."

"From Marti Wallace, I expect." She smiled again. Our rural mail carrier, you see, is a wicked gossip.

The door banged back against the wall, I jumped, and a woolly mammoth carrying a briefcase stumbled sideways into the cabin.

"I do wish you people would take the time to shovel instead of just stomping down a path," it grumbled from somewhere deep inside. "Hey, Willie. What you got this time?"

"Pretty much what you see, Doc. Meet the late, unlamented Frenchy Plourde."

The fur-lined hood flipped back from the mammoth's head and revealed longish white hair and a corresponding beard crowning a body that was easily a head taller and fifty pounds heavier than me. He reached over Frenchy and shook my hand. He had some grip!

"Eimon Jeffreys, boy Medical Examiner," he rumbled. "Legally dead, I'd say from preliminary examination. At least he still looks relatively fresh. Got pictures yet?"

"I'll go get the camera out of the cruiser," Willie said. "Looks pretty straightforward though. I don't think we'll have to call in the troops."

"Probably not." The doctor wheezed and coughed into his elbow. "But I'll have a look anyway. Need to earn that massive fee." He smiled and bent down over the body as Willie went out the door.

"Whoa!" he said with a surprised grunt. "This is something you don't see a lot of in Franklin County. Rictus Sardonicus. I think maybe old Frenchy here finally pissed off the wrong person."

"Huh?" I said.

"That look on his face is called a poison grin. Usually strychnine if I remember right." He shook his very large head. "I'm beginning to think that maybe we should call 'the troops' after all."

"They had to light the fire and warm the place up enough to scrape him and the dog off the floor," I told Nadine, the half owner of Sally's Motel and Bar and Live Bait and Convenience Store, about two hours later over my first Shipyard. "They took them both down to Augusta for autopsies."

"So they think somebody did it in for him?" Nadine looked mildly grossed out but interested, as did the two guys in nice, clean, brand-new snowmobile suits sitting at a table by the front window. Together they rose and slid in on either side of me at the bar.

"Maybe," I said, warming up to the audience. "The State Police detective team came in behind us and kicked me and Deputy Willie out as soon as they got there. She looked a little pissed to be put on traffic detail."

"That'd be Willie Brackett, Jim Brackett's daughter from down in Phillips," Nadine said, shaking her head with a smile. "She's a little corker, that one. About a month ago she cleaned this place out single-handed when the Martinos got into it with the Regan brothers. Handcuffed Dutch Regan so fast he didn't realize it until he was out the door. Then she came back and used some kind of judo move on Finn Martino that had him crying like a baby."

The snowmobilers edged closer and the older one who smelled like a cigar offered to buy me another beer, which I happily accepted.

I guess I was walking a little close to the middle of the road on my way home some time later, because Marti Wallace had to pull into the left lane and blow her horn to get my attention when she found me. Luckily there was no oncoming traffic. There seldom is. She shoved me into the back seat of her canary yellow Jeep amongst all the mail and her turnout gear and drove me the last hundred yards or so home.

"Ya got yourself hammered again, din't ya?" she said, shaking her head as she climbed out what should rightly be the passenger side front door. Did I mention she's a "BMW," a "Big Maine Woman," and she had no trouble extracting me and walking me into my kitchen? Of course I had to tell her the whole story all over again, which pleased her no end but made her late finishing her mail route because she had so much fresh news to distribute.

I swear it happens every damn time. Just when Helen Hunt is about to finally slip out of that tiny little tank top something wakes me up. Pam's probably laughing her ass off somewhere, wherever she is.

"Sorry, Hon," I said to her picture on my nightstand.

My Fire Department pager was screaming like a banshee in heat. Lummox, my cat, headed for the hills. From the length of the sequence of different tones I could tell that this wasn't going to be a little chimney fire. I started pulling on my long woolies.

Dallas Plantation doesn't really have its own Fire Department and, like everything else in my life, I'm not really a firefighter. About fifteen years or so ago, back before I moved here, the insurance company that covers the ski slope up on Saddleback Mountain realized that the nearest fire truck was about ten miles away in Rangeley and that the entity hereinafter to be known as "The Mountain" was accumulating a lot of really expensive and flammable equipment, not to mention all those combustible skiers who were paying to sleep (or party hearty) in their fancy trailside condos, each of which has its own rustic, fully stocked fireplace. "The Mountain," which is actually in Sandy River Plantation next door, went to our Board of Assessors because we've got a population center—sort of—that's closer than their own on the far backside of Saddleback Mountain itself. Through their professionally attired and outfitted legal representatives they reasonably proposed that we needed a fire truck in the worst way. As the Assessors were themselves all tax payers, they balked up tight until "The Mountain" offered to pick up most of the tab. As a result we now have the permanent loan of old Engine Five from Rangeley, along with enough money each year to insure her, keep her in diesel and oil, and heat the Town Garage enough to keep her water tank from freezing up. Fifteen or twenty good citizens who always wanted to be firemen as kids usually show up for monthly meetings at Sally's and about half of those actually show up for the infrequent fire or traffic accident. All us taxpayers have to do is pay the insurance premiums and minimum wage to the ones who do report.

The screaming subsided and all over Franklin County men and women lifted their pagers to their ears to see which of them could go back to bed.

"Attention, Dallas Fire. Attention, Rangeley Fire. Attention, Phillips Fire. Attention, Northstar Ambulance Rangeley base. Report of a structure fire, fully involved, at 3700 Hog Road in Dallas Plantation. Dallas Chief is on the scene. Phillips, respond one mutual aid tanker and stand by at the station. Time out zero four forty-five."

Since I live across the street from the town garage, I usually drive the truck and run the pump. I had more than enough firefighting experience and training in the Coast Guard to know I'm no longer interested in charging into burning buildings. There are enough young kids around who get a charge out of that, so I'm content to pass on the actual grunt firefighter stuff. Besides, I like running the old American LaFrance; she's a real gamer for her age.

"Frenchy Plourde's place." Snort Benson shouted, piling into the passenger seat as I hit the starter. "Weren't you just over there, Bobby?"

"Yeah, Snot. I was." I hit the lights and siren as the old girl warmed up and pushed the shifter toward first gear. "Sounds like Marti called it in on her paper route. The woman never sleeps!"

Snort's nickname's been pronounced Snot since grammar school. He hates it. Marti is also our fire chief. She's good at it.

"Dallas Five to Franklin. Enroute with two, uh, make that three," Snot said into the mike as Bear MacGillicuddy landed next to him and slammed the door shut. Cozy.

"Ten-four, Dallas Five." Franklin County Dispatch replied.

Snot grunted as the right turn out of the garage pushed Bear over onto him. Bear's big. Snot isn't. *Real* cozy.

We made it to the late Frenchy's ex-cabin without further incident and set up to pump three main lines at Marti's direction. Nobody and nothing of consequence was in imminent danger so we adopted the ancient, accepted and safe fire-fighting strategy of "surround and drown." With help from Rangeley's pumper and the tankers from Rangeley and Phillips we efficiently reduced the cabin to a few standing charred timbers in about half an hour. With precise hose handling from the nozzle men, we actually managed to stop the flames from reaching the outhouse, a feat which, everyone knew, would later be loudly and proudly celebrated at the incident debriefing at Sally's. Curiously the cabin's stove pipe remained standing. Backed by the rising sun it was twisted into the shape of a question mark, as if the old place's last comment was, "WTF?"

"Might's well wrap it up," Marti shouted to me as I throttled down the engine to disconnect the power takeoff to the pump. "The fire marshal will be up later to look for a cause and the sheriff's sending a deputy to stand by."

"Hope they find something to go on," I said as the old engine settled back to her gently purring idle.

God, I love this machine!

"I think they will. I met a big, black, one-ton pickup with two snow machines on a tilt body booking it out of here just before I came on the fire," Marti said. "No front plate I could see but I think they were Massholes 'cause one of them gave me the finger."

"Gotta be Massholes," I agreed, grinning. "Nobody from around here would dare!"

About then I stepped down wrong and slipped on the ice that had accumulated under the pump's output connector. Gracefully I landed on the left side of my face, splitting my lip. My first thought was that the OSHA and Workman's Comp paperwork was going to take a week. My second thought was *"What the hell is that?"*

Lodged in the ice under the truck was what looked very much like a cigar butt.

A couple of days later I was sitting in my front room working on my flies when a sheriff's cruiser pulled into my dooryard. Buck Champagne taught me how to tie fishing flies my third year in the plantation. It's a real good way to stay sane and at least semi-sober from November through April on the mountainside. Later on I took an Adult Ed course about the Internet at Rangeley High School and the kids there taught me how to set up and run a simple website. Believe it or not, I now sell my Wytopitlock Wooley Booger flies all over the US and Canada.

I watched as Willie got out of the car and walked up to my front door. I rapped on the window between us and waved her on in.

"Mister Wing," she said with a nice smile. "How've you been? How's your lip?"

My day was improving by the minute.

"Healing. I've had worse. And it's Bobby. Mister Wing was my Dad."

She hung her parka on the hook on the kitchen wall and I waved her into a chair and poured her a cup of coffee.

No rings.

"I wanted to thank you for preserving that cigar butt and remembering those two snowmobilers at Sally's," she said. "I managed to get a tentative ID on one of them from Nadine's room registration records and the parking lot surveillance camera. They gave Nadine false names and a bogus plate number but the camera gave us a good one. The truck was a rental from Worcester, Massachusetts. It's still missing and the Mass State Police have just listed it as stolen in NCIC. The guy who rented it had to show ID. They told the rental agent they were going to Maine to pick up some snow machines for a guy in Vermont. We think they actually stole the machines down near Portland. If they are who we think they are they're players on the Boston docks involved in all kinds of stuff like fencing stolen property, smuggling, dope, you name it. Anyway, the DA says thanks to you we've got a good chain of custody on the cigar butt and the lab's doing DNA as we speak. With luck we'll be able to place the cigar guy at the scene in a week or two."

"I'm sure Frenchy would have been pleased," I said.

"That's another thing. Doc Jeffreys called me this morning to tell me that the State Police have closed his death as a natural causes case."

"Natural causes? It sure as hell didn't look natural," I said.

"Agreed. But it turns out that one of the other causes of that facial expression is tetanus—lockjaw. He probably caught it off the ax he was using to split kindling. Doc says it's a really painful way to die, with violent muscle spasms and seizures. Frenchy'd probably been alone in that cabin, sick, for a week or more before he worked up enough strength to fill the stove and light it. Doc thinks he had a seizure just before he lit the match and suffocated. He was probably conscious and at least vaguely aware of what was happening until he passed out from lack of oxygen and died."

"I'll be damned," I said, actually beginning to feel a little sorry for Frenchy. "And the fire . . .?"

"Was definitely set, probably by our Massachusetts friends," she said. "We don't know exactly why yet, but there may be a connection between Frenchy and one of them through Frenchy's prison time. Again, if he is who we think he is, the older guy was in Windham at the same time Frenchy was. I think they were looking for something in the cabin and couldn't find it. They burned the place to cover their tracks. Alcohol, Tobacco and Firearms agents have also gotten involved because of the arson and the interstate connection."

"I'll be damned again, most likely," I said softly. "Who would have thought . . . way up here in Dallas Plantation, Maine . . . of all places." I shook my head, feeling suddenly, somehow, vulnerable again.

Willie laughed. "Come on, now, Mr. W . . . sorry." She paused, still smiling. "Bobby. I get the feeling there's more to your act than you let on. I heard you were in the service for almost as long as I've been alive. I bet you've seen things, done things . . ."

I'm not sure what I looked like just then, but whatever it was she picked up on it, along with my admittedly uncharacteristic silence.

"I better get going," she finally said with a soft little frown. "I've got a meeting this afternoon on this case with the DA and all the agencies involved. Maybe there'll be some new developments. I'll let you know."

"You don't have to. I'm just the local yokel."

"Who's been a big help to us all. See you later." She smiled again, a bit sadly I thought, and left.

You know, she looks just a little like Helen Hunt.

Turns out Willie was right. The cigar guy was positively ID'd through the DNA on his butt, putting him at the scene of the fire. Franklin County Court issued a warrant for Arson (of a Residence), Class A, for the two of them and the younger one caved as soon as the ATF agents walked into the Boston PD interrogation room and showed him their badges.

Along with a lot of other stuff, they'd been in the business of procuring dried bear gall bladders for Chinese men who think they're an aphrodisiac and then shipping them off the Boston docks in a clandestine manner. You can apparently make a mint doing that but it's illegal under federal law. Who knew?

The cigar guy was in prison with Frenchy and offered to buy any bladders he could get. Frenchy had called a couple of weeks before and said he had some ready, but they found him dead when they got there. They tossed the cabin and left the night before, before the snow. After they heard my story at Sally's, they went back for a second look, but still couldn't find anything. They dowsed the place with gasoline and tossed the cigar into the fumes to set it off.

Willie got a commendation from ATF and Federal Fish and Wildlife. She got her picture in the paper shaking hands with the sheriff.

She looked pretty good.

About March, the Board of Assessors got tired of fielding complaints from "The Mountain" about how bad the fire scene looked to their customers headed up to spend money lavishly on clean rustic Maine recreation, so they voted to take the property for taxes (Frenchy had never paid any) and "eliminate the eyesore," as they told me.

When things had melted off in May, I rented an excavator off M & H Logging in Rangeley and went over to the Hog Road to reestablish the harmonious beauty of nature. I was almost done when I tipped over the outhouse, and a canvas bag that had apparently been hanging under the seat fell onto the now-uncovered pile of now-stinking crap.

I shut the machine off and sat in the warm spring sun and stared at that bag for a long while. I thought about money, and happiness, and Frenchy, and fear, and Chinese men, and dead bears and dogs, and Willie, and Helen Hunt, and Pam. Then I covered the hole all up, graded it off and planted some grass seed.

Author's Note: Dallas Plantation, Maine is a real nice place but the characters, places, names and situations in this story are figments of my imagination. If you think it's you or someone you know, it's not, so don't get your nose out of joint!

Sanford Emerson: After retiring from a thirty-five-year career in law enforcement and corrections in Franklin County, Maine, Sanford Emerson operates a Christmas tree farm and a woodworking business in Wilton, Maine. Despite having written thousands of official reports over those years, this is his first published work of fiction. (Really!)

Baker Street, Boston

Louisa Clerici

I've been in love with Sherlock Holmes forever. There, I've said it. Maybe since I was thirteen years old and read *The Hound of the Baskervilles*. I was supposed to be asleep, but under a cave made of blankets in my bedroom every night I read pages by flashlight. I was afraid to stop reading and let this world of whodunit and fantasy escape from me.

At sixteen I wanted to *be* Sherlock. I thought I could solve everything. It's all in the details I knew; a trace of chalk on a shirtsleeve, fingernail polish chipped, but only on the ring finger.

I longed for a cold corpse and a dark mystery. At eighteen as my friends were going off to college, I dreamt of the life of a private detective. I looked like Sherlock's true love, Irene Adler, all chestnut red hair, scarlet lipstick and too-high heels. But I liked to think I had the heart of Holmes and maybe the soul of Watson.

My family thought I was a fool so I reluctantly went to secretarial school, culminating in a job as a receptionist at a fitness club. I was bored. I knew deep in the ice of my bones, it was a crime to settle for a suspense-less life, so I moved to the big city. I longed to live on Baker Street in London but Boston, Massachusetts would have to do.

My roommate, studying to be a counselor at Sunset Valley College, thought maybe I just needed a hobby. "Life could be worse," she said. "You're smart, pretty, making a decent living staring at well-hung jocks all day. What is your problem?"

My life had no surprise. I was stuck in the thriller-less limbo of 9 to 5. At least until Halloween arrived that year. The night when the veil between worlds is thin and magic is afoot.

It finally happened. I came home from work to find the police at my apartment building door. A real dead body had finally crossed my path. Myrtle Stroud from 4B had been stabbed in her sleep, no suspects, no leads, just an old lady with an enemy. A wrinkled body waiting for a grave. The slum we lived in had drug dealers and single moms, a dominatrix and college kids, but no one who had anything against Myrtle. It was a scene straight out of a Dickens rookery, no killers, but loads of folk carrying around a secret on their backs. Forensics said one bone on her big toe had been shattered. *Curious*, I thought.

My investigative mind flew immediately to Mr. Carlos Von Kitteridge, my landlord. You'd pick him out of any lineup. He wore plaid blazers in summer and track shoes in winter. He walked around with his wire-rimmed glasses perpetually on the end of his nose. There was something slimy and odd about how he always looked away when you entered the elevator with him in the morning. I'd long suspected him of something . . . bank fraud, no fashion taste, bad breath or worse. Now I wondered why he had savagely killed poor Myrtle. Did he have a toe fetish, a hankering to steal some of her chicken soup or perhaps they were having a torrid affair? I could see it all . . . Carlos and Myrtle tangoing in the laundry room . . . making love under the stars on our rooftop deck. Carlos reaching to unbutton Myrtle's worn wool cardigan, accidentally pulling on the pearl choker she always wore, tiny iridescent beads springing forth to land in crevices and stairwells, shining under the light of the moon, clues.

But alas, in a packed lobby scene that Inspector Lestrade would have envied, the police informed us that Myrtle had simply turned over. Turns out she always slept with a steak knife under her blanket—bad neighbors and all and when she awakened to find blood dripping on her sheets, she stumbled from her bed and fractured her toe. Once again—all in the details.

I have to admit, I was a little disappointed, the suspense had kept me going for a week of my normal dreary life. But I think I learned a lesson, elementary, dear fiction reader, murder isn't a fantasy, and death isn't a plot but a departure from this world of books. And the moral of the story—get a life, literary or private eye, because the surprisingly sweet scent of mystery, the everlasting tango of solving the crime—it's in your blood. Or maybe your head and that's when I decided to go to college and become a writer. All the macabre crime I could think of would live only on a clean white page.

Louisa Clerici's fiction has been published in anthologies and magazines including *Carolina Woman Magazine* and *The Istanbul Literary Review.* Her non-fiction book, *Sparks from the Fire of Time* is based on her work as a hypnotist. Louisa Clerici C.Ht is a writer, hypnotist and behavioral sleep coach who teaches workshops and sees private clients at her practice in Plymouth, Massachusetts. www.clearmindsystems.net

Dear Manuel

Judith Green

Dear Mami and Papi,

See, I write to you in English! School is good, and I learn very much. I like my host family very much. The soccer is all gone for this year, and still is a long time before the baseball. But soon will be snow. I want very much to see snow! Snow for the Christmas!

Y en espanol. Me gusta la escuela, pero le futbol esta fini por el ano, y estara mucho tiempo antes de el besbol. Pero quiero ver la nieve—la nieve para la Navidad!

Mucho amore, su hijo, Manuel

Season's Greetings to our family and friends!

This has been an exciting year for us, with Melanie off to college at Bates, and Tommy and Jenny moving up to 11th and 8th grade respectively . . . and we have a new family member! Manuel Rodriguez Jimenez is with us for the year from the Dominican Republic. What a great addition he has been! Right now he's dreaming of a White Christmas . . . he's never seen snow! So Merry Christmas and Happy New Year to you all, and let it snow, let it snow, let it snow!

Love from the Easton family

MELANIE

Miss me? I miss you

    BRENT

    Miss you bad, babe

MELANIE
OMG, it's a shock to be home
from college, my brother and sister
make more noise than a whole dorm full
of girls! And now this exchange student,
too, Manuel, I told you about him,
although he's pretty quiet. I think mostly
he's hoping to be discovered in the spring
by a baseball scout.
          BRENT
          National sport in Dominican Republic.
          And a real good way to get to America
MELANIE
Anyway, he's a nice kid, and he kind of keeps
an eye on Tom. But I can't believe it's two
whole weeks until next semester starts and
I see you again. I'm gonna go crazy!
          BRENT
          Counting the days

TO DO
Pick up flowers
Warm socks for Manuel
Stocking stuffers
Call Ginnie
Xmas Eve 5:00, Choir practice 4:00, white shirt, black pants
Don't forget! Take turkey out of freezer!

TOM
Hey guess what Im
texting u from?
Smartphone!!!
          SAM
          Sweet

TOM
Pulled this baby out
of my stocking & I
literally fell over

TOM
Hey, texting u on
new smartphone!
Wuz in my stocking!
    CYRUS
    Nice. All I got
    was clothes

TOM
Check it out new smartphone!
    KOBE
    About time you joined 21st century

Dear Grandma,

    Thank you very much for the beautiful sweater, it is nice and warm!!! It was nice to have Manny here with us for Christmas. He says they don't have a Christmas tree at home, but they have a poinsettia *tree* in their front yard!!!! He told me he had never seen so many presents, I think maybe his family is very poor, when he came he didn't have very many clothes, Mom had to give him a bunch of stuff that Tommy had outgrown. Remember how in "Little House in the Big Woods" Laura was all excited about getting an orange at Christmas? Well, Manny doesn't care about oranges, he gets them all the time at home, but he loves apples!! But mostly he wants snow. I hope we get some soon.
    Love, Jenny

SHOPPING LIST
Bread
~~2 gals~~ milk 3 gallons!
Spaghetti sauce
Yoghurt
Apples
Cheerios
Ice cream

TOM
Thx for invite, see u New Yr's Eve
Gonna bring Manny, OK?

> SAM
> Do u gotta bring Manwell?
> He's a dirtbag

TOM
I no u r still pissed about soccer, yah it
wasnt fair Manny got MVP instead of u

> SAM
> Yeah, cuz Manwell only here for
> 1 season

TOM
Yeah but . . . well we did win the
championship haha!

> SAM
> Wtf? Shut up u sound like Coach.
> Thought he'd have heart attack over
> that trophy. He wuz like in love with
> your little Mexican

TOM
Manny from Dominican Republic.
Not Mexican

> SAM
> Whatever

TOM & MANNY:
HEADED FOR MY MEETING EARLY TO BEAT THE STORM.

SHOULD BE A COUPLE OF INCHES BY THE TIME YOU GET
UP. SNOWBLOWER GASSED UP & READY TO GO, SO USE
IT! HAVE FUN, MANNY! WE TOLD YOU IT WOULD SNOW
SOMETIME.
    DAD

TOM
Dude, finally got snow! u shoulda
seen Manny. Woke up & saw snow
& ran outside in his sweats. Thought
he could walk on TOP of snow cause
he stepped off porch and fell right in.
Didn't brush himself off so it melted
all down inside his clothes.
    SAM
    Wish you had it on video!
TOM
Yeah. Well, gotta go snowblow the
driveway for the old man. Teach Manny
how so HE can do it haha

MELANIE
I'm surviving the fam . . . but just barely.
Little Bro can't talk about anything
except his new smartphone, Little Sis
is prancing around reciting her part in
the school play until I'm ready to puke,
and now Manny (exchange student)
came inside all upset that his hands were
paralyzed
    BRENT
    Paralyzed??
MELANIE
All it was, he was out there snowblowing
with no gloves on, so his fingers got a little
stiff . . . guess he's never been cold before in

his life. Then he got upset all over again
cause Jenny and I started putting the
Christmas decorations away. I guess where
Manny's from, they do Christmas right up
until Epiphany, which is in January, when
the 3 kings came, or something. Will this
vacation ever end? Still miss me?

MOM—
MANNY AND I FINISHED DRIVEWAY & SAM CAME OVER
AND HUNG OUT WITH ME AND MANNY FOR A WHILE BUT
THE GIRLS WERE MAKING A MESS WITH THE CHRISTMAS
TREE SO WE WALKED OVER TO KOBES BUT MANNY
DIDN'T WANT TO COME. HAVE YOU SEEN MY PHONE?
PRETTY SURE I LEFT IT ON THE TABLE.
    T

Dear Aunt Ginnie,
    Thank you for the necklace, it's so pretty I wear it every day!! I
wish school would start soon so I can show all my friends. Also I wish
school would start soon because my family is driving me crazy!!!!
Melanie is like I'm so sad I miss my college boyfriend, and Tommy
can't find his new smartphone he just got for Christmas and he's like
it's everyone else's fault that he can't remember where he put it, and
Manny our Domican Repubblic guy is like I wanted to see snow and
now I've seen it I don't want to see it anymore. Like he didn't know
that snow was going to be cold!!!! Plus now he can't find his lucky
baseball that was signed by some famous Domican guy. So I will be
glad when school starts again and are you coming to see our play?
    Love, Jenny

MELANIE
I gotta get out of here, Brent. I miss you, plus
this family's driving me crazy. Tom lost
his smartphone and it's like it's the

end of the freaking world. He swears
he left it on the kitchen table, but I think
he probably dropped it in the snow and
he and Manny probably ran over it with
the snow blower and shot it into the woods
in a million pieces. And now Manny can't
find his favorite baseball, which I hope
Tommy didn't take it in some kind of
retaliation.

MELANIE
I can't believe tonight is New Year's Eve
and I'm not going out! Wah!

MELANIE
Miss me?

MANUEL—
WENT OVER TO KOBES HOUSE AND WE PROBALY WILL GO
STRAIT TO SAMS OR IF YOU WANT TO GO TO SAMS PARTY
CALL ME. EXCEPT YOU CAN'T CALL ME CAUSE I DON'T
HAVE A PHONE, YA KNOW. TOM

Dear Aunt Marilyn,
    Thank you for the new book, I am reading it and I like it a lot!!!!
School started again yesterday, and Melanie went back to college
today, and Tommy is out with his friends and Manuel is upstairs in his
room, so its nice and quiet and now maybe everything will get back
to normal. Are you going to come see my play? I hope so.
    Love, Jenny

Apple Hill High School
Guidance Department
January 6

Dear Mr. and Mrs. Easton,

I am writing to express my concern about your student, Manuel Jimenez. His teachers have noticed a marked change in him since before the Christmas break; he seems to have withdrawn from his classmates, and his schoolwork is deteriorating. Please call my office to make an appointment at your earliest convenience.

Sincerely yours,

Cliff Roberts, Guidance [F-M]

Honey—

You need to speak to your son.

Margery

To: Jennikins22@gmail.com

Subject: What's happening?

Hi, Jenny—

How are things at home? Did Tommy ever find his stupid phone? Does he still think Manuel took it? What do you think??? Brent and I kind of broke up, but I guess that's OK. I hope your play is good. Well, gotta go study. X Mel

To: EMelanie@hotmail.com

Subject: Re: What's happening?

Dear Melanie,

Im sorry about brent, he sounded nice!! Oh well!!! I don't know about Manuel. He just stays in his room. So maybe he feels guilty? If he broke the phone? Or maybe took it? Anyway I'm sorry about Brent, maybe you will find someone even better. Love, Jenny

Apple Hill High School

Guidance Department

January 26

Dear Mr. and Mrs. Easton,

Manuel Jimenez has requested that I arrange for him to go

home. He says that he misses his family, and that the cold weather is bothering him.

I know that you and your family have made every effort to accommodate him, so I hope you will not feel responsible for his lack of success.

Sincerely yours,
Cliff Roberts, Guidance [F-M]

East Stratford Times Register

January 29
BREAK-IN AT APPLE HILL HIGH SCHOOL

Custodians arriving early Monday morning discovered a break-in and considerable vandalism at Apple Hill High School. A person or persons evidently entered the building by breaking a window in the auto shop area. Vandalism was limited to the front lobby of the school, particularly the trophy display cabinets. Many trophies were damaged, and missing was the newest trophy for the Regional Championship in soccer, won during a miraculous turnaround season which saw the Apple Hill Tigers, led by Dominican exchange student Manuel Jimenez, surge to victory for the first time in Apple Hill history. The only clue was an autographed baseball found lying in . . .

To: braasmusen@applehillschooldistrict.edu
Subject: Manuel Rodriguez Jimenez
Dear Mr. Raasmusen:
I cannot believe that you allowed the Sheriff's Department to interview and fingerprint Manuel at the school without my husband or myself being present. We are his legal guardians while he is in the U.S. This must not happen again!
Margery Easton

JETBLUE
ITINERARY: Portland ME—Santiago, Dominican Republic
Passenger: Manuel Rodriguez Jimenez

February 5
Depart PWM 9:10 a.m. Arrive JFK 10:17 a.m.
Depart JFK 12:56 p.m. Arrive STI 5:03 p.m.

TOM
Rents bought me new smartphone! So
they finally caught on that old Man-well
took it, even if dumb Sheriff couldn't
prove anything about the trophy & stuff.

> SAM
> Hope they checked his suitcase
> before he left, probably find our
> trophy, haha

TOM
Glad the little jerk is gone, anyway

Dear Mr. and Mrs. Easton,

I write to say I have come home safe and thank you very much
for everything you did for me and I am sorry that you maybe think
I am bad person but really I try to be good son to you. And good
brother to Tom and Jenny. Well, goodbye and God bless you.

Manuel Rodriguez Jimenez

To: EMelanie@hotmail.com
Subject: What's happening?
Dear Melanie,
Its so quiet around here without Manny. Poor thing he looked so sad
when he left, like his heart was breaking. He felt like everyone in
school hated him, and now he'll never probably never play baseball
like he wanted to that was supposed to be his life career. I can tell
Mom and Dad feel read bad about him going away, and Tom is gone
all the time with his stupid friends, specially Sam, and my play is
over and I didn't even really care about it. Love, Jenny

To: <u>Jennikins22@gmail.com</u>
Subject: Re: What's happening?
Dear Jenny,
I feel bad about Manuel too. I can't believe he would break into the school and steal the trophy. I just can't. I wish there was some way to prove he didn't do it. Hey, I just met someone new. I can't wait for you to meet him, maybe at spring break. X, Mel

PLEASE PASS THIS NOTE TO KYLEIGH AND DON'T READ IT!!!!
Kyleigh, I got to talk to you after science class, okay? About Manuel, you know, our exchange student. Jenny

PLEASE PASS TO JENNY EASTON
Jenny, I can't stand the way Mr. Kelly just talks & talks, it's like he doesn't know we're in Middle School, he thinks we're in college. Who cares about cells 'n' stuff, anyway? So what happened with that Mexican guy you had? My brother Sam says he was a real jerk. Kyleigh

PLEASE PASS TO KYLEIGH RIGHT AWAY!!!!
Kyleigh, Not Mexican!!! From Domican Republic. Don't you know anything? And he wasn't a jerk, no matter what your stupid brother says!!!

PLEASE PASS THIS TO STUPID JENNY
Yes Manwell was too a jerk!!! Sam should have been MVP for soccer, he played for years and years, and then this Mexican guy comes along and plays a couple of games and everybody thinks he's some kind of hero but so what, Sam should have been MVP.

PASS THIS TO STUPID KYLEIGH
Yeah, but the soccer team lost every game until Manny came along. Losers! Maybe it was your brother who broke into the high school. On account of he was jealous. Maybe he's got the trophy under his bed!

PASS THIS TO THAT IMBECILE AT THE END OF THE ROW
Shut up shut up shut up. If you don't shut up I'm going to tell Mr.
Kelly your passing notes and then you'll be sorry.

I will not pass notes in class.
I will not pass notes in class.
I will not pass notes in class.
I will not pass notes in class.
I will not . . .

East Stratford Times Register

February 20
BREAK-IN CASE SOLVED

Following an anonymous tip that originated at a public pay phone
at Apple Hill Middle School, members of the Sheriff's Department
have solved the January 28th vandalism at the high school, and
recovered the prized soccer Championship trophy. In an interview
with the lone perpetrator, a minor who is a student at Apple Hill High
School, deputies discovered that . . .

Dear Manuel,

Feliz Navidad! I am writing to wish you and your family a very
Merry Christmas. I can't believe it has been almost a year since you
were here with us. I hope that you are having a good year in school,
and that you are still practicing your English.

I thought of you this afternoon when we got the Christmas
decorations out of the attic, and what do you think we found at the
bottom of one of the boxes? Do you remember the smartphone that
Tommy got for Christmas last year? It must have got scooped up
when the girls put things away last year. I know that Tommy was
upset when it disappeared, but now that mystery is solved.

We are all well, and having a good year. Tom didn't play soccer
this fall, but he's looking forward to spring and the baseball season.
Melanie is . . .

Dear Mama Margery,

It is nice to get your letter. I am glad you are well. I am also glad you found the phone belongs to Tom. Maybe also police could give back my baseball? It was signed by the famous Dominican baseball player Fernando Garcia Vega. Say hello to Jenny and Melanie and Mr. Dad. If you get the baseball maybe you could send it to me?

Muchos gracias,
Manuel

As a former Adult Education Director for an eleven-town school district in rural western Maine, **Judith Green** has written twenty-five high-interest/low-level books for adult students. Her mystery stories have been chosen for each of the anthologies of New England Crime Stories published by Level Best Books. "A Good, Safe Place," published in 2010 in *Thin Ice, Crime Stories By New England Writers,* was nominated for an Edgar®.

The Bucket List

A. J. Pompano

The first time I laid eyes on the well-seasoned lovebirds was in a hotel lounge overlooking the Boston Common. Her lipstick too red and his lapels too wide for 2015, they were having the time of their lives doing the Bossa Nova like it was still in style.

They seemed to have the joy of life that I wished for my parents who have decided to sit out their retirement in front of the TV set. I was so taken by them that I told the bartender to send them a drink. The server pointed to my table and they ambled over followed by waves of Opium and Jade East. The woman said they were the Gilberts; Virginia and Ted.

"That was very amiable of you, Miss . . ."

"Nike DeNardo." I held out my hand.

"Oh, what a beautiful name. After the goddess?"

I shook my head. "Actually, after the missile. My grandfather named me. He was in aerospace."

Like most people, Virginia seemed taken aback by my unusual name, but Ted took it in stride.

"Even if you were named after the shoes it would still be beautiful. We thank you for the drinks."

He held up his drink and we clinked glasses. "I hope you don't mind. You seemed to be having such a good time that I assumed you were celebrating some occasion."

"We are," Virginia said.

I asked if they would like to take a seat. To my surprise they did.

"So what are you celebrating?"

"Just being alive." Virginia winked.

"It's actually a little more than that. We're working our way through our bucket list," Ted explained.

"You mean the things you want to do before you die?"

"That's correct as rainwater."

"What Ted is trying to say is that we made a list of all of the things we talked about over the years but never got around to doing. After we retired we decided it's now or never."

Ted put his arm around her. They reminded me of teenagers on a first date. "That's right. We want to see what we've missed of the world while we still have the energy. We started last year on our forty-fifth anniversary."

I wished that my parents could take some lessons from these two. "That is all kinds of awesome. There're tons of things I'm going to do someday."

Virginia patted my hand. "Honey, don't wait too long. You may be half our age now but before you know it you'll find you're pushing seventy too."

I wasn't sure if that was supposed to be a compliment or not, but she was so sweet I let it go. "So, tell me about your list."

"Goodness, where to begin? Last Christmas Eve we visited the Austrian church where 'Silent Night' was written. We also saw the Northern Lights in Iceland."

"Don't forget the Roman Forum." They glanced at each other with a look that said, *What happened in the Forum stays in the Forum.* I turned away not wanting to spoil their moment.

"Never." She giggled. "Oh yes, I took a picture of Ted watching the sunrise at Machu Picchu."

"And I took one of her at the Key West sunset."

"Now we've learned how to take selfies like the youngsters do. He doesn't like computers, but I even have a Facebook page where we share our adventures."

"That's what I love about my Ginny. She keeps us young."

"Anyway, Ted always wanted to come to Boston to see the Freedom Trail. We had ten must-do things on the list. This is one of the last." For a second I thought I heard a note of sadness in her voice. "Look at this photo." Virginia took out a cell phone and showed me an off-center-selfie of the two of them by the Swan Boats. "But enough about us, what do you do?"

Next to theirs, my life was pretty dull. "I'm a one-woman detective agency."

"A one-woman detective agency." Something flashed across Virginia's face. I get that sometimes. To some people the word detective is a sign to step back.

But, Ted was very interested. It may have been the novelty of a lady detective.

"What are you working on?"

"Nothing really that interesting. I'm only staying at the hotel for a few days while I testify in a divorce case."

"I'm sure we've bothered Nike enough." Virginia stood up from the table and put her hand on Ted's elbow to bring him to his feet as well. "Besides, we have a swing dancing lesson in ten minutes. Again, thank you so much for the drink."

It was about 10:30 when I heard a knock on my hotel room door. I hadn't ordered room service. It was Virginia.

"Nike, you have to help me." Her eyes were red and her face was creased with worry.

"What's wrong?" Her behavior made me uneasy and I crossed my arms across my robe.

"Someone is going to kill Ted. Please help me. When I heard that you were a detective I just knew you were heaven-sent. I don't know who else to turn to."

"What makes you think anyone wants to hurt your husband?"

Her bottom lip quivered. "I hired a man to kill him."

"A hit man?" What had I gotten into? I should have known that my pay-it-forward would turn around to bite me in the ass.

"Yes, I guess that's what it's called. You see, Ted is dying. That's why the bucket list is so important. I always held us back because I thought we would need the money for more important things. We've missed our whole lives because I was worried about saving for our old age. When we learned of Ted's illness I saw what a fool I'd been, so I convinced him it was his idea to tackle our bucket list."

"But why hire someone to kill him?"

She began to cry. I pulled some tissues from a box and handed them to her.

"We did just about everything. Now he doesn't have much time before he'll be in a bad way. We've known our doctor all of our lives and he said that Ted doesn't have much more time before whatever it is in his brain will strike. It will be horrible. He doesn't deserve to suffer so I hired someone to . . . you know. I was promised it would be painless. But I changed my mind. I want us to go through this together. Who knows? Miracles happen every day. "

I wanted to dismiss Virginia's ranting as dementia, or a problem with her meds, but something made me believe her story.

"Then call it off."

"The problem is I don't know who I hired. It was all very secretive. I need you to stop it from happening."

I was hearing her words but coming from such a sweet old lady they were a total mind-botch. I wanted to make sure I understood. "Tell me everything. How did you find a hit man? I mean, you don't look like the type to have those connections."

"I learned how to use a computer at the senior center. You can find anything you want on the Internet if you look hard enough."

"True. But how am I supposed to help you?"

"I told him on the computer that I changed my mind, but he said a deal is a deal. I have to give him $15,000 in the Public Garden tonight at 11:30 after Ted goes to sleep. I'm afraid that if I don't pay him, he'll tell Ted what I did. He said he has copies of our chats. I'm scared. Can you at least come with me?"

"You realize that even if you pay him you're opening yourself up to blackmail for the rest of your life."

"I have to do what I can to save Ted even if he doesn't have much time. I'll take the consequences."

"You never met the man. How will you know who to give the money to?"

"He'll find me. I'm supposed to wear a yellow scarf and wait on the lagoon bridge."

I looked at my watch. "Give me the scarf and stay with Ted. I'm going in your place."

The cool fog in the Public Garden misted my skin and the air smelled fresh, a bit like the sea. The murkiness hid the top of the George

Washington statue and haloed the lights on the path to the lagoon as if I were wearing glasses made of wax paper.

I waited at the railing of the bridge. A couple came hand-in-hand out of the vapor, walked by without seeming to notice me, then disappeared again in the cloud at the other end of the short span. I waited looking over the side. The fog allowed me to see only one of the Swan Boats tied up below. I thought of how happy Virginia and Ted looked in their off-center selfie. After fifteen minutes or so I was about to leave when a man in a white rain shell materialized next to me. His thin face needed a shave.

I touched the scarf and his eyes followed my hand. He nodded slightly and smiled. A meth-mouth if I ever saw it.

"You waiting for someone?" His breath reeked of weed.

"I am."

"Anyone in particular?" His eyes darted around as if he were looking for someone else to come out of the fog.

"I think I've found him."

"Well, that's good. Have a nice night." He started to walk off the bridge.

"I have something you want." I touched the scarf again. Once more his eyes followed my hand, but this time he scoffed and shook his head.

"Not from you sister."

"What's wrong?"

"You don't think I know entrapment when I see it? I smell bacon."

"I'm not a cop."

"Whatever. The age isn't right."

Was he that dumb or that desperate for money that he didn't realize he was practically admitting he was up to no good? "You can't expect an old lady to come out here at night. She sent you this." I pulled an envelope of money from my pocket. Meth-mouth looked interested but still wary.

"Keep talking."

"The money is yours. But she doesn't want the service."

He raised his eyebrows and turned his hands palms up. "We had a deal."

"I'm going to give you the money. But forget the job. Understand?" I had a problem with paying him but my priority was to save Ted's life. "Just take it." I handed him the money. "Now that's the end of it. We don't want to hear from you again."

"I'm afraid it doesn't work that way." He pulled a knife from his pocket. "These jobs are all about balance. You have something on me. I have something on you. You hire me to kill someone. I kill someone. See what I mean? You can't rat on me, I can't rat on you. Without that balance I have a real problem. I've done dozens of these jobs and someone always has to be killed. Unfortunately, in this case it is going to have to be the person who can identify me—you."

At that point I was glad that I didn't let Virginia meet with him. It was obvious that he would have killed her.

He lunged at me, trying to throw me over the rail. I kneed him and, as he doubled over, I cuffed him on both ears. He straightened up, knife still in one hand, envelope in the other. He seemed off balance like a marionette with broken strings. His arms spun in circles. The envelope dropped, but not the knife as I was hoping. He went backwards toward the railing. I tried to grab him but couldn't make it and fell to my knees as he went over the side. A woman screamed. I scooped up the envelope and stuffed it in my pocket before getting up.

The couple who had walked by earlier ran over. "Are you all right?" the fellow said.

"We saw him attack you with a knife. It was amazing how you defended yourself." The girl leaned over the railing to look. "He's in the Swan Boat. I think he landed on the knife. He looks dead."

Virginia looked like she had gained ten years overnight when I spoke to her in the hotel lobby the next morning. "What happens now?"

"Nothing as far as the police are concerned. He was wanted for murder. Witnesses saw him attack me and he died by his own actions." I knew I was sidestepping her question.

"And me?"

"You should continue to take care of Ted and finish as much of that bucket list as you can."

She smiled. "Thank you. There are a few things that we never got to. Can you imagine a couple of old goats like us on a zip line?"

Actually I could. I thought about the Gilberts a lot over the next few weeks and followed Virginia on Facebook. Every once in a while a picture of them doing something from their bucket list appeared on my newsfeed. After a time the postings stopped and I knew Ted had probably had his last adventure. I thought of contacting Virginia but got involved in work and never did.

It was almost a year later when I was following a trail of laundered money for a client that I spotted Ted at an airport in Costa Rica.

"Ted, I'm so glad to see you. You look so well." I caught myself from saying more. He didn't know that Virginia had confided in me concerning his health. "What brings you here?"

"Zip lining through the rainforest. It's one from the list that we had overlooked. I'm with that group over there." He nodded toward a group on the other side of the lobby.

"I don't see Virginia."

His face changed.

"I'm afraid she's not here. She passed away six months ago. I'm the oldest one in the bunch but I'm doing this for her."

"Dead?" I had heard of this before. The caregiver dies before the person they are taking care of.

"I know what you're thinking. She must have told you I was dying."

At first I thought of denying it, but Ted would have seen right through me. "She was stressed and confided in me."

"I don't doubt it. But the truth is, I wanted to have her experience everything she had missed in life so I told her I was the one who was dying. She never would have done the bucket list if she thought it was for her. She was too practical."

"How did you keep it from her?"

"She had arthritis in her neck and they picked up what they called a glioblastoma in an MRI. It was in a place they couldn't operate on. I know our doctor well. He wasn't blessed with a good marriage like I was; mostly through his own fault. You know how it is in a small town. I had enough bad stuff on him to persuade him to tell her I was the one that was sick. There wasn't much he could do anyway. He gave her every new treatment he could between trips right down to the newest tetanus shot therapy. The tumor showed no symptoms for over a year so she thought her shots were for arthritis. You know the rest.

I expressed my condolences. "I think Virginia would have been very happy that you are here."

Ted nodded and walked toward the zip line group.

I doubted that he knew that Virginia had almost had him murdered. He wasn't going to hear it from me. Sometimes couples have secrets from each other that are best taken to the grave.

A.J. "Ang" Pompano has many published stories including mysteries in the anthologies *Still Waters, Deadfall,* and *Stone Cold.* He also writes academic pieces on detective fiction. He is on the New England Crime Bake Planning Committee and is the treasurer of Sisters in Crime New England. Ang lives in Connecticut with his wife, Annette, and his dog, Quincy.

The Intruder

Deborah Dolby

The moment I walked into the kitchen I sensed a strange unfamiliar atmosphere. It was as though some unseen presence lent an peculiar energy to a place that usually felt warm and welcoming. Happy. Was it a smell? Or something missing, or added, or out of place?

And then I saw it. Just in between the range and the kitchen island the body lay sprawled on its side, mouth open, eyes bulging, legs akimbo, a pool of dark blood just under its head, dead without a doubt. My hand stifled my scream as it came out sounding like more of a whimper, as I looked to the ceiling, thanking my luck stars I hadn't been here when the wildly scruffy unknown intruder had entered our home. I put my package down and closed my eyes. It took me a moment to catch my breath, feeling my whole body zinging with adrenaline. I felt as I had once when experiencing a life-or-death near miss while driving, needing to breathe deeply while studiously avoiding the sight on the floor.

Yet as I regained my equilibrium, my eyes, unbidden by my conscious self, slowly returned to the gory sight. I was compelled to take a closer look at death. The stillness of the atmosphere hung silently as I examined the body. I'd had no knowledge of the living version of this corpse, and so felt no emotion as I leaned over to see it more closely.

I looked at the dark eyes and wondered: had there been a foreknowledge, was the death blow seen as it came crashing down? Was the moment life ended a surprise? Was there any sense of loss? Or was there just life as usual, as if invading my home and kitchen were usual, and then nothing.

And who? Who had done this rough deed? Who had lain in wait perhaps, or come upon the intruder, and let defense of home and family trump sanctity of life? The small wooden slab, the metal bar, were indisputable signs of premeditation. My husband of course. It could not have been anyone else. Peter did this for me. I know I will never have to worry about my safety or sense of security with him in my life. But I will ask him to let me know beforehand when he next gets out the cheddar and sets a trap.

Deborah Dolby and her husband Peter Martin have been receiving guests at their Sampler House Bed & Breakfast, and the Elderberry Lodge vacation rental in Milton and Georgia, Vermont for over thirteen years. She visits her children in Seattle, San Francisco, Jacksonville, and DC, and enjoys writing, watercolor painting, gardening, playing bridge, and working alongside Peter as they remodel old houses.

Gone But Not Forgotten

Leslie Wheeler

Betty stood awkwardly on the lawn by the tent set up for the fiftieth reunion of the class of 1963 at Hargrave College. Clutching the glass of white wine her husband Chip had fetched before joining a huddle of his frat brothers, she scanned the crowd for a familiar face. Not that she expected to find one. Hargrave had been Chip's college. Her parents couldn't afford the tuition at this small private institution with Ivy League aspirations and a bucolic setting in upstate New York. She'd attended the SUNY campus in Potsdam, the hometown she shared with Chip.

Chip had dutifully invited her to big events like homecoming—she was his girl, after all. Yet there was plenty she didn't know about his Hargrave years. He'd say things like, "The brothers and I did the craziest thing," but when she asked what it was, he invariably replied, "Trust me, you don't want to know."

This was the first reunion they'd attended. In the intervening years, Chip had lost contact with most of his classmates except for the small group of brothers he was hanging out with now. She knew those men by name only; their annual weekend get-together at a camp in the Adirondacks was a stag affair. Aside from Chip, the only person she'd spoken to this Friday evening was the caterer who kept asking if she wanted another mini quiche.

Betty had just accepted her fourth—or was it her fifth?—serving of the fattening little tidbits when a female voice at her elbow said, "We've met before, haven't we?"

Betty peered down at a petite woman with a cap of silver hair and bright, inquisitive blue eyes. "Maybe, I'm Betty Blackburn."

"Of course! I've heard so much about you from Chip."

"Oh?" Betty stared at her.

"Trudy Endicott. Class correspondent since 1963.

"Ah, so what did Chip . . .?"

Trudy didn't answer. Her eyes had shifted to the throng under the tent: the men wearing khaki pants and blue blazers, the women, cocktail dresses and heels. Betty spotted a few trophy wives in the crowd, but most of the couples looked to be in their seventies.

"I can't believe how we've all aged," Trudy said wistfully. "But with age comes accomplishment. There are more than a few movers and shakers here. Recognize him?" Trudy indicated a tall, distinguished-looking man with a full head of wavy gray hair.

Betty had no idea who he was, but she didn't want to admit this. "Oh, it's . . . Sorry, I can't remember his name right now. Must be having a senior moment."

"George Fredericks, a frequent commentator on PBS."

No wonder Betty didn't recognize him. She only watched the local news channel.

"He's the emcee for the memorial event we're having tomorrow for our deceased classmates," Trudy said.

"In the chapel?"

"No, George wanted an informal sharing of memories rather than a religious service. We're holding it in a meeting room at the campus center. I hope you'll come, though you may not have known many of the people we'll be talking about."

"I'll try."

Betty's gaze shifted to a couple who didn't fit the almost cookie-cutter mold of the rest.

The man was slight of build, without the paunch so many of the men, including Chip, sported. His face was unlined, his hair dyed a reddish brown. He wore a striped jacket with wide lapels and striped pants. With him was a sultry blonde in a mini-skirt who looked young enough to be his daughter, and probably was, given the strong facial resemblance between them.

"Who's he?" Betty tilted her head in their direction.

"Park Avenue plastic surgeon."

"And the young woman with him—his daughter?"

"Not by a long shot, though he's done her face to look like his."

"She was . . . a patient of his?" Betty was stunned.

"Patient turned fiancée. Did the same thing to his three other wives."

"Really? That's kinda—"

"Ghoulish, if you ask me," Trudy declared in a loud voice.

The plastic surgeon turned to glare at Trudy; his fiancée looked upset. Putting his arm around her, he guided her away.

Trudy went on to provide the low-down on others in the crowd, some of it nice, some not-so-nice. At least she was more discreet about the not-so-nice stuff than she'd been with the surgeon. Otherwise, Betty would have felt really uncomfortable. She already felt ungainly standing beside Trudy. Six-feet-tall in heels, she towered over the other woman, and she was full-figured, unlike Trudy, who looked like she could easily fit into minus sizes. Big Betty and Tiny Trudy. Still, she was grateful to Trudy for befriending her.

"Which table are you sitting at?" Trudy asked when dinner was announced.

"We don't have one," Betty confessed. "We'd barely arrived when Chip went off with his frat brothers."

"Sit with us then." To Betty's amazement, Trudy marched over to where Chip remained in a tight circle with his friends and said, "Break it up, boys, it's time for the buffet. And Chip, after you've filled your plate, bring it to that table over there, where your wife and I will be waiting."

After dinner, they were invited into the college president's house for a sing-a-long with the president accompanying them on the piano. He led them in a rousing rendition of the college fight song, followed by a number of old favorites. When he stopped for a break, the plastic surgeon's fiancée took over. She played a classical piece Betty didn't recognize with dramatic flair. Whether drawn by her playing or her youth and beauty—Betty suspected the latter—an admiring group of men, including Trudy's husband, gathered around her. The surgeon lounged in a nearby chair, a proprietary smile on his face.

"You're lucky your husband has the sense to keep his distance," Trudy said at Betty's elbow. She gestured toward a far corner of the room where Chip was convulsed with laughter at something a brother was saying.

Betty was lucky, indeed. But it hadn't always been that way. In high school, Chip had barely noticed her. He'd been attracted to girls like the blonde at the piano and probably would have married one of them, if it hadn't been for his mother. Mrs. Charles Blackburn II had "discovered" Betty at an athletic awards ceremony, where Betty and Chip were both receiving trophies—she as the star of the girls' basketball team and he as most valuable football player. The discovery led to a rather clumsy dinner invitation from Chip, along the lines of "my parents would like to meet you." After dinner, Chip's mother told Betty how much she and her husband had enjoyed Betty's company. With a pointed glance at Chip, she added, "And I hope we'll be seeing lots more of you." From then on, Mrs. Blackburn did her best to foster a romance between them, through what combination of gentle persuasion, bribery—Chip sported a new Porsche soon after they began dating—or outright arm-twisting Betty didn't know. Nor did she care; she was simply happy to have her prince.

"Just look at them," Trudy proclaimed in a voice shrill enough to be heard over the music, "a bunch of old farts making fools of themselves over that little tramp."

The surgeon's smile faded. His fiancée's fingers crashed down on the keys. She left the room in tears, the surgeon hurrying after her. The men who'd been hanging around the piano, stared at Trudy with a mixture of surprise and annoyance.

Trudy shrugged. Seizing her husband by the arm, she dragged him toward the door, declaring in the same strident voice, "All that excitement isn't good for your heart. We need to find a less stressful form of entertainment. Want me to round up your hubby, too?" she asked Betty.

Betty shook her head. She didn't need Trudy or anyone else to ride herd on Chip. Not now nor during nearly fifty years of marriage. The only time he'd ever given her cause to worry was during that awful period right after graduation when he suddenly announced he was taking a year off to travel around the world. This had come as a bitter disappointment for Betty, since it had been more or less understood that as soon as Chip finished college, they'd get married and he'd go to work at his father's insurance company.

"He just needs to satisfy his wanderlust," Chip's mother reassured

her. "Then he'll settle down, and you two can start raising a family."
Betty, however, was afraid Chip would fall under the spell of some
beautiful but dangerous woman in an exotic locale who would lure
him away from her.

To keep herself busy as well as make money, she took a job at
a local dress shop. In her spare time she did a lot of knitting. She
also wrote Chip long letters and mailed them care of the American
Express offices in the various cities on his itinerary. She never knew
if he actually received her letters, because his infrequent postcards
contained such generic messages as "Having a ball" or "Wish you
were here." Still, she saved them all in a scrapbook she labeled
"Chip's Wanderlust Year."

Betty liked to think her devotion had been rewarded on a beautiful
summer day when Chip's mother called with exciting news. Chip had
telegraphed his parents he was arriving on a Pan Am flight to John
F. Kennedy Airport the following evening. Just like that. Out of the
blue, he was coming home. "Did he give any reason why, all of a
sudden, he's returning?" Betty asked.

"No, but I suspect it finally hit him how homesick he is, and
how much he misses us, you especially, Betty," Mrs. Blackburn said.
"Charlie and I are driving to JFK to meet him. Why don't you come
with us?"

Betty hadn't needed any persuading to accompany Chip's parents
on the long drive from Potsdam to Queens. When they arrived at the
gate, his mother nudged Betty forward so she was the first person
Chip saw when he walked off the plane.

"Betty? Omigod!" He ran toward her and collapsed into her
arms, shaking and sobbing, almost as if he'd come from the killing
fields of Vietnam, as he might have if a heart murmur hadn't enabled
him to avoid the draft. Chip's emotional outburst surprised Betty;
he'd never acted this way before. When she asked if he was okay, he
said he'd simply missed her and was glad to be back.

Betty teared up at the memory.

"What's the matter, Honey?" Chip slipped an arm around her
from behind. "I hope you're not upset I've spent so much time with
the boys. I haven't seen them in awhile, and—"

"No, it's fine," Betty assured him.

The next day brought a whirlwind of activities. Before Betty knew it, it was five p.m. and time for the memorial gathering. The room had begun to fill when Betty and Chip arrived, but she found seats near the front in the row just behind Trudy, who turned to smile at Betty. While they waited for the program to begin, Betty studied the flyer she'd been given. The cover read: "Gone But Not Forgotten, Hargrave College, Class of 1963." Inside, arranged alphabetically, were small black-and-white photos of the deceased classmates that had been taken from the yearbook, beside their names and dates. Scanning the entries, Betty focused on the death dates. As she'd expected, most were fairly recent, but she found several from years ago. The men were probably casualties of Vietnam, but what about the woman who'd died in June of 1964, only a year after graduation? She stared at the accompanying photo. Sheila Logan had been an attractive girl with a blonde flip and a big smile. Betty turned to Chip. "Honey—" Chip put a finger to his mouth and pointed at George Fredericks, the PBS commentator.

"We're gathered here to remember our classmates who couldn't join us because death intervened," Fredericks said. "We'll start with those who've told me you'd like to share memories of a particular classmate."

Some of the stories, especially those involving college hi-jinks, were amusing; others, poignant. When Fredericks finished with the people on his list, he said, "I'm going to read through the names of classmates nobody has spoken about yet, in the hopes someone can share a memory."

When Fredericks reached Sheila Logan, there was silence. Betty could tell Fredericks was ready to move on when a man seated several rows behind her rose and said, "I didn't really know Sheila, but I couldn't help noticing her—she was so lovely and full of life. This may sound strange, but I've often thought of her in the years since." He paused to clear his throat. "I've thought of all the things she missed by dying so young: marriage, children, grandchildren, involvement in her community, maybe building a career, getting together with old friends, making new ones, and taking part in this reunion. That's all."

"Thank you, Paul," Fredericks said, as the man sat down.

Betty found herself moved almost to tears by Paul's words. As Fredericks spoke the name of another classmate, Chip made a choking sound, clamped his hand over his mouth, and charged from the room. Betty rushed after him, catching up when he was about to enter the men's room. "Are you all right?"

"No," he groaned, "something I ate at lunch, or too much . . ." She couldn't make out the last word. The door shut behind him and she could hear him retching. She was tempted to go in, but knew he wouldn't like it. She waited until the retching stopped and she heard a toilet flush. A minute later, Chip staggered from the restroom, wan but composed. "Think I got rid of the bad thing in my system, but I'm going back to the motel to lie down. If I'm feeling better, I'll join you at dinner."

He'd barely left when Trudy burst from the meeting room. "What's wrong with Chip?"

Betty repeated what Chip had told her.

"Really? I thought maybe it had to do with something else."

"Like what?" Betty asked.

"Well, he *did* become ill right after Paul spoke about Sheila."

"So?"

"You know what happened to her, don't you?" Trudy's bright, inquisitive eyes bore into Betty.

No, but I bet you're going to tell me.

Applause issued from the meeting room, then the noise of scraping chairs. The gathering was breaking up.

"Sheila was murdered," Trudy stage-whispered. "In Bombay. Wasn't Chip—"

Before Trudy could finish the sentence, Betty broke away, stumbling into the crowd leaving the meeting room. "Sorry!" she mumbled to someone she bumped into.

"Are you all right?" It was Paul, the man who'd spoken about Sheila.

"Yes—no. I just—"

"Why don't you sit down?" Paul steered Betty to a nearby seat and sat next to her. His brown eyes behind horn-rimmed glasses were filled with concern.

"I don't know what came over me," Betty murmured.

"Occasions like this can stir up a lot of emotions," Paul said.

"I liked what you said about Sheila Logan," Betty blurted. "It was very moving."

"Thanks."

They were silent a few moments, while Betty tried to decide whether to ask Paul for more information about Sheila—information she might have gotten from Trudy, except she didn't trust Trudy not to gossip about their conversation. Paul, however, seemed like a sensitive, caring person.

"I heard she was murdered," Betty ventured.

"Yes," Paul said with a sigh.

"What happened?"

"Another stewardess found her strangled in her hotel room in Bombay."

"That's awful. She became . . . a stewardess?"

"Sheila had an adventurous spirit and wanted to see the world. After graduation she went to work for Pan Am."

"Was her murder . . . ever . . . solved?" Betty had trouble getting the words out.

Paul shook his head sadly. "As far as I know, it wasn't."

"Too bad."

"Yes." Paul's tone was somber. Another silence fell between them. Finally Paul took her hand. "Ready to face the world?"

"Uh-huh." She'd face it all right—just not Trudy. At the cocktail party, Betty surrounded herself with other people, moving to a different group whenever Trudy approached. When Chip joined her for dinner, Betty made sure they sat at a table as far from Trudy as possible. She managed a few pleasantries with her table mates before the questions roiling in her brain took over.

Had Chip been involved with Sheila Logan and taken his wanderlust year so they could meet in various places around the globe? Then they'd had a falling-out and he'd . . .? Betty wouldn't allow herself to even think the word. Unbidden, an image swam into view. It was the last page of her "Chip's Wanderlust Year" scrapbook, where she'd pasted the telegram from Bombay, telling his parents he was coming home the next day. Betty could see it as clearly as if she held the book in her hands. And there was the date: June 19, 1964, the same day Sheila died.

Oh dear God! Blood roared in Betty's brain, so loud she was sure others could hear it. She glanced furtively around the room to see if anyone had noticed her distress. Her eyes met Trudy's. Betty looked quickly away. She needed to calm down. She didn't want to betray herself, as Chip had earlier—at least as far as Trudy was concerned. Betty took several deep breaths and let them out slowly. She looked at Chip and saw the man she'd always loved. Could something that had happened years ago erase everything that had come after? All the truly good years of their marriage when Chip had shown himself to be a devoted husband and father. Betty knew Chip hadn't loved her at first, but she believed he'd grown to love her and had worked hard to make their marriage a success. That was what mattered, wasn't it?

Betty stole another glance at Trudy, now having an animated conversation with a woman seated next to her. Trudy's eyes darted back and forth between this woman and Betty and Chip's table. At one point, she even stabbed a finger at Chip. The other woman's mouth popped open with surprise.

Betty's gorge rose. Trudy was spreading ugly rumors about Chip just as she had about the plastic surgeon. She wasn't simply a gossip, but a scandalmonger, who didn't care whose lives she destroyed with a flick of her malicious tongue. She could've begun to connect the dots between Chip and Sheila before the reunion. Then she'd befriended Betty in the hopes Betty would provide the missing links. Trudy was like a dog, digging and digging, throwing more and more dirt into the air until it blocked the light. She had to be stopped.

Betty scrawled a message on the back of a napkin. Excusing herself, she dropped the napkin by Trudy's feet as she walked past.

The lights were turned down in the room where the memorial gathering had been held. Betty made her way through the dimness to the far side. Moments later, the door cracked open, and Trudy's sylph-like figure slipped inside. "Betty?" she whispered in a conspiratorial tone.

"Over here."

"This is about Sheila?" Trudy asked, scurrying toward her.

"Yes."

When Trudy was inches away, Betty drew herself up to her full height, taking advantage of the difference in their sizes.

"Chip was in Bombay when Sheila was killed, wasn't he?" Trudy's eyes glittered and her voice vibrated with excitement.

"No," Betty said firmly, looming over Trudy. "Chip never even went to India. What makes you think he did?"

"Someone told me, I don't remember who." Trudy's voice quavered.

"Whoever it was, was wrong."

"But—" The word came out a squeak, but it was a protest nonetheless.

Betty clamped her hands on Trudy's shoulders, holding her in place. "It's nice that Sheila was remembered today. But she's been dead for nearly fifty years now. She's gone, Trudy. Gone and best forgotten."

"But . . ." Fainter this time.

Betty's fingers closed around Trudy's neck, gripping tightly.

Trudy gurgled.

Betty applied more pressure. "Got that?" Trudy's chin jerked down in a desperate gag of agreement.

"Good," Betty said. "Now, go back and enjoy the rest of the evening."

"I hope this weekend was fun for you," Chip said later that night, as they relaxed on folding chairs watching a brilliant display of fireworks light up the sky over the quad.

"Yes," Betty replied. "Interesting, too."

"Oh?" He turned toward her. "What was so interesting?"

"Trust me." She smiled. "You don't want to know."

An award-winning author of American history books and biographies, **Leslie Wheeler** has written three "living history" mysteries and is at work on several new book-length projects. Her short crime fiction has appeared in a number of Level Best anthologies, and her essays and articles have been published in such magazines and anthologies as *American History Illustrated, Montana, the Magazine of Western History,* and *Dead in Good Company, A Celebration of Mount Auburn Cemetery,* edited by John Harrison and Kim Nagy.

"Relax, It's Not Loaded"

Mark Ammons

"!!*@%*#&^#!!…"

Mark Ammons, Level Best co-editor, Edgar® nominated writer and Robert L. Fish Memorial Award winner, is finally at a loss for words.